Praise for *Deadly Obsession*

"This is an exceptionally well-written novel. It's Clark's third book about the lives of the compelling Kinncaid brothers, but it easily stands alone. The main characters are subtle and complex from page one, especially the particularly strong, emotionally full-ranged heroine. The dialogue is outstanding, and the pacing both realistic and highly suspenseful."

— *Romantic Times*

"*Deadly Obsession* is the third story about the Kinncaid family and is a heart-wrenching tale. A well-written, in-depth romantic suspense, Jaycee Clark's *Deadly Obsession* is one of those stories that will linger in your mind and heart long after the story is over."

— *Romance Reviews Today*

"*Deadly Obsession* is the third book in the Deadly series and is an absolute must-read! Jaycee Clark has delivered a masterpiece! *Deadly Obsession* is accurately titled as this story is chilling and terrifying in the wake of one man's obsession. *Deadly Obsession* is simply remarkable! I could not put this book down. This story just draws readers in on so many levels. *Deadly Obsession* can be read as a standalone, but in this reviewer's opinion is even better when read with the previous two titles, *Deadly Shadows* and *Deadly Ties*. The highest of praise to Jaycee Clark, *Deadly Obsession* is outstanding!!!"

— Fallen Angel Reviews

"Ms. Clark has the uncanny ability to draw the reader into the story right away. She has you sitting on the edge of your seat, reading furiously to find out what happens next. The suspense resonates throughout the whole story. She writes wonderful four-dimensional characters that you can relate to. The villain is wonderfully written. Ms. Clark writes a fast-paced plot with plenty of action. This is an exciting, breathtaking ride."

— Love Romances

Books by Jaycee Clark

Angel Eyes
Firebird
Talons (coauthored with Shannon Stacey, Mandy Roth, Michelle
      Pillow, and Sydney Somers)
Black Aura
Ghost Cats (coauthored with Mandy Roth and Michelle Pillow)
Ghost Cats: Revenge
The Dream
Deadly Shadows
Deadly Ties
Deadly Obsession
Deadly Games
Phoenix Rising II (coauthored with Donna Grant and Mandy Roth)
Ghost Cats 2 (coauthored with Mandy Roth and Michelle Pillow)

Deadly Obsession

Jaycee Clark

Beyond the Page Books
are published by
Beyond the Page Publishing
www.beyondthepagepub.com

First digital edition copyright © 2004 by Jaycee Clark
First print edition copyright © 2004 by Jaycee Clark
Material excerpted from *Deadly Games* copyright © 2005 by Jaycee
Clark
Second digital edition copyright © 2011 by Jaycee Clark
Beyond the Page/CreateSpace print edition copyright © 2013 by
Jaycee Clark
Cover design and illustration by Dar Albert, Wicked Smart Designs

ISBN: 978-1-937349-51-6

Acknowledgments

Thanks to the girls for reading yet another Kinncaid story and Jules for her brutal honesty, as always.

Thanks for putting up with me, A. & A. ~ You're the best part of my life. Love ya.

To my siblings:

Bobby — the old man, who used to threaten all boys away; Dan — the ever-cool one that spoiled me rotten and let me drive his T-Bird; & Boyd — the proverbial big brother who loved to scare me any way imaginable, but taught me to swim to the bottom of the pool while playing James Bond. Awesome big brothers. And Kristie — the blond, annoyingly perky little sister who thinks like me, way too much. Awesome sister. Love you guys.

Prologue

He'd found her. Finally, after all this time.

The opera CD he'd put on soared to a crescendo—and he remembered. The music stirred the memories within him. Strains filled his mind with thoughts, yearnings so strong he could scarcely breathe, could all but taste the sweet nectar.

Her soprano voice, young yet worldly, released all the emotions known to man within notes and keys appreciated only by a few.

And she had been his.

No.

She was his *still*. She would always be his. He'd promised her that.

He opened his eyes, his leather chair squeaking slightly as he shifted. The smoke from his Cuban cigar drifted up from the Waterford ashtray, the taste sweet with a hint of citrus behind the robust tobacco flavor.

Her face stared up at him from the photograph. That smiling picture had sat at the corner of his desk for the last eight years. It was her in youthful beauty, the innocence still there in the soft lines of her face. Except for her eyes.

Those smoky gray eyes had always seen too much, understood too much. Those eyes haunted him.

With one finger, he traced the line of her mouth, remembering what it felt like beneath his, what it had tasted like, the music that could come from those lips. The glass protector was cool to his touch.

His sigh carried with it tension and elation. Carefully, he set the photo so that the edge of the frame was an inch from the corner of his blotter and just a finger length from the family picture. In the photograph, her hair was the color of dark winter wheat. He'd loved the long tresses, the smell of them, the feel.

She wasn't to cut her hair.

The man took a deep calming breath and heard voices drift down the hall.

No matter, no one would disturb him.

He opened the top drawer to his right, the moan of wood on wood familiar, the jingle of the handle dropping back down

1

unnoticed.

His fist clenched atop the polished mahogany as he withdrew another photo from the drawer.

His angel.

He'd know her anywhere.

Somehow, he'd known all along she wasn't dead. But to find her again . . .

Ahhh . . .

He shook his head sadly. A shame, all her beautiful hair, cut short now, in some feministic stylish flip. The shortened tresses were darker and made her round eyes even larger. Her straight nose, slightly tilted at the end, was the same. At least she hadn't had a nose job. And he had to admit the new hairstyle accentuated her long, graceful neck. He traced the swan-like column, remembering how soft her skin was just there. The lines of her face were not as soft as in the other picture. Time had sharpened them to an edge, prominent cheekbones and her stubborn, arrogant chin. His fisted hand relaxed, and he curved it around the crystal-faceted tumbler sitting on his desk.

She should have long hair, and not this deep brown color. What had she been thinking? Did she dye it? Probably.

He sipped his brandy, the taste full and rich on his tongue, swirling away and melding with the taste from his Havana best.

Always was too smart for her own good, which was why he was drawn to her. Her brain, her looks, her voice.

She was older now, more worldly.

Her young voice shimmered from the speakers as she held a note, as she drew it out.

Kinncaids. She was with the Kinncaids. A more noble, honorable family he could not think of. Strange, them being so old to the Washington, D.C., area, yet none of the elite family had ever had a thing to do within political circles. A shame really. With their money, brains, and ambitions the possibilities would be endless. Or could have been.

Christian Bills. She was going by that deplorable name. Christian, Chris. He'd hated it, as, he recalled, did her mother. And Bills? It was so very low-class, so incredibly common. Though he suspected it stemmed from William. She always was the daddy's, even granddaddy's, girl. Christian Bills? No.

Josephine. She was his Josephine.

And she always would be.

He'd let her think herself safe, for now.

He smiled. The cat's advantage to the mouse was in the fact the cat knew of his prey's existence. Unfortunately, from the mouse's point of view, the rodent was all too often unaware of the feline until just before the pounce.

Cat and mouse.

A game they knew well.

Eight years.

Full circle.

The game was just beginning.

He grinned, touched the lips of the woman, caressed her cheekbone, the column of her neck. His lungs filled with his sigh, just as blood rushed to fill his veins, his passion. It would not be long. Not long at all.

Opening his eyes, he tapped her lips one last time before he gently placed the photo in the top drawer and locked it. Footsteps neared his door.

In one gulp, he finished off the brandy and hit the remote. The opera and Josephine's voice silenced. Carefully, he set his empty glass on the desk just as the door opened.

"There you are. I'd wondered where you'd gone." She propped her hands on her trim hips. "Come on. You can't hide out here all night."

No, he supposed he couldn't, but he would dearly have loved to. He stood and inwardly longed for the house to be empty. Then, he'd be able to go up to his private, hidden room and enjoy the memories and plan for the future. Wasn't to be.

Smiling, he ran a hand down his jacket, straightened the black bow tie and held his hand out to her.

"I just needed a moment, darling."

"Hmm. Well, come on then. There are guests waiting. Don't want to give the wrong impression, do you? The constituents should be placated."

A glance over his shoulder and his eyes landed on the photo on the edge of his desk.

Gray eyes.

It was her. He'd found her. His angel.

The music from the terrace drifted down the hallway as he turned and led the woman away.

He'd found his Josephine and he was never again letting her go. No one else would have her.

Ever.

Chapter 1

"Don't look at me like that," Brayden said on a sigh.

Christian cleared her throat. "I'm sorry, how am I supposed to look at you?"

She would not cry, she would not.

Just because she'd finally overcome her fears, finally reached for what she'd wanted when it was offered, finally made love to the one man, the only man she wanted, did not mean she would fall apart when he acted as if it were a mistake. Just because it had been the most wonderful night of *her* life did not, obviously, mean it had been *his*.

Brayden Kinncaid's cobalt eyes bore into hers before darting away. He rose from the bed and grabbed the quilt. Not that he needed it. She knew his body now as a river knew its streambed. Tall, well muscled, he'd always reminded her of a professional football player. Wide sculpted shoulders tapered down to a toned and trimmed torso, long tan legs dusted with his dark hair strode along as he paced. His six-foot-four-inch frame moved as fluidly, as powerfully without clothing as it did within his custom-made suits. Ebony hair, cut neatly short, caught and held the rising sun.

Christian pulled her knees up and tucked the sheet under her arms.

"Look," he said, turning to her. "I'm sorry, this—" He gestured at the bed. "This never should have happened between us. What the hell were we thinking?"

A knot lodged in her throat. She wished she could curl up under the covers and hide from the eyes that would not meet hers.

Taking a deep breath, she braved, "Why? What was wrong with what we did? If memory serves, it didn't seem to bother you last night."

The night of lovemaking had been exquisitely sweet. Passionate and cherished, hungry and tender—so much more than she ever would have, could have, dreamed. It had felt honest. Open. Right.

His jaw tensed as he leveled a look at her, his eyes widening, black brows winging up on surprise. "What was wrong with it?" He shook his head. "What was wrong with it?"

Had it really been that bad?

Forget it. She didn't want to know the answer. Scrambling off the bed, she wrapped the sheet around her until she spotted her silver evening gown.

"Sorry it was obviously such a strain for you, Bray," she tossed, letting go of the sheet as she grabbed the silk dress. "Though last night, I don't remember you complaining in the least. In fact, at one point, I do believe you begged."

The gasp of breath behind made her glance over her shoulder.

His eyes were lightning, blue-edged lightning.

Could it be that simple? Standing naked and holding the gown in her hand, she faced him squarely, though it took all the courage in her to do so. "What? Oh, I guess I should cover up, huh? Wouldn't want you to see something that might be *wrong*."

She slid the dress down over her head, the silk gliding over her skin, reminding her all too clearly of Brayden's hands. As her head broke through the neck, she noticed he had moved forward with his hands fisted at his sides.

Turning her back to him, she propped her hands on her hips. "Zip me up, and I'll leave."

His heavy warm sigh brushed the back of her neck, as his fingers grazed her backbone. The zipper slid up slowly from the small of her back before it was yanked quickly to the top.

She tilted her head to the side, caught him looking down at her, his hands hovering over her shoulders. Taking a deep breath, she took two steps away before facing him again.

"Was it really so bad?"

His silence hung heavy between them.

"You know, I guess this goes without saying, but last night . . ." She stopped. Licking her lips, she continued, "It was — it was —"

"What? It was what?" his deep voice coaxed, though she caught the strained edge.

What the hell. Closing her eyes, she admitted, "It was the best night I ever had. More than I had thought it could be."

He couldn't know, no one knew, just what last night had meant to her, the hurdle she'd finally overcome, the deep fears that had finally been banished.

"It shouldn't have happened," he repeated, sitting down on the edge of the bed.

"Why?"

His eyes when they met hers again were tumultuous. "Because, it's just not right. You're practically my sister! Tori thinks of you as her mom!"

Christian rolled her eyes. That didn't make a bit of sense. Temper started to simmer beneath the pain of his regret. "Your sister? First off, Brayden Kinncaid, I'm not your damn sister — or, for that matter, any relation to you at all. The things you said to me, did to me last night —" She waited a beat. "It wasn't to a sister." Thank God. "And how dare you insult us both, demean us both by that simple, stupid statement.

"Second," she started, the anger warming even more. "I think of Tori as my daughter. I've seen her grow from a month-old baby. She's as much mine as she is yours, regardless of whether or not I gave birth to her." Then an idea shimmered. Cocking her head to the side, she whispered, "Or maybe that's part of the issue here. I'm not JaNell, Brayden." His eyes flashed. She hurried on, "But other than that, I really don't see what Tori's view of me, or my view of her, has to do with you and me, with us. Don't," she added when his head shook, "shake your head at me. There is an us. There always has been in one form or fashion, and if you say otherwise, you're lying. Not that I would be surprised with the excuses you're spouting this morning."

A muscle bunched in his jaw as his eyes narrowed. Temper now fueling her, Christian walked toward him.

"I don't know what changed from a couple of hours ago." She leaned down into his face. "The words I said to you last night, I meant every one of them."

I love you. Now, she couldn't believe she'd told him. "And, you said them back to me." Hot and sweet in her ear as he'd brought them both to pleasure, the words still echoed in her heart, in her soul, in her very being. "You said them back."

The blue of his eyes shifted. She couldn't define the emotion in them, the feelings behind them.

"We were both drunk," he said.

"Drunk?" She straightened and laughed, but her heart skipped, cracked. "Drunk? That's the road you're going to take now? When a few hours ago you were whispering about perfection and beauty."

"Look, Christian." He stood and she stepped back. "It never should have happened."

"Why?" She crossed her arms over her chest and hoped to hell he couldn't see them tremble. God, why?

He paced away, ran a hand through those soft wavy locks, and muttered to himself. Finally, he stopped. The confusion on his face tied her nerves even tighter.

"We crossed a line last night, I know that. I'm just trying to figure out what the hell to do about it."

He would worry it, analyze it, and dissect it to death. She hoped to hell he would.

"Fine," she said tightly. "When you figure it out, you let me know. Stubborn ass."

Taking the bull by the horns, she walked up to him, leaned up on her bare toes, grabbed his face between her hands, and kissed him.

Brayden rocked back, the feel of her wonderful against him. He started to push her away, but could no more do that than he could stop his next heartbeat.

Her body, soft and pliant against his, roared the memories from the night before to life in his mind. Shifting and caressing, they teased his mind, his senses. Just as his hands got lost in her short, cropped hair, she pulled back from him.

"There," she whispered, licking those luscious lips, "maybe that'll help you figure things out."

She stood barefoot before him, gowned in wrinkled silver with hurt and anger shifting in the depths of her smoky gray eyes. God, he loved her eyes.

As she turned to go, he grabbed her arm. The skin, soft as satin, glided under his fingers.

One dark brow arched in question.

"We're not through with this discussion," he calmly told her.

He wanted to kiss her again, and that only aggravated him more, made the tension in his voice more pronounced. "It shouldn't have happened."

Her eyes flashed at him. "Have you bothered to ask yourself why it did?"

He opened his mouth.

One elegant finger rose between them. "Do not use the drunk excuse again, or I swear I will hit you."

Brayden had known this woman for well over eight years and could count the number of times she'd lost her temper or even raised her voice. The fact she was clearly close to doing both now fascinated and warned him.

"I wasn't. I will admit, I think the alcohol only pushed the foolishness to the front, but—"

Her deep in-drawn breath and slight narrowing of her eyes told him that was the wrong thing to say.

They shouldn't even be having this conversation. What the hell had he been thinking? Well, it was obvious, he hadn't been. That was the damn problem.

"Maybe it was just—we spend a lot of time together, you and I. And as you pointed out, we've both raised Tori, in the same home, around the same people. We even work together. Maybe we've been playing house for too long."

Both her dark winged brows rose on that one.

"House? We've been playing house?" The strain in her voice sharpened her tone to a fine edge.

Why wasn't she understanding? On a curse, he looked down, his disbelief, his self-disgust at what had happened between them, what he had *allowed* to happen between them, simmering into anger. There was no way to go back to what they were.

"I hired you to help raise my daughter, my parents see you as part of this family, as a daughter of their own, my brothers think of you as their sister. This should not have happened between us." He punctured the air with his finger.

She jerked her arm free of his hold. "Well, Mr. Rochester, I'm so sorry, my lowly, employed self aimed, dreamed of better things. Yes, I should know better."

Women! How did they manage to twist everything so damn illogically?

Christian strode to the door, anger radiating out of her like the ripples cause by a boulder splashing into a pond.

There, she turned. "You can be such an ass, Brayden Gallagher Kinncaid. You know what your problem is? You've painted every woman with the brush JaNell handed you. And I could almost hate you for that alone. I'm not her. I didn't lie last night. Part of me wants to believe you meant the words you said. But this morning has shown me you are either a liar or a coward." Her eyes locked with his. "Maybe even both. I never thought you were either."

On those words, his bedroom door slammed shut.

Frozen, he stood there. What the hell? A liar? A coward?

He stalked to the door and all but ripped it off its hinges. The outer suite door slammed shut as well.

In the middle of the living quarters, he stopped. Anger tempted him to go after her, but his pride wasn't about to let him traipse out into the damn outer hall wearing a bed quilt, for the love of God.

He stood glaring at the door of his suite, willing her to come back so he could—he could what?

Try to make her see reason, see what they had done was not only wrong it was—it was . . .

Damn it.

Right, so damn right, it made his breath catch to think of how it had been between them. Never had it been like that with any other woman—except JaNell. Maybe Christian was right. He was measuring her by another woman. God. He rubbed his hand over his face. He needed to think. Or a drink.

Looking across to another door, he was silently thankful Tori, his eight-year-old daughter, elected to sleep in her grandparents' suite a few doors down the outer hall.

He bit down on his temper and frustration at the situation, at how hopeless it was, as he walked back to his room.

In fact, the whole damn mess was beyond hopeless. No matter how much he cared for Christian, how great the night with her had been, it would not be again, and shouldn't have happened in the first place.

So, he had looked at her in the last couple of years in more than a sisterly fashion. No harm there, she technically wasn't his sister, regardless of what the family thought of her. Or what he told her.

Then what the hell was the problem? He stared himself down in the mirror and realized the problem was staring back at him.

She was right, he was an ass, and would probably continue to be so. He'd learned the hard way, women and commitments weren't for him.

* * * *

Christian stood, barefoot, waiting on one of the private elevators. At least she'd remembered to grab her purse.

Come on, come on. Surely it didn't take that long for the elevator to get up here.

The idiot! The jerk! Who the hell did the man think he was? A Kinncaid, that's who. She'd been with them long enough to know, whatever a Kinncaid wanted, a Kinncaid got. It wasn't just Brayden; they were all that way — strong, arrogant, powerful men. Handsome men who were loyal to a fault.

She wiped a tear away and realized she was actually crying. God, her heart hurt. After everything, *everything* this was how it ended?

Last night had been . . . Wonderful. Loving. *Healing.*

And now?

Footsteps sounded down the hallway.

Without turning around, she all but snarled, "If you think I'm changing a thing I said or meant, you are dead wrong." Silence greeted her, but the footsteps neared.

"I don't care to talk to you right now. Leave me the hell alone!" She turned to glare at the man, her anger charged and ready to zap the blind, denying idiot, and stopped short.

Quinlan Kinncaid stood a few paces to her left looking straight at the elevator doors.

Shit. Shit. And shit again. Bring the whole damn family into it. Good God.

Christian inwardly sighed and closed her eyes. The ping of the elevator doors jerked her back.

Quinlan stared at her with those green eyes he'd inherited from his mother, his hand holding the door.

Without another look at him, let alone another word, she walked into the elevator. Stepping in beside her, he punched the lobby button, and just as the doors started to close, she saw Aiden Kinncaid walk out of his suite and holler, "Wait up."

Thankfully, Quinlan let the doors shut and the elevator went down. The entire Kinncaid clan was here at their hotel, the Highland Hotel, since they'd celebrated Gavin and Taylor's awaited wedding reception. When the two had married several months ago, there had not been time to have a celebration. After Taylor healed, and the kids were doing better, the family threw a giant ball in honor of the new couple in the family hotel here in Washington, D.C. The night of dancing had ended in one of love. Or so she had thought at the time.

The sunrise apparently changed the mind-set of Brayden. Idiot.

Quinlan cleared his throat.

She glanced at him out of the corner of her eye. His were locked on her. She could smell the aftershave he'd always favored and that always made her think of watery forests for some reason.

"I didn't think you'd want another one of us asking you what was wrong," he said.

Was it possible to fade into the wooden paneling?

His head cocked to the side. "Want to talk about it?"

"No."

Silence stretched between them. But then he cleared his throat again. "Not that it's any of my business, but from the looks of things you're rather upset. Bray being an ass again?"

She didn't snicker at the pun. "Isn't he always?"

"What did he do this time?"

Turning, she faced this youngest Kinncaid, who was still a few years her senior. "Do you think . . . That is . . . Never mind."

His tongue ran around his teeth. "You two were awfully close last night." He shoved his hands into his pockets, his dark suit jacket caught behind his wrists. "I know you left together, which isn't really anything new, but I have to admit, seeing you barefoot, dressed in last night's dress and your hair all a mess reflects a little close to a lovers' spat."

She felt her face heat at the words and that damn cocky grin of his slid across his face. She should have just gone to her own room, but then she still would have been in Brayden's suite. And they'd probably still be snarling at each other because Brayden could never just leave it alone. No, she had to get out and if she looked tumbled, well . . .

"And the hickey on your collarbone. I wondered how long it would take you two."

Great. This just kept getting better. "Hell," she muttered. "You know what, I don't care. Tell me, do you think, since you obviously noticed something between us, do you think it's only there because we've been playing house?"

She crossed her arms over her chest and tapped her foot. It was beside the point she was beyond embarrassed, mortified more like. What if Brayden did have a valid point and she just couldn't see it? No, that couldn't be right.

Russet brows rose at her question. Out of all the Kinncaid males, Quinlan was the only one to take after Mrs. Kinncaid, his mother, in coloring with his eyes, green as Ireland, and his hair as burnished as autumn leaves.

One long finger scratched the corner of his mouth. "No, I don't think . . . Playing house?" His eyes narrowed on her.

The disbelief in his words mirrored her feelings. "Never mind, you answered my question." Then an idea came to her. "Maybe I should find my own place."

"What?" His voice sharpened. "Did he say that to you?"

The more she thought about it, the more the idea bloomed. Playing house. No way. Let the man see what life without her was like. 'Course, she might be spiting her nose to save her face. And she would miss Tori dreadfully, but if—and that was a giant if—Brayden was actually right, that meant he would eventually find some other woman and she couldn't very well sit back and watch as someone else slid into the role she was used to playing. She could never be the passive little nanny.

"Christian?" Quinlan's voice pulled her back. "Did you hear what I said?"

She shook her head. "I need you to do me a favor and be quiet about it."

"First, answer my question. Did Brayden tell you to find your own place?" His eyes were as sharp as emeralds.

"What?" She waved her hand at him. "No. I just need you to do something for me."

"Well, that depends on what you want me to do." The elevator reached the bottom level. The elevator was hidden behind a wall of gilded mirrors. The occupants inside—the Kinncaids—could see out into the lobby, but no one could see in until the outer mirrored doors were opened. The men said that as owners of the Highland Hotel, they didn't want to be predictable. This gave them the advantage of seeing what was going on, on the floor, without anyone the wiser.

Quinlan didn't open the outer doors, nor did he look at the floor; his gaze was centered on her.

"What do you want me to do, Christian?"

Taking a deep breath, she said, "I want you to keep quiet about me looking for a place. I don't need anything fancy, just an apartment, somewhere between here and Seneca. That way I'm close to the shop and close to home, too."

His eyes studied her, made her feel like squirming.

"Why?" He crossed his arms.

She raked her hands through her hair. "Because, maybe he's right. Maybe we just got lost up in the moment. No. That's not it either. That can't be it. I don't know. Maybe if I was gone, he'd see that . . . that . . . Hell, I don't know. Just keep quiet, will you? Be a pal, a brother. Help me look. It doesn't mean I'm going to actually get it, but I might."

Another moment stretched between them. "Have you thought about Tori in all this? Or Mom and Dad? I think you need to think this through."

She loved this family, she really did, but they were all so damn protective, so — so — Kinncaid!

Reining in her frustrations at the males of this clan, she said, "Yeah, I have. If he's so set that I'm not the woman for him, that means that he will one day find one. What am I supposed to do? Sit back while she starts doing all the things I've always done? With a family I consider mine — and I'm not talking all you guys. I'm talking about Brayden and Tori. And if that does turn out to be the case, then in the long run, my moving will help Tori. I won't be in the way for whomever, or whatever he decides he wants." She stopped, his expression hadn't changed. "I'm a grown woman, Quinlan. Have you ever known me to leap without looking?"

"Before this morning? Or maybe last night? No. But need I remind you why you're concocting this brilliant plan of yours in the first place? Did you leap or look before . . . Before . . ."

"Before what? Before I made love to your brother?"

His eyes slid closed and he pinched the bridge of his narrow nose. "I don't want this picture in my mind."

"You're the one that brought it up. I don't want it there either." Planting her hands on her hips, she said, "What do you think? I just hopped in bed for a damn one-night stand?"

His head shook. "No. I'm just trying to point out—"

A shadow fell over the doors. Aiden, the eldest Kinncaid brother, stood glaring in. In seconds, the mirrors slid back.

"Why didn't you hold the elevator? I know you heard me." He glared from one to the other, but his cobalt gaze, darker than Brayden's, zeroed in on her. "What's wrong?"

"Nothing." She started to shove by him, but he blocked her way and turned the stare on Quinlan.

"What did you do to her?"

Quinlan's hands rose, palms up. "I'm just trying to talk some sense into her."

"Will you both just stop!" This time, when she shoved Aiden, he moved. "I have things to do."

"You're not wearing shoes," he muttered. And she heard his whispered, "She had a hickey on her neck!"

Rolling her eyes, she didn't look back, but hurried across the foyer of the grand hotel and out into the warming sun. Already into September, the mornings were cool here and the cement chilled her feet.

The valet brought her Volkswagen Bug around. She climbed into the gray vehicle, cursing all males in general and left, merging with the early Sunday morning traffic.

There were things she needed to think about, things to decide.

Maybe Brayden, even in his stupidity, had been right. Maybe they did spend too much time together. They lived together, had built a life together, hell, they worked together. The Kinncaids had been Heaven sent to her, in her opinion, and perhaps it was time to move on. Grow up and move away.

Well, not grow up. She'd grown up one wintry night years and years ago.

But moving on, moving away was realistic. The problem was she didn't know if she was ready. Was she ready?

The small town of Seneca, the old family Kinncaid home, the hotel, the entire family, offered and blanketed her in a security she did not take for granted. She'd known a family like theirs once, long ago, but time, events, and people changed all that.

No, she wasn't going there, not now, not this morning.

Back to the matter at hand.

Should she get her own place? And if she tried, what excuse would she give?

What about Tori? That would be hard. No, more than hard. She was used to seeing the little girl every day. Morning routines before school, picking her up from school, listening through music lessons if it was her turn, bed times, sick times . . . She hadn't lied when she said she thought of the little girl as her own.

But—and God knows she didn't want to think about it, yet the doubt crept in anyway—what if Brayden didn't feel the same way about her as she did about him? What if he didn't really love her? What if he'd just said it in the heat of the moment? Then one day he would find someone and that someone would be Tori's mom. That woman would get the breakfast routines with them both and the school work and the piano practices and the fights about vegetables before cookies.

That hurt, hurt so bad her skin prickled and her breath caught.

Christian shook her head, blinked the sudden stupid tears away and gripped the steering wheel. No matter what, she had to know what he really felt about her.

Perhaps by putting some distance between them, she, he, they could figure it all out.

So distance it would be. A place of her own.

On her own. She hadn't been on her own since she'd come to Washington, D.C., and Seneca, Maryland—since she'd met the Kinncaids.

The past slithered through her memories, but she shoved it aside. All that was behind her, and ghosts couldn't hurt her. Besides, *he* was still in Oregon, completely across the country and he had no idea where she was.

Yes, she could live alone. She was a grown woman and it was time to stop living in fear.

Chapter 2

Two months later

Oh, God, he'd found her.

Christian took a deep drag of albuterol. It had been months since she'd had to use her rescue inhaler. Fall netted over the air, a golden, amber web chilling and promising the winter to come. The heater blew at full blast in her car, and even with her long woolen coat, nothing stopped the shivers sliding through her bones.

This was not happening. Not again. Why? Why now? After all this time?

She glanced over at the passenger seat as the tightness in her chest loosened a bit from the albuterol and she could breathe. Photos today. Large glossy eight-by-tens in black and white. She'd found the brown envelope under her wipers when she came out of Dr. Trevor's office. Her name was printed in bold black letters across the front.

But inside . . .

Inside she was caught on individual freeze-frames. Frozen moments of her life stilled in photos. There were pictures of her doing everything from swimming to laundry, coming and going to the shop, the store, her apartment. He knew everything about her. Everything she did. Where she worked. Where she lived. How she spent her time and who she spent it with. Like shopping with Tori.

Oh, God, Tori! That picture pierced her heart.

She leaned back against the leather headrest, tension throbbing behind her eyes.

A chill had wrapped its cold arms around her and held her fast for the last month. These were not the first photographs she'd received, but she hoped they'd be the last. First had been the postcards. Two words scrawled in that hand she knew all too well. *My Angel.*

There was one in the envelope now.

My Angel.

Her high school photograph, years and years old.

My Angel.

Then every few days a packet with photos recording her activities arrived. Last night was a phone call. All she could hear was that damn opera in the background.

The breath hitched again in her lungs. Fighting the panic back, she left the envelope in the car and got out, locking the doors. Her gaze slid over the growing and lengthening shadows.

Was he out there now?

A bell from the door jingled, pulling her attention to the shop's entrance. *Kinncaid Antiquities* was written in black letters across the door and picture window.

Brayden stood there with his hands on his trim hips, dressed in a dark button-down and black slacks. "You're late."

"I'm here, aren't I?" Deep breath. Shoving her hands in her coat pockets, she ducked her head and passed him. Hopefully she looked all right. Sometimes he could be so perceptive.

She'd left here at noon to meet with clients in Virginia, then rushed back to D.C. for an appointment with her shrink, but Brayden didn't need to know the last part. It was the first counseling session she'd needed in over five years.

"I—I got held up in Virginia then stopped at a few country shops to see if I could find any decent deals."

The antique industry was Brayden's contribution to the family business. He owned this shop and supplied the Kinncaid line of hotels with either the best original antique and vintage pieces or reproductions. Christian understood antiques, she'd grown up with them. After she moved here and Brayden realized she knew what was what with the old pieces of furniture, glassware and sculptures, she'd started working here at the shop. She'd then gone to Georgetown U and earned her business degree with a minor in art history. Both helped her with her job here in the family shop.

Christian walked around behind the counter. Antiques stood still, waiting for someone to come in and claim them like lost orphans hoping for another home. The shop smelled of musky old wood, beeswax and lemon oil, a soft familiar smell that mixed with the sandalwood-spiced cologne Brayden favored.

For the first time since seeing that brown envelope on her windshield, she sighed, something calming her. Or rather someone. Brayden.

"What took so long today?" His voice had always been deep and soothing to her, like unfathomed depths of a lake. "I was starting to worry. It's not like you to meander back to work, or browse country stores," he said, shutting and locking the door.

She was late; it was almost six and the shop closed at five, but after seeing the envelope she'd panicked. She'd just driven and this was where she'd ended up, even though she knew the shop was closed. Some part of her had hoped he'd still be here. Not that she could tell him anything.

Brayden walked toward her, but stayed a distance away. The same routine since that morning a couple of months ago; he got close enough to inquire, yet far enough away to run.

"So I decided to stop at a few shops. It's not a big deal," she lied, looking over some notes and receipts in the basket by the old-fashioned register. "I'm sorry I didn't make it back earlier."

"I don't care about that," Brayden's voice barely registered.

She darted a glance at the window. Was she being captured in freeze-frame now? There had been a photo of her here at the shop, the coffeehouse, her car. He knew everything! Everything. How had he found her? How? Already she was losing sleep and her appetite. The windows only showed her the busy street beyond. A man waiting on the light looked over to the shop.

Absently, she rubbed her neck. Could he be the photographer? She had no idea what her stalker looked like. The man following her, taking the pictures, documenting her life, was not the man she needed to fear. No.

The terror came from the one who hired him.

My Angel.

A shiver danced down her spine and she wiped her damp palms on her dark, pin-striped pants.

"Hey, you okay?" Brayden's roughened voice inquired.

Not meeting his eyes, she shrugged. "Sure."

"Christian."

The fear, the terror, the past all rolled together. She turned the storming emotions into anger, biting out at him. "What do you care? You no longer have a say in anything I do."

The corners of his mouth thinned and his eyes hardened, darkened in their blue as they studied her. "I have a say, simply because I do care."

"Hmmm."

He stared at her in that intense gaze he'd inherited from his father, Jock Kinncaid. Finally, she looked away, but her neck tingled where she knew his eyes bore into her.

"Christian," he repeated in a steeled tone.

Her eyes slid closed. She could *not* tell him. He'd ask questions. Questions she couldn't answer, wouldn't answer, because the threat was too great.

The truth had gotten her nowhere before. And asking for help had led to unbearable consequences. Not again, never again. She'd deal with it on her own.

Maybe she should just move away—leave as soon as possible.

My Angel.

Her chest vised and she gasped for breath. Again, she jerked out her inhaler and tried to fight off an asthma attack.

"Look at me."

Slowly she drew a breath, fought her demons and turned to face the man she loved with all her heart. For the first time since she'd left his penthouse suite two months earlier, she was almost glad he'd turned away from her. Almost.

His gaze ran over her face, down her body, and she remembered what it was like to be held in his arms. To feel safe.

Safe? That was an illusion.

There was no safety for her. There never would be.

"You'll always be mine, Josephine. Always," the voice from the past whispered through her memories.

"What's with the inhaler? You haven't had an asthma attack since the mess with the kids months ago. And before that? I can't remember you using one in years."

Brayden wondered at the vulnerability he saw in her, the worry in her eyes.

Christian was one of the strongest women he knew. She gave what she got, usually in spades. For the last two months or so they'd bantered and bit at each other. But lately she'd seemed distracted. Too quiet and withdrawn. He noted the darkened circles under her eyes, worry creasing her brows. Her pallor contrasted starkly against her short dark hair, her charcoal pantsuit. Had she lost weight? Her collarbone, more prominent than he remembered, peeked out of her white button-down. Bones protruded from her delicate wrists as her French cuffs shifted. Had he brought her to this?

Well, she was the one who decided to move out of the family home. Not him, and he damn sure hadn't chased her away like his brothers seemed to think. Everyone blamed him for her move to the city: his daughter, his parents, his brothers and their wives.

Himself.

No, it was not his fault she'd up and decided to leave. He'd told her he would move to the hotel. After all, he was in town most of the time anyway.

She wanted her own place, her own space. So out she moved while his mother tried to understand, his father barked and snarled, his daughter cried, and his brothers glared at him.

Now he felt like glaring at himself.

Ironically, it felt like a marriage separation, or what he figured one would feel like. He'd taken her for granted, he supposed. The housewife who helped with his business as much as the child would allow. They'd been so much a part of the other's life for so long and now . . . Now she wasn't there.

He missed her. Missed breakfast with her, listening to her clear laughter mix with Tori's, hearing her voice, seeing her around the house when he was there, missed their talks about the important, the silly, the nothing-at-alls. He just missed her.

Loneliness was a strange thing at thirty-four, creeping upon the wary. Her perfume, Calvin Klein's Obsession, drifted on the air between them, the sweet smell reminding him of a dark, sultry, tangled night.

She looked as lonely as he felt. Brayden hadn't seen that haunted look in her eyes for a long, long time, those darted hurried looks. Other than that nightmare months before—when Tori and her cousin, Ryan, had been kidnapped—he honestly couldn't remember the last time Christian had needed to inhale albuterol. Fear shifted along her features as she glanced again out the window, the pulse furious in her long slim neck.

"Christian?"

She rubbed her arms.

"What's wrong?" he asked.

She shook her head, one long-fingered hand running absently

through her short, slightly curled hair. He caught the tremor as she dropped it down to her side.

He sighed. There were walls between them, there always had been, but most had crumbled the longer she'd lived with his family. Some had gone up after their night together. Recently, it was as if she were carefully fortifying some inner sanctuary.

Different tactic. Nonchalantly, he leaned against the counter and crossed his ankles and arms. "Mom called yesterday. She's worried about you. She said she and Dad hadn't heard from you much lately and when she did hear from you, there was something in your voice."

Her eyes wouldn't meet his and she busily ruffled through a stack of papers he'd been looking over as he'd waited on her.

"I'll—I'll have to call and talk with her. Everything's fine. Fine. I've just been really busy and had a lot on my mind." Her voice seemed sincere, but there was something—tension—just under the surface.

"Such as?"

She took another deep breath. "Just—just things, Brayden." Finally, she looked at him and leaned back against the counter, but she was hardly calm. Her boot heel tapped on the floor. "I've been doing some thinking lately. Well, longer than lately. It started last summer when you and I talked about opening a shop in the London hotel."

She cleared her throat. He noticed her fingers fidgeted within the confines of her pockets. And why did she still have her coat on?

"Anyway, I've been thinking about my career and life in general," she finished on a huff.

"What do you mean?"

Her head tilted to the side and very quietly, she asked, "Did you know I was going to go to Juilliard? I don't think I ever told you. I had a scholarship and everything. I used to want—never mind. Anyway, life moves on, not always the way we planned, and I've been thinking. That's all."

Juilliard? No, she'd never told him. For as long as Brayden had known her, a runaway who had shown up on his parents' doorstep years ago, he suspected the reason behind her flight had been a bad home life. Not that any of them knew for certain. Christian could be open about many things, but others — it was like trying to see a clear picture in a black murky pond. She'd never told them about her life before, and they'd eventually quit asking. She was twenty-eight years old and she did what she wanted to.

So she was musically talented, he did know that much, if not the Juilliard bit. Why she was suddenly telling him this, he couldn't figure out. He took a deep breath; he'd just stay quiet and see what else she decided to tell him. Maybe she'd eventually get around to what was bothering her.

Frustration laced her sigh and a sad smile played on her face. "I wanted Broadway. I guess maybe that's why I still take a theater and music class every semester. Who knows."

He still had no idea what she was leading up to.

Turning her back to him she said quietly, "I used to be really good at that sort of thing. I grew up like Tori, for the most part. Voice lessons, ballet, art classes."

Brayden still didn't understand what was troubling her. And troubled she clearly was.

She turned to him. "I'd always thought music heals."

Heals? He tucked that bit away for now.

"Okay," he drew out. "What does all this have to do with the London shop?" A suspicion grew, but he tossed it aside. She wouldn't.

"Music doesn't heal everything," she whispered.

"What do you want it to heal?" he asked just as quietly.

For a long moment she stared at nothing, and the pain in her eyes, the sheen of tears, made his breath catch.

She opened her mouth, then snapped it shut.

"Christian?" He reached out to her, but she jerked back.

Finally, she smiled. "Nothing. Doesn't matter. Sorry, I haven't been in the best of moods lately." She waved a hand. "I don't know why I'm going over all that. I just wanted to talk about the idea of opening the shop in England."

Her smile was too bright and he didn't miss the fact she kept looking out the window.

"You're suddenly interested because?"

"I thought . . ." She licked her lips. "That is . . . I thought maybe I could go over and open it. I know enough and —"

"Stop right there." Move to England? He wasn't even going to go there. Trying to understand what the hell was up with her, he changed the subject. "Tell me why you're not sleeping. You look like hell, and you just fought off an asthma attack. If you don't take care of yourself, Mom and Dad will have you moved back home in no time and London won't be an issue."

Actually he liked that idea. Not that it should matter to him either way, but it did. He wasn't about to stand by and watch her run herself into the ground. Or let her move to London, for God's sake. London?

Already she was shaking her head. "I won't move back to Seneca."

"Why?" Damn stubborn woman.

"I have my reasons."

"Is this all because of us?" he braved.

Her look singed him on the spot. "Us? You mean there's actually an us now, Brayden?"

He counted to five. "Not like that. What happened *between* us."

She closed her eyes and an idea slammed into him. Pale, losing weight, off-kilter. "Are you sick?"

A small grin played at the corner of her mouth. "No, why?"

He took a deep breath, then strangled out, "Are you pregnant?"

Her eyes shot open. "What?"

He watched her, watched the surprise in her eyes. "Are you pregnant?"

The shocked look on her face should have been enough, but it wasn't. He'd been down this road before.

"Would it matter if I was?" she asked quietly.

His stomach rolled, fluttered, and twisted. "You're coming home."

She laughed. "God, Brayden. No."

"Yes, you are."

She cocked a brow. "Excuse me? First off, I'm not yours to order around, and if you don't like that, too damn bad. Two, if I was pregnant, I'd still tell you, though I might not move back home. And three, it hardly matters since I'm not pregnant."

Relief warred with more disappointment than he'd expected. He stared at her; she seemed to be telling the truth.

Her eyes narrowed. "I told you before, I'm not JaNell. Stop comparing me to her."

Brayden blew out a breath and shoved his hands in his pockets. "You sure?"

"Yes." She shook her head. "Yes, I'm sure."

He shoved a hand through his hair. "Damn it, Christian. What am I supposed to think? You're not acting right, losing weight and pale all the time and —"

The knock at the door had him turning, but not before he'd noticed Christian jerk.

Well, damn.

Inwardly cursing the gods of timing, he walked to the door and mouthed through the glass to the couple, "Sorry, we're closed." They nodded and moved on down the walkway.

What had Christian so jumpy and contemplating moving an ocean away? And what was with the past revelations? He'd learned more of her past in the last few minutes than in the years he'd known her.

He glanced at Christian. Her gray eyes flashed with a hidden challenge, for a moment overshadowing the fear he was certain he'd caught in their depths.

"Where were we?"

Christian walked to him and slid around, unlocking the door. "I should have just gone home. I'm leaving."

He put his hand on the door above the lock. "We're not through."

She turned those haunted gray eyes on him. Leaning up on her toes, she kissed his cheek and said, "Yes, Brayden, we are."

His gut tightened. Hell.

Brayden grabbed his long woolen coat off the antique rack, shrugged into it, and cut all but the track lights. He watched her as she walked out the door. Christian was normally quite composed — graceful came to mind usually. But not today. He frowned and caught her quick look over her shoulder out to the street, the tight way she held herself, the way she held her keys in her fist, the metal keys bladed out from between her fingers. But always the darted looks, almost as though she were afraid of . . . Of what? Or who?

His eyes locked with Christian's and something tightened within him even as he knew she wouldn't welcome him. And he couldn't really blame her.

The cold November air swirled down the street. For a minute more he held Christian's smoky stare until the woman he couldn't get out of his mind turned and walked to her car. At his own vehicle, he opened the door, but his eyes kept watching her.

Again, she glanced around, looking over her shoulder.

What was with her?

It didn't matter. Something was wrong and it had nothing to do with work or music or whatever else she'd tried to tell him—including London.

Christian was afraid and he wanted to know why.

* * * *

Several days later, Christian parked her car in her allotted slot in front of the condos. She'd spent the afternoon with Tori, who chatted about Ryan and music and school and her next recital.

Kaitlyn Kinncaid had asked her to stay out at Seneca, at the family estate, and Jock warned her of the drive, but Christian drove back here to D.C. anyway.

Why? Did it really matter? Brayden hadn't been there. He'd been out doing God knew what with God knew who and she shouldn't give a damn.

Brayden's parents both dropped hints that it would be better if she were around more. They tried to talk her into moving back out to Seneca, back into the family mansion with them and Brayden and Tori. They were worried. Jock informed her she looked haggard. Lovely. Just lovely. She was not only letting her man get away in her absence, but she was looking haggard.

On a sigh, she got out of the car, locked her doors and started for her condo.

The night was cold. A bone-slicing wind sharpened through the air and she pulled her coat tighter as she walked down the lighted walkway.

She really liked these condos. They had a security gate, though she now wondered how good it really was. Maybe she could get an alarm system installed.

Her boot heels clicked on the bricked path. Already she had her keys out.

A car door shut in the night and voices floated on the air.

Hurrying to her door, she glanced around and stopped.

The large brown envelope against her door immediately stole her attention. She looked over her shoulder, but the darkness cloaked what might lie beyond the realm of light.

Goose bumps pricked her skin.

Her breath hitched, but she closed her eyes and thought through her breathing exercise. When she opened them several moments later, her chest, thankfully, didn't squeeze up, but still fear slithered through her dark and dangerous.

Steeling herself, she knelt down, almost afraid to touch it.

Pick it up. Just pick it up. Or throw it away.

No, she wouldn't throw it away. How long had it been here? All day? On a deep breath, she picked up the package. Without standing, she slid a finger under the metal brad, folded the ends together and opened the envelope. Pictures slid into her hand as she turned it to empty the contents, and a white postcard fluttered to the concrete.

My Angel.

Her hands shook. Why the hell wouldn't he just leave her alone?

She grabbed the white card and stood, anger and fear warring within her at what he was doing to her.

"Hi."

Christian whirled at the male voice. The photos flew out of the open envelope and splattered across the ground as she staggered back a step.

Her heart slammed against her chest.

A man stood a few feet behind her, holding a laundry basket. A familiar man, he stepped closer and the last of the shadows left him.

"Lieutenant Morris?" she gasped. What was he doing here?

He smiled, a quick flash of straight teeth. "Yeah, I live a few condos down. I was doing laundry." He settled the basket on his hip and held his hand out. "I'd heard Drayson and Geoffery talking about the new girl who moved into Drayson's condo. I had no idea it was you. How do you like it?"

He dropped his hand back to his side.

"F-fine." Drayson and Geoffery were her next-door neighbors. Drayson taught theater music at Georgetown University, which was how she'd found this place. He'd moved in with his partner, who managed the condos. Lieutenant Morris worked the special crimes division of the Washington, D.C., Police Department. They'd met under strained circumstances several months ago.

"I'm sorry I startled you." Morris had a well-modulated voice. Probably went with the job. His dark hair was cut short enough, she wondered why he just didn't get a buzz. He was the same as she remembered him from a few months ago during that nightmare with Gavin and Taylor, when Ryan and Tori had been kidnapped.

Morris bent down, setting his laundry basket by her door.

The photos. Shit.

"Oh, don't worry about it, I can—I can get it." She tried to shuffle and grab all the photos, but he already held several in his hands.

Dark eyes narrowed on a frown as he looked from the pictures in his hands to her.

"Where did you get these?" His voice wasn't well modulated now. More like a sharpened blade.

A cop. He was a cop. She didn't want to get into this. There would be questions. Things she couldn't say, couldn't answer, and she knew she wasn't a very proficient liar.

Without looking at him, she gathered the rest up. Just as she was reaching for the white square on the ground, his hand darted out and snatched it up.

"*My Angel?*"

Her hand trembled as she slid the eight-by-tens back into the envelope. She shrugged. "Yeah, some guy, I guess, has a crush on me."

Trying to take the photos from him proved useless. He didn't release them. Finally, her eyes met his, in what she hoped was a glare.

"Can I have my pictures back, please?"

"When you answer my question. Where did you get these?" He looked down and flipped through the ones he held. "Walking to your car, talking to a kid on a park bench, working in that antiques shop, eating at a restaurant, and you looking over your shoulder at a red light. Here's one with you and the little Kinncaid girl." His dark brown eyes leveled a look at her, and she almost squirmed.

"Care to explain these?"

"No." She stood and held out her hand.

Sighing, he too rose, and she realized he wasn't much taller than she, not like Brayden. Morris was more along the lines of average in her opinion. In a pair of heels she'd look him in the eye.

"Are these the only ones you've gotten?"

"Yes." No, but he didn't need to know that. She'd gone to the cops before and it hadn't done her any good.

One single brow cocked and his look said he knew she was lying. "Have you reported these pictures? That someone is clearly stalking you?"

Christian propped her hand on her hip. "Are you always the cop?"

He nodded. "Yes."

Figured.

"And as an always-cop, I notice you didn't answer my question. So here's some professional advice from my line of work: Report this. The sooner the better. Carry some mace or pepper spray with you, and always keep a cell phone handy."

"I'm sure you're making more out of this than—"

"Don't be stubborn. Have you taken any self-defense classes?"

Christian sighed. Nothing would stop this man from her past, not mace or pepper spray or self-defense classes. She turned and put her key in her lock. Morris's hand covered hers.

"Do you mind? Call it occupational hazard, but I'd rather know that everything is as it should be inside, rather than let you waltz in there."

She returned his stare. "You don't have a wife or girlfriend, do you?"

He smiled again, his square jaw softening just a bit. "Why, Miss Bills, is that a come-on? You're not very subtle."

"More subtle than 'let me check out your place for ya, babe.'"

He ignored her, shoved her door open, and flipped on the lights, moving past her into the condo.

Christian rolled her eyes. "Besides, I just meant you obviously don't have a significant other, or you would know women don't like to be ordered around. Do this . . . Do that . . ."

He walked out of the open living area and into the kitchen. Not that she'd admit it, but she was glad to know there was a cop not too far away and that he was looking to make certain no bad guys lingered in the shadows. As he came out of the kitchen, he took the stairs two at a time to the second level. Christian shrugged out of her coat, hung it in the closet and leaned against the wall. Morris bounded down the stairs and stopped in front of her.

"Catch the bad guys?" she quipped.

For a moment he said nothing. Then, "I saw two more brown packets in the living room and one in the bedroom. Not that I opened them, but I'm betting they hold the same thing that one in your hand does."

Not a thing came to mind to tell him. What would she say?

"This is serious, Miss Bills."

Yeah it was. "I will handle it, Lieutenant Morris."

"Call me Gabe."

"As in Gabriel?" she asked.

"Gabe," he answered.

There they were in her entryway, she hoping he would leave, yet glad he'd checked things out, and him studying her in an easy, yet sharp way.

Finally, she cleared her throat. "Okay, Gabe, though I think Gabriel fits better."

"I'm serious about reporting this."

She shook her head. "It's nothing."

His gaze remained steady and it was easy to understand what some people meant when they said they could spot a cop. Something in his carriage, his stance, was warning. She shifted to her other foot as he stared at her.

"If you knew how many times I stood over . . ." He shook his head. "Don't be stupid. Report it, get some mace and be on the lookout. Call the cops or even me." He dug a card out of his wallet and handed it to her. Looking around, he grabbed a pen off her entry table and scribbled on the back.

When he handed it to her, she saw it was his home number.

What the hell did she do?

Looking him in the eye, she only said, "Thanks."

The corners of his mouth hardened. "You're done talking about this, aren't you?"

She nodded. "Yes."

"Fine, but I warned you."

He strode to the door. "You might think of having your locks changed. The photos show he knows where you live, he could have gotten a key somehow."

She hadn't thought of that.

He continued to stare at her. "If you change your mind about reporting this, give me a call. At least get some damn mace."

"Aye-aye, Captain!"

His glare made her grin. He was easy to rile; in that he and Brayden were the same.

"What do the Kinncaids have to say about this 'infatuated' guy?" He paused out on her stoop.

At the door she said, "Good night, Gabe."

"You haven't told them, have you?" His muttered curse was colorful and inventive. "Why?"

"Good night, Gabe."

"What kind of game are you playing, I wonder?" he asked as he grabbed his laundry basket.

She slowly shut the door.

A deadly game. One she'd played and lost before, and was terrified she'd lose again.

Chapter 3

He leaned back against the cushions of the couch.

The latest pictures slid easily from one to the next as he flipped through them.

Josephine might have cut her hair and moved clear across the country; years may have passed, but he still knew just how to play her. What buttons to push, how to string the game along. Anticipation only heightened the experience. He knew the postcard would tell her who he was.

A soft chuckle escaped him.

This picture clearly showed him his game was a success thus far. In it, Josephine was looking through some of his pictures when the cameraman snapped a photo. Frozen on black and white paper, her fear excited him.

He had the power. He always had. Always would.

She had just forgotten that.

Anger flickered and glared within him, but he shifted past it because it only clouded thought and reason. Her time would come. But for now? Now, he was having fun.

Looking at the clock, he noted how late it was and reached for the marker. Time to up the stakes. He only had two days before his flight back.

Presentation was everything. Everything. Set the stage for his entrance.

The hotel room was dark, save for the small desk lamp.

A grin lifted his mouth.

The Kinncaids definitely knew how to run a first-class hotel. Only the best for certain guests, and he'd always liked the best of everything. He toasted their success with his watered scotch in his Highland Hotel crystal glass.

Standing, he turned and looked out the window. He knew just what to do next, and it was certain to gag her into silence should she decide to tell after their meeting.

What a meeting it would be.

He had years to make up for, and so little time to do it.

He'd been given the opinion to just let her have an accident, something to end it cleanly. After all, truth was, Josephine was a threat to his career, but he wasn't ready to let her go yet. He'd waited too long to find her. Now that he had, he wasn't about to discard her. She'd been perfect once. Only and completely his. And she would be again. He was simply reminding her of that fact.

Turning back to the desk, he picked up the black marker and set to work.

* * * *

Kaitlyn Kinncaid walked down the long hallway toward the room she'd shared with her husband for well over forty years. As she passed Brayden's hallway, she paused and sighed. Things simply were not the same anymore. Not since Christian left. Stupid boy.

She shook her head; those two were meant for each other. She still had no idea what happened between the girl that had become their daughter and their son, but she was trying not to meddle.

A sliver of light came from beneath Brayden's door. Frowning, she walked down the hallway of Brayden's wing and gently knocked on his door. She might not meddle, but that didn't mean she couldn't give a faint push when needed.

"Yes?" his voice came from inside. "Come in."

She eased the door open, propping her mug in one hand. He was dressed in sweatpants and a T-shirt, and judging by the scattered papers and laptop, he'd been sitting in the seating area before the fire. Now he stood before the darkened window. "What are you still doing up?"

His mouth lifted in a rueful grin. "Couldn't sleep."

"Hmmm." She walked in, shut the door and sat in one of his chairs. Of all her sons, he was the most complex. Aiden without a doubt had been the easiest, but both Aiden and Brayden had always shared a serious, deep streak that the others didn't possess. "Have you talked with Christian?"

He startled. "Mom."

She shrugged. "I just thought you might have learned what was bothering her." She took a sip of her tea and pushed a graying strand of hair back. "Do you think I should color my hair?"

"What? Why?" And just like that, he looked as baffled as his father.

Kaitlyn laughed and waved a hand. "Never mind. So tell me, what's bothering you?"

He opened his mouth, then shut it. "Nothing."

Time for the nudge. "I went by to see Christian yesterday and she doesn't look good. Of course, I met her hunky cop neighbor."

He whirled around from the window he'd been looking out. "What?"

"Morris. You remember him? Nice gentleman. He stopped by and talked with her for a few minutes." Now that she thought about it . . . She frowned. "He seemed very protective."

Brayden walked past her to his desk, then back to the window. He stopped, turned to her, then walked back to the desk.

"Do you miss her at all?" she asked softly. "I don't mean to be like your father. He tends to get a bit in his mouth and that's all he sees." Like with Brice and Aiden. Or years before like Brice and Ian.

"What? Miss her?" He sat heavily in the other chair, his eyes closing as he leaned back. "Yes, Mom. I miss her."

"Then what, pray tell, are you going to do about it?"

He sighed.

"She's not JaNell, Brayden." JaNell Thomas had been Tori's biological mom. The woman had been nice and sweet and had given the baby to her father. For that alone, the woman would have Kaitlyn's thanks. But JaNell had also ripped Brayden's heart out. He was old-fashioned with old-fashioned ideals, and he'd been madly in love with that young, driven girl. JaNell had died in a plane crash not two months after Tori's birth. Worried about stability for his baby daughter, Brayden had sold his apartment in town and had moved back out to the family mansion in Seneca, Maryland, with his parents. The family home was just that, a family home, no matter how many wings it had. And Kaitlyn was full of love and gratitude and so much pride for her son and the wonderful father he was.

On a frustrated sigh, he raked his hands through his hair. "I know that. I've never really thought she was JaNell."

Kaitlyn cleared her throat. "Maybe not intentionally." She rose and patted his hand, yawning. "God only sends us so many blessings. It's up to us to recognize them, and if we don't, He rarely sends them again."

"Mom, sometimes you talk like a damn fortune cookie."

She leaned over and kissed his cheek. "We mothers are wise souls." She caught his grin as she walked to the door. There she saw he'd picked up his laptop and was grinning at it.

"I'm not the only one up," he said to her.

So her other heartsick one was up as well.

"Tell Christian I said hello, and to make certain she gets enough rest and a good breakfast."

He nodded. "Yes, Mom."

She shut the door and walked to her room. Inside their apartments, her husband sat leaning against the headboard, his white hair standing in disarray. "You bring me anything?"

"No, I thought you were asleep."

"As long as we've been married and making love, you'd think you'd know by now I like a snack after loving my wife."

She grinned and handed him a cookie from her robe pocket.

"What took you so long?" he asked, pulling her down into the crook of his arm.

"Nothing. Brayden's up."

He humphed. "You wouldn't be meddling now, would you?"

Kaitlyn decided not to answer.

* * * *

Christian rubbed her eyes. She'd typed up her latest acquisition reports for several clients and still needed to do the bid proposals for the North Carolina estate being sold next week. She'd gotten behind since her theater class started rehearsals.

She didn't exactly have the time, but theater was a love she just couldn't seem to let go of. Though this particular play, about a stalked woman who comes back as a ghost, stirred up old memories she thought she'd finally put in the past. But that was before the notes, the photos and the midnight calls. How the man got her number she would never know. She was unlisted, but still he called. There were hang-ups on her machine, breathy whispers in the dead of night, and always that stupid opera in the background. A shiver danced down her back. At least he didn't know her cell number.

If she believed in fate or karma she'd think she was just royally screwed.

His Angel.

Something popped against her window and she jumped. Her hand flew to her chest as chills raced down her spine.

Damn her nerves. Before long she'd be on Prozac or Xanax. Either one would be fine with her. That'd be good. She could smile when she found the next batch of photos, and who knows, she might actually get some sleep. Or at least do some day-to-day things without feeling like a cold hand hovered just above the back of her neck.

God, she was tired, but in sleep the past mixed with the present and the nightmares were as exhausting as staying up all night. She signed on to her messenger.

Oldshopkeeper popped up with a message.

A soft sigh escaped and she grinned.

Brayden.

Clicking on the message, she answered.

Broadway_Babe: *What are you doing up at this hour?*

Oldshopkeeper: *I asked you first.*

Truth or lie? Better yet, neither. Simple.

Broadway_Babe: *Couldn't sleep.*

Oldshopkeeper: *Obviously.*

For several seconds she looked at his message and could imagine him sitting in his bed, the notebook propped on his lap. What she wouldn't give to be there at Seneca with him, sitting in his room talking about anything, everything, or nothing at all.

Those days were over. If Brayden hadn't pushed her away before, she'd be pushing him away now.

She had to.

He had found her. Her phantom to his angel, like in Leroux's classic. When *he* was around, those close to her died.

But God, she missed Brayden, the way his voice soothed even though it was roughened and gruff. How his eyes could cut a person in half with just a look. She missed his smile that totally transformed his serious face into a charming rascal.

She missed him, Tori, everyone. Kaitlyn came by yesterday and pounded her with questions. Why wasn't she eating? Was she not sleeping? Kaitlyn had seen the inhaler. That launched a lecture and a dozen questions on stress and health and overall well-being. Christian missed her family. Now more than ever.

This I'll defend. The Kinncaid motto echoed in her mind. She could tell them what was going on, move back home, and they'd do everything in their power to help her.

But.

She wasn't about to do that to them. The man stalking her, terrorizing her, was selfish and dangerous. Christian couldn't bear it if something happened to them because of her. Like before.

The last photos.

There had been a family picture and on all their faces *he'd* marked an X. Christian wasn't stupid. She knew what it meant. Stay away from the Kinncaids, or they'd get hurt. Because of her.

Like he had hurt Danny.

Like he'd hurt Susan and her whole family.

Oldshopkeeper: *Hello? Are you still there or did you go to sleep on me?*

Emotions that she didn't know how to handle warred within her. Finally she typed back.

Broadway_Babe: *No, I'm here, just thinking.*

Oldshopkeeper: *About what?*

Chaos. Hell. A living nightmare. She wished she could talk about this with him so she'd know what to do. She raked her fingers through her hair. For a moment she didn't do anything.

Broadway_Babe: *Have you ever taken a turn and couldn't figure out how to get back to where you were going?*

Oldshopkeeper: *Yeah, I turn around and go back.*

Go back? To the past? Not that she had to. It was coming to her in spades.

Oldshopkeeper: *Can I ask you a question?*

Broadway_Babe: *What?*

Oldshopkeeper: *What's going on with you? And not just us, or this thing with us, not music, or work. It's something else. You're afraid of something. What?*

Her breath huffed out. How in the hell could the man figure that out an hour away on a computer and not realize his emotions or how they tangled with hers when they were in the same house? Not that the latter mattered anymore.

Broadway_Babe: *I just have lots on my mind lately.*

Oldshopkeeper: *Lots of what? Whatever it is, it's serious enough to bring on asthma attacks. To isolate yourself from your family. We haven't seen you much lately.*

Isolate yourself. Isolate.

Isolation.

He wanted her isolated. All to himself. Just like before.

She leaned up on her elbows, her hands on her mouth. Either way she lost.

Separate herself from those she'd die to protect and do what *he* wanted. Or ask for their help, their belief, and run the risk of them not believing her or worse, of something happening to one of the Kinncaids.

No. No. She wouldn't risk it. They meant too much to her.

Maybe she could move. It worked before, and unlike before, this time she had funds.

God, why was this happening?

Oldshopkeeper: *What is going on? Can't we even talk anymore?*

Her eyes slid closed. Sighing, she typed.

Broadway_Babe: *I wish we could. God knows I wish we could.*

Oldshopkeeper: *We can. Tell me.*

Her fingers hovered over the keys and she stared at her screen.

Oldshopkeeper: *Tell me. If you don't, I'll just call you.*

The man would.

Broadway_Babe: *I can't.*

Oldshopkeeper: *Why?*

Broadway_Babe: *It's nothing, really. I'm just stressing about work.*

For a moment nothing happened. Then she saw he was typing a message back.

Oldshopkeeper: *You're lying. Don't lie to me.*

Christian chose to just let that one go. She'd learned that often she could just wait him out and he'd change the subject. Or let her.

Oldshopkeeper: *Does this have to do with your new neighbor?*

New neighbor?

Broadway_Babe: *Drayson or Geoffery? How do you know them?*

Oldshopkeeper: *More guys? Why couldn't you have found some female neighbors?*

She smiled.

Broadway_Babe: *Do I detect a hint of jealousy? And if not them, then who did you mean?*

Oldshopkeeper: *Jealous? Of course not. I'd just feel better knowing you were safe. Females are safer.*

She quirked a brow. Where did he come up with this? Shaking her head, she set to typing.

Broadway_Babe: *Not jealous? I'll leave that one. And my next-door neighbors are nice, polite gentlemen. As far as safety and females, need I remind you of the female a few months ago that made all our lives hell? But don't worry, you can rest your little mind. I have a cop.*

A full minute passed before she got a reply on that one.

Oldshopkeeper: *A cop?*

He knew. She would bet her condo he knew.

Broadway_Babe: *Morris. Remember him? He lives a few doors down.*

She thought for a moment. What the hell.

Broadway_Babe: *Gabe's been really helpful.*

Oldshopkeeper: *Gabe? Helpful? What the hell does that mean?*

She could all but see the bite in his words. If he'd asked the question aloud, his voice would deepen and gruff over words when something got to him more than he was willing to admit.

Broadway_Babe: *Just that he's helpful.*

Someone knocked at her door downstairs. She glanced at the clock and saw it was almost three. Who the hell would be knocking this time of night? A chill danced down her spine. *He* knew where she lived.

Oldshopkeeper: *And that means what?*

Again thumping echoed from downstairs. Should she answer it? No. No, definitely not.

Thump. Thump. Thump.

The sound reverberated through the quiet night. At this rate whoever was knocking would wake the entire complex. She closed her eyes and took a deep breath. She was not going to let the man reduce her to hiding under the covers.

Broadway_Babe: *Brb. Knock on door.*

She noted he was typing as she stood and hurried downstairs, leaving the lights off.

Another small yet looming nightly war. Lights or no lights? Lights allowed her to see if anyone were in her condo. After all, she could hardly see in the dark. But lights also allowed those outside to see in. Carefully, she looked through the peephole.

No one.

"Who's there?" she called.

Silence.

Gnawing on the inside of her bottom lip, she stared out at the distorted view of the night, then dropped back down onto her heels, staring at the door. Christian drummed her fingers against her thigh. Who knocked? She was tempted to fling the door open to prove to herself she was only letting him get to her.

Reason won out. She might be paranoid, but that didn't mean someone might not be out there.

Carefully, she looked out the side window beside the door. The sheers really didn't do much in the way of blocking her view, but still she shoved them to the side. She saw no one.

Goose bumps pricked her skin.

It was nothing and no one. Probably just some kid out knocking on doors.

Sighing, she turned and headed back upstairs.

Thump. Thump. Thump.

She jumped, almost losing her balance on the steps. A glance out the side window showed her a blur moving quickly past.

"Who's there?" she yelled.

Licking her lips, she thought about what to do. If she opened the door, what? What would happen? And if she didn't, would he continue to knock?

He?

Who was he? Was it *him*?

Stop it. Stop it!

She took a deep breath and walked to the door. This time she hit the outside light. Nothing happened. Had her bulb burned out?

Grumbling about her fate in general, she craned a look out the window again. And saw the package sitting at her door.

Her chest tightened. No. No. No. She was *not* going to let him do this to her. Damn him. Closing her eyes, she counted, concentrated on her breathing. She could win this, she could.

Sighing, she sat on the floor and stared out the window. It was a big package. What had he sent her this time?

Tears stung the backs of her eyes, but she refused to let them fall. Enough! Blowing out her tension, or what she could of it, on a huff, she grabbed the door handle and pulled herself up.

The man was *not* going to reduce her to the terrified girl he'd controlled years ago. She'd gotten away from that once, there was no way she was going to let him drag her back. He wanted her afraid and she'd be damned if she'd give him the satisfaction.

If she didn't open the door, she let him win.

Cool metal rested against her palm as she cupped the doorknob. With her other hand, she flicked her lights on. If her porch light didn't work, she'd illuminate the stoop with what she had.

On another inhale, she unlocked the bolts and opened the door.

Cold night air blew in and chilled her where she stood. Whatever it was almost fell on her. The package was wide, tall and thin. She caught it as it fell into her entryway.

Terrified that at any moment someone was going to leap out of the dark at her, she pulled the awkward package into her entry. It wasn't too heavy, but weighed enough that when she lost her grip, it slammed loudly against her door and inner wall. Cursing, she heaved until it stood upright in her entryway.

She turned to close the door, when an outer light pierced the stoop and she heard the door next to hers open. The condos were set up so that two doors stood side by side, and her entry, living room and part of the kitchen shared the wall with her neighbors.

"Christian?" a voice asked, faintly British.

Drayson.

She thought about pretending she hadn't heard him, but he stuck his head around her door frame and knocked on the open door.

"Luv, what in the Almighty are you about at this bloody hour?" he asked.

Propping her hand on her hip, she said, "Exercising."

"What in the world have you got there?" he asked, still leaning into her doorway.

She looked from the robed, handsome man to the brown-papered package leaning lopsided against her wall. It went over halfway to the ceiling.

"Actually," she said on a sigh, "I have no idea."

"Where did you get it?"

From a monster? "Someone knocking on my door left it."

"Did you—" He broke off as she heard a muffled yell from next door.

Great. Wake everyone up.

"Yes, Geoffery," Drayson said. "She's right here." He stood in her doorway. "Sorry, luv, we were worried about you. All that bumping and thumping. It looked like you had every light in the place on."

So she did.

Shaking her head, she motioned him in; might as well have a drink with some friends. She could open the thing later. As he crossed over her threshold, another man joined him from next door. Drayson was young, in his mid-thirties with blond hair, fair eyes, and a long narrow face ending in a perfectly trimmed goatee. Drayson was a director with the university theater. Geoffery, on the other hand, was a bit older, with gray-streaked dark hair and crinkling eyes. He worked at one of the many government jobs in the city. Both stood in her entryway wearing navy robes.

"I called Gabe. I told you to wait before just barging over here. The world is not the place it used to be, Drayson. Hello, Christian. What's that?" Geoffery asked.

Gabe? He called Gabe? Well, hell.

Just then the phone rang.

Three a.m. and she was having a party. At least it took her mind off of other things.

It rang again.

"Are you going to get that?" Geoffery asked her.

"No, I'll just let the machine pick it up."

On the third ring, her voice echoed from the kitchen. When it clicked, the condo blared with the strains of an opera distorted from the volume. But she recognized it. His song. His song for her, of her. An aria from Puccini's *Tosca*.

Chills raced down her spine as her own voice filled her condo.

"What the hell is going on?"

She whirled around to see Gabe standing in her doorway; the music softened, silenced until she heard a chuckle and a click.

Her eyes looked away from the three pairs of questioning ones that stared at her.

"Hello? Did anyone hear me?" Gabe asked again.

Christian fisted her hands to keep them from shaking, but it was no use.

"Not now, Gabe," Drayson said, walking to her and putting his arm around her. "Can't you see she's upset? Christian, luv, you need to sit down. You're looking a bit pale. Who would call and leave that on a phone machine at this ungodly hour? And that chuckle was beyond polite."

She stopped and stared at the package against the wall. Shrugging off Drayson, she walked to the present and ripped it open, the brown paper rippling and giving under her nails. The sound of tearing paper rent the air, overshadowing Geoffery's quiet voice as he tried to explain things to Lieutenant Gabe Morris.

A cop, she had a cop in her house and . . .

"What is that?" Geoffery asked.

That was a painting.

The last of the brown wrapping paper fell to the floor. One large canvas. The colors were dark: grays, blacks, and blues. In the center was an angel, standing with long flowing hair and too-large gray eyes. The angel's mouth opened on a scream, her arms thrown high and wide. Framing the figure were faces, hands, shoulders, elbows, body parts, bare and naked. But it was the face, the same face. Her face. Gray eyes looking down, looking out, looking back, wide in shock, or narrowed. Her body parts. The macabre disjointed appendages alone were bad; painted strategically together, they framed the canvas and the solitary figure in the center. A morbid frame painted on the canvas.

Black roses fell from the angel's hand. At first glance, it seemed the angel was standing on orange, red, and yellow flowers, but a closer look showed they were flames. In the flames were faces.

Danny.

Susan.

Papa.

Christian jerked back, her hands flying to her mouth. The trembling started as she stared and understood.

Chapter 4

Brayden pulled away from the window and looked back at the monitor of his notebook. Still nothing from Christian.

What the hell had she been thinking? Answering a door this time of night. It was after three now, and she still wasn't back on.

Worry fueled his anger.

He strode to the phone and snatched it up. What if everything was fine? What if he made a fool of himself? The phone weighed in his hand.

Did she even have another phone line? Or was she using it for her computer? He'd never thought to ask. Now that seemed really important. Most everyone had wireless, but there were a few holdouts. What if she used dialup?

He shook his head. Who used that anymore? Making himself insane, that was what he was doing.

Quickly he punched her number and waited as it rang, and rang, and rang.

Brayden hated not knowing what was going on. And where Christian was concerned, he was learning there was a whole hell of a lot he didn't know.

His grunt filled the silent room as he stared at the clock.

Fine, he'd give her a few more minutes. He was probably just overreacting anyway. But the worry didn't go away. He thrummed his fingers on his thigh. He tried her damned cell as well with no answer. Straight to voice mail.

Forget it, he'd call her again on the way. Stop at her place, then head to the hotel and finally, over to the shop. If everything were fine, he'd simply say he decided to get an early start on the day—it was hardly important that it was only after three. Who the hell needed sleep anyway?

First, he left a note for his parents on their apartment door to please see Tori got to school. One good thing about living in the same house with family, there was always someone there when needed. He checked the clock in his room. He'd give her two more minutes. He'd be dressed by then anyway.

* * * *

"It's almost beautiful in a contradictory, morbid sort of way," Drayson commented.

"Part celestial, part pagan," Geoffery agreed.

Evil. It was evil.

She looked to them and noticed they were studying the picture.

Gabe, however, was zeroing in on her with his dark eyes. "It's weird as hell to me."

Christian looked back at the painting. A painting she knew *he'd* done himself. There were others in his private collection. She'd seen them, been forced to pose for them.

But this one was different. This one was new, a reminder of who he was, what he could do, and how he controlled it all.

Her chest vised and she gasped for breath. This time when she closed her eyes, the breathing exercise didn't help. Her lungs tightened, until she wheezed a breath out.

Patting her side, she realized she didn't have her inhaler.

"Luv, you're scaring us. Come on, calm down. Come sit down in the kitchen." Drayson took her arm to steer her there.

She needed her inhaler. Looking to the stairs, she shrugged him off as her hand rubbed her breastbone. All she could hear was the pound of her heart and the wheezing of her own breath fighting out as her expanded bronchial tissues closed off the escape of carbon monoxide.

"Christian?" Gabe was in front of her.

God, she needed to breathe. *Don't panic. Don't panic.* Her gaze locked over his shoulder to the painting standing obscenely against her white walls. The faces in the fire. Black roses from her hand.

Gasp. Wheeze. Gasp. Wheeze.

It was as if *he* were squeezing the breath from her.

"Calm down," Gabe said.

She motioned that she needed her inhaler.

"Asthma?" he asked.

She nodded.

"Where is it?" he asked.

She pointed upstairs. His feet pounded up the steps. Geoffery and Drayson led her into the kitchen. Just as they sat her in a chair,

Gabe handed her the metered-dose inhaler.

The mist hit the back of her throat and within seconds she felt the bands loosen around her bronchial tubes. Though she was still breathing too hard, she could at least take a breath and not wheeze. She held the inhaler tightly between her palms to try and calm the shakes. But it didn't help.

The painting.

Her body. His angel bringing death and destruction to those she'd loved.

Susan. Danny. Her own father.

Oh, God.

Why wouldn't he just leave her alone, let her go?

She hated this. Hated it!

Someone handed her some water and she sipped the cool liquid.

Drayson cupped her hands in his. "Luv, it's only a painting. I take it you didn't choose it?"

She just glared at him.

"No," he continued, "I didn't think so. Someone's sick idea of a joke. Don't let it get to you so. I'm sure they didn't mean for you to become so upset."

Oh, yes. Yes, they did — he did. She could see him, sitting calmly in his chair, that smirk playing on his mouth, while his eyes held *that* look.

A shiver danced down her spine, chilling her blood.

"I'll take care of this," Gabe said. "Why don't you two go on back to your place."

Christian just wanted everyone out, but wanted them to stay. She wanted them gone so they wouldn't see how upset she really was, but didn't want to be alone either.

She looked at Gabe, and for the first time really saw him. His simple jeans and a T-shirt molded his muscles. Though he had a very nice chest, it was the gun shoved in his waistband that held her attention.

The cops.

What if *he* was watching and knew there was a cop here?

The faces in the fire.

She'd gone to the police before and no one believed her. No one, but Danny. No one but Susan. If they had . . .

They should all leave. All of them, before she hurt any of them. Or someone else she cared about.

"Did any of you see who delivered the package?" Gabe asked.

She shook her head, as did Drayson and Geoffery.

"We just heard all this knocking," Geoffery offered. "And then thumps, and we noticed Christian's lights were on. Drayson decided to make certain she was all right. And in this day and age, you can never tell."

Gabe's eyes cut her where she sat. "You didn't see anyone either, I presume?"

Again she shook her head. Clearing her throat, she tried, "No, I just—someone just knocked on my door. When I went to answer, no one was there, but I saw the package through the window."

That was mostly the truth.

Though her heart raced and blood pounded through her veins, she held Gabe's inquisitive stare.

"I don't think we should leave you alone," Drayson told her. "After that note on your car tonight at the theater and now this."

"What note?" Gabe asked.

Damn it.

Drayson shrugged his shoulders. "All it said was '*My Angel.*' Reminded me of *The Phantom*, but it was weird. Maybe a jealous undergrad you beat out in casting." He patted her hand and smiled.

"What?" Gabe asked, confusion clear in the word.

"My Angel. *The Phantom*?" Drayson rolled his eyes. "Honestly, Gabriel, you need to get out more. *The Phantom of the Opera*, the Broadway musical, the old 1940s movie. Gaston Leroux's book? The phantom and his angel." He launched into the chorus of the Phantom's song. His baritone voice carried throughout the kitchen.

Christian normally laughed at Drayson's antics, but now it wasn't even remotely funny. It was too close to the truth.

The past.

"Josephine, you will be the best." Long fingers tapped on the piano. She hated his fingers. Hated his hands. Hated him. "Again from the top."

And as she sang her pieces, his eyes watched her, burned with a fire she didn't want to name, didn't want to know. His was a look, a knowledge she feared and burned the pit of her stomach.

Then he smiled and his fingers stilled, the last note of the piano stringing through the air.

"Josephine, my angel. Like the production we saw the other night. Theater isn't exactly opera, and a high school production is hardly worthy, but I do have a fondness for pieces that spin off Leroux's work. It's almost seductive. Wouldn't you agree?" She didn't answer and he continued. "The phantom's angel. Yes. I think I'll call you my angel, my Josephine. Mine."

"Christian. Christian!"

She jerked back at her name.

"You didn't join in," Drayson said. "Luv, you need some rest. Why don't you come over to our place and crash?"

She shook her head.

"Drayson's right, I hate to think of you worrying over here all alone. Joke or no, this is hardly funny," Geoffery agreed.

Again, she shook her head. "Sorry, you guys. I didn't mean to wake you up. Or you," she added to Gabe.

She patted Drayson's hand. "Thank you for coming over. You're great, go on home. I just freaked out over that painting and the weird phone call. You're probably right, Dray, it's just some flunky. I'll talk to Gabe and see what we can come up with."

His expression said he was trying to figure out if he should indeed go. But then he glanced to Gabe, to the gun, and back to her.

"All right, if you say so, but you call me. At this rate, you won't even be rehearsing tomorrow."

His brow furrowed in what she knew was his "I'm-about-to-lecture-and-be-the-director" mode.

Hurriedly, she said, "I'll be there tomorrow afternoon like we discussed, just as planned."

Still he watched her. Finally, he nodded and said, "Fine. But you're riding with me. Then we won't have to worry about you getting notes on your car or something else."

That probably wouldn't work because she was spending the morning at the shop and then going to rehearsal. "We'll see. Go on to bed."

Drayson leaned over and kissed her on the cheek before leaving. As the door clicked shut, she could feel her nerves tightening.

Gabe cleared his throat as he sat across from her. He didn't say a word, and neither did she, they just stared at each other. He must be a nightmare in an interview or interrogation. With his stare alone criminals probably admitted to fictitious crimes. A muscle ticked in his jaw.

"You know, I checked today, and there have been several stalkers reported by women. None of the reports were filed by you."

She stood and walked to the counter. "Would you like something to drink? Coffee? Tea? Juice?" She fiddled with the canisters waiting for his reply.

"Have you told the Kinncaids? The one you have a thing with?"

"A thing?" Christian turned to face him and leaned back against the counter. "You mean Brayden? There's not a 'thing' with him." *Lie. Lie. Lie.* Is that all she did anymore?

Gabe only nodded in that "yeah, right" kind of way. "I thought there was something between you two. Brayden's the shop owner with the little girl, right?"

His gaze was so intense, she could only hold it for so long. Nodding, she agreed. "Yes, that's him. Brayden and Gavin are twins. Brayden owns the shop and Gavin is the doctor. I thought there might have been a 'thing' too. Maybe there could have been something." Shrugging, she gave it up. "I don't know. I just don't know and now it hardly matters."

"Well, Brayden is one stupid guy." At his words, she cocked her head. "That shocks you, I see. I wonder why."

The phone rang.

Jumping at the sound, she grabbed the cordless before the second ring sounded.

"Hello?"

Silence.

"Hello?"

Softly in the background music played, and she knew.

"Josephine. Josephine. Josephine," his voice *tsked* over the phone.

Ice pierced her heart and nausea greased her stomach. She turned her back to Gabe. "My name is Christian. Christian."

His chuckle did an evil dance in her ear. "So many men this time of night? Shame on you. You know I don't share. I've never shared."

"I'm not yours to share or otherwise."

Something clicked through the phone and she imagined him lighting one of those cigars he preferred.

"Leave me alone." She cursed the tremors of her hands, then

stabbed the OFF button.

A glance over her shoulder told her Gabe wasn't ignoring her conversation. Carefully, she set the phone back on its stand, then turned to face him, just as the phone rang again.

It rang again.

The answering machine picked up.

"I don't like to be ignored," he bit out, his voice filling the air around her.

She'd managed to get to him. When angry, his voice flinted to a fine edge.

"But I suppose it's all been a bit of a shock tonight." His words, like black oil, slithered from the machine through her kitchen and she started to shake.

"Did you like the painting? Rather good, I thought, considering. I know it's hardly my best, but I think it served its purpose." Silence and a huff. She could imagine him blowing a stream of smoke out. "Those asthma attacks are pesky annoyances, aren't they?" His gravelly laugh echoed.

Asthma attacks? Her gaze, still riveted on the answering machine, darted around the room. How did he know? How?

Was he that close?

His laugh trailed off. "Worried? You should be."

The line went dead. He'd hung up.

Her chest tightened and she bumped the table. She grabbed her inhaler and took another puff, fighting the constriction back before it started.

Her hands shook and she couldn't get past the realization that there was no privacy here. None. There never had been with him.

"You should sit down," Gabe told her, walking to the machine and staring down at it. "Oh, for the days when there were little tapes to pop in and out."

The phone rang again; he picked it up from the base. Christian leaned over and grabbed it out of his hand.

She was tired of this. Tired of cowering. She just needed to figure out what to do without telling.

The phone rang again.

Anger and fear warred within her as she threw the phone to the floor. Cursing, she jerked the base away, ripping the cords out of the wall, and heaved it across her kitchen. The plastic shattered, chips and wires exposed, like a childhood radio kit.

"Why won't he just leave me alone!" she whispered furiously.

She covered her face with her hands, rubbing as if to wipe images from her mind. Sliding her hands back through her hair, she looked at the cop leaning against her doorjamb.

"I really wish you hadn'ta done that. I could've taken the base and analyzed the voice. Tell me," he said, crossing his ankles. "Why haven't you reported this guy? All the pictures? And if you haven't reported this, I'm betting the Kinncaids don't know about any of it. I'm wondering why." He shrugged. "Maybe you think it's Brayden or one of the others?"

"What?" Christian propped her hands on her hips. Was he for real? His no-nonsense frown said he was. "This is not Brayden. Or any of the others. It's not."

"How do you know?"

Shit. "I just do."

"Then you know who it is?"

Praying he didn't see more than she wanted him to, she held his stare. "No, I don't know who it is."

"Then you have told Kinncaid about the photos? About the phone calls and notes? How long has this guy been calling anyway?"

She only shook her head, and caught his mumbled curse. There was hardly any use in denying it. She had told no one. The only one that even remotely knew anything was standing, calm as you please, in her kitchen. And though the surface was unrippled, she sensed the currents running beneath the smooth façade. He wanted answers.

"I'll take your silence as a no. The question in my mind is that if you really care for Brayden and for this family, which you seem to be a part of more or less, I can't help wondering why you'd keep this from them." His dark eyes narrowed in their study of her, until she looked away. "The Kinncaids all love you, from what I've seen. I've got two sisters, and I'd be pissed as hell at one of them for keeping something like this from me. Or my parents."

She didn't say anything, just turned around and busied herself with making coffee as she filled the carafe.

"There is someone out there doing their damnedest to terrorize you." She heard his footsteps as he walked toward her. "He's letting you know he's watching you. He knows everything about you. He's starting to send you gifts. He's calling you. Cases like this only escalate."

Escalate? To what? An attack? She already knew what this monster's worst was.

"Have you changed your locks?" Gabe asked her, the switch in topics momentarily catching her off guard.

"The locksmith is coming Monday morning. I couldn't get anyone sooner and had to pay extra to bribe my way to Monday," she admitted to him.

Gabe ran a hand through his dark brown hair.

He grinned at her then, a small, half grin. If she were interested in him, she might find it attractive. But she was only interested in one man. Had only felt safe with one man. Brayden.

"You are a stubborn woman."

Christian shrugged but couldn't hide her grin. "So I've been told."

He shook his head. "You need to report this. No one can help you if you don't. And you're going to hurt your family by keeping this from them."

He was right. Brayden was already wondering what was going on and . . . Oh, hell. The computer.

She hurried out of the kitchen. Brayden would be so pissed. The stairs were cool under her feet as she dashed up them. Her computer sat on her bed silent and waiting. She saw that *Oldshopkeeper* was no longer online.

Quickly, she scrolled back through his messages.

Oldshopkeeper: *Don't answer it.*

Oldshopkeeper: *Damn it, Christian, it's three a.m.*

Oldshopkeeper: *Are you back? Who was it?*

Oldshopkeeper: *If you're not back on in a few minutes, I'm calling you.*

Oldshopkeeper: *You didn't answer — either phone. I'm coming to town.*

That was the last message. Hell.

Why hadn't she gotten his call? Unless Brayden called while *he* left a message on her machine. What was the time of the last message? Well over half an hour ago. Hell, he'd be here soon. She grabbed her mobile off the nightstand where she charged it every night and turned the volume down so it wouldn't wake her. Sure enough. Five times? He called that many times? Of course he did.

She whirled around and saw Gabe standing in her doorway. "Problem?"

"Yeah, Bray's coming. I went to answer the door and well . . . I never got back to instant message him, so he's coming."

"Maybe he's not so dumb after all."

Men. She rolled her eyes. "Could you do something else for me?"

"Well, I could wait around and piss off a wealthy powerful guy and his brothers because I'm here with you in the wee hours of the morning. That ought to be fun. Or I could let it slip some twisted man is staking a claim on you. But what did you have in mind?"

Christian shook her head, brushed past him and hurried downstairs. She had to get rid of the painting. If it was here when Brayden arrived, there would be all sorts of questions.

"I was wondering if you could use those muscles of yours to take that—that—thing." She pointed to the entryway.

He stepped beside her and stared at the object she was referring to. "You mean the artistic masterpiece?" Gabe scratched his jaw. "On one condition."

"What?"

"You tell me what you see in the painting. Because you saw something the rest of us didn't. And then I get to take it and do with it what I want, no questions asked."

Christian met his gaze directly. Her muscles tensed and she thought about what it meant, what he wasn't telling her. But then realized how hypocritical that thought was.

"You want that in your house? What the hell are you going to do? Hang it over the stairwell?"

His eyes narrowed. "No, take it to the lab."

"Fine. Whatever. But not now, I'll look at it later. Tomorrow or something. Or Sunday." She needed to get it out of here now.

His brows furrowed and he only shook his head. "You are hiding something, Miss Bills. Or maybe even someone." He sighed and hefted the painting up.

Hiding? If he only knew.

She turned, opened the door for him and yelped.

Chapter 5

"What the hell is going on?" Brayden asked, his voice tight. He looked from Christian's shocked pale face to the man in her entryway.

One Lieutenant Morris of the DCPD.

He was a fool. All this time he'd been worried about her and . . .

"Brayden?" Relief flashed across her features and he noticed the tremble in her voice. She leaned into the door.

Morris only cocked a brow, and awkwardly carried a canvas toward the door.

"What are you doing here?" Brayden asked the man.

Christian opened the door further and motioned him in. He caught her scanning the darkness before she shut the door. And the darted look to Morris.

Hell.

She cleared her throat. "Well, my neighbors called him. Uh— yeah. My neighbors woke up to the pounding and saw all my lights were on. They got worried, me being a single female, so Geoffery called Gabe while Drayson made certain all was well," she said in a light tone.

He wasn't buying it. Nor did he look at her; his gaze was focused on the cop. Who didn't look away, only smirked.

Brayden wanted to wipe it off his face.

Finally, the lieutenant looked at Christian. "I'll call you later. I think you two need some time alone. Remember what I said."

She nodded and reopened the door.

What was with the painting? All he saw was the back of the canvas.

When Morris was even with him, the man stopped. "It's about time you got here. You might not be as dense as I was beginning to think you were. In this day and age, single attractive women living alone are just too tempting for some of the more twisted of our society . . ."

"Good night, Gabe," Christian said tightly.

The look Morris sent her was hardly lover-like. More like notched arrows. Then again, what did he know? Maybe he was a fool and they were in the middle of some fight. And . . .

"What?" he finally asked, Morris's words registering. "What did you mean, tempting twisted—"

"Good night, Gabe," Christian interrupted and all but shoved the cop out the door. "I'll call you tomorrow about that appointment."

The entryway echoed softly with the latch as the door closed.

Brayden took a deep breath and tried to get his bearings. He'd broken several speeding laws to get here in the time he had.

"Why didn't you answer your phone—either one of them?" he whispered.

Christian didn't immediately reply. Her hair was standing up in disarray, the way it did when she was frustrated or nervous and ran her fingers through it repeatedly.

She'd lost weight. The pale skin on her face seemed taut, her eyes sunken, or maybe it was the darkened circles beneath them.

Finally, she shrugged. "I had some phone trouble. And I didn't hear my cell. I always turn the volume to silent at night."

She walked past him and into the kitchen. Brayden followed. Christian was a contradiction. She sounded fine, played the situation as though it were the most normal event for him to show up at her door at four in the morning to find another guy there. But he'd caught her relief and the tremble in her words. Her posture was seemingly normal, but it was almost too perfect, too coiled, as if waiting to spring.

At the kitchen, he followed the black cord like a dark snake and saw the phone lying shattered on the white tiled floor.

Phone trouble?

He leaned against the doorjamb and watched as she sat the coffee carafe on the machine and clicked the button. She was wearing those blue and gray pajama bottoms he liked with a tight little camisole top. She wore her favorite comfy blue cardigan, too.

"Christian."

Her shoulders stiffened.

"What is going on? Don't bother telling me nothing. What were you doing answering the door at this time of night? And why in the hell didn't you answer your phone? I've called I don't know how many times." He'd tried to keep the anger out of his words, but he'd been so damn scared at the idea of something happening to her. All the way into town, dark images danced in his head. Then to find her whole and safe in her entry with another guy. Well, it was no wonder he couldn't control his tongue.

She didn't say anything. He was tired of this. She'd scared the hell out of him.

"You just type you're going to answer the door in the middle of the night and then you don't bother to call me or get back to IM to let me know you're okay. Do you have *any* idea what was going through my mind? What *is* going through my mind? Damn it, Christian."

She turned to him then, and he saw the sheen of tears in her eyes. Slowly, he straightened away from the doorway.

"I want to know what the hell is going on. Now." His steely words left little room for argument.

Sighing she said, "I've just been getting some weird phone calls. You must have called while he did or when I broke the phone."

"Weird how? He who?" He walked toward her, but she backed up and he stopped.

Her tongue darted out, licked her chapped lips, and he saw the tremble of her hand as she raked it through her hair.

"Just—just weird. You know, midnight creepy phone calls. He was calling a lot." Her shoulders lifted on a shrug. "And tonight he left me a present. Gabe came over and took the thing."

"A present?" Brayden asked. He waited, but she didn't elaborate. Distance be damned. His shoes clicked softly on the floor as he crossed to her. Her bent head rose when he stopped in front of her. He placed his hands palm down on either side of her, trapping her against the counter. "Some wacko is calling you, leaving you gifts, and you don't tell me?"

She hadn't said a damn word.

Her in-drawn breath was ragged, and she looked away from him. If she would just . . .

"No, I didn't. It's not that big a deal. That's all. I'm a big girl now. I don't need to rely on you or your family for every little thing. Some things I have to do alone," she whispered.

"What the hell are you talking about? This has nothing to do with *me* or *my* family, which is yours too, by the way. I'm talking about us."

Us. There, he'd said it. Us.

"What about it all being a mistake?" she asked softly.

Brayden sighed. "I don't know. But." Truth or lie?

"But?"

Tonight he'd been terrified some rapist had knocked on her door and had all but murdered her. He hadn't been this scared since Tori and Ryan had been kidnapped.

Truth.

"I miss you."

Her head jerked up and her eyes met his. Disbelief and hope reflected in them. Or did he just imagine the hope?

"I miss you," he repeated.

"Oh." Her eyes darted away. The floral scent of her shampoo drifted up between them, reminding him of the night he hadn't been able to forget.

Christian, the night they'd shared, was like the tide against the rocks. It was constant and wearing; at the edge of his mind during the day, pounding at him during the night. He'd been stupid and the lying coward she'd called him. He missed her, and he was afraid he was losing her. Losing whatever connection they'd always seemed to have.

To hell with this.

Brayden took a chance. He reached up and cupped her face.

"I'm sorry," he said.

"For what?" Her brow furrowed.

Brayden bit down. "For being stupid. For pushing you away. You were right, I'm an ass. I'm not like . . . I can't always say . . . Hell."

The frown between her brows deepened.

Sighing, he tried again. "I was wrong, that morning. I was wrong. You were right."

Her eyes searched his and he wondered what they saw. And still, she didn't say anything.

"I miss *you*." God, did he miss her. The smell of her, her smile, her laugh.

Her smoky gaze narrowed before she slid her eyes closed.

Please don't let it be too late. Brayden leaned closer, stretched his hand around to lose his fingers in the short hair at her nape and noticed it had grown since the last time he'd held her so. He grazed the curve of her ear with his thumb, felt her pulse bounce in her neck.

He lowered his mouth to hers. Her lips, her skin was as soft as he remembered. Slowly, he traced her mouth with his tongue, daring her to kiss him back. On a trembling sigh, she opened her mouth. Brayden pulled her close, held her tight as he deepened the kiss. She tasted just as sweet as he remembered, like a dark forbidden fruit. The kiss lengthened, deepened, and she twined her arms around his neck. Her curves pressed against him, and images from a night spent in her arms flashed unbidden in his mind. He knew the paleness of her breasts, the way her skin dipped near her hip bone, the mole on the right buttock cheek. The way she kissed, tasted, smelled. All the memories slammed into him and Brayden wondered absently what the hell he'd been thinking to turn her away before.

Just as he tilted his head, her hands came up and pushed against his shoulders. She broke the kiss. "We can't do this." Her eyes looked at his mouth.

"Why?" He held her in the loose circle of his arms. She fit perfectly. She took a deep breath and he rested his forehead against hers.

"There's just—there's just—there's too much going on right now." Her whispered words warmed against his mouth.

"Like what?"

The silence between them stretched. Why wouldn't she open up?

"Talk. To. Me. We've always talked about everything."

And they damn well would again. Then, another thought occurred to him. She'd broken the kiss. She'd pulled away, pushed him away.

Brayden straightened and stepped back, shoving his hands in his pockets. "Is there something between you and Morris?" His breath huffed out. Not that he had anyone to blame but himself if there were. The thought tightened his gut.

She shook her head. "No. Gabe's just a friend."

A friend? A friend who came over in the middle of the night? So if that wasn't it, then what? She wouldn't meet his eyes, always darting away. Nervous and scared.

"I don't know what is going on with you, but I wish to hell you'd tell me. And it's not just me who's noticed. Is it this wacko calling? Who the hell is he? Do you know him? What damn gift did he leave you?" Brayden paced away from her and turned back.

Christian bent down and picked up the pieces of the phone.

"If that's the only damn phone you have, I'll get you two more." Then she could answer it in whatever part of the condo she was in.

"No, there's one upstairs, but I keep the ringer turned off, just like my cell. I'm normally sleeping in my room, I don't want a phone in there ringing all the damned time."

He grunted. "Mom and Dad want to know what the deal is with you. They all blame me for it, and they're right. Tori wants to know when you're coming home and Jesslyn and Taylor are pissed at my idiocy as they refer to it and—"

"This has nothing to do with you." Her words jerked him back. He stared at her across her kitchen.

Why? Why couldn't he get past her walls? Get even a glimpse inside her fortress? Her words hurt more than he would have thought. Not have anything to do with him?

"Do you still mean the words you said to me?" he asked, though he hadn't meant to.

"What words?" She dumped the shattered plastic and wires of the broken phone into the trash.

"That night. The next morning." *I love you.* Had she meant it?

She paused, and though her back was to him, she stiffened. "I'm not answering that. I'm not talking about that."

Brayden cursed, his worry turning to a simmering anger. "You're not talking much about anything these days, are you?"

When she turned to face him, his breath caught. Her eyes were haunted pools of pain.

"Talk to me," he said yet again, slapping his hand on the counter. "Tell me what the hell is going on with you. I can't stand to see you this way."

She shook her head, but her eyes filled and tears fell over her cheeks.

Brayden couldn't handle her crying. He walked to her and pulled her to him.

"Ah, Chris, don't. Don't. Come on, baby, tell me. Talk to me. I'll help you. Whatever's going on, I'll fix it." Or he'd find a way to.

"I—I can't."

He slid his eyes closed and pulled back, cupping her face in his hands. "You mean you won't."

Even as he reached up to wipe the silvery trail of tears away, she shook her head.

Brayden didn't know if he wanted to kiss her or shake her.

"I think—I think you should go," she told him, pulling out of his hold and walking to the sink.

Go? He could only stand there. "I'm not going anywhere until you tell me what's going on with you, Christian. And if you don't, by God, I'll find another way to discover whatever it is you're hiding."

Her hands shook as she placed them on the countertop, fisting them until her knuckles were white.

What inner battle was she waging?

"Please leave."

Brayden looked to the ceiling, as though hoping the answer to all his questions would appear there. But no floating hand appeared to write a single blessed thing.

"Are you going to tell me about these creepy phone calls? And this midnight present?"

"No."

Damn her.

"Why the hell not?"

"Because I want you to leave."

"We don't always get what we want," he told her, wishing she'd turn around.

"Geez, ya think? Look, Brayden, I'm really tired. I just need some time—time alone, to think. Okay? I can't eat, I haven't slept. I can't think straight." Her fists beat on the countertop and he could see the tension in her shoulders from here. "I just want everyone to leave me the hell alone!" Her voice rose on the end.

He didn't know who was more shocked at her outburst, him or her. She wanted him gone. Fine. For now. At least until he figured what the hell to do. And he was damn well going to do something. She couldn't keep on like this.

"I'll go, if that's what you really want."

For one long moment she didn't move, but then ever so slowly, she nodded.

Brayden could have hit something. Instead, he cleared his throat and counted to five. "Fine. I'm going to the hotel, then the shop."

"I can open the shop," she said.

"Don't interrupt me. I'm not in the mood. Don't step foot in the shop today. You look like you're sick." And still beautiful as ever. "Rest. Get some sleep. Whatever is going on is there for all to see, we just can't figure out what the hell it is." He paused. "But I will."

At the doorway he stopped, slapped his palm on the jamb. "Are you coming up to the house tonight?"

A moment passed and he heard her swallow, saw her wipe again at her eyes.

"I don't know . . .," she trailed off.

The leash he'd had on his anger snapped. Damn her. "You're coming up there if I have to come here and drag you. I don't know what's going on that has you acting this way. You won't tell me. Fine. If you're mad at me, then fine. You can hide from me, be pissed at me, whatever at me. Do not take this out on Mom and Dad. They love you and care about you. I won't make any excuses for you with Tori, and I won't stand by and watch you disappoint her."

Her head fell to her chest, the lights from the kitchen glinting off the deep mahogany tresses.

More than anything, he wanted to pull her close and tell her everything would be fine. Kiss her until she smiled. Love her until she confided in him. But he couldn't do that, wouldn't do that until she told him what was going on.

"I'll be there," she whispered, though he heard it. She cleared her throat, and still didn't turn to face him. "I have rehearsal, it might run a little long, but I'll be there tonight, maybe by seven or so."

"Fine. Do you want me to wait on you? We could drive up together."

She shook her head. "No, but thank you."

Brayden counted to five again and ground his teeth. "I'll see you then."

With one long look at this stubborn woman, he turned and strode out of her condo.

She might not tell him what was up, but he bet the neighborhood cop knew. He'd just drop Lieutenant Morris a visit later today. He wanted to know more about these midnight phone calls and presents. Was this what had her so scared? Or was it something else?

* * * *

Christian rubbed the exhaustion out of her eyes as she put the key in her door.

Rehearsals had been over for two hours. After they'd practiced for most of the afternoon, she'd left to clear her mind.

The clean air around the Mall had done the job. The morning's fight with Brayden had shoved some of the rubble out of her mind. He might not always have flowery words, but that's who he was, that's who she loved. And he was right. She missed him, missed them, what they had, the dream of what they could. As she'd walked along the Reflecting Pool, she'd decided to take a chance.

Calling Gabe, she'd agreed on a meeting to report the stalking, the photos, the calls, and the gifts. Gifts, plural. Today inside her car, in the passenger seat, he'd left a small wrapped package with a red bow. That he'd gotten into her car was the final straw. In the velvet-lined box was the silver locket she'd left on her bed eight years before.

Josephine, my angel.

She still didn't know how to report the crime without reporting the criminal. Therein lay her problem. Maybe she'd figure it out in the shower.

Shrugging off the chill, she looked at her watch. There was enough time to take a shower, get to the station to talk to Gabe and then drive to Seneca. It was five now. So she might be a little late, but she'd get to the family place around dinner.

Seneca. Everyone was going to be there. Pumpkin carving. The family tradition. The weekend before Thanksgiving, they carved pumpkins for the fun of it and then cooked the vegetables to make the puree for the holidays. She'd tell them tonight. Then she'd be done with it.

Anxiety skittered along her nerves. One minute at a time. First, shower, then the station, then confessions with the family.

Sighing, she opened her door, stepped inside, and shrugged out of her coat. After tossing it on the banister, she turned and slid the dead bolt home.

Something to drink. Maybe a glass of wine to calm her. No, she didn't want to smell like a cast of Pinot Grigio when she went to the police to report this. Water, she'd get a glass of water.

Shadows deepened early this late in the year. She flicked on the hallway light and walked toward the kitchen. Her boot heels echoed eerily in the silence. Light filled the room as she flipped the switch. Just as she stepped into the kitchen, an arm snaked around her middle.

"Welcome home, Josephine." His words, warm against her ear, froze her blood in her veins and hitched her breath.

Oh, God.

She heard and felt him inhale as he took a deep breath.

He was here. Here in her home. In her condo. And they were alone. She started shaking.

No.

Think. Think.

Christian kicked back with her boot heel. He grunted, and relaxed his hold enough that she twisted out.

Whirling, she backed away from the handsome man in her doorway.

His pale green eyes sparked with that fire they always had when he looked at her.

Her stomach rolled, the greasy feel of nausea immediate. Though her chest tightened, she fought off the attack.

"Josephine, that wasn't a very nice greeting," he said and started toward her.

She looked around but saw nothing. A basket of fruit, the stale coffee in the carafe, her hanging pot rack.

"Here I've been waiting on you for almost an hour." He shook his head.

The knife block. Not very practical, his arms were longer than hers, but it was better than nothing.

She backed toward the center island.

His eyes narrowed. "I told you I don't share. I've never shared. You are *my* angel. I won't share you with anyone. Not the cop and not that Kinncaid boy. Didn't you learn before?"

Boy? She'd never heard of anyone calling six-foot-four-inch Brayden Kinncaid a boy.

He stalked her, slowly, calmly, as if he had all the time in the world.

"What—what do you want, Richard?"

Though she knew. Some part of her had always known he would

find her one day.

Richard's taupe-colored suit covered his wiry frame and was as pristine as his white shirt and blue tie. A long narrow face was as she remembered it, the cheekbones prominent, the eyes sharp, the nose hawk-like. He'd always reminded her of a bird of prey. The only difference she saw was his neatly combed chestnut hair was not only silvered at the temples, but dusted throughout.

"What are you doing here?" She looked to the side table for the phone. Damn it. She'd broken it. If she could just get upstairs.

"You didn't know?" He slapped a hand against his chest. "I'm truly shocked. I won the representative election. I needed to see to some things here in D.C. I'll be living here come January."

She shook her head.

He smiled and nodded, his grin straight as a blade.

"You need to leave. I don't want you here," she said. Her voice trembled, but she couldn't help it.

He cocked a perfectly arched brow, the grin growing. "You'd like that, wouldn't you?" he asked quietly.

Quick as a snake, he struck. His arm darted out, his fingers closing over her arm as he shoved her into the island. She reached back behind her. The hilt of a knife fit her palm.

"Richard, I don't want this. I don't want you here. You should leave." His face was inches from hers. Though she almost choked, she tried reason. "Congratulations on your election. You don't want to ruin your career by being here. Leave. Just leave me alone."

The dark light of passion flashed in the depths of his eyes. An evil spark. His laugh grated between them, and she leaned back from his warm minty breath laced with tobacco and brandy. "Oh, I won't ruin a thing. You won't tell. If you had, I wouldn't be here. You wouldn't risk that nice family you've found. Such upstanding and righteous individuals, aren't they, the Kinncaids?"

Her breath hitched.

"No, you won't risk something happening to any of them." One long finger trailed down her cheek, ice following in its wake, as his gaze watched his caress. "And you know something terrible would befall them if you said anything." Those eyes, like shards of jade, locked back with hers. "Anything, Josephine."

He grabbed her hair and pulled, no longer caressing; the fingers held her hair tightly. She could feel his other hand bruising on her arm.

"I don't like this new look."

He lowered his head and slammed a kiss down on her, bruising her mouth.

She bit his lip and pulled the knife free, slashing out with it.

He stumbled back, hissing. "You little bitch."

Blood lined the cut along his upper arm. Christian kicked out again, catching him in the groin. He bent over, puffing.

Quickly, she hopped onto the center island, intent on putting it between them. His hand grabbed her ankle and jerked her down onto the floor. She slid, scraping her ribs along the edge of the chopping board. Oranges and lemons bounced around her and the basket hit her shoulder.

"You're not going anywhere," he bit out.

She kicked with her other foot until he let go. Then she stood, holding a hand to her ribs.

The door, she had to get to the door. Her boot heels echoed down the hallway, mixing with his curses and footsteps.

Hurry. She had to hurry.

The dead bolt. Why had she thrown the dead bolt? She tried to unlock it, wasting precious seconds. Just as the door cracked, and she reached through it, he slammed against her. She barely had time to jerk her hand with the knife back through. The doorknob bit unmercifully into her aching ribs. His body against hers shut off her exit, knocked the air out of her and trapped her against the door.

Christian screamed and sliced back with the knife.

His hand fisted in her hair, the other digging into her jaw.

He pulled her head back, arching her neck so that she was looking up at him, even as he maneuvered away from her knife.

"You're going to pay for that. You're going to pay for everything, Josephine."

Her eyes locked with his, saw the twisted and sick intent in them even as he slammed her head against the door.

The world went hot white, then black.

Chapter 6

He set the empty syringe aside and stared down at Josephine as he held her across his lap, sedated. They were in her upstairs bathroom. She'd taken so long, there had been plenty of time to prepare for her arrival.

The scent she wore was nothing like what she should be wearing. Josephine didn't wear this heavy fragrance. She should have something softer, lighter, more floral.

Leaning back, he studied her face, the unchanged lines of perfection. So beautiful. In the harsh glare of the bathroom lights, her pale skin was almost translucent. The beat of her pulse jumped in the long column of her throat.

He glanced at his watch. He needed to hurry. She would be out for a while, but there was still much to do. Carefully, he dabbed the washcloth to the cut on her forehead. She'd run. Did she actually think she'd get away? The cuts on his arm and thigh stung, but he'd take care of them later.

Smiling, he got to work. He hated this dark hair color. Hated it. It was *not* his Josephine's. Reaching over, he picked up the pitcher of water he'd set there earlier. Carefully, he wet her hair, making certain her head was draped over the tub. No need to dirty the bathroom floor.

When it was wet enough, he opened the tube of hair color he'd set on the back of the commode earlier.

Honey Wheat Blonde. It was the closest thing he could find to her old color—a darker blonde. It would have to do. He'd memorized the instructions and knew exactly what to do.

As he slathered the thick tubed cream into her too-short hair, he realized his leather gloves were ruined. Good thing he had a second pair. It didn't take long to comb the dye through the short mop of hair. He snapped the plastic covering on the tube, then stretched over and rinsed the cream off his gloves.

Her scent taunted him. As he leaned over to rinse his hands, he was so close to her that her breath warmed his neck.

He wrapped his arms around her and held her close.

His angel. His angel. After all this time, he had her in his arms again.

He kissed her brows, finely arched, her closed lids, her cheeks, and finally, finally, her mouth. It was soft and pliant under his. Giving beneath his.

Her heartbeat pulsed against his fingers on her throat. He gazed on her beautiful face. Eyebrows. He blinked. Her eyebrows were dark.

He'd almost forgotten them. Carefully, he applied the hair color to those as well.

While he waited for her hair to change back to its blonde color from that horrid dark brown, he stared around her space, dreamed of the rest of the evening. Or what time he had of it.

The thought of what was to come excited him, rushed his blood through his veins.

When twenty minutes were up, he turned on the tap and rinsed the coloring off. It was an awkward job, and he half expected her to awaken, but of course she didn't. Finally. The wet strands slid through his leather-clad fingers. He imagined them as dampened silk.

Her hair would be as it should be.

He grabbed the towel off the back of the toilet and rubbed her hair, drying it.

Josephine's head hung limply on his arm, as he turned and carried her into the bedroom. The shades were already lowered, the lights dimmed, the covers removed.

He sat on the edge of the bed and undressed her, his excitement growing as bit by bit he revealed her skin.

When she was only wearing her lingerie, he laid her in the center of her bed.

Should he remove them? Or wait till she was awake? Still undecided, he pulled one arm up and tied it with the nylon cord that was already there. It worked well that she ran late today; he'd been able to set things up perfectly.

Leaning over her body, he stretched her other arm up and tied it. The lingerie had to go. It would be nice to see her fear when she awakened, but the terror of not knowing what he'd done, what he could do, would be so much better.

He tied one of her ankles and reached for the other one. So soft.

He slid his hand up her leg. No, not now, wait until she woke up. He stood at the foot of her bed and stared at her, at her beautiful, long curvaceous body that had once been solely his. Only his.

He demanded perfection and rarity. She hadn't been his exclusively for a long, long time. Josephine was no longer perfect.

She was flawed.

He stopped, frowned, thought. She was flawed. If something of his became imperfect, he destroyed it.

There was a thought.

No, he wasn't ready to destroy this treasure of his yet. Josephine was his angel, even if she was a fallen one. He'd have to think on how to perfect her once again.

Quickly, he reached again for her other ankle and tied it tight. He picked up another syringe he'd set on her nightstand. This counteracted the sedative. She should be awake—he slid the needle into the vein on the inside of her right elbow, depressing the fluid into her—any minute. He counted off one minute, halfway through another. She moaned and he smiled.

A poem danced through is mind.

The mouse ran to, and the mouse ran fro.
Crying and squeaking: which way, which way.
Didn't matter, and the cat only smiled.
For it was time for the cat to play.

Indeed. Time for the cat to play.

"Come, come, my dear. Wake up."

Again she moaned, and he jerked on her ropes. No slack. Perfect.

"You've been a bad girl." He straightened and stared down at her, watched as she slowly came to. "It's time you remembered who you belong to. Unfortunately, our time is limited." He walked to the side of the bed. "Such a pity really. I have a plane to catch." He slapped her thigh, and thought of his own; the sting had faded to more of a throb.

He'd pay her back for those too.

Taking one of the silk scarves he'd brought along, he sat beside her and tapped her face.

Before he gagged her, he leaned down and whispered against her lips. "Wake up, my angel. Jo-se-phine." He drew her name out. "Josephine. Wake up. It's time to play."

* * * *

"Daddy," Tori asked, "is Chris coming home tonight?"

Brayden looked up from the board game and into his daughter's eyes.

"She said she would be here around dinnertime. She might run a little late because of rehearsals or something." He looked at the clock; surely she wouldn't be too much longer. At the latest it would be another hour.

Tori nodded her dark head and studied the game again.

Brayden hadn't called Christian all day, though he'd wanted to. He figured she'd left the ringer off her upstairs phone and he assumed she hadn't had time to get a new one. Again, he looked at the clock. Had she left yet?

He'd tried to reach Morris today, but that hadn't worked. He should have just gone over to the guy's condo this morning, but he hadn't known which one belonged to the lieutenant. This afternoon when he'd closed the shop early, he'd gone by the station, but Morris had been out.

Brayden shook his head and tried to concentrate on the game with his daughter, but his mind kept wandering.

He should have stayed that morning and forced Christian to tell him what was going on. Another look at the clock told him it was well going on six. Like he'd ever been able to force that woman to do anything?

Well, force or no, willing or no, they were damn well going to get to the bottom of things this weekend. He reached up and rubbed the back of his neck, wishing he felt at ease where Christian was concerned.

* * * *

Christian heard a voice thundering in her ear. The words pierced her brain, but she couldn't make them out. God, her head hurt. Nausea swirled in her stomach.

Someone moaned.

Was that her?

"... It's time to play." His voice slithered over her, through her. A nightmare.

Wake up. Wake up.

His laughter danced across her face.

Scattered bits and sharpened pieces, scenes floated through her mind. Why couldn't she think? Move?

Then everything fell into place and she remembered.

Oh, God. No!

She tried to sit up, her eyes flying open and pain radiating through her head.

Ropes bit into her wrists, held her legs immobile.

The room was spinning and spinning.

Her chest tightened.

Breathe. Breathe.

It was a dream. *Please let it be a dream.*

A sob caught in her throat.

She focused on the face above her.

Oh no.

Richard. He was leaning over her, grinning down at her struggles.

Oh, please no. Please no. Her chest vised, but she closed her eyes again, prayed and pleaded to not have an asthma attack now. Not now. She fought the tightness back just a bit and opened her eyes.

She would not beg. She would not. He loved that. What had he given her? She felt light and heavy at the same time.

The son of a bitch had drugged her. She remembered the feeling, the games he liked to play.

When his lips touched hers, softly, lovingly, bile rose hot in her throat.

Again she jerked her wrists and the ropes didn't slacken. Or was she not trying hard enough? Her arms were heavy.

This was not happening. This was not happening. Not again, please, God, not again.

He pulled back, and caressed her face. "Still so beautiful."

Christian jerked from his touch.

Richard tsked. "Now, now." He tapped his bottom lip. "Remember? Tit for tat, my dear."

With that, he leaned down and bit hard enough on her lip that she tasted blood.

She couldn't keep the whimpered cry locked in her throat.

"You know my rules," he told her, wiping her blood off her chin. The red liquid glinted in the lights, catching her attention as he rubbed it between his fingers.

His green eyes flickered as he stared from the drop of blood on his gloved hand to her. Then, his look raked down her body.

Her clothes! He'd taken her clothes off! What had he done? She was completely and utterly exposed to him. No. No. No. Twisting and tugging did no good, but she didn't stop. The ropes bit into her wrists, the pain shoving the fuzziness of the drug aside.

"You gave me something. What did you give me?" She twisted her head and saw the syringe by her lamp, by the telephone. "You're a sick, twisted bastard! A low-life son of a bitch!" She spat at him. "I hate you! I hate you!"

He backhanded her, right beneath her eye. Pain exploded in her cheekbone.

Richard reached down and grabbed her hair. "Be quiet and be still." The bed gave under his weight. He straddled her, his legs locking around her torso. "I need you quiet."

She saw the long piece of material he held in his hand. The silk gag pulled the corners of her mouth tight as he tied it roughly behind her head. She smelled him on the material, tasted him, and almost gagged. She closed her eyes, not willing to give him the satisfaction of looking at him.

Again, she worked her wrists, moved her feet, but it did no good. No good. He'd always tied the knots tight.

He laughed. "You're shaking, my dear."

She was. Even though she knew, *knew* he only fed on her fear, she could no more stop the trembles than the tightening around her chest.

Please not now. Not now.

Her head was spinning again. Damn him.

Carefully, she pulled air in through her nose, even as she heard the swish of silk again. She managed to see his black leathered hands holding another white scarf before he wrapped it around her eyes.

This time her whimper turned into a muffled yell.

She was not going to let him do this to her. Thrashing her head from side to side dislodged his blindfold.

Again pain burst in her cheek as he hit her in the same spot. "Be still."

Her chest tightened and she tried to breathe calmly. He tightened the blindfold and she felt her hair pull at her temples.

"Now, now. Calm down. I don't want you passing out. That would hardly be enjoyable."

His hands slid down her stretched arms. To her chest. "And I so want to enjoy this."

She heard something clatter from the nightstand. What did he get? The syringe again? Something else she hadn't seen?

"You cut me," he said, his breath warm on her face.

She heard him moving around the room.

"Do you know how long I've waited for this, Josephine? How very long I've planned our meeting?" His voice arrowed to her, a fine cutting edge evident.

"People were constantly asking questions on why you disappeared."

He was pacing. He'd only paced before when he'd been enraged, and enraged, he was so much worse. So much.

Oh, God. The bands in her chest tightened, but she held them back. She couldn't have an attack now. Please not now.

"Your grandparents and brother tried to file murder charges on me. Me! As though I were no one." He continued to mumble and pace, but his words gave her courage. Joshua? Grandmere? Granddaddy?

They'd believed in her, even if they'd known nothing, they'd blamed him. If she could have, she would have smiled.

Christian had no idea how much time passed. He continued to pace and once he went downstairs. What he was doing, she couldn't begin to guess. Then she heard her piano, the tiny ping as he hit a high note, then the lower base notes following. Chopin. She hated Chopin because the composer was a favorite of his.

She pulled and jerked and tugged on the ropes, but it did no good. The more she moved, the more she focused, the more she could think. The sluggish feel of the drug was thinning. Her wrists were sticky when the piano silenced and she heard his footsteps coming back.

What was she going to do? What?

What about Drayson? Geoffery? Were they at home? No one was here to help her. No one. It would be hours before Brayden came looking. God, she'd been so stupid, so perfectly stupid. All but setting herself up. She should have told Brayden. She wouldn't be tied to a bed now if she had just talked to him.

And Gabe?

Gabe. He was expecting her at six. Six. What time was it?

Footsteps hushed across the carpet to the bed. Christian stiffened.

"Your hair is the wrong color," he whispered furiously. "This can't be right! What . . ." he trailed off. She heard a slap. "Never mind, it doesn't matter. Too red, damn it." Then he yelled, "Blonde. Your hair is supposed to be blonde! Not this trashy tarnished color."

She jerked at his raised voice and pressed herself into the mattress as she heard him near the bed.

Something cold slid onto her chest, his hands on either side of her face. He jerked her head up, and she felt the pull of metal along her neck. The locket.

"You were supposed to have this on. I found it in your purse downstairs." Carefully, he worked the chain around and settled the locket between her breasts. He jerked on her hair, muttering to himself. She felt the mattress rise as he moved away. The squeak of her closet doors filled the air. What did he want in her closet? Who cared. As long as he stayed away from her. Mutters and mumbles lost their way to her.

Tearing material, the slice of fabric rent the air.

"I don't like the looks of your clothes, Josephine, any more than your hair. Don't know what happened. Red. Cheap. You look cheap." His words were hurried and clipped.

He was cutting her clothes. He'd done that before too. That last night. He figured if she had nothing to wear, she couldn't leave. And she wouldn't have, if Susan hadn't shown up and helped her. Susan.

Danny.

Oh, God.

Rips and tears mixed with his furious whispers and curses to her. "Whore's clothes . . . trashy . . . what were you thinking?"

Wood moaned on wood. Her dresser. The same ritual happened there. The rustle of material, the jerk of drawers, the slicing click of scissors. Finally, silence settled and it was more terrifying than the sound of bladed objects cutting her things.

What was he doing? Where was he?

She could hear his breath, hurried and fast.

Something sharp poked her chest and she froze.

"Did you know I was advised you should have an accident?" he told her quietly. "You probably will, you know. Eventually, you'll have to. You're rather a liability." His sigh filled the air. "It's a shame you're no longer perfect. I have to decide what to do about that, you know. I tried to get you back to you, but I wonder if it'll ever happen." His fingers ran through her hair. She sensed rather than saw his shrug. "But right now, now I want to have fun with you. I've missed you."

I miss you. Those similar words had filled her with hope and longing earlier. Brayden. Oh, please. Please. Tears wet the material at the corners of her eyes.

I've missed you. Now they stabbed her heart with terror.

Something clicked softly. More like a shushed click. Again. What was that?

Again the snap continued. On her right side, then around to her left. His chuckle danced from the end of the bed. One more snapping click, then silence.

What was he doing?

She could sense him to her right. Cold metal grazed the tops of her breasts, clinked against the necklace he'd put there. "I could kill you so easily right now, and no one would know who, let alone why. No one."

The asthma attack she'd been fighting roared to life.

The knife! It was cool where he slipped it between her breasts. She half expected him to stab the thing into her chest. But then, pain seared across the underside of her upper arm as he cut it.

"Tit, tat."

Her stomach muscles tightened as she felt the steely point graze over her abdomen, past her navel.

She couldn't hold the whimper in.

A slashing sting burned across her thigh. Once, twice, three times.

Tears leaked out the sides of her eyes to absorb into the silk scarf of her blindfold.

Please. Please. Please. She jerked and pulled against her bindings.

Her chest tightened unmercifully and she tried to breathe through her nose.

He laughed. "You wouldn't be wanting this, would you?"

She heard the puff of her inhaler. Again the misted sound filled the air.

Calm down. Calm down. She had to think, breathe.

* * * *

Lieutenant Gabe Morris looked at his watch. It was almost six thirty. He glanced at his partner, Emma Laurence.

"What's up?" she asked him.

"Something." He had a bad feeling. Miss Bills should have been here by now.

"What?"

"Come on," he told her, standing and grabbing his coat.

In the car he filled her in.

"We can't help her if she doesn't report the crime, Gabe."

He flicked his blinker and switched lanes. "I know that. And this could be nothing. But she said she was coming in to report it and file a complaint by six. She called at four thirty, said she was going home to pack for the weekend. She'd stop by the station, do what had to be done, and then planned to tell her family this weekend."

The message that Brayden Kinncaid had stopped by to see him reached him too late to do anything about. He didn't figure theirs was a conversation to have over the phone anyway.

Holding the wheel with one hand, he dug through his stash of business cards in the console.

"You're gonna kill us in this traffic," Emma told him. "Who the hell are you looking for?"

"Brayden Kinncaid, or Gavin. The family home number is on the back."

Finally, she rattled off the number. Gabe punched the digits into his phone.

When the other end was answered, he asked to speak to Christian Bills.

As he'd figured, she wasn't there.

Damn.

He asked for Brayden.

"Brayden Kinncaid."

"This is Morris. Is Christian there?" he asked, as he maneuvered through the traffic, heading to the condos.

"No, why?"

Gabe caught the tension in the question. He weighed his options. He could blow it for Christian now, or give her the benefit of the doubt and let her tell her family everything. For now, he'd go with the "which-one-of-us-will-get-the-girl" routine. "I just got a message she'd tried to reach me. I thought she mentioned heading up there for the weekend."

Silence paused between them. "Did you try her cell?"

"No."

"Well, when she gets here, I'll have her call you."

Gabe nodded, felt bad for lying to the guy. "You do that."

The click sounded in his ear.

* * * *

Brayden set the phone down and stared at it. That was a line of bullshit if he'd ever heard one. What the hell was going on?

He picked the phone up and dialed Christian's cell.

Probably just overreacting. But where she was concerned, he couldn't think straight. She'd more than likely walk through the door at any minute; it was almost seven now.

When her voice mail answered, he hung up. Maybe she just turned her phone off.

Weird phone calls . . . creepy phone calls . . .

Damn it.

He dialed her condo. If she didn't answer this time . . .

It rang, and rang, and rang.

* * * *

The ringing phone startled her and she jerked. Her phone never rang up here. He must have turned up the ring volume.

"Help is so close," he said and chuckled, "yet unattainable."

The phone rang and she smelled the albuterol as it puffed

uselessly in her face. Tears soaked the cloth covering her eyes.

"Don't you just hate that? And the phone is what? Eight inches from your hand?" His cultured voice taunted her, the smile in it, the humor, the excitement whispered through. "The medicine to help you breathe? Only two inches from your face."

Her chest was so tight it hurt to even try to breathe. The puff of her inhaler sputtered.

"Oops, it appears you need to refill your prescription." She heard the inhaler drop to the floor, the sound of crushing plastic as he must have stepped on it.

One leather-clad hand trailed over her chest. Christian bucked and jerked, strained against the ropes until her muscles shook.

The sound of his laughter rang in her ears as his hand traveled lower and lower.

She tried to scream, but the wheezing sound was lost in silken fabric.

* * * *

Gabe parked beside Christian's VW Bug. Geoffery and Drayson were walking to their door.

"Oh, Gabe." Geoffery's gaze looked at the parking space and back to him. "New slot? You know tenants are supposed to park in front of their condos."

He didn't care about proper parking rules.

"Yeah, I know. Any more trouble next door?" he asked as Geoffery slid his key in.

"No, should there have been?" Drayson asked.

Gabe shrugged.

"Did you learn any more about that ghastly gift and strange caller?" Drayson asked.

"No." Gabe smiled and stood in front of Christian's door. He could hear a phone ringing. And ringing.

Why didn't she answer it? Maybe she was just in the shower.

He knocked.

"Christian!"

Nothing.

"Christian!"

Something crashed inside.

"Christian!" He moved back and noticed the long fresh groove in the door facing.

He pulled his gun and motioned to Emma. To Drayson and Geoffery he said, "Stay back, get in your condo."

He banged with his fist again.

"Christian! Christian! Open the door. It's the police!"

Still nothing.

* * * *

Damn it! He looked down at the woman of his fantasies, at his angel, and cursed.

His erection was painful and he wanted to sink it deep inside her.

Someone banged on the door again. If only he hadn't thrown the phone. It'd hit the wall and broken a vase.

Richard grabbed her by the throat and with the other hand twisted the locket tighter and tighter. "If you say anything. Anything. One single word, the Kinncaids will die. The first will be Brayden and his little girl." He ripped the locket from her neck and shoved it in his pocket.

Quickly, he rose, grabbed his wet pair of gloves off the floor where he'd thrown them, and hurried down the stairs.

Just as he eased out the sliding door in her kitchen into the darkened courtyard, he heard the shots shattering the front door lock.

The shadows covered him as he slithered through the darkness, hopped over the back fence and hurried through the alleys. Sirens screamed in the night.

He walked a block down to his car. Inside, he pulled off the gloves.

Thrumming his fingers on the steering wheel, he tried to figure out what had gone wrong. How had the police arrived?

It didn't matter. He'd find out.

Right now, he needed to get to the airport.

* * * *

Brayden hurried down the stairs. She hadn't answered. At the door he pulled on his coat and grabbed his keys.

"Where are you off to?" Aiden asked coming from the living room, where everyone else was.

"To town."

"Why?" Aiden stopped in front of him.

Brayden didn't have time for this. "She didn't answer."

"So?" His brother crossed his arms. "Maybe she's out with another guy. What do you care?"

"Christian is . . ."

The corner of Aiden's mouth twitched, but his eyes narrowed. "Don't pull another stunt with her like you did after Gavin and Taylor's party," Aiden warned, his voice low.

"What?" He couldn't believe what he was hearing.

"You heard me."

Brayden closed his eyes. "I don't have time for this."

"Why are you rushing off to town?"

Damn it. "Because she said she'd be here and she's not!" he yelled.

Aiden stepped back and lowered a look at him.

He sighed and raked a hand through his hair. "Something is wrong, Aiden. Really wrong."

"Fine. What do you think is wrong?"

"Someone's been calling her. Creepy, midnight calls, she said. Last night the guy left her a gift. Whenever I see her, she's always darting looks over her shoulder. Have you even seen her lately?"

Aiden nodded and frowned. "Yeah, she didn't look so good. I was pissed at you. Figured it was your fault."

Brayden smiled. "Yeah, well, I did too at first. But now, after this morning . . ." He shook his head. "I don't know, Aiden. Something is off, way off. I never should have left her. I should have waited on her and driven her up here myself. I should have gone back to town hours ago." He stopped and looked at the floor. "I've got a really, really bad feeling. Like the time Tori was taken."

There, he'd said it. The churn of sickness coated his stomach. He stuck his hands out and saw they trembled. "She should be here. I'm going to town."

Aiden studied him for a minute, then reached around and into the coat closet, retrieving his own black woolen coat. "I'm going with you. Let me tell Jessie."

"That's not—"

"I'm going."

He reached for the door.

He stepped outside and into the cold wind that slapped and stung, a vengeful woman full of fury.

Chapter 7

Gabe looked around the hallway, his gun sweeping wide, Emma right beside him. She'd radioed in as soon as he'd shot the locks. In the kitchen he saw blood on the floor, the scattered fruit.

"Christian!" Turning, he ran down the hall, took the stairs three at a time.

His heart raced at what he might find. Had the guy taken her?

Why wasn't she answering? He didn't want to think about that. Too many bodies bloodied his memory with grotesque images at what could have happened. Sirens pierced the night.

Please, let her be okay.

He turned the corner to her room and stopped, frozen at the sight before him.

She was tied, spread-eagle on the bed. Rage pounded through him and then the freeze-frame snapped and he moved. Emma swore behind him and shifted to check the bathroom.

"Clear," she said.

No one. The closet doors stood open, torn and ragged clothes falling out. The place was empty.

Lowering his gun, he walked to the bed and saw her chest panted fast and furiously. Thank God. She was alive. He tried not to look, but the image seared into his mind. Tethered like an animal, she was exposed and at the mercy of whomever had done this.

On the floor lay her crushed inhaler. On the bed beside her, a bloodstained knife. Folded neatly in the chair were blankets and sheets. He jerked one of the blankets off and threw it over her, but not before he'd registered the multiple bruises and cuts covering her. Her wrists were bloody and bruised, the skin peeling back where she'd rubbed against her bindings.

"Christian?" he whispered. He reached up to untie her gag and blindfold. As soon as his finger grazed her cheek, she flinched away, the whimper squeezing his heart.

Damn the bastard.

Voices called out.

"Up here!" he yelled. Trying to ignore the way she stiffened, he untied the gag and blindfold, ripping them aside. Her wide terror-filled eyes stared at him for a long second, then slid closed.

The wheeze of her fighting to breathe filled the air.

"Do you have another inhaler?"

She didn't answer.

He looked up at Emma. "Don't forget to get that knife and syringe. We need them bagged as soon as the crime tech guys are done." He stopped; Emma knew how to do her damn job. There was blood on the knife. He saw the slice that dribbled blood on her arm. Had seen those on her thighs.

She was shaking, he could feel the bed tremble.

He jerked out his own pocketknife, leaned over, and cut the ropes that bound the woman to the bed. Pristine white nylon dangled, marred with crimson.

"Hang on, Christian. Just hang on." He started to touch her, but didn't.

He looked at her trembling on the bed. What the hell was she doing here alone? If she were his, he damn well wouldn't have left her alone for one second.

Emma came back from the bathroom bagging more evidence. "The ambulance is on the way," a uniform said from the doorway.

He nodded. "Good, keep the neighbors back and away from here. I want this entire place picked apart."

Gabe's gaze was locked on Christian curled tightly in the center of the bed.

* * * *

The hospital noises were sharp and loud, yet distorted. The harsh glare of florescent lights stabbed and prodded her headache, teased the nausea. She'd been given albuterol here and in the ambulance. At least her chest didn't hurt anymore and she could breathe from the nebulizing treatment. Though not too deeply; her bruised ribs pulled and all but moaned if she did.

Slowly, she slid off the exam table.

"Since you didn't have any clothes, you can put these on," the female doctor said, laying a pair of folded blue scrubs on the end of the bed.

They were at Sibly Memorial Hospital. Aggravated sexual

assault. They performed a rape kit. The doctor didn't think the attacker had time to get to that part, thank God. Christian couldn't remember everything, and what had he done to her while she was out? She didn't say no when they asked for her consent, and she signed the form. For almost two hours she answered what questions she could or would and endured all the poking, probing, and exposure she could stand. Maybe, maybe he left something else behind, he'd touched her enough. She did remember that.

A violent shiver shook her. Oh, God. This wasn't happening. Not again.

Clicking. The clicking. They'd taken pictures to put in the reports. It was no less humiliating now than it had been eight years before.

The clicks. He'd taken pictures too.

That's what the slight clicking noises had been, and beeps. Had there been a beep? Digital camera? Bile rose again in her throat. She'd already thrown up the water they'd given her. And the pain meds.

She couldn't quit shaking. God, she was freezing.

"You should stay tonight for observation," Dr. Ripley said and cleared her throat. "Did you call your family?"

The doctor knew. Most didn't connect her with the Kinncaids, but this woman did. No big surprise. With the Kinncaids and two of them doctors, some people knew her.

Christian only shook her head, her gaze focused on the white bandages around her wrists. The edges of her vision were still blurred, thanks to whatever he'd given her. It was like looking in a tunnel. The wraps on her wrists mirrored the one on her right thigh. One of the cuts was deep enough she'd needed stitches.

Dr. Ripley sighed. "I would advise you to talk about this with them. Hiding something like this doesn't help."

The white strips stared back up at her. They reminded her of the ropes. Voices yelled from out in the ER, machines and trays clattered and clanged, shoes squeaked as they ran down the hall. She was surrounded by people and felt utterly isolated.

Pictures and phrases danced chaotically through her mind. She didn't really remember the ride here. Just the terror. Words. His voice.

. . . *Anything and the Kinncaids will die* . . .

Her hands shook as she slid the scrub uniform on.

"You can take a shower here, if you want."

A shower. But what if someone came in while she was naked? What if someone saw her? It was a public place, what if he was here waiting for her. What if . . . No, the hotel. She'd lock the door and shower there. Hot, very, very hot. It was safe there.

Christian shook her head at the offer. She just wanted out of here. Away from all these people, their questions and the pitying looks.

Dr. Ripley continued, "If you're going home, I'll write you a prescription for the pain and another for a measured-dose inhaler. Though I'd rather you not take the Percocet, painkillers, for at least another four hours if you can handle the pain. You've got a nasty concussion and your tox levels are still not as clear as I'd like them to be. But I'll send you enough to get you through the night. Get this prescription filled in the morning." The sounds of scribbling filled Chris's ears. "And to be on the safe side, have someone wake you up every hour or so."

The rip of paper made her jump. She turned and took the prescription and little white bag Dr. Ripley held.

The doctor held a card out. "Here's a group. We meet every two weeks. Survivors of sexual crimes. If you need someone to—"

"Thanks," Christian cut her off, snatching the card. Taking a breath, she took small steps to the door and opened it. The floor was cold beneath her bare feet.

Gabe and Emma leaned against the wall. Geoffery and Drayson with them. Oh, God.

Emma Laurence had been in the room during part of the exam asking questions and taking notes until Dr. Ripley told her to leave. Or at least she thought so. It was hard to remember.

"Are you . . . how are you . . . Do you want to talk to us now?" Gabe asked her, not moving any closer.

She didn't want him closer.

"Lieutenant, she needs to rest," Dr. Ripley said, coming up behind her. "Chris, do you want me to call you a cab?"

Christian nodded.

"No, I'll take her," Gabe said.

Dr. Ripley looked at her for her decision.

She darted a look at Gabe, but didn't hold it long enough; she didn't want to see the look in his eyes. "I just want to go to the hotel," she whispered.

"How 'bout Seneca?" he asked softly.

Seneca. Home. The Kinncaids. Oh, God.

Tears pricked her eyes, but Christian shook her head. Cleared her throat. "No. No, the hotel. I want a shower. I have to take a shower. And some clothes."

A moment passed, noises shuffled around them, and she felt like she was part of some movie, invisible while the world moved slowly around her.

Finally, he answered, "Fine."

His phone rang. Jerking it out, he walked away from them.

"Luv," Drayson said, reaching out to her.

She backed away.

Someone cleared their throat. "Honey, if you need anything, anything at all, just give us a call, all right?" Geoffery asked.

All she could do was nod.

She heard them walk away.

Dr. Ripley placed a hand on her arm. "I need to know where to call. I'd really prefer you stay the night."

She shook her head no.

"Okay, then I'll ask you to come in, in a couple of days, but I'll call you. Check on you tonight. All right? You should also follow up with your own gynecologist."

Christian hated this place, words and sounds sharpened and droned on. "I—I don't know where I'll be. Probably the hotel."

Dr. Ripley only raised a brow. "Don't go through this alone."

Alone . . . alone . . . alone . . .

She had to be. Just like before. He hurt her friends and those closest to her.

. . . *Say anything and the Kinncaids will die . . . will die . . . will die . . .*

Gabe walked up to them. "You ready?"

She jumped and nodded. He offered his jacket, but she didn't take it.

Her bones felt brittle. If only she could get warm.

Dr. Ripley wrapped a blanket around her. "It's cold outside."

"Come on," Detective Laurence said.

She followed them out the door and into the unforgiving, bitter cold.

* * * *

Brayden slammed to a stop in front of the ER. Nausea rolled in his stomach.

He should have gotten here sooner. But the damn wreck on the interstate had traffic backed up for over an hour.

When they'd finally reached Christian's condo it was to find the place swarming with cops, and all they'd been told was the resident of number nineteen was at Sibly Memorial. Some sort of attack.

What the hell had happened?

He ran through the double doors, hearing the faint swoosh behind him as they closed.

At the nurses' station, he thumped the counter with his fist. "Christian Bills?"

The nurse looked at him and tapped some keys and shook her head. "No, sorry. I just came on about two minutes ago and she's not listed."

Brayden slowly counted to five. "Will you check again please? We were told she was here."

"Brayden? Aiden? What are you doing here?"

Brayden turned and saw a doctor he'd met with his mother several times.

She smiled. "Dr. Ripley. You just missed Christian."

"What happened?" he asked.

Her look darted away, then down at the chart she was holding. Ice skittered through him. Finally, they rose back to him. "You know I can't discuss patients."

"Is she okay?" She must be if she left. "You said 'missed her.' Where is she?"

Dr. Ripley sighed and motioned them to the side.

"Yes, she was here. I would have preferred she stay the night, but she refused."

"What the hell does that mean?" Brayden snapped. Where was she? This was like before. Cops, hospitals and no one telling him a damn thing.

"Dr. Ripley," Aiden said, "is there anything you can tell us?"

"I heard her mention the hotel. Detectives Morris and Laurence gave her a ride."

Brayden barely heard the last of it; he was already hurrying to the door, dodging a gurney and the persons pushing it.

By the time they reached the car, Aiden was on his phone talking to Quinlan, who was still at the hotel overseeing the setup for a large convention.

"Quin, just keep your eyes open for them." Pause. "I don't know." Pause again. He could hear Quinlan's voice through the car. "We don't know. Yeah, we'll be there in a few minutes."

Brayden felt sick. He should have stayed. He should have stayed. He knew it! Damn it!

He slapped the steering wheel with the palm of his hand.

Taking every shortcut he knew, he raced through the traffic. Aiden never said a word, not that he would have noticed.

He had to get to Christian.

* * * *

In the elevator, she braved, "Did you call him?"

One long moment passed before Gabe cleared his throat. "I tried to, he wasn't there and I didn't leave a message."

Christian closed her eyes, relief trickling through the fear, yet she wished he were here. Part of her wished for the safety she felt with Brayden, even if it was only an illusion.

But even if he were here, she wouldn't know what to say or do. She didn't want him to see her like this. She didn't want anyone to see her like this.

Weak, frail, beaten.

She was strong. She survived before, she would again.

She would again.

The doors slid open and she stepped out into the quiet, dimmed hallway. The plush rugs, laid out in the entry, swallowed her footfalls. At apartment 3B, she stopped. Her key. Her key was in her purse and . . .

"I picked this up at the condo. I figured you'd need it." Detective Laurence held out her purse.

Christian reached for it, but stopped. The locket. The locket had been in her purse. He'd been in her purse.

She shook her head. "No. No. I don't want it. I'll call down and get another one."

"I can get it," Gabe volunteered.

"No!" she yelled. "He—he touched it. I don't want it." The shaking wouldn't stop. She hurt, hurt all over. She just wanted inside, inside where it was safe. Away from him. With nothing he'd ever had his hands on.

"He was in your purse?" Laurence asked.

She nodded, reached up and felt the side of her neck, where the chain had bitten the flesh as he'd ripped it off.

"The locket."

"What locket?" Gabe asked.

"The one—the one I called you about today." She looked to the door in front of her. "He got it out, put it on me when—when—when . . ." She took a deep breath and closed her eyes.

The ping-swish of the elevator doors startled her. Her heartbeat speeded up, but she didn't turn around.

"Thank God."

Brayden.

No. Oh, no. Not like this. Not like this. Please.

Christian pulled the blanket tighter, stared at the closed door and kept the bruised side of her face away. She had no idea what it looked like; she hadn't wanted to see, but she could imagine.

Footsteps neared. More than one.

"Mr. Kinncaid. Mr. Kinncaid. And another one, I presume? If you don't mind, we'd like a moment of your time," Laurence tried. Christian felt the cop move to stand between her and them.

"I do mind." Then he was there, pulling her against him. "God, I've been worried sick. When I couldn't get hold of you. When I couldn't . . . I kept thinking about . . . What happened? All they said was that you were at Sibly. Something about an attack. And then you weren't there. God, are you okay?"

She could feel him trembling, or maybe it was her.

It didn't matter. She was dirty. Dirty. She pushed him away, brought the blanket up with her hands to shield her face.

Out of the corner of her eye, she saw him raise his hand, and she stepped away.

His hand hovered there. "Christian?"

Silence settled around them. She was so cold, she couldn't stop shaking.

"Let's go inside," Gabe said.

Brayden didn't care about going inside. He wanted to know what the hell was going on. When he'd seen her standing there between the cops, relief had rushed through him. She was okay. She was fine.

But as he'd gotten closer, he noticed the posture of the cops, guarding—hers, tightened. The changed hair color, a burnished blonde-brown color. And the relief slid away into worry.

She stood there, trembling before him, her head bowed in the blanket.

"Christian?"

Still she didn't lower the blanket and Brayden didn't move.

Slowly, he reached up to the bunched material hiding her from him.

Her head shook back and forth, but she didn't jerk away.

"Don't look at me. Don't look at me," she whispered. If he weren't standing so close, he wouldn't have heard her.

"Christian." Carefully, he pulled her hands down.

Her head was still bowed. He saw the white butterfly bandage on her forehead, the dark bruise contrasting around it, the large knot bumping under the contused skin.

With one hand, he crooked a finger under her chin, noticed her stiffen, pull into herself. What had happened?

"Look at me."

She shook her head.

"Baby, look at me."

Her eyes slowly rose to his and he felt his world tilt, quake and shatter.

"Jesus." The entire right side of her face was bruised, swollen and red. Dark purple marks colored her jawline. Gently, he moved her chin to the side. Her lip was swollen and split.

He heard Aiden's in-drawn breath, Quinlan's curse.

"What the hell happened?"

The hands, hidden beneath the blanket, held in one of his, started to shake. The trembles shook her entire frame, until she quaked violently.

"Bray, let's go inside. Get her inside and sit her down before she passes out," Aiden said.

Her eyes wouldn't meet his and she ducked her head. He shifted out of the way as Aiden unlocked the door, wrapping one arm around her.

Still holding her hands in one of his, he pulled her closer and walked her into their apartment.

He cupped her arm with one hand to steer her to the couch, but at her grimace he let go.

She stopped and stepped away from him, looking at the floor. "I'm going to take a shower."

A shower? He reached out to her, but she stepped further away.

"D-don't. I'm dirty. Please don't—don't touch me."

The words sank home, the possible meaning behind them. No. No. God, no.

Christian turned to walk to her bedroom and stopped. She stood in front of the hallway mirror. He saw her reflection, the shock on her face. Her trembling hand rose to her hair.

"Look," she whispered. "Look."

He was and his stomach pitched at the bruises on her face, her swollen eye. An accident?

I'm dirty . . . don't touch me.

Brayden swallowed.

The bandage around her wrist flashed at him. White against white skin. Her other hand came up and the blanket dropped.

Holy Mother of God.

Her neck was scratched and scraped. A bandage wrapped around both wrists and her upper arm.

"Look at my hair," her voice trembled. Tears trickled over her cheeks.

"Honey, it's okay. It's fine," Aiden said calmly from behind him.

Brayden didn't give a damn about her hair, it was the rest of her, abraded and bruised, that shook him, made him fist his hands at his sides.

Her eyes rose to his, then locked on Aiden. "It's not fine."

Brayden saw the fear, the anger in the gray depths.

"It's *not* fine!" Her fingers ran through her discolored hair. "He—he did this." Her eyes looked back to the mirror, to herself. "He—he—he . . . Oh, God." She swayed.

Brayden moved and caught her before she crumpled to the floor.

Rage pounded through him. Disbelief warred with the bruised and battered woman in his arms. Her body shook so badly, so deeply, he wondered that her bones didn't snap.

"Who?" He held her, gentled his voice even though he wanted to yell.

She stiffened, pushed away from him. "Don't—don't touch me. Don't. I'm dirty. I have to take a shower. I have to get him off. I can't . . . I don't . . ."

He reached out, but dropped his hands back when she shook her head and stepped away. All he could do was watch helplessly as she took small steps to the door of her rooms. He fisted his hands at his sides until they shook, bit down till his teeth hurt.

At her door, she stopped. Without turning, she asked, "Could—could you get me—get me some clothes?"

Brayden could see her trembling from here. "Anything. Anything you want. Anything you need."

She nodded. "Clothes. I need some clothes. He—he . . . I need some."

With that, she shut her door and he heard the lock slide home, click back open, then slide home again.

Brayden stood staring at the door, refusing to see the picture her voiced and unspoken words painted.

He moved his jaw back and forth, grinding his teeth. Taking a deep breath, he turned to see the cops standing in his foyer. Aiden paced by the couch. Quinlan stood by a chair.

He asked Morris, "What the hell happened?"

Morris rolled his head on his neck, his jaw moving side to side as he walked toward Brayden. His eyes narrowed. With no warning, Morris threw a punch, catching him right on the jaw.

Brayden shook his head, the pain not registering.

"Morris? Are you insane?" the female officer asked.

"That's what I'd like to know," Aiden added. "Interesting way to help your career."

Brayden's gaze locked on Morris's dark one.

"You don't deserve her. Damn you. Why the hell did you leave her alone?" Morris bit out. "You showed up at her place last night, middle of the damn night. You saw her then. You know she was afraid. How could you just leave her alone?"

"Gabe. Calm down." Stepping between them, the short woman held her hand out. "I'm Detective Laurence."

Brayden barely spared her a look, but when he did, he asked, "I want to know what the hell happened and I want to know now."

* * * *

The scalding water filled the bathroom with so much steam she couldn't see herself in the mirror. Just as well. She didn't want to see. Didn't want to see the bruises, the cuts, the marks he left on her.

She didn't want to see Josephine staring back at her.

The skin on her arms was pink, almost raw from the pumice stone she'd used, and the entire bar of soap.

And still she scrubbed. The water heated her already reddened skin.

She'd taken off the wet gauze from her wrists. The spray bit into the raw skin, stinging at first, until it grew numb.

Water ran off her hair, down her face. She stared at the cream tiles, the steam so thick on them, water trailed down.

What was she going to do?

. . . first will be Brayden, and his little girl . . .

Oh, God. What did she do?

A sob choked her, tore out of her throat.

She leaned back, slid down the wet wall. With her knees to her chest, she bowed her head and tried to stop the tears that washed away her shame as uselessly as the hot water beating unmercifully down on her.

Chapter 8

Brayden paced outside her door, down the hallway and back.

He looked up and regarded the other men in the room. Aiden stared out the window, Quinlan poured another drink at the bar. The cops were on the couches.

A heavy silence cloaked everyone.

This couldn't be happening. Not to her, not to Christian.

Morris filled them in. Aggravated attempted rape, from preliminary tests, with a deadly weapon. Then there were the drugs in her system. They'd have to wait on lab results to verify, but apparently Gabe had showed up before the bastard had . . . had . . .

Brayden stopped, shoved the heels of his hands into his eyes. But the black images danced behind his eyelids.

Tied to the damn bed, like a fucking animal.

Rage and fury roared through him, beating him into a red haze. Blindly, he swung out and punched the wall. The drywall gave with a satisfying thud against his knuckles.

He bit down on his clawing temper and leaned his forehead against the wall.

He'd failed her. Him and his stupid twisted pride, his questioning sense of what was between them. He should have stayed in town. Should have driven by and picked her up. Should have made certain she was okay. While she was beaten and terrorized, *he'd* been playing with his daughter.

"Bray."

He opened his eyes, straightened and turned. Aiden had come away from the window, and stood not far away.

His gaze locked onto his brother's. As if to no one in particular, he bit out, "I want this bastard found."

The message passed between them, unspoken yet heard. He saw Aiden's barely discernible nod.

"Brayden," Aiden said, "he will be. I'm sure the police are doing everything they can."

The police. He looked over to the couch and nodded curtly to Morris.

"Bray, she needs you right now. She needs all of us, but you more than anyone. Don't let your anger at this bastard scare her into a corner," Quinlan told him. "She needs you."

Why was it the youngest was the most levelheaded? Quin was right, but the anger and fury roared within Brayden. It wasn't often he lost his temper. He'd learned early on that large males and tempers often gave the wrong impression. But right now he wanted to rip something apart with his bare hands. Preferably the man who had done this.

Sighing, he rubbed his hands over his face.

"You saw no one, Lieutenant?" Aiden asked Morris.

Morris, to give the man credit, seemed to care more than was professionally necessary. And thank God for that. If he hadn't . . .

"Do you think I would be sitting here wanting to talk to her, make her go through it all again, if we had something to go on?" Morris answered, his voice steeled on the edge of anger.

Brayden looked at her door, then at his watch—over an hour. She'd been in there over an hour.

The phone rang.

"Mom," Quinlan said.

He hoped not. Brayden strode to the phone and answered on the second ring, "Hello?"

"Did you find her?"

How the hell had Quinlan known? Brayden sighed and thought about what to say, what not to say.

He scratched his head. "Yeah, Mom, we—uh—yeah, we found her."

"Oh, thank God. Your father and I are worried sick. Becky said a Lieutenant Morris called here looking for you. Tori and Ryan were asking questions, and Gavin and Taylor are trying to keep us all calm. But I know . . ." His mother's voiced trailed off. "I know something happened. Tell me she's okay."

Lie or truth? Closing his eyes, he did something he'd rarely done to his mother. He lied.

"She, uh, she will be, Mom. There was a bit of a . . ." He sighed. "She'll be okay."

"Oh, my God! What happened?"

Brayden bit down, ran his bottom lip between his teeth. Quickly he said, "We're not really sure, Mom."

"We'll be there . . ."

"No!" he all but yelled. Then more calmly, "No, we'll be home later, she wants to come home," he said, not knowing if she did or not. "The police are still asking a few questions."

"The police?"

"Mom, please just stay there. We're coming home as soon as this is all wrapped up."

She sighed on the other end and he knew she was trying to read what he'd said and what he hadn't.

"Let me talk to Christian," she said.

He rolled his neck. "She's in the shower. She had a few scrapes and bruises. When she gets out, there are some questions that need clearing up and then . . . Then we'll head out there."

"What exactly happened to her?" she carefully asked.

Hell.

"I—it. Mom, the police are still here talking to us, we'll call when we head up there." He needed to get off. "I'll call you back in a bit. Bye, Mom."

With that, he hung up and puffed out a sigh.

"Grown men lying to their mother. Do you boys do this a lot?" Laurence asked.

"She can't speak to them, Mom is worried and you are here still wanting answers. What part of that is a lie?"

"Mom would disagree," Aiden answered for them. "But for now, it served its purpose. Mother would worry and descend."

Silence settled again.

Brayden's gaze landed on the bag from the downstairs boutique. Quinlan had run down and grabbed something. Brayden hadn't wanted to leave the apartment. He walked to the bag and picked it up.

Maybe she was done and needed her clothes.

He looked back at the door. Was she all right? Well, no, but he was worried about her. At her door, he knocked. No one, nothing.

Again he knocked. "Christian?"

Still nothing, and his feeling that something was wrong grew.

This time he knocked harder.

"I could go in and check on her, if you want me to," Laurence volunteered, standing behind him.

He almost handed her the bag and agreed. But he didn't. He needed to see Christian, see she was all right.

Shaking his head, he turned back to the door and drew his master key out of his pocket. The family suites were designed so that the front door key could open any door in that apartment.

On a deep sigh, he slid the key across the lock and opened the door.

The bedroom was dim and silent. Carefully, he shut the door and set the bag on the bed.

"Christian?"

Silence greeted him, or almost silence. He could hear the hum of the built-in heater in the bathroom and the spray of water.

He raised his fist to knock on the bathroom door then lowered it, shoving his hand into his pocket. Perhaps she needed the time alone. But he'd left her alone before, stepped back, and look what he'd allowed to happen.

The water sprayed in a constant uninterrupted stream.

He frowned at the door, ran a hand through his hair.

If she were in the shower, wouldn't he hear the change in the water?

Pausing, he raised his hand, then took a deep breath and knocked. "Christian?"

Nothing.

He tried the knob, it was locked.

"Baby, are you . . ." He trailed off. Of course she wasn't okay. "Do you need anything?" he asked against the door.

Not a muted sound drifted from within.

He didn't want to invade her privacy. One last time he tried knocking. "Your clothes are out here."

Still not a single sound.

He stared at the door, then turned to go, but stopped. She might hate him, but be damned, he had to know she was all right in there.

He pulled his key out again, unlocked the bathroom door, and pushed it open. "Chris . . ."

Thick hot steam rolled out, engulfing him. It was hotter than a sauna in here. The room was a muted wall of heated mist; most of it escaped out the open door.

"Christian?"

Still no answer. His heart slammed in his chest. The water ran ceaselessly. The bathroom was empty.

"Christian?" he asked louder, striding to the shower stall.

She wasn't in there. Fear shot through him and he jerked the door open. Hot stinging spray splattered out on him.

She was curled on the bottom of the tiled floor. Mumbling a curse, he reached in through the scalding water and shut it off.

Her skin was bright pink and heated as he touched her.

She didn't even flinch as he stepped into the shower and scooped her up against him.

"Oh, baby. Come on. It's going to be all right. You're safe now."

The heat and water from her soaked through his shirt. She slumped in his arms, boneless. Holding her close to him, he reached out and grabbed her robe hanging by the shower.

For a moment he looked around, then sat on the toilet, with Christian on his lap.

He leaned her head back, her eyes were closed. Fear slammed through him. Didn't she have a concussion?

"Christian?" Reaching to the side, he grabbed a washcloth and soaked it with cold water. Gently, he feathered it over her face, careful of the bump on her head, her swollen, already blackening eye. He bit down at the sight of her abused face.

Still she didn't stir.

"Christian, baby, talk to me." He placed a soft kiss on her forehead. "You're scaring me here. Come on."

She was hot, too hot. He kept up his nonsensical words. "I bet you just got overheated."

A moan drifted passed her lips and her eyelids fluttered, though only one rose. He rubbed the cool cloth over her neck.

Her eye stared at him, but she didn't stiffen as he expected her to.

He sat the cloth on the counter and gathered her robe up. "Can you stand, just for a second? I want to put this on you."

Her gray stare was blank. As easily as possible, he shifted her so that they were both standing. He held her up with one arm and tried to put the robe on with the other.

His gaze ran over her, her body that haunted his dreams, a body he loved. One that should be cherished, cared for . . . protected.

Now, bruises darkly contrasted against her pale skin. Some part of him catalogued the damage someone had inflicted on her, but a red haze threatened the edge of his vision, blacked the border of his sanity and temper.

Christian didn't need his rage.

Taking a long breath through his nose, he studied her. The entire right side of her rib cage was shadowed, one large bruise covering several ribs. He gently reached out and ran a hand over them; her stomach muscles tightened under his fingers.

"Sorry." He took his hand away, but looked at her. "Are they broken?"

Her eyes looked away and she shook her head.

Round purple marks marred her upper arm, just above a cut. He'd seen the cuts on her thigh, the blackened stitches obscene against her pale skin.

Biting down, he shoved the air out of his lungs. As carefully as possible, he helped her put the robe on. He tied it gently, mindful of her bruised ribs. Then he noticed the marks at the collar of the robe. He traced the violet contusions along her jaw and neck, the reddened cuts on both sides, heavier at the back. What the hell was that from?

She didn't move, didn't look at him. With every new mark, bruise, and laceration he discovered, fury roiled his blood.

Finally, he dropped his hands away from her and turned so that she sat on the toilet. She swayed for a moment, but then leaned back. He stood there, staring at her.

What the hell did he do to help her? How could he . . . What was there . . . Did she even . . .

On a silent curse, he flicked the water back on and filled a glass. He held it up to her lips. "You need some liquids in you."

She drank the entire glass down.

When she lowered her hands, a hiss escaped her. Brayden knelt beside her.

"What? What is it?" he asked quietly.

Christian shook her head, but mumbled, "My wrists. The robe hurts my . . ." She trailed off.

Brayden reached out and took her fine-boned hand. Carefully, he pushed the cuff of her terry robe up.

The abraded and peeling skin was scabbed in places, purples mixing with blues, reds, and mottled yellows. A glance down showed him her ankles with the same violent marks.

"Christ." All he could see when he looked at those wounds was her tethered and struggling, trying to escape.

On another curse he rose, all but ripped a drawer out of the vanity.

He shoved things out of the way and tried the next drawer. There was a box of bandages and a tube of antibacterial ointment.

Again he knelt in front of her.

His hands shook as he applied the clear cream to the bandage. Then he wrapped the white gauze around her wrists. When they were taped, he stared at her hands.

Ankles. He reached for one ankle, but she pulled it back.

"I can do it," she whispered.

The control on his emotions almost snapped. "Let me —" Biting down, he held his hands palms out to her and slowly rose. Looking at her bent head, he said, "I'm sorry. I'm so damn sorry. I didn't mean to make you uncomfortable, or anything like that."

Damn it all to hell. What did he do? How did he help her?

She nodded, though she still didn't raise her eyes to his. "I know that. Thank — thank you for . . ."

"Don't," he said through his teeth.

This time her face rose to his, and though he knew what he'd see, his breath still caught in his chest, his blood still froze in his veins. He'd kill the bastard.

Her one good eye looked at him, confusion clear in its gray depth.

"Do *not* thank me. For God's sake, Christian." He paced away from her toward the door, fisted his hands and shoved them in his pockets to keep from ripping something apart. "Do *not* thank me. I didn't do shit. I didn't . . ." He closed his eyes and took a deep breath. "You're so precious and I can't stand the thought of how hurt you are."

Christian sat there looking at him. Her face hurt. Hell, her entire body ached, pulled and jerked.

Brayden stood before her, hands balled in his pockets. Such a tall man, proud and strong. The lines on his face were hard and unforgiving.

When his eyes opened, her breath caught again at the storming rage lighting his eyes from within.

"I should have . . . I wasn't . . . Damn it all to hell," he finished on a sigh. "Tell me what I can do to help you."

A muscle jumped in his jaw, the corners of his mouth tight, and then she saw the shine in his eyes and something inside her squeezed.

"I want to fix this and I'm afraid to get too close to you."

Her heart dropped. She had told him she was dirty. Shame came in a hard, fast wave.

"I'm afraid I'll scare you. I don't want to scare you," he said softly. "I just want to . . . to . . . to . . ."

"To what?" she asked.

She saw him swallow; his jaw moved back and forth. "I want to hold you and tell you everything's going to be okay. I want to take all your pain away. I want to go back to this morning and . . ." He stopped and shook his head. "I don't want to frighten you. I never want to frighten you. I don't want you to hurt anymore, in any way."

Relief crested and rolled in her. She shook her head. "I could never be scared of you, Bray. Never."

The muscle bunched in his jaw, once, twice, and again. Slowly, he walked to her. He stood in front of her, but she didn't look up, instead stared at the silver buckle of his belt. His knees popped when he squatted back down so that he was at eye level with her. Gently, he reached up and cupped her face, his thumb caressing her cheek with the softest touch. Carefully, he leaned forward and kissed her hair. When he straightened, his gaze locked with hers.

His eyes said it all. Determined fury mixed with the promise of retribution. His voice roughened over the words, "What can I do? What do you need?"

Christian took a deep trembling breath. "Clothes. I need some clothes."

"They're out on the bed." Quickly, he rose, turned, and in seconds he was back holding out a bag from downstairs.

She held the bag on her lap.

"Do you need some help?" he asked.

Christian shook her head.

Still he stood there a few feet away. Finally, he cleared his throat. "Morris and his partner are still here." A beat passed. "They want to talk to you. But if you'd rather wait until tomorrow or another time, that's fine and we'll just go home."

Home. She closed her eyes. What to do? She still had no answers.

"No, that's fine. I'll—I'll talk to them," she said softly. Oh, God, please help her.

"Okay. Why don't I wait out here in the bedroom while you get ready. I don't want you falling over and hitting your head or something."

"No, I need some things out of the bedroom. You go on ahead."

"What do you need, I'll get them?"

She told him and listened as he rummaged in a drawer and brought back her underwear. The sounds reminded her of earlier and she jumped when he came back in.

Instead of bringing them to her, he said, "I'll put them here on the counter."

She could only nod as she waited. Finally, the door clicked shut.

Slowly, she rose. Without looking in the mirror, she dressed in the charcoal chenille sweater and black pants from the bag. She'd have to forgo the bra he'd gotten from her armoire. It hurt to put it on. The sweater was a turtleneck and covered her from just below her ears to her thighs. Soft. Though the sweater was thick, it did little to warm her as the cold started to seep back into her bones.

She pulled on the boots Bray had brought from her closet. For a moment she sat and stared at the black shoes and wondered when she'd purchased them. The thought seemed so stupidly important. On a sigh, she shrugged it off. It didn't matter. Nothing mattered.

Closing her eyes, she said aloud, but quietly, "I survived before and I'll survive again."

A shiver danced down her spine. It could have been worse. Richard could have finished what he started. He could have actually raped her. The calls and photos were bad enough. But the whispers, the helplessness of it all, on top of all the buried memories . . .

The trembling started again.

"I am strong. I am strong. I—I—I *am* strong." She nodded, wiped the tear from her eye, then stood and faced the mirror. The sight made her tremble.

"I'm okay. I'm okay. I'm okay," she repeated, hoping she would believe the mantra.

But the woman staring back at her reminded her too much of a girl she'd tried to leave behind.

Richard may have tried to break her, but he wouldn't. He *wouldn't*. She might crack and tremble, shake and fear, but she would —not—break.

* * * *

He sat in the terminal at Chicago O'Hare waiting for his next flight. It wouldn't be too much longer.

Carefully, he ran down the list of numbers he'd copied from her little black book he'd taken from her kitchen. Lists organized things, and hers was so unorganized.

People worried about "valuable" possessions when there was a break-in, or credit cards when wallets and purses were stolen. They should be more worried about the personal items; one could learn from such simple things as an address book or a calendar.

He now had every number, every place he could find her. He'd already known her schedule, though he would gamble that timetable would no longer hold.

He knew who her doctor was and when she had her period. Women thought no one could figure out what the little *x*s meant for a week across the calendar.

Richard chuckled. At least this way he knew when *not* to pay her a visit.

So where would his angel be?

Again he ran down the list of numbers.

His finger tapped on the hotel. Glancing at his watch, he decided to wait a few minutes.

Then he'd give her a call, just to let her know how much he enjoyed tonight.

He grinned widely, and nodded to the woman across the way, who apparently thought he was smiling at her.

The black book shut with a snap and he tossed it into the briefcase.

He thought about the call, and knew just what he would say.

* * * *

The cup of coffee warmed her palms. The boys had tried to get her to drink some tea, but she'd wanted coffee. She shifted on the couch again, the pull in her ribs catching her breath.

Quinlan and Aiden stood off to the side somewhere. Brayden's body next to hers was a warm comfort, and so was his arm across the back of the couch. Though at times, she stiffened at his touch. And she hated that, even as she couldn't seem to help it.

Gabe cleared his throat. "Christian, would you rather do this alone?"

The black coffee jiggled when she jerked.

"We'll be in the kitchen," Aiden said. She heard his steps mix with Quinlan's across the hardwood floor.

Brayden shifted, but she reached one hand out and laid it on top of his on his thigh. She looked at him. "Stay. Please." Then she realized how he might not want to, so she added, "If you want to. If you don't that's . . ."

"I'm right here. I'm not going anywhere unless you ask me to go." He turned his hand over and laced his fingers with hers.

She didn't know if she was more relieved or nervous. Taking a deep breath, she nodded, though she didn't look at any of them.

"Miss Bills," Laurence said, "can you walk us through what happened? From the beginning?"

The coffee cup jerked in her hand again, and she leaned up to set it on the coffee table, but hissed at the pull in her ribs. Brayden took it and set it aside.

"I'll try," she told them.

"What happened when you came home?" Laurence asked.

Again she took a deep breath and started her story. Jerky at first, but smoother as the words came forth. She gave them what details she could without revealing too much.

"You pulled the knife on him? From your own kitchen?" Gabe asked her.

She nodded.

"At any time during this encounter did you recognize him?" he asked.

Christian looked down at her fisted hand. Until she knew what proof they had, it would do her no good. No good, except endanger those she loved. She'd gone to the police before, but there had been no proof, and what little there was had strangely disappeared. No, she had to wait. She couldn't risk the Kinncaids . . . *Brayden and his little girl . . .*

She closed her eyes and cleared her throat. "N-no. He was—he wore one of those black ski masks. I could see his eyes." She could tell them that. "He had green eyes."

Scribbles filled the air from the two cops taking notes.

"What about hair color and build?"

She answered as best she could, detailed, yet vague.

"Okay, you grabbed the knife, then what happened?"

Her hand shook in Brayden's and he tightened his hold on her. Licking her lips, she started again. With each word, she was aware of the man next to her tightening, coiling his energies, ready to strike out.

"That's it. That's all I remember," she said.

"How long do you think you were unconscious?" Laurence asked softly.

The cold had settled in her bones again, and Christian could feel the tremors start. "I—I don't know. I don't know." Then she thought. "Long enough for him to do this." She ran a hand through her hair.

"All right, and as a bottle woman myself, I'd say that took at least twenty to thirty minutes. The sedative he gave you was more than likely for that purpose alone."

Christian didn't look at the woman, just held on to Brayden's hand.

"Then what?" Gabe asked her.

"I don't know. I don't know what he did to me while I—while I . . . When I couldn't." She took a deep shuddering breath and wiped a tear from her cheek. "When I w-woke up. Things were foggy, fuzzy. I couldn't focus." She blew the breath out and whispered, "I—I was already . . . He'd already . . . I was tied down."

She brought her free hand up to shade her eyes, cursing the fear that roared like a clawing beast within her and the trembling of her voice.

"Did he say anything?"

Did he say anything? Oh, he said a whole hell of a lot. But she couldn't tell them all that. Instead, she said, "I don't—I don't wan—want to talk about this anymore, please."

She bit down and wished the tears would stop.

Brayden pulled her close and she felt his lips against her head. Even as she stiffened.

"I don't want to talk about this anymore," she whispered into his chest.

The phone rang and she jerked, then moaned as pain shot from her bruised ribs.

"Aiden, grab the phone!" Brayden hollered.

It rang again and she only started.

"I'm sure it's Mom wanting to know —" Aiden started.

"No!" Christian yelled, pushing back from Brayden, as Aiden reached to answer it. "No," she repeated, shaking her head. "I don't want her to know. Not yet. Not yet. Please."

Aiden looked at her as the phone rang a third time. "I won't tell her, honey. Not if you don't want me to."

"No, please."

"Just let the machine get it, then you won't have to lie to her," Brayden volunteered.

The machine clicked.

Silence.

Then a sigh.

"The mouse ran to, and the mouse ran fro. Crying and squeaking: which way, which way. Didn't matter, and the cat only smiled. For it was a *fun* game that the cat did play."

She could hear the smile in his calm voice. The trembles shook her and she gasped for breath.

No. No. She shook her head back and forth.

She heard Gabe, "Don't answer that!" Saw Aiden freeze at the edge of her vision, and felt Brayden tighten his hold on her.

"Tell me, did you like our game? Such a luscious body you still have." He tsked. "I thought it ended much too soon. Till next time, my dear."

Brayden leapt off the couch. Christian alone heard that evil chuckle fill this safe place.

Slapping her hands over her ears, she squeezed her eyes tight and rocked.

He couldn't hurt her, she was strong, she was strong.

Brayden wrenched the phone up. "You're dead, you son of a

bitch. You better pray I never find you . . ."

The man laughed in his ear. "Such passion." Silence settled between them.

"She is mine, Mr. Kinncaid. *Mine*. She always has been and she always will be. I'll kill her before I let anyone else have her."

Brayden looked at the woman he loved rocking on the couch, curled into herself as if warding off a blow. "Over my dead body."

The man laughed. "That too can be arranged." The line clicked in his ear.

Brayden swore and threw the phone across the hall. His eyes met Aiden's.

"We'll find him," Aiden promised. He jerked his head toward the couch. "Get her out of here and go home. I'll call the car downstairs for you."

Brayden walked to the couch and leaned down. Carefully, he picked her up and cradled her against his chest, feeling her body shake. He heard Quinlan and Aiden talking, their voices mixing with Morris's and Laurence's.

Aiden walked with them to the elevators. "I'll take your car on ahead and explain things. You two take the limo. You don't need to worry about driving and she needs you."

Brayden nodded. The rest of the ride was silent save for Christian's hurried breath against his chest.

If anyone looked at a large man carrying a woman in his arms across the lobby of the hotel and out the front doors, Brayden didn't notice. At the long black car, Aiden held up a little white bag. "Laurence gave me this. Painkillers and a new inhaler." He tossed it into the interior of the limo, then said something to their driver, Tom, while Brayden maneuvered them both into the car without releasing Christian.

Doors shut and the car pulled away from the hotel. Brayden held Christian in his arms as the lights of D.C. slid past their windows.

She was burrowed into him. At a light, he leaned over and retrieved a bottle of ginger ale. Without moving her, he jostled one of the white oblong pills out.

"Here, baby. You need this."

"Can-can't. Doctor said four hours. Drugs in my system. Concussion."

Why in the hell wasn't she in the hospital?

"You should be at Sibly."

"No!" Her hand shook as it covered his with the pill. "Please. I hate those places. Please."

"Okay. Okay, whatever you want." Since Mom was a doctor and so was Gavin and he figured they were both out at the house, he wouldn't press her.

He put the pill back in its bottle and held the ginger ale up to her lips and watched as she took a drink. Pulling back, hissing, her tongue darted out to lick the cut on her lip.

"He knows, he knows everything," she murmured, curling up in his lap.

"It doesn't matter." Brayden held her close, yet loosely. "It doesn't matter. He's never getting near you again."

Let the bastard come. Brayden wanted the man. Wanted to rip the monster apart piece by slow piece. It didn't matter how damn long it took. One day, he'd find the son of a bitch, and when he did, he'd make the bastard beg for mercy long and hard before he finished with him.

No one, but no one hurt the woman he loved and got away with it.

Chapter 9

Aiden Kinncaid, the eldest of his brothers, tapped the steering wheel and waited for his phone to ring. He'd left in front of the limo, driving Brayden's Hummer.

Come on, Ian, call.

Ian Kinncaid was their disowned brother, though still for reasons unknown to Aiden. As far as most knew, Ian had no contact with the family. But Aiden knew differently, and had for years. There was a number to call when things came up. Never names given, at least not until Ian called back.

Aiden didn't ask exactly what his brother did; he figured he was probably better off not knowing. But he had a feeling, maybe something in the government, or even, God forbid, as a mercenary. Occupation aside, Ian was a Kinncaid, and Kinncaids stuck together.

The phone rang. Aiden jabbed the TALK button and spoke into the hands-free headset while he maneuvered through traffic heading out of D.C.

"Yeah."

"What the hell is going on now?" Ian's resigned voice asked.

"It's pretty bad," he told him, taking the Seneca exit.

"What? Who? Dad?"

"No, Christian." Aiden sighed, ground his teeth. "Someone broke into her condo and tried to rape her."

"What?" Ian asked.

He took a deep breath. "Some son of a bitch almost raped our sister."

Ian cursed. At first Aiden heard French expletives, but then he thought there might have been German and Russian thrown in. The last of the obscenities was muffled and beyond him.

"Explain," Ian said, his voice different, cold and hard.

"I don't know that I *can* explain. She's been acting off lately. None of us thought much of it, what with her and Brayden's . . ." How to explain that one? "Relationship thing."

Trees were a darkened blur on the roadside. Headlights came and whizzed past.

"Anyway, she's been getting some strange phone calls. I don't know what all went on, but apparently the guy . . ." He bit down.

"Is she okay? I mean, he didn't . . ."

"No, she's not okay, he roughed her up pretty bad. Granted, it could have been worse." He flicked on the blinker and turned into his parents' drive. "Then the bastard called the hotel room. Left a message. All hell broke loose. I've never seen Bray like this. Not even with the Fisher incident." And that had been bad. For over a day they couldn't find Tori or her cousin Ryan when they'd been kidnapped. Brayden and Gavin, the twins, had been beside themselves trying to find their kids.

A sigh came over the phone. "Tell him I'll call. I need some more details. I'll call in the morning, or later tonight. Hell, I don't know. I'll be in touch."

"Ian, he wants this guy found." Aiden pulled to a stop in the drive and checked the rearview. It wouldn't be long before Brayden and Christian got here.

A harsh chuckle spiked through the earpiece. "Oh, I'll find him." Ian's voice held no quarter of doubt. "I'll find him."

With that, the line went dead in his ear. The front door stood open and light flooded out, outlining his mother and father.

How the hell was he going to explain this? He'd called Gavin's cell earlier so he wouldn't have to risk Mom or Dad answering the phone. At least one doctor of the family, Gavin, was still here, though his brother had had Taylor take the kids home with her. He had no idea if his own wife, Jesslyn, was still there with the twins or if she went home.

Wearily, he climbed from Brayden's Hummer.

Kaitlyn Kinncaid watched as Brayden's SUV parked in the circle drive. Her heart thumped against her ribs, and Jock's hands on her shoulders were a comfort.

"Something's wrong. Something is very, very wrong," she whispered.

Jock squeezed her shoulders. "Don't borrow trouble."

At least they were home. She waited, but only one person got out . . .

Aiden. Why was Aiden alone?

Her heart skipped, her stomach twisted, and suddenly she didn't want to know . . .

His shoes echoed against the stones as he walked up the walk. When he stood close enough, he leaned down and wrapped her in a hug.

"Wh—" She cleared her throat and pulled back. "What's going on? Where's Brayden? Where's Christian?"

He motioned them inside and she got a good look at his face. Harsh, pulled tight, and she knew then whatever it was, was bad. He hadn't looked like that since Colorado.

"Aiden?"

He rubbed a hand over the back of his neck. "I need to tell you all something. Brayden and Christian will be here in a bit and you need to know before they get here."

Without another word, he turned and walked to the living room.

Jock gave her shoulder another squeeze and muttered, "Why they can never just spit it out is beyond me."

* * * *

The car pulled to a stop in front of the family mansion. Brayden climbed from the car and leaned down, reaching toward her.

Christian shook her head. "No, I'll walk. I want to walk."

With his hand on her elbow, he helped her up. She really wished she'd taken the Percocet. Pain pulsed through her body. Letting out a long shallow breath, she grabbed his arm and stared at the lighted house before them. She didn't want to go in. She didn't want them to see her like this.

"They're worried, and will be more so since Aiden came on ahead. They'll need to see you're all right," Brayden said, his voice deep and soft, reading her thoughts.

He was right, but it still didn't change the fact she wanted to curl up under a mound of covers in a dark room and sleep for a long, long time. Just forget. Pretend it was months ago and life was fine. Pretend it was yesterday morning and do everything over, but she couldn't.

Finally, she nodded and let him help her along the walk. The night air was cold around them, their breaths clouding in the dark air. By the time they reached the front door, she was trembling. Neither of them had on a coat. Why didn't Brayden have one? She had to ask him. Some part of her mind told her it didn't matter, like her boots. But she kept focusing on little, unimportant things that suddenly loomed to monumental proportions.

With one hand he opened the door and helped her inside, quietly shutting it behind him. The soft click of the latch seemed to thunder in the silent entryway.

She could hear voices from the living room. Brayden, one arm gently wrapped around her back, walked her along, but she stopped.

"I—I can't."

Damn the tears, she could feel them sliding down her cheek. She started to reach up, but Brayden cupped her face, his thumb brushing the wet trail away.

"I'll be with you."

She closed her eyes and nodded.

Together they walked down the hallway to see their family.

* * * *

Brayden eased her down on the couch. The sky outside blushed with the promise of dawn. Carefully, he tucked the thick blanket around her and stood, simply staring at her.

With one hand, he brushed a lock of hair off her forehead. The rage he'd felt all night bit at his controlled temper.

Quietly, he looked up. His mother stood in the doorway with a cup of coffee.

"I thought you might have talked her into lying down," she whispered as he came closer.

Brayden shook his head. No, Christian had been terrified at the mere mention of lying on a bed. So he'd held her all night on the couch. Tried to calm her and himself as thoughts and images ricocheted through his mind.

His mother sniffled and wiped a tear from her swollen eyes. He leaned over and kissed her cheek.

"Will you watch her for a minute?" he asked. "There's something I need to do."

She nodded and gave him a smile. "Beat the hell out of it."

His mother knew him too well. Without a backward glance, he left his living room and headed to the private gym at the back of the house.

He didn't change, he simply ripped his shirt from his pants and tossed it to the side. Nor did he bother to grab a pair of gloves. All he saw was the punching bag, and when he looked at the black leather, all he saw was some faceless bastard. Christian scared, Christian crying, Christian beaten and helpless.

Fury roared through him and he let it loose. His punches sent the heavy bag rolling and spinning and he pummeled it time after time.

Suspicions danced in his head, as they had all night.

She is mine, Mr. Kinncaid. Mine. She always has been and she always will be. I'll kill her before I let anyone else have her.

Harder and harder, faster and faster. Thump, swing, thump, swing.

. . . Such a luscious body you still have. Still have . . .

He stopped, catching the swinging heavy bag.

. . . always has been . . . still have . . .

The bastard knew her. He knew her, or thought he did.

Muttered voices finally pierced the black-edged cloud that blinded him to all but his fist connecting with a solid object.

He whirled, his chest heaving, his hands fisted at his sides.

All three of his brothers stood in the doorway staring at him. Aiden obviously decided to brave the wrath and stepped further into the workout room.

The other two followed, and Gavin shut the door.

"We were trying to decide which one of us should be stupid enough to draw your attention," Aiden volunteered. "Quin and I thought it should be Gavin. I mean, with his face identical to your own, you might halt before you reared back and knocked him flat."

"I told them that never stopped you before," Gavin quipped.

Brayden didn't give a shit why they were here. Sweat ran down his back and chest.

He looked down and saw blood on his knuckles and hands.

"How long have you been knocking that thing around?" Gavin asked, coming closer and reaching for one of his hands.

Brayden jerked it back. "Not long enough."

"Did you break anything?"

He shook his head at his twin. "Always the doctor." Flexing his fingers, he winced at the pain that was beginning to spread. "No, they're fine."

Quinlan handed him a towel.

"What do you want?" he asked without preamble.

"Hell if I know," Quinlan said. "These two knocked on my door and told me to get my ass down here. As the youngest, I've learned to please or face the consequences."

Brayden glanced at his watch. Damn, he'd been down here for almost an hour. "Is Christian awake?"

"No." Aiden, dressed in what looked like fresh clean clothes, lounged on one of the workout benches. "We need to talk. And let little bro here in on some things."

Bray huffed out a breath and collapsed in a chair, which sat against one of the many mirrors in the room. Raking his hands through his wet hair, he looked back up at Aiden and asked, "Did you get hold of him?"

"Who?" Quinlan asked.

Months before when Tori and Ryan had been kidnapped, Brayden and Gavin had learned the value of their absent brother, Ian, and his shadowed life. Brayden still didn't know what to think about his mysterious brother. The man had a way of solving problems and finding out information. Brayden didn't care what tactics Ian used as long as he found out what Brayden wanted to know.

And all he needed was a man's name.

He listened while Aiden filled Quinlan in on their secret, making him swear not to tell Mom and Dad. No one outside the room knew about Ian or any contact any of them had or didn't have with the black sheep of the family. As far as society and their parents were concerned, Ian had left years before without a glance behind or a word to any of them. Brayden figured it was probably wise to keep it that way.

Questions were answered and Quinlan fell into a brooding silence, for Brayden knew the look on his youngest brother's face.

Brayden asked Aiden again, "Did you reach him?"

"Ian said he'd call you, or me. Either way he'd be in touch, probably sometime today. He needed some details. Which brings me to topic number two." Aiden leaned forward, his elbows resting on the end of the bench. "Are the cops coming today?"

Brayden nodded. "Yeah. Becky said Morris called last night and they'll be here around nine to talk to Christian again. We didn't exactly finish last night."

"Okay," Aiden said. "Listen carefully. Try, if you can, to remember everything she says. Ian, I have a feeling, will be in grilling mode. He was rather pissed."

Brayden was well accustomed to the feeling. After a few minutes he rose. "Do you think . . ." He stopped, twisted the towel between his hands.

"What?" two voices asked at the same time.

"That phone call, last night." Bray turned and looked at his eldest brother. "Did you catch what the man said?"

Aiden held his stare, arching a brow. "I wondered if you caught that. And if you did, then chances are Morris did too."

Quinlan nodded. "He knows her."

"What the hell are you all talking about?" Gavin asked, at a loss.

Aiden quickly explained how the caller last night spoke as if he'd known Christian for a while.

"Or maybe he just thinks he knows her," Brayden muttered.

Silence settled around them. Finally, Aiden cleared his throat. "As much as I hate to be the one to say this, we really don't know that much about Christian. She didn't want to talk about her past and we never pushed it."

Abruptly, Brayden tossed the towel away and said, "I'm going to take a shower. I don't want to be away from Christian for too long."

As he got to the door, he heard Quinlan ask, "Exactly what does Ian do?"

Aiden chuckled. "I've never asked, and I don't intend to. I'd advise you of the same."

* * * *

Christian sat in the living room on the couch. Everyone, save Brayden, was scattered around the house somewhere and not present.

The cops were here and she was supposed to answer questions. Gabe Morris seemed more tense than normal, but then again, what did she know about tension. Let alone normalcy.

"All right," Emma Laurence said. "We got a bit into this last night before the phone call. We have no way of knowing where it came from, the conversation was too short. Gabe mentioned this man had called you at your residence night before last while Gabe was there."

She nodded. "I sort of threw the phone and base and parts scattered everywhere. Sorry."

"No problem. We just like to lay out a schedule, a timeline. And if we had a copy of that recording, we could match the voices."

Her voice was straight and to the point, yet calm all the same.

"You mean," Christian asked, "if you find this guy, if you get him to talk, you can match that person to the person who called last night?"

"The one who attacked you, yes."

Another nail in the bastard's coffin. She had some of her own. But those might take time. For now, she would give what she could.

"All right, do you want to start at the beginning again, or would you rather pick up where we left off?" Laurence asked.

"I want her to start at the beginning," Lieutenant Morris interrupted. "She might have remembered something and doesn't even realize it until she says it aloud."

Or she could screw up. What had she said last night? She couldn't really remember. Then again, what she did remember was garbled and hazy at best.

Rubbing her forehead, she nodded and again started from when she came home.

As the events unfolded, Brayden stood and walked to the window. His arms crossed. From here, she could see the tightened cords in his neck shift and bunch, the jump of muscle in his jaw.

Laurence said, "So when you awoke you still didn't see him?"

She shook her head. "No, my head hurt and I was trying to figure out what had happened, where I was." She remembered his voice, teasing, calm and daring. She rubbed her hands over her arms. "Then I-I heard him. He grabbed my hair and kissed me. I tried to pull away and that's when . . ." She trailed off.

"That's when what?" Laurence prompted.

Christian swallowed and looked down at the throw over her lap. "That's when I realized I couldn't move." Taking a deep breath, she went on. "I still didn't see him. Things were blurry and out of focus, but he said I was beautiful. Then he said tit for tat."

"Tit for tat?" Gabe asked.

She nodded. "He kissed me again, but bit my lip."

The rest of the facts she relayed as she could. When she'd awoken this morning, she'd convinced herself she could get through this. She could. Just relay the bare facts with a few omissions. Not that hard.

But the fear and the helplessness of it all clawed at her like a tiger playing with its food.

"The phone kept—kept ringing. I remember wondering when I'd turned the ringer back on. He must have because I couldn't remember. He'd just laugh when it rang."

Help is so close, yet unattainable.

She heard the click of Brayden's shoes as he crossed to her. A shiver danced down her spine. The pain pill was wearing off. Brayden perched on the arm of the couch, his arm around her. She stiffened, knowing she wasn't through with the story, but she didn't want him to leave either. She held on to his hand, as though he somehow gave her strength to go on.

Silence netted around them.

"Okay, what happened when the phone rang?"

"He just laughed," she repeated. "Just laughed, teased me. I couldn't see, but he told me the phone was so close."

"Bastard," Brayden muttered, but she heard him all the same.

"Then what happened?" Laurence asked.

She couldn't do this, she couldn't go into this with Brayden sitting right here beside her. Shame filled her, made her shake with humiliation and self-loathing. Anger sparked deep within her, but she buried it. Buried it until later.

She closed her eyes, raised her hand to cover them.

Laurence cleared her throat. "Would you rather Mr. Kinncaid leave?"

She felt him shift, start to stand, but she tightened her hold on him, holding his hand with the both of hers. She didn't know what she wanted.

"He—he was wearing gloves," she whispered.

"What kind?" Laurence asked, just as softly.

"Leather."

Leather. She would never forget how that warm material almost felt like a heated hand trailing over her, touching her, violating her.

"I know this is difficult for you, but . . ." Again Laurence cleared her throat. "During the exam last evening you didn't talk very much or answer many questions. With what happened, that's understandable."

Christian closed her eyes. She could feel Brayden tense beside her. Maybe she should have let him leave, but she couldn't. If he was here, no one would hurt her.

Laurence asked more questions, probing—probing for answers, for details.

What she'd already told them turned her stomach.

Bile rose hot in her throat.

"I'm going to be sick," she said quickly, trying to get off the couch.

Her ribs pierced through the nausea and had her gasping. Brayden helped her up and she all but raced to the nearest bathroom. She could hear his furious voice lashing out at the cops as she shut the door down the hall.

After the heaves stopped, she leaned into the counter and tried to catch her breath. Her cupped hands shook so bad most of the liquid escaped before she could rinse her mouth with water.

What was she doing? Was she making the same mistakes as she had before by keeping silent?

No. No. No.

She'd told others before and it got her nowhere. Nowhere, but pain. He won. He'd always won. And he'd pay her back, not only by punishing her, but by hurting those she cared about.

Danny's body in that cold casket flashed through her memories. Susan and her mother helping her onto the train. Susan's father as he rode with her. Papa as they'd lowered his coffin in the ground.

Her eyes slid closed and her bruised face faded from her sight in the mirror. She could survive what he did to her, but if he hurt any of the Kinncaids or her family, there was no way she'd ever forgive herself. She'd rather him just kill her.

This was her home and her family.

The Kinncaid motto echoed through her: *This I'll defend.*

It wasn't just the Kinncaids. She still had a brother who would never expect the maliciousness Richard was capable of. Grandparents in Louisiana too old to be a match for this monster.

The first will be Brayden and his little girl.

Tori. Oh, God.

Her hands shook as she dried them off and opened the door.

Kaitlyn stood in the hallway. "Are you okay, sweetie? Do you need anything?"

Christian shook her head and tried to take a deep breath.

"You might want to get back in there. Brayden is threatening to throw them out and they're adamant about talking to you about photographs."

Photographs?

She walked with dread back to the living room. Now everyone was in there, and on the coffee table were packets. Brown manila envelopes—she knew what the contents were.

Gabe only arched a brow at her. "Shall you do the honors or shall I? No one here seems to know what's in them. But you do, don't you? And I do."

Why was he angry?

Gabe ripped open the top one and dumped the contents across the small table. Glossy eight-by-tens slid out across and onto the floor.

He opened the next one.

Brayden and Aiden stooped to pick them up.

"What is this?" Brayden ask, first her then Gabe.

She stood to the side of the boys and across from the police.

"Well, now," Gabe said, "this, or rather, *these* were found in her condo. Neatly labeled and dated, complete with his calling card." He flipped one up in a plastic bag. *"My Angel."*

She saw Brayden turn to her, but kept her eyes on Gabe's raging ones. "Look, Christian, these good boys don't seem to know what the hell's going on."

The flutter of the photos swished through the air as someone flipped through them.

"I never told them," she admitted.

Gabe shook his head at her.

"Why? How long have you . . . When did all this . . . How the hell long has this been going on?" Brayden finally managed to ask.

She looked around to him, at everyone staring at her.

Taking a deep breath, she said, "Since about a week after I moved into the condo."

The skin across his face pulled taut, and his eyes narrowed on her. "Why, in the ever living hell, didn't you say something?" he asked quietly, too quietly.

She dropped her gaze from his and could only shake her head and shrug.

"Want my opinion?" Gabe asked.

No one answered him.

"I think this guy knows her, which means she probably knows him. I can't help wondering if she's not protecting this man. Then I ask myself who would she *want* to protect and more importantly *why*. Only people she has contact with are you guys. Maybe it's one of you."

Christian could only stare at him. "I told you before, it was none of them."

"Why not?" he asked her. "The youngest has fair hair and green eyes. His build seems about right from what you've described."

"What?" She couldn't believe this.

"Excuse me?" a male voice asked. Christian didn't take the time to see who it was.

"Maybe you and young Quin here had something on the side and he's pissed 'cause you chose his older brother. Not wanting to tear the family up, you keep silent and . . ."

"That's enough!" a voice lashed out.

She turned and saw Jock glaring at the cops. All the men were lined together behind her, Kaitlyn just to the side of her.

"I will *not* have you insulting or implying something so horrible about a single member of this family," the patriarch said.

Gabe ignored him, and turned to look at Quinlan. "You have an alibi for last night?"

"It's *not* him! It's not! God!" she said, striding to Gabe, anger radiating out of her. Never would she allow anyone to defame this good family. "I told you before it wasn't them, Gabriel, any of them. Why are you doing this?"

"I want the truth."

She didn't understand his fury. "Are you pissed at them?" She pointed to her family behind her. "Or me?" Her voice wavered and caught.

His dark look was flat as a shark's. "I want to know why you never told them someone was following you, photographing you, sending you sick and twisted gifts and calling you," he said just as straight as his unwavering stare. "Why you never told them you were being stalked."

"I don't know!" she yelled. "I don't know. I don't know. Is this an 'I told you so,' Gabriel? Do you think—think I don't know I made a mistake?" She slapped her chest with her hand. "God, I'm slow, I'll give you that. And with what happened, it's probably a given I'm st-stupid."

Tears streamed down her face. "I should have told them. I know that. It doesn't matter I was coming to file an official complaint yesterday with you, does it? No, I should have done that before. And it's beside the point I'd planned on telling them last night."

The coffee table stood between them. Tears choked her, and her chest tightened with another attack. "I thought it would go away. I hoped it was a stupid joke and if I ignored . . . I know I made a m-mistake. I think I realized it about the time the bastard slammed my face into a door. Or, no, wait, I did get an inkling before that when he grabbed me in the kitchen."

Rage volcanoed out of her. "But it became blindingly clear to me, Lieutenant, when I was tied to a damn bed and couldn't stop the son of a bitch from copping a feel or jabbing his fingers or hands where-the-hell-ever he pleased. I made a mistake. A mistake. I can't go back and change it! I wish I could, but I can't. I can't." A sob caught her off guard. "Oh, God."

Tears blurred her vision, and someone reached for her, but she shook her head and backed away. Her knees hit the edge of a chair and she crumpled, the emotions twisting her tighter and tighter until all she could do was release them.

"It's past time for you to go," Brayden said right beside her. "And if you can't find the damn door, I'm sure one of my brothers can find it for you."

She felt his arms go around her, stiffened within the embrace, then gave into the storm raging within her.

His scent engulfed her and she let herself lean, took from the shelter he unconditionally gave as sobs rocked her.

Chapter 10

Venice, Italy

Brayden shut down his computer. He'd just finished chatting with Aiden after he'd opened an email from Rob Roy. Ian. At least he assumed the email was from Ian. The police admitted they found blood and hair that didn't match Christian, and they were doing DNA tests. That was hopeful. And in the background, Aiden was quietly pressing Mom and Dad about Christian's past to see if they knew anything.

The feeling wouldn't go away that she somehow knew this guy. Somehow, somewhere she had crossed his path.

As soon as the police had left their house the morning after the attack, Brayden arranged to take Christian away. Italy appealed to him, and he knew she liked Venice. So to Venice it was. They'd been here for almost a week and he'd tried to get her out to see the city. But she wouldn't leave the palazzo he'd rented near the Grand Canal.

Instead she was silent and withdrawn—understandable, but it was killing him. He'd removed the two phones installed in the palazzo. The only phone he used was his mobile and he kept that on him. The first night here, she'd had a nightmare that the bastard was calling them. She had dozed off out on the couch. He'd told her over and over there were no phones, but it had taken forever to convince her there wasn't a phone ringing. He figured it was the pain medication she took.

Brayden stood and rubbed the back of his neck.

Maybe tomorrow he could get her out to see Saint Mark's Basilica. Tomorrow would tell.

It was after midnight and he couldn't sleep. The sitting room between their two bedrooms was silent, only marred by noises of the occasional *vaporatto* on the canal below. The palazzo was big enough to house his entire family, but he wanted to be close to her. So he chose rooms that adjoined, for the most part.

He stretched, realizing he wanted a glass of wine. He started for the kitchen but stopped at the muffled sound.

Where?

There it came again.

He strode to Christian's door and pressed his ear to it. If she was asleep he didn't want to wake her up. She was hardly sleeping at all.

Again the noise shifted from within. Another nightmare?

He knocked, "Christian?"

The door, unsurprisingly, was locked. She always locked it.

"Christian?" He rattled the knob.

A whimper from within rose into a scream. Damn it. He reached over and lifted the plant on the side table. A key lay beneath.

"Christian?" Brayden unlocked the door, for the first time invading her privacy since coming here.

The room was lit from a lamp she'd left burning. His gaze landed on the bed. It was empty and his heart crashed in his chest.

"Christian! Answer me, damn it!"

The whimper, just a whimper.

He hurried around the bed and almost stepped on her. Quick reflexes saved them both.

She was lying on the floor, tangled in a quilt. Had she fallen out of bed? Then he noticed the pile of blankets under her.

On the floor, she'd been sleeping on the damn floor.

"Ah, baby." Gently he squatted down and reached out. "Christian."

She moved away from him.

"No, no. Stop," she pleaded, gasping for breath.

Brayden sat beside her and gathered her to him. "Shh. Shh. It's just a dream. Only a dream. You're okay, Christian."

She struggled within his hold, caught in whatever demons plagued her.

"Let me go! Let me go! You son of a bitch!" She pulled and strained in his arms. "I hate you. Hate you. I always have and I always will!"

Her voice was hoarse, barbed with malice.

"Christian." Softly, he kissed her forehead. "Come on, baby, wake up. Shhh. You're safe. You're safe here." He rocked her, anger and helplessness warring within him.

Finally, finally, she stilled. Brayden leaned back as she opened her eyes. Panic coated the smoky irises and she bolted in his arms even as her breath wheezed out. Another asthma attack.

He let go. "You were having a bad dream," he told her softly.

She stared at him with almost vacant eyes. Then, hugging herself, she rocked.

He looked around, didn't see her inhaler. "Where's your MDI?" he asked, looking for her metered-dose inhaler.

She reached under her pillow and pulled it out, taking a deep breath of the medicine. Tears wet her cheeks and he reached up to wipe them off, but she shied away. On a sighing growl, he dropped his hand back and sat with her on the pallet. He was completely lost here. He had no idea if he was helping her or making things worse.

"So, felt like camping out, did you?" he asked.

What might have been a snort huffed out of her.

"This floor is hard. No wonder you don't sleep." He glanced at her. Tears still shimmered in her eyes. "Why the hell don't you sleep out on the couch if you don't want to lie in the bed?"

She didn't look away, but shrugged. Her bottom lip trembled. "I —I didn't want you to know."

Well, why didn't she just hit him?

"Why?" he asked softly.

Again she shrugged. "I feel like such a—a—a coward," she finished.

Counting wasn't going to help. "A coward?" He couldn't believe this. "Why in the hell would you . . ." No, she didn't need his anger. With more calm than he thought he had, he said, "Sorry. Why would you ever think something like that?"

Tears trailed down her cheeks and her eyes were hazy pools of pain. "Look at me, Brayden! I'm a mess. A mess." Her eyes were still glazed and he noticed her voice wasn't normal, not quite slurred, but not . . . not . . . well, normal.

"Are you hurt?" he asked her.

"Percocet," she mumbled.

Silence settled between them and this time he waited her out. "I don't know what to do," she whispered. "I don't know what to do." Christian wiped her face on the knees of her pajamas. "I hate this. Hate this. Maybe I can fix-fix it. But I just panic."

Again he waited, but this time, she didn't continue. His feet were getting cold. Picking up the quilt, he stood and wrapped it around him, then sat, leaning against the bed. He tucked Christian up next beside him, the quilt engulfing them both. Her head rested on the crook of his shoulder. The scent of her shampoo drifted to tease him. He ignored, or tried to, the way she immediately stiffened. He could all but feel her forcing herself to relax. He absently wondered how much she would remember in the morning. She remembered some of the first night in Seneca but none of the plane ride and little of the first day here. But he didn't care. He talked.

"First off," he started, "no more sleeping on this cold hard floor. You don't want to sleep in the bed, fine. The couch is out in the living room." He started to say she could sleep with him if she got scared, he'd keep the demons away. Probably wasn't the right thing to say. "Second, and let me make certain you understand this, I never, never want to hear you call yourself a coward again." My God, that she'd even think it. He tilted her chin up so that she was looking at him. "What you are is a survivor. Remember that."

Her eyes were haunted as she blinked. This close and at this angle of light, he noticed the size of her pupils, large and round, edging out the gray of her irises. She probably wouldn't remember a bit of this tomorrow. He needed to remember to ask her about it and how the medicine affected her.

"I can't get him out of my mind, Brayden. He's there. He's always there. Just waiting, just like before. He won't let me go, he—Ri—" She stopped and tucked in her chin.

Ri . . .? What was that?

. . . always have. I always will . . .

. . . just like before . . .

His pulse leapt.

"What were you going to say?" he asked her softly, even as she settled against his shoulder.

She shook her head. "Nothing, nothing. He's just always right there. Right there," she mumbled.

Brayden digested that and didn't believe it. Right—long *i* sound. She'd started to say something else. Something with a short *i*. A name maybe?

Tightening his hold on her, he said, "Don't keep anything from me, Christian. Not even sleeping on the floor. I'm right here. You don't have to do this alone."

For a long time she was silent, so still and quiet he thought she was asleep.

"Sometimes I have to," she whispered.

"No, you choose to. There's a difference."

He felt her swallow, heard her ragged breathing and felt a tear drop as it fell on his hand.

"The—last . . . He was angry. So angry. Banging on the door. Grabbed my throat and ripped the stupid locket off. Hate the locket. Hate it. Know what he said?" she asked shakily.

Grinding his teeth at the pictures her jumbled words evoked, he answered softly, "No."

"He—he said—he said." She was crying. More tears fell on his hand holding hers.

"Shh," he told her.

Her head shook on his shoulder. "Can't tell anyone. No one. Not a word or the Kinncaids will die."

What? He tried to push back, but she latched on to him like a lifeline. Her fingers clawed at his hand and chest as she burrowed against him. "First—first would be you and T-Tori." Tremors shook her.

Smart bastard. Very smart.

Pulling back, he turned so that he could cup her face.

"Look at me."

When her eyes rose to his, he said, "This I'll defend. Do you think I wouldn't defend you and Tori? I'll admit I've done a shitty job so far, but never again, Christian. Do you hear me? Never again. You're mine. Not his. I protect what's mine. You're a Kinncaid."

She nodded, then leaned her head against his chest. "I know, that's why I can't tell."

Brayden held her, thinking about what she might know and simply be too scared to say. Too scared? No, the bastard had her so utterly terrified she even covered up slips of the tongue in a drugged state. That might explain it.

But explanation or no, no one used his family in any way.

"Relax," he whispered. "I'll hold you. You won't have any more nightmares tonight."

He'd make certain of it.

* * * *

He paced as the rage roared through him. Where the hell was she? They—those Kinncaids—had *his* angel somewhere.

The question was location. He had to find her. After all this time, he could not bear to lose her again. Not again. Never, never again.

Josephine was his.

On a muttered curse, he stalked to the desk and sat down. His leather chair sighed as he leaned back, tapping a letter opener on the edge of his desk.

Where? Where? Where?

He threw the letter opener across the room. It embedded into the wall, the hilt vibrating.

He took a deep breath through his nose, ran his hands through his hair. He had to think, calm down and think. Anger and rage only clouded reasoning. Grabbing up the remote to the stereo, he clicked it on. Mozart's requiem drifted softly from the speakers. The somber mood fit his present frame of mind.

God, Josephine was still so incredible, so beautiful, so . . . so . . . succulent. Her body, her pliant luscious body.

Closing his eyes, he smiled and let the music fill him, allowed the memories of her beneath him to heat through his blood.

Her soft skin like ivory velvet teased his senses, the taste of her haunted along his tongue.

He opened his eyes and sat up. Lovingly, he picked up the photos atop his desk.

They didn't show her at her best, but were arousing all the same.

Richard ran his fingers over the glossy surface, remembering how her naked skin had caught and held the dim lights, how it was warm through his gloves. As if caressing her, he rubbed his thumb over her stomach.

One day he wouldn't have to tie her down. He'd broken her before and he would again.

First, he had to remove her safety net, her comfort zone. For a moment, he played with the idea of taking out the Kinncaids. All of them. It wouldn't be impossible—difficult, but not impossible. But the media fallout . . .

The politician in him shuddered.

No, something else. Something more subtle.

Sighing, he flipped through the harsh pictures. He needed the perfect one. The perfect one. There. That one. A smile tilted the edge of his mouth up. This would make a lovely Christmas gift. The question was, to whom did he send it?

The knight, or the damsel?

He heard the click of heels down the hallway. Quickly, he stacked the photos and put them in his briefcase. The lid snapped shut just as his wife opened the door. As always, and befitting her station, she was perfectly groomed in her tailored suit, pearls and coifed hair.

"Richard, Senator Lend's wife just phoned me. Have we found a place to live yet?" She crossed the Persian rugs, her heels muffled in the plushness. "I really think it would be unseemly for us to stay in a hotel come January. Don't you? And what about Christmas and New Year's? Mrs. Lend invited us to their party, you know."

Like a light, she shone the way. Poor misguided woman. He gave her a benign smile and pecked her cheek with an air kiss.

"Yes, dear. I've been looking into some places. You know I like my privacy. I don't want right in the middle of town. There are several places I'm checking on. Maybe we'll fly out next week and look at them. How is that?"

With enough money, he could find what he wanted.

So subtle no one would realize it, no one but her.

With a silent chuckle, he already calculated how much this investment would cost him.

It didn't matter. In the end, he always obtained what he wanted.

* * * *

The Venetians called it *La Serenissima* — the most serene — and Christian supposed they did so wisely.

The city echoed with sounds, not normal metropolitan sounds, but simple noises. Voices carried on the briny wind mixing with the lap of water against centuries-old buildings. There were no blaring horns or the rumble of engines. The city seemed stolen from a time almost forgotten.

The morning was chilly and she sat wrapped in a sweater, out on one of the balconies. Christian studied the scene in silence, almost calm in the early morning light. Gondolas slid seamlessly through the waters, sleek as black snakes.

It would be nice to ride in one. She loved gondola rides.

For the last few days Brayden had been badgering her to get out of the palazzo and see the city with him. She knew she ought to, knew the fear was unreasonable. But it was easier to hide inside.

She heard the scrape of his shoes on the stones as he crossed to the little table, speaking in rapid Italian to the maid. He was probably ordering breakfast. Italian was one of those languages she just couldn't seem to grasp for some reason. The cup of coffee warmed her palms. She looked away from the scene below to Brayden.

His studying gaze was not new to her; behind his shades, she couldn't see it, but she could feel it.

"Morning," he said.

"Morning."

Moments stretched to minutes and the silence remained. She didn't know what to say to him. How to talk to him. Unlike the days before, Brayden seemed quiet today, as though his mood followed hers. It made her twitchy, and she was already off enough between her emotions, lack of sleep, the nightmares, the pain meds and stress in general.

Finally, she asked, "What?"

The wind off the canal was cold and she pulled her sweater tighter against her.

"Hmm?" he asked, his gaze studying the scene below.

"You seem quiet this morning," she ventured.

He shrugged and leaned back. "Just thinking."

"About?"

She watched as he ran his tongue around his teeth. Without looking at her, he only said, "It'll keep."

All she could do was stare at him. It'll keep? What did that mean?

"Fine," she said, standing.

"In a minute." He patted the seat beside him. "Sit back down, I want to ask you something."

"What?" Dread tightened the muscles in her neck and nerves twisted her stomach, but she sat. The seconds stretched.

Brayden cleared his throat. "I didn't want to bring it up because of how upset you got with Morris, but I have to ask . . ." He raked a hand through his hair, then turned to face her fully. "Why didn't you tell me about the photos? The calls? The gifts?"

His voice had never been a humorous one, and had been known to cut a person with a scathing word, herself included. But now, now his voice was different. She caught the underlying edge of angered steel, laced with disappointment, and the hurt rang clear through her.

What did she tell him?

"I always thought we could talk to each other about anything. We always did before. Did I hurt you so badly you couldn't even talk to me about this? I knew I was stupid that morning in the hotel, knew it as soon as the door slammed, but I don't . . . I can't . . . Ah, hell," he finished on a frustrated sigh. "But I can't understand why you never said anything."

Brayden stood and stepped to the railing, gripping it as if it supported him. "Maybe I should coddle you. Not that I've ever been the coddling type of guy. Don't even know if I know how, and I'm afraid if I do, I could lose you, that you'll just fade into—into this quiet unseen person." He continued. "I know if I push too hard, you'll just shut down on me. Or, God forbid, something breaks in you that I can't fix," he whispered, "and I'll lose you either way." He turned to her. "I don't want to lose you."

That's what he thought? She sighed, and knew she couldn't argue with him. She didn't know anything herself, how could she tell him what to do, or not do.

"What do you want me to do?" she asked.

"You need to get out of the palazzo."

"I am out of the palazzo. I'm on the balcony," she told him.

Brayden walked to her and squatted beside her. "Outside these walls. I want to show you Venice. I know you love it."

And she did.

"Today is market day," he tried. "Fresh fruits and vegetables. The Basilica. The Bridge of Sighs."

She smiled, and it felt good. "Maybe. You know, you're not doing a bad job."

"At what?"

"Coddling."

"Am I? I wonder."

He sat back down beside her, his hand coming up to cup the back of her neck. "Even now," he continued, "you're tense at the thought of talking to me. I wish you weren't."

"Brayden." She tried to pull away from his hold, but he only moved closer. For a moment her heart skipped, but this was Brayden. Only Brayden. She sighed.

"Don't shut me out. I'm sorry, Christian. I am every kind of fool and stupid coward you called me that morning and I don't plan on being one again. I want to know, to understand why you kept this from me."

Brayden was a man who analyzed everything and was, she knew, blaming himself.

She licked her lips and looked down, his hand gently massaging the cords of her nape.

"I don't know. I do, but I don't. At first I just ignored it all, or tried to. Then I thought, well, I wanted to move out and get my own life and here was something and my first thought was to run back home and tell you. But I didn't. I didn't. I should have, but things were messed up between us. Not just because of you, but me as well, and I couldn't . . . I didn't . . . I know that makes no sense," she admitted. God, she wished she could tell someone. Quiet stretched between them as if he waited for her to continue, but she didn't. What could she say?

Brayden cleared his throat. "There was a picture in several of the packets, an older picture of you with longer and lighter color hair."

Oh, God. She'd forgotten about that one, her high school picture. Her hands shook in her lap and she fisted them.

"We never pushed you on where you came from or what you ran away from," he said quietly. "Or maybe who?"

Too close, he was getting too close. She closed her eyes. She couldn't talk about this, not here, not now.

"Things he said on the phone, things you've said, make me wonder . . ." He trailed off.

Wonder he would. Brayden gave tenacious a new meaning, and observant was an understatement when describing him.

What had she said? When would she have said it? That first night? She couldn't remember too much of it; there were glazed pieces but nothing solid to hold on to other than feelings. On the plane? Some other time?

"Did you — did you come into my room last night?" She couldn't remember that either, or she could, but it was mixed up and fogged.

His huff of breath brushed warm against her face. "Yes. You had a nightmare, don't you remember?"

"The Percocet, it makes things fuzzy. I can't remember what's real and what's not." Nightmares meshed last night. She remembered her father with a gunshot wound smiling at her, Danny yelling at her, Susan crying, and Richard. Always Richard. She rubbed her arms, goose bumps prickling the skin.

"What do you mean?" he asked her.

"My dreams run into reality. I kept thinking I was awake and something would happen to make me realize that I wasn't. I couldn't get away and then I saw your face but it kept shifting into Rich—" She ground to a halt, closing her eyes. Stupid. So damn stupid. She could only shake her head.

"Rich? Now I wonder, is that a name?" he asked, his voice deceptively soft.

Think, think. "Uh-uh. No. No. I just thought how crazy it would sound if I finished, so I didn't."

"Please do."

She wasn't fooled by the quiet, calm words or even the gentle touch on her neck. He'd paused for just a second.

Looking out over the water, she said, "I told you I see strange things. Your face kept shifting from you to this rich blue fabric that changed into . . ." Into what? Hell.

"Into?"

"Oh, forget it," she said quickly and stood. "Just forget it. I sound certifiable enough as it is. I don't want to talk about this anymore."

His hand shot out and grabbed her wrist. It didn't hurt, but she could tell he wasn't about to let go.

"We *are* going to talk about this. Not right now. I'll count my ground gained, but I'm telling you, I will get to the bottom of this."

Her hand trembled in his. That's what she was afraid of.

Chapter 11

They sat in a little room with a fireplace, overlooking the lighted canal below. She could see the Grand Canal and the lighted St. Mark's speared up in the night.

Fire crackled in the hearth. It was a cozy dinner setting, but as tense as the day between them had been. Every day between them was tense. The atmosphere was still heavy with unanswered questions.

I could kill you now and no one would know who or even why . . . Richard's voice echoed through her thoughts.

She shoved her plate away, intending to leave, but Brayden's voice stopped her.

"I don't understand you," he whispered.

Perched on the edge of her chair, she waited.

"Can't you see I only want to help?"

Yes, she could see that.

"Why won't you let me?" He slammed his fist down, rattling the dishes on the table.

As if her bones were too weary, she sighed and leaned back in her chair. "You can't take on all my battles for me, Brayden."

His eyes rounded. "All? Hell, woman, you won't even let me take on one!"

Not this one, no. But she didn't say that. Didn't even shake her head.

"What is it? What is it about all of this that keeps you so locked into yourself that you won't let anyone too close?" he asked, leaning forward.

"It's not just the attack," he remarked, jabbing a finger at the tabletop. "You were quiet before then. Thought, for some absurd reason, you had to keep quiet about the photos and the gifts and the calls. The more I think of it, the more I go over everything in my mind, the madder I get."

"At me?" she asked. He'd get mad at her sooner or later.

"At me, at you, at this nameless, faceless monster who has you believing you're protecting Tori and me. Hell, you think you're protecting the whole damn family with your silence!"

She stood abruptly, turning to the door. But he'd stood too, and now blocked her path.

His hands settled on her shoulders, squeezing once, twice before settling. Gently, he said, "You're helping no one but him, Christian. No one but *him* by keeping quiet." Cobalt eyes bore into her, his expression fierce. "Don't you see that?"

She opened her mouth. How did he know that? Did she tell him? What else did he know that he wasn't mentioning? Oh, God.

His eyes pierced through to her soul. Such beautiful eyes . . .

"Talk to me," he coaxed softly.

All she saw were his eyes. It would be so easy to lean . . .

"Baby, talk to me," his whispered.

"He — he —" Flashes of memories pierced her.

"Seems your little knight — what was his name, Danny — had a slight accident, Josephine." Richard tsked. *"I told you what would happen if you told anyone what was between us. No one will believe you anyway. What did you do to him? Sell your body for his support?"*

He'd leaned forward and grabbed her chin. "I don't like to repeat myself . . ."

. . . Local Policeman and Family Dead in Gas Explosion — Susan . . .

Brayden watched the emotions play across her face. He could almost see the walls weakening, watched as she opened her mouth and shut it, then opened it again as if searching for words. But then something shifted in her eyes, and he saw terror and fear in their depths before she slammed her defenses back up.

Christian jerked out of his hold. He inwardly cursed.

"Leave me alone." She shoved hard against his chest, and he backed up. "Leave me alone! You know nothing. Nothing about any of it," she said furiously.

He stepped out of her way as she flew past him. The slam of a door echoed in his heart.

Damn it. Maybe he pushed her too hard. No maybe about it.

Sighing, he reached over and picked up his wine, downing it in one long gulp. Hell. The stem broke in his fist and he hurled the remnants of the glass away, the quiet night shattering as it connected with the wall.

Brayden rubbed both hands over his face.

He'd wanted answers. He still didn't have any. No, he did, just not the one he wanted. He strode through the door and up the stairs to their suites. Stopping, he glanced at her door. Should he go talk to her?

No.

Give her a bit to cool off.

His gaze landed on his laptop. Well, there was something he could do. Sitting so that he could see whether she came out of her room, he booted up and dropped Aiden an email.

Scan the old picture and see if someone with the name of Richard/ Richmond/Rick? crosses her path. All I got was "Rich" before she stopped and came up with some lame cover-up. She still won't tell me a damn thing, though the harder I press, the less she forgets to deny.

I agree with Morris, I think she knows this guy. He's just got her so terrified, she believes she's protecting us all by keeping silent. Bastard was smart, told her the first to die would be me and Tori. I don't like to be used, especially by this son of a bitch. I don't know how much harder I can press her. I think I went too far today. Let me know if you find anything.

Bray

He reread what he wrote then hit send. Either they would find something or they wouldn't. Hopefully, they would.

Richard? That was his best guess. He didn't know of any other name that started with "Rich."

Something thumped from inside her room and he looked to her shut door, but no one emerged. Had he made a mistake? His gut told him no, or maybe that was the part of him that wanted this guy.

She'd finally smiled again this morning. Would it be square one again for them? He hoped not.

That morning, out on the balcony, the wind had teased her short tendrils of hair, the sunlight played off her delicate profile. He'd been so close to pulling her to him and kissing her. But he knew it was too soon. He missed her.

God, he missed her even before she'd moved out and into her condo. And he hadn't lied to her today when he'd told her he knew he'd been seven kinds of a fool. Christian haunted him, the feel of her, the taste of her, the way it had been and could have been between them. The way he wanted it again.

There was no way of knowing if he could get that back for them, but he was damn well going to try.

So how did he now make tonight up to her?

Music drifted through the open balcony doors, from someone's open window, reminding him where they were. Venice, Italy. And there was more to do in Italy than either one of them could imagine.

It was time to get her out of the palazzo.

* * * *

Christian worried her lip as she paced her room. For the last few days she and Brayden had hardly spoken. She didn't realize how much she had come to rely on him. The sound of his voice, the quiet smile he'd send her, just sitting on the balcony watching the sunset. Him simply there was something she'd come to count on.

The words he'd lashed at her had made her angry. He didn't understand. She was right about that, but then the guy could hardly understand when he didn't have a clue what was going on. His words had haunted her for days while he'd dragged her around various sites in the city.

"At me, at you, at this nameless, faceless monster who has you believing you're protecting Tori and me. Hell, you think you're protecting the whole damn family with your silence!"

"You're helping no one but him, Christian. No one but him by keeping quiet."

Like annoying song lyrics they echoed in her thoughts, kept her up at night, and mocked her during the day. At first she'd been angry, simply angry. But then reason peeked through and part of her wondered if he wasn't right.

Terror messed with your mind. She knew that. She'd been in victim groups before where some were so scared they completely shut down. Hell, she'd been one of them. Lack of control, lack of hope, lack of help—they were all sharp points on the mace of fear. And the hand wielding that weapon was power.

Terror was about power.

Abuse was about power.

Rape was about power.

Richard had the power.

She stopped, the truth slamming her in the chest.

Richard had the power and she was as good as handing it to him on a platter.

He'd expected it.

God.

She covered her face with her hands and took several deep breaths.

At least she wasn't completely stupid. She had started to gather her resources before the attack. After the arrival of the first batch of photos, she'd begun researching DNA, and had sent letters to two people: one to a doctor in a small clinic in Arizona and the other to a forgotten man in San Francisco. She needed evidence. Now more than ever. Who knew if the two could help her.

She stood by the bed, tired and wanting to sit. Just as she connected to the mattress, she all but leapt up.

The revelations were one thing to deal with.

Resolutions were another.

Something small, yet meaningful. Something to let her, herself, know that she *wanted* the power back. *Wanted.* No, *demanded.*

But first, small steps.

She stared at the bed with its neatly folded blankets and fluffed pillows. There was nothing wrong with it. She could sit on the bed. She should force herself to. Or try to sleep on it. The thought coated her stomach with a greasy film.

No. Too big. Her hands were shaking as images flashed in her mind and tears burned her eyes. Okay, something else. Something else. The room suddenly seemed too small, too confining.

"I want the power," she whispered. "I want my life. I want the power."

Sad, it was very sad. God, she was pathetic. What good were revelations if you couldn't even act on them?

At least she'd started to. In the last two nights she started looking up websites when Brayden was in bed. She'd located the Justice Department in Oregon and a list of statute of limitation bills that had been passed. She'd found that the first night she began looking and the elation she'd felt still thrummed through her blood. Since she'd been under eighteen when the crime was committed, and if she could prove DNA evidence, Richard could still stand trial and be convicted for what he did then. Not to mention what he'd done now.

She'd searched other sites as well, whose mottos and themes are all the same: *Report crime. Silence only gives the violence power. Break the cycle of abuse.*

Sighing, she shrugged off the thought. She had something she might look up tonight if Brayden's laptop was still out on the coffee table. She leaned down, grabbed a pillow and blanket, but caught her breath at the pull in her ribs.

Stupid. That was her own fault. She should have been paying attention. Carefully, she picked up what she needed and straightened, carrying her linens with her.

The living room was dark save for the moonlight streaming through the windows. With a place this size, she could have chosen one of many rooms, but Brayden wanted her close, so they shared these rooms and the little breakfast room downstairs for the most part. That was fine with her. Security was a nice thing, even if it was a fleeting thought.

Holding the blankets to her, she stared at his door. Yeah, it was nice knowing he was right there if she needed him.

So why did she keep pushing him away?

A smile caught her completely off guard. Brayden was Brayden. It didn't matter how much she pushed, or how hard. He was still right there.

Right where she needed him.

"I've really missed that smile. What are you smiling about?"

The soft words jolted her and she spun around, dropping the bedding.

"Damn it, I wish you wouldn't do that. You're too big to be that quiet," she told Brayden. Her chest squeezed at the panic racing through her. Idiot. "Where the hell are you? You scared me." She searched the darkness and tried to breathe past the looming attack.

Brayden watched her rub her breastbone. "Sorry, I'm on the couch. I didn't mean to frighten you." He should've turned on a damn lamp.

"I know that," she answered, annoyance clear in her voice.

He stood and walked to her, bending down to pick up the blanket and pillow.

He'd gotten off the phone with Aiden, who was emailing him a file. He'd sat here in the dark wondering what the hell to do, wondering how to fix things, when she'd stepped out of her room and into the moonlight.

All he could do was watch her.

The moonlight washed her face white and he studied her while she stared at his door. The intense frown on her face as she nibbled the inside of her cheek, as she had a habit of doing when involved and concentrating, was familiar and heartening to him. Then her face had softened and a small smile had lifted one corner of her mouth. The smile had eased something in him.

"Couldn't sleep?" he ventured, standing back up with the bedding.

"No."

"How come?" he asked as he walked to the couch and dropped the linens. He flipped the blanket open and settled it over the back of the cushions and tossed the pillow on the armrest.

"Just thinking."

Answered but vague. She had the concept down to an art.

He sat down and Christian did as well.

"What are you doing up?" she asked. "I thought you'd be asleep."

He tried to read her eyes, but couldn't in the low light. Something was different. Something he couldn't quite put his finger on.

"No, I called home earlier. Everyone sends their love. Mom wants to talk to you," he told her.

Brayden watched her as she eased down on her side, settling the quilt over her. He thought about the email he'd received from Rob Roy. Ian wanted to meet them here in Venice. Some schedule break. He'd send the details later.

"What are you smiling about?" she asked, turning his words on him. He shook the thoughts of his brother off and concentrated back on Christian. Time to gamble.

"Our trip," he told her.

"What trip?" she asked.

"Oh . . ." He purposefully trailed off. He moved, giving her more room to stretch out. His hip was beside hers, his arm on the back of the couch as he leaned over her.

"Did I forget to mention that?" he asked her as he caught the slight scent of her shampoo and the lotion she used.

She nodded. "I think so, yes. Unless you told me while I was conked on my painkillers."

He grinned at her, saw the curious look on her face washed in moonlight.

She didn't seem as tense, and if he wasn't mistaken some of the fear was gone.

"Trip?" she prodded with a raise of eyebrows.

He smoothed the discolored arches of her brows, ran a hand over her hair, sighing. He hated this stupid color. Shrugging off the thought, he leaned over and gently kissed her cheek. As he rose, he whispered in her face, "Venice is an awesome city. I want to see it with you, experience it with you."

"We've been here before."

"On business or with the family. Never by ourselves."

She stared at him and stared some more, her eyes black and dark silver in the moonlight. Then she frowned.

Was he making a mistake? "We're going on a tour tomorrow if I have to drag you. Then we're going to eat *gelatos*. And ride in a gondola. Maybe go to a few shops. You could use another jacket."

"I do love Venice," she whispered on a heavy sigh.

She reached up and touched his face, a small smile at the corner of her mouth. It was the first time she'd reached out and touched him. The simple contact squeezed his chest, made the muscle bunch in his jaw. He placed his hand on top of hers on his cheek, turned his face slightly and kissed the inside of her wrist.

"I know," he whispered back.

"I want to tour the bridges."

"If that's what you want." He kept his voice as low as hers.

He loved to see her smile. Taking a chance, he kissed her again on her cheek. "Good night, baby. I'll see you in the morning."

He straightened and walked across the living room to his door.

She, without a thought, had reached up and touched him.

He sighed.

"Brayden?" she asked.

He stopped and turned back. "What?"

"Thank you."

"For?"

A slight chuckle danced in the air. "Not coddling—too much. Good night."

He stood there staring into the darkened living room, heard her shuffling around on the couch. A smile creased his face as he turned and went to his room, cutting off the light, but keeping the door open.

She might need him during the night.

* * * *

For a man who didn't think he could coddle, Brayden was doing a damn good job.

In the last week, she'd become more relaxed, or maybe it was her revelation and the decision she'd made. Either way, the days here were becoming a warm comforting dream. During the day they toured the city and at night they would either sit and talk about work and the shop, about Tori, or just watch the nightlife from their balcony while sipping wine.

She breathed deeply and leaned her forehead against the cool pane of glass.

They'd been here for weeks, though the first was still a blur to her, either because of the shock or the pain medication or both. The bruises were fading and with them some of the terror, but not the resolve.

Yesterday she talked to Kaitlyn and Tori on the computer. She missed Tori, horribly. And she was ashamed to admit she felt as if she'd somehow failed the little girl. Not that Tori said or acted that way. Conversations with Tori Kinncaid were always the same, like a burst of rainbowed sunshine through a cloudy day.

The thought made her smile.

Sly child that Tori was, she asked if Christian and Daddy were having fun yet. Christian hadn't answered, but instead asked what Tori wanted for Christmas. Tori informed her that since they were away together maybe they could just get married and come home and be a family. That was what she wanted for Christmas.

Kid didn't ask for much.

Once upon a time . . .

Christian sighed. Ironic, when she dreamed of him, wanted him and would have done anything for the man, Brayden hadn't seen her, at least not like he did now.

140

Now that her life was chaotic, to put a nice neat term on it, Brayden was all she ever dreamed he would be.

The times when he reached for her hand, the way he held her when she was scared and lost . . . The way something in her sighed when he kissed her hair.

She picked up her coffee cup. Time to get ready. She wanted to visit a church today. One with a priest. Now she just had to inform Brayden.

* * * *

The church was quiet and dark. Out of the way. Why she'd chosen this one to visit was beyond him. She told him she liked these forgotten chapels on dead-end streets. They'd toured dozens yesterday, but she'd wanted to see them again. So they stopped at this one. Christian even told him he could go take a walk.

Like that was going to happen.

The woman went into a confessional.

Brayden stood at the back of the chapel. What the hell did she have to confess?

He knew something was up as soon as she wanted him to take a walk. She never said anything, but he was aware of the way she was always within hand's reach of him. The only time they were really apart was at night when she slept on that stupid little couch and he in the bed. But if it worked for her, he wasn't about to make an issue of it. He'd noticed the ease in her the last few days, the genuine smile and occasional laughter. All of it loosened the noose strangling his heart.

Brayden sat in one of the back pews. A woman to his left lit a candle and crossed herself.

He realized then he hadn't been to mass since last Christmas. Grammy would be so disappointed, strong Irish Catholic that she was. He'd known Christian was Catholic, one of the few things he actually knew about her. She'd told him once when he'd asked her.

The woman who had lit the candle was gone, an old man taking her place.

Why did people do that? Did it really help them? Christian had lit one. He'd lit a few in his life, not many, mostly when he'd been much younger and had gone to mass with his mom. Now? He really didn't think a candle was going to help him. He turned and looked at the front of the chapel, the large crucifix hanging from the ceiling.

The pew creaked as the old man sat beside him. He looked at the stooped man out of the corner of his eye as he heard a chuckle.

That was odd.

"So serious, Brayden," the man said.

Brayden looked at him, but his face was hidden behind a weathered and tattered fedora.

"Excuse me?" he asked.

The man turned to him then, a wooden cane in his hand, but Brayden didn't know him. No, wait, something . . . something about the man was familiar. White scraggled hair stuck out under the hat, his weathered face creased with deep wrinkles.

"I don't have all damn day here. Who knows how long she'll be confessing whatever sins she thinks she has." The man nodded to the confessional.

Brayden knew that voice.

"Ian?" he whispered.

His brother shook his head. "I always thought you were the smart twin."

"Good God," he muttered. He'd looked directly at the man, watched as he'd lit the candle, sat right, *right* beside him and had not recognized his own brother.

Even now, if he hadn't spoken so clearly, there was no way Brayden would have known who it was.

"That's downright creepy," he told Ian.

A gravelly chuckle answered him. "I told you I was meeting you sometime today."

"I was thinking more along the lines of the hotel, the Rialto, Piazza San Marco."

It was incredible. Brayden reached out and touched a weathered hand.

"How . . . why . . . what did . . ."

"Still so articulate, too." Ian shook his head. "Don't. It's not important, but it is necessary. That's all you need to know."

Brayden sighed and sat back, still looking at this brother of his he could have passed ten times on the street and not even known it.

Passed? Hell, he could have shaken his disguised old hand and not known he was touching related flesh.

"If you keep staring someone could notice." Though the smile softened the features, the words were hardly misted with amusement.

"Sorry," Brayden muttered and looked back to the little door Christian had gone into.

"How is she doing?" Ian asked quietly.

"Better." He clasped his hands between his knees, leaning forward. "Better."

Ian also leaned forward so the pew in front of them shielded them somewhat.

"What have you found out?" Ian asked him.

"Not much more than what I've already emailed you."

Ian gave some incoherent guttural reply. "Nothing else?"

"I think something . . ." He looked back to the confessional and lowered his voice. "She's been looking up stuff on the computer for the last week. Usually when I'm in the shower or after I've gone to bed."

"Very inconspicuous, isn't she?"

"Anyway, I wanted to know what was so important," he admitted.

"For shame, brother dear," Ian retorted.

"There's a bunch of Justice Department websites. One in Louisiana and the other in Oregon."

"Oregon?" Ian asked, his eyes lost behind makeup and fake lenses.

Even after he'd taken the hat off and gray hair stood up on an age-spotted bald head, Brayden still couldn't discern the color of Ian's eyes. Realizing he was staring, he glanced away.

"Yeah, Oregon." He raked a hand over his hair. "It was a statute of limitations website."

"What all was on it?"

"Sexual assault and murder. For the most part."

Ian scratched his deceptively wrinkled throat and wiped the makeup from his nails off with his thumb. "That was the Oregon site?" Ian whispered.

"Yes."

"What about Louisiana?"

"I have no idea, that one is all over the place."

"What else has she been browsing?"

Brayden rolled his neck and bit down, the constant taste of anger filling his mouth. "Rape and sexual assault websites. Women help groups."

Ian grunted. "I hope they help."

They both looked to the confessional.

"Hire her a personal trainer to teach her some self-defense moves," Ian advised.

Brayden immediately thought it was the best idea he'd heard in a while and could all but hear the silence that would greet him if he told her.

Chapter 12

Ian watched his brother, the black of Brayden's hair glinting in the dim lights of the chapel.

"How are you?" he ventured.

Brayden smiled, rather self-deprecatingly, and only raised a brow. "Great, just great. You?"

Ian stared into those dark blue eyes. He asked again, "How are you?"

Brayden looked away, stared at the large crucifix above the altar. Ian thought he might have cursed, but wasn't sure.

Himself? Well, God would be sending him to Purgatory for more than just a slip of the tongue on holy ground.

"I can't get it out of my mind, Ian."

Ian sighed and thought about his words. "No one's asked you to."

"When I close my eyes . . . I can't help but think . . . I just wish I could do something, anything! I feel useless and not worth a damn." Brayden's chest rose and fell and Ian caught the telltale glistening in the corner of his brother's eye even though Brayden still stared straight ahead.

Ian didn't say anything, just sat still and quiet. Brayden had always been one to hide his feelings. In that they were very much alike.

Brayden's voice pulled him back from his comparison of genetics. "I didn't protect her. First Tori, and now Christian." Finally, Brayden turned to look at him and Ian's breath caught at the raw emotion on his brother's face. "What kind of father am I that I let my daughter get hurt? What kind of husband am I that I let Christian . . ." He stopped and quickly looked away.

Ian hid his smile. Husband, was it? "Is there an elopement I don't know about?"

Silence greeted him and he saw Brayden's hand swipe viciously under his chin before Brayden turned back to him.

"I was stupid enough to let her walk away from me before. She offered everything and I was . . ." Brayden sighed. "Never again. I won't ever make the same mistake again. Christian is mine. I don't care what this bas—monster thinks of her."

Ian did smile at his brother's thought to their location.

"Christian is mine."

Ian wasn't about to let on what he already knew. Well, not for certain. He suspected his brother didn't know Miss Bills as well as Brayden thought, not facts. Most of the information Ian was finding out through Aiden, that the family knew, was useless or false.

He'd run checks on missing persons files and had a few still left to sort through. There were several possibilities. No, Ian knew Brayden only needed to know facts that were solid, not what-ifs. And with his brother's current frame of mind, it was probably safer. Christian didn't need her *husband*/fiancé/whatever locked in jail for going after someone that *might* have had something to do with it.

Ian shifted, the padding under the gabardine pants scratching his waist. Disguises often were very uncomfortable.

"If I find out who . . ." He let the sentence hang.

When he finally locked eyes with his brother, Brayden said, "I want him."

Ian wondered if Brayden knew exactly what he wanted or if it was just emotions talking. He would take nothing away from his brother, not if he was certain.

Time would tell.

"Well, that can be arranged," Ian said, and noticed not so much as a flicker in Brayden's eyes.

After a moment, Ian asked his brother other questions, moving to other topics.

Ian glanced at his watch and noticed he'd been here for almost an hour. If Christian took that long asking for forgiveness he'd be in one of those little boxes for several years. On that thought, the deep red velvet confessional curtain ripped back and Christian tore down the side aisle.

As she passed them, Ian saw the tears trailing down her face, her complexion pale in the dim church.

The priest came right behind her but she was already hurrying away. The black-robed man, older than Ian's disguise was to seem, shook his head and genuflected, but Ian saw the tears in the old man's eyes.

Muttering, the priest said, "*L'oh, Dio. Che un bambino dovrebbe*

soffrire cosi . . ." Then he started in on a prayer to some saint.
L'oh, Dio. Oh, God, that child should suffer so . . .

* * * *

Christian ran blindly out the doors and tripped going down the steps. She sat, not caring who saw her, the ancient stones cold through her pants. Sickness rolled through her, the truth, black and greasy. She leaned over and retched up the coffee she'd drunk that morning.

She'd thought she could do it, just tell it and get it over with. But she couldn't. She'd gotten through most of it, all the hard, degrading details—the murder, the molestation, the beatings and rapes, the choking silence—all of it. All of it. But for some reason when she started in on how Susan's father had helped her escape, she'd just choked up. Just started crying and couldn't seem to stop.

The confessional had been warm and stuffy and she needed air, needed to breathe.

The priest . . .

He'd never given her absolution, but then maybe she didn't deserve it.

"Here." Brayden stood on the step above her.

Christian wiped her mouth and looked up through the cold, foggy morning to him as he squatted, holding out a handkerchief that he'd wet from his bottled water.

She took them, wiped her face and rinsed the bitter taste of sickness from her mouth.

When she handed the bottle back to him, her hand trembled. His covered hers on the bottle and he helped her stand up and face him.

She stared at the wide expanse of his chest, covered in a cream pullover.

It would be so nice just to lean, just to be held, to know someone was there for her, no matter what. She took one deep trembling breath, then another, and wrapped her arms around his waist.

"Hold me, please, Brayden. Just hold me," she whispered.

His arms came up around her, tight and strong—protective.

"Always."

Here she was safe, here nothing could harm her. Here, Richard couldn't touch her.

Brayden's cologne, sandalwood and spice, held her as surely as his arms did. His lips pressed against the top of her head and his arms tightened even more.

"It's okay, Christian. Whatever it is, you're okay." The words were warm against her head.

She finally leaned back and brushed absently at the makeup stain now marring his shirt. A sigh huffed out before she looked up at him.

"I'm sorry. I'm sorry."

The corners of his eyes narrowed. "For?"

She shrugged. "Everything."

It was hard to tell if the sound he made was a growl or a grunt. "Why is it you can piss me off as easily as flipping a switch?" he softly asked.

"I'm—"

He put his finger to her mouth. "Don't apologize again."

Christian studied him, really, really studied him. For the first time, she noticed he looked tired, worried, confused. And just shimmering beneath those was anger. How it must be for him, not to be able to do anything.

Her boots creaked as she leaned up on her toes and cupped his cheek. "I—Thank you. Thank you for being here, for always being here."

He tucked his chin down and pulled back a bit.

"I don't know what I did to deserve you," she said, watching his brows rise. Her teeth clicked as she ran them together. "I love you. If nothing else, please know I love you."

The muscles in his jaw moved and bunched even as his chest rose on his inhalation. His arms tightened and pulled her to him again. "God, I've been so . . . I didn't think . . . I'd wondered if I'd ever hear you say that to me again." His chest fell as his breath huffed warm against her hair.

"I love you, too." He pulled back, cupped her face in both his hands and bent his knees so that they were looking at each other at eye level. "I love you, don't forget that. I'm here. Right here."

She was being so unfair to him by not telling him what she knew. She looked away. "I know you're disappointed in me," she whispered.

"Why do you think that?"

"I don't think it, I know it. You want me to be honest with you, and . . . I want to tell you," she said. Then she shook her head. "No, that's not right, I don't want to tell anybody. I don't want anyone to know." Her words caught on the knot in her throat as more tears spilled down her cheeks.

His thumbs brushed them away. "Want and need are often two different things."

He was right.

"I know. I will, I'll tell you." She would. One day. "Just not now, not today."

"You will?" His ebony brows arched.

Could she? Look what happened with the priest, who was an unseen stranger.

"You will?" he asked again.

She nodded.

The corner of his mouth pulled, but not really into a grin. "That's all I ask. I'll try not to push you. I know I'm impatient, and with something like this . . ." He trailed off. "When you're ready, baby. When you're ready."

He leaned forward and kissed her forehead.

As he pulled back, she grabbed his face and held it still. Looking into his eyes, she leaned forward and chastely placed a kiss on his cheek.

This time, he did grin.

Her spirits lifted at the sight of it.

"Can we go to the spa?" she asked him, clearly catching him by surprise.

"The spa?" he asked.

"Yes, the spa." She hated this hair color. It wasn't a bad color, but it was a mark Richard had put on her and she wanted it off.

"The spa?" He sighed. Shaking his head, he held the expression every male must when a woman says any of those mysterious words like salon, spa, manicure, or makeup. Why it was such an anomaly to them, she would never know.

His head shook again, catching the light in the dark strands. "I can hardly wait."

"I just . . ." Christian took a deep breath. Her eyes locked with his. "I want my hair back." Her voice caught. "I want his mark off me."

Whatever humor had been on his face was immediately slain by rage, but even then as his hand came up and ran through her discolored strands, it was a gentle touch.

"I think that's a great idea," he told her.

She caught the look he threw over his shoulder to an elderly gentleman at the top of the steps.

Hand in hand, they walked down to the dock and waited for the *vaporatto*. She looked back to tell Brayden something and noticed the same old man stood a bit behind them.

"What?" Brayden asked her, blocking her view of the man in the weathered fedora.

"Nothing." She looked back at the water gently lapping at the edge of the dock. Brayden stood directly behind her.

"You know, I think you should go straight red, more red than Mom's," Brayden said, his voice low and deep.

She tilted her head back and around to look up at him. "Why is that?"

His grin flashed at her, charming as always, yet she saw it didn't quite reach his eyes. "I always wanted to date a redhead."

"Again, why?" This time she turned fully to face him.

His tongue poked in his cheek before he said, "Well, you know what they say about redheads."

Was he flirting? "No, I seem to have forgotten, what exactly do they say?"

"They're great in bed."

Great in bed.

"Your memory must have slipped," she told him, turning back around, crossing her arms over her chest.

He leaned over, his breath warm on her ear. "What makes you say that?"

She turned and their noses almost touched. "I don't recall you complaining before."

His eyes darkened as they ran over her face and dropped to her lips. "Why do you think I said you should dye it straight red?"

She couldn't help it, she laughed, and realized it felt good. No, it felt wonderful.

"God, I've missed that sound," he told her, grabbing her chin between his thumb and forefinger. This time he lowered his head to hers, his lips lingering softly, undemanding. Christian started to stiffen, but closed her eyes, Brayden's scent surrounding her.

Straight red?

She grinned against his mouth as something in her slowly loosened and unfurled.

* * * *

Richard shook his head at the moving technician. "No, no. Not there, the desk needs to be in front of the wide windows."

What were these people thinking? Idiots every last one of them.

"Darling?" his wife's voice rose from out in the foyer.

"Yes?"

"I think they might have lost our living room furniture."

Richard closed his eyes and counted to ten, thinking of being anywhere else than here. "If they did, they can buy us more!"

The movers set his desk down with a hard thud. Sunlight slanted through the windows behind them.

"Is that centered?" he asked them. "Fix it. It needs to go down about a foot."

He turned around and unpacked the box in his hands, setting the framed pictures in the chair. He paused at the picture of Josephine. If the imbeciles could ever get his desk in the right place, he'd set the photo on its corner.

His gut tightened as it always did when he looked at it. Anger raced through his blood. Four damn weeks. She'd been gone for almost *four* weeks.

The corner of the frame bit into his palm until he felt the skin break.

Where the hell was she? He could find nothing out. Not a damn thing, and he'd tried. The Kinncaids were loyal to a fault. And he knew they knew where she was.

That shop owner was gone too and had been the entire time Christian was absent.

Richard was not a stupid man. No. He knew Mr. Brayden Kinncaid was with her. With *his* Josephine somewhere.

He wondered how he could bring them out, bring them back. Or maybe he should wait for them to come home and then strike.

That would work.

Carefully, he took a deep breath through his nose.

"Is this the exact spot ya wanit in?" asked one of the movers.

Richard shot a glare in the man's direction. How dare he interrupt. With an absent wave toward the door, he barked, "It's fine. Leave."

When the door closed behind them, he carried the photos to the desk and set them up.

An inch from the corner of his blotter and a finger length from the family picture.

There. He smiled at the smoky eyes staring back at him.

She would come home. She had to, and when she did, she would be his.

His angel, his Josephine would never, *never*, be anyone else's.

Chapter 13

Christian looked at Brayden as they walked back into the palazzo.

The symphony he'd taken her to was spectacular, and the dinner wonderful. She might have consumed a bit too much champagne, but that was okay, too. She hadn't been on any medication for several days now.

Brayden shut the door behind him, standing there in his black tux, perfectly tailored for his tall frame, and her heart skipped a beat. He was so incredibly handsome.

"Did I tell you how great you look tonight?" His eyes ran over her from the top of her — once again brunette — head to the hem of her satin dress. That smile hiding at the corner of her mouth sent a shiver down his spine.

She couldn't help but grin as she ran a hand over her curls. Finally, she looked like herself. "Thank you. I think so, about a dozen times. You don't look bad yourself."

Brayden's smile was soft, as though he held some secret he wasn't sure he wanted to share.

"Thank you for the dress. You didn't have to . . .," she started.

One ebony brow rose over those cobalt eyes. "You don't like it?"

Not like it? How on earth could she not? The beautiful A-line, strapless dress, made of heavy ice-blue satin, fit as if it were made for her alone. The bodice rode just above her breasts, with only a hint of cleavage showing, the hem floor-length. The only adornment on the entire thing was the sheer, beaded inlay, decorated with silver embroidery and beads, that went from her waist to the floor, an inverted V.

"It's beautiful," she finally answered him. Turning her back to him, she said, "And so is the necklace. You really shouldn't have."

He'd also given her a pendant. The necklace was a sapphire, the size of his thumbnail, or maybe a knuckle, and hung from a twisted rope of silver.

His gaze ran over her. "Why not? What's wrong with getting you presents?"

She thought, or tried to. There had to be a reason. "I don't know."

"Hmm."

A chill danced down her spine, and she didn't know if it was from the open window letting in the cold night air or the hot look from Brayden's blue eyes.

"I should . . . uh . . ." The champagne danced through her bloodstream.

"Should what?" he asked, walking slowly toward her.

Should what? Who should?

Oh. "I should go change."

He offered her his arm and helped her up the stairs. She tripped and giggled.

His chuckle glided over her nerves.

"You, baby, drank too much champagne."

Again she giggled. "Maybe. No, probably. Yep, I think I did."

Once in their suite, she let go of his arm and started toward her room. "You know what?"

"What?" he asked.

"I feel good. Thanks for tonight. It was wonderful."

She shut the door and sighed.

Tonight . . . tonight was . . . a dream. A dream come true. A candlelit dinner, presents, a symphony. Beautiful, like a slow-rising tide in the summertime.

She faintly heard the pop of a cork through the door.

Pushing from the door she reached behind her and tried to undo her dress. It laced down the back. No zipper, no buttons, just one long silk ribbon that ran through loops. She'd had to ask for Brayden's help to do the dress up earlier.

Now her fingers fumbled again.

Sighing, she opened the door and walked back into the sitting room.

"I'm sorry, but I need help with my dress. I can't get it undone myself."

He looked at her for a minute, not moving, a flute in one hand, a champagne bottle in the other. He set the flute on the coffee table, the bottle in an ice bucket, and she turned her back as he walked to her.

His hands were warm as they weaved the long piece of silver satin through the small loops. Every now and then, his knuckles grazed her backbone and she felt it all the way to her toes.

She heard him breathing behind her and turned her head to look up at him.

His eyes rose from what he was doing to hers. His fingers froze and then trailed from her shoulder blade up to her neck.

"I had no idea, this dress would be so . . ." His gaze dropped to her lips.

She watched his Adam's apple bob as he swallowed.

"Difficult," he finished.

What was difficult?

Slowly he lowered his head, his hand and fingers caressing from the back of her neck, around her jaw, to tip her face further back.

Again she shivered.

His eyes stayed open as he came closer. A breath away, he whispered, "I want to kiss you."

Licking her lips, she tasted the scent of his aftershave on the air between them. Never breaking eye contact, she said, "Okay." Slowly turned to face him.

His eyes held hers as his lips touched her mouth. She slid her eyes closed as his lips lingered undemanding on hers.

She relaxed with him, and though only their lips touched, he flooded her senses. His gentle coaxing tempted her until finally she kissed him back.

She wound her arms around his neck and pressed against him.

Everything was Brayden. Simply Brayden. His arms, tight around her; his mouth, cherishing; his scent arousing and comforting at the same time.

Slowly, he pulled back, his hand smoothing from her cheek, through her hair.

His heavy sigh wafted against her lips even as his eyes looked deeply into hers. She wondered what he saw.

"Was that . . . I didn't mean . . . Are you okay?" he finally asked.

She smiled. "I'm wonderful because of you." Christian ran her finger down his cheek and tapped his chin.

His brow cocked and he grinned. "I can deal with that."

"Thought you might." She turned her back to him again. "Could you get this undone, now?"

Some sort of guttural growl came from him, but she didn't look back as his fingers deftly unlaced her gown, but left the long ribbon in the loops.

With a jerk, he pulled back. "There."

She let go of the dress and it stayed in place. Reaching back she realized he hadn't undone it all the way, just part of the way and loosened the rest. She watched him walk to the coffee table, where his flute of champagne sat. She licked her lips, one hand holding up the front of her dress, just in case.

He looked up at her and raised a brow.

"Thank you." She couldn't seem to move. "I should uh—I should probably . . ."

Alcohol swam through her veins, heated her, swirled pleasant memories of her and Brayden together . . . Pleasant, happy, passionate memories.

He strode to the silver bucket holding a champagne bottle. After pouring another flute, he handed it to her and said, "No, thank you, Christian. For the best night I've had in a long, long time." He looked at the flute, then said, "Actually, you've probably had enough."

She sighed. "I love the way you say my name. Don't know why, it's just different when you say it."

His eyes widened.

"I was thinking the same thing," she said, and snatched the flute from his hand. "Not about the champagne, but about tonight."

There was that charming smile, dancing all the way to his eyes. "Were you?" He raised his own flute. "Well then, to new beginnings."

How could anyone know her so well, without really knowing her at all? Swallowing past the emotion, she looked straight at him and clinked her glass to his. "New beginnings. I like that."

Christian took a sip of the effervescent wine. She was warm all over and not just from the champagne. Looking out the window, she watched the city.

Venice was complex at night. It reminded her of a harlequin, a *dottoro*, an elegant *countessa* all at the same time. The fun and excitement of the jester seemed to mirror in the reflected lights of the canal, the secrecy hidden within the shadows masked what was and what could be, the age-old elegance of her sitting through the tides whispered on the breeze.

New beginnings. She really liked that. There was still so much between them, so much it sparked a pull deep within her, and she was tired of hiding from it because of Richard.

Damn the monster.

She didn't want to think about that, not about Richard, what he'd done, or what she was doing. All she wanted to think about was Brayden and how she felt safe and happy with him.

"I love you," he said to the side of her.

The words jerked her around.

"Why?" she blurted out.

The grin flashed before his deep laughter rumbled across the air, around and through her. "God, woman! Hell if I know." Shaking his head, he set his flute aside and took hers from her. His palms were warm as he cupped her face. "Hell if I know, but I do."

He did. She knew he did, some part of her knew, but another part worried and doubted.

Brayden watched the anxiety and questions dance in her eyes. "Why do you doubt that?" he asked, tracing her jaw with his thumbs.

She shrugged. "You don't know me."

Well, when the truth came out of her, it just sort of slammed down between them.

"True," he told her. "I know the important things, Christian, or I think I do."

"What things?"

"You're loyal, kind, you love my family as much as I do and Tori —"

"You said, before, that it was because we'd been playing house."

He closed his eyes. "Forget what I said before, I was a dumb ass. Just forget it all. Well," he amended, "not all, just the stupid stuff."

She tried to turn back to the window, but he held her, her face still between his hands.

He watched the long column of her throat work as she swallowed.

"I don't know what to think about anything anymore, Brayden," she whispered.

"You know I love you." He dropped his hands to her shoulders, and he noticed the shiver as it danced through her muscles. "I'm not just saying that, Christian, if that's what you're thinking." He could see it might be, the doubt flickering there in those smoky eyes. "I'll admit I'm slow, and you already know what an idiot I can be. But I love you."

Her eyes looked down, her lashes sweeping to shutter her gaze from him.

He sighed. "Have you ever known something, deep inside, it just takes you a while to realize it?"

After a beat, her gaze rose back to his. "Yeah."

She held her dress up with one hand. Damn, he should really let her go change. Looking at her bare back was bad enough, but something about her just holding that satin against her . . .

"Yeah—um—Well, that's me."

Finally, he saw her lips curve at the corner.

"You think too much," she said

"Isn't that the pot pointing to the kettle?"

Her smile reached her eyes, but then she glanced away and the smile faded. "Can I ask you something?"

"Anything."

Taking a deep breath, she looked back up at him, and he felt her straighten under his hands, her shoulders going back just a bit.

Her tongue darted out to lick her lips. "I've no right to ask this of you. I know that. But I have to. I want to because . . ."

"Because?" he prodded when she trailed off.

"While we're here. Here in Venice, can we not . . ." She took another deep breath. "Can we not talk about the other?"

"Other?" he pressed.

"The—the attack." She closed her eyes. "It's too beautiful here, too special, and I only want this to be us. We have to go back soon and then it'll all be . . . Can the time we have left here be just us? Here and happy?" Her eyes opened and he caught his breath at the intensity in them. "Only us. Please?"

He thought about it, not that she talked about the attack anyway, so he would play along. Besides, something in him loosened at her words and he smiled. "I thought you mentioned something about there not being an us."

"No." Her grin answered his. She tapped his chest. "That was you."

"Well"—he waved it away—"that was one of those stupids."

She shook her head then asked again, "Please?"

Brayden picked their flutes back up, handing hers back to her. "I'll try. Sometimes it's hard, but I don't see a problem with Venice just being us, if that's what you really want."

"It is. I know you get aggravated with me. Just please, try and be patient." She huffed out a breath and mumbled, "I've no right to ask you that either as you've already been so patient."

The woman made his head spin sometimes. "I'll be patient. That's my middle name."

Her laughter rang out. It had always reminded him of darkened pleasures, velvet and chocolate, something sought after because it seemed almost forbidden. The full, rich sound tightened his gut. He'd missed that sound. Missed it so much, his chest squeezed.

She raised her flute. "To us?"

Brayden pulled her to him with one arm, clinking their glasses just before she came back into contact with his chest. Her satin bodice whispered against his shirt.

Us. She wanted Venice to be about them and only them. The gods were smiling on him tonight.

Looking into her eyes, as he had before, he chanced another kiss.

"To us." Then he lowered his head to hers, catching the spark of something deep within her eyes before they slid closed.

The kiss was chaste, just a gentle press of lips, but he wanted more. When she sighed in his arms, he opened his mouth and teased the seam of her lips with his tongue. He waited for her to stiffen, but she only leaned into him.

Gently he waited, teasing . . . asking . . .

Finally, her lips parted beneath his, and though he wanted to kiss her with everything in him, he didn't.

Brayden held back, waited and prayed.

When the tip of her tongue touched his, he couldn't hold the grunt in or the smile that spread across his face.

She angled her head and he let her deepen the kiss, take it as far as she wanted to go.

Oxygen was important. Some part of him remembered that as they both pulled back from the kiss.

Her smile, twinkling in her eyes, was all he needed to see.

"That was — nice. Yeah." Her eyes were locked on his lips. "Nice."

Christian took a breath and grabbed the back of his head. With a jerk, she locked her lips on his, eager to make him understand what he meant to her, the kiss was all raw need . . . need of safety, of cherishment, of love and banishment of terror. She wanted the power back. One of them gentled the kiss, she had no idea who, and it hardly mattered.

She angled her head and deepened the kiss, thrusting her tongue into his mouth, demanding he kiss her back. The black strands of his hair were silken tresses between her fingers. His arms slid around her and wrapped around her back, pulling her hard against him.

Christian's heart thundered, roaring blood through her veins, but it had nothing to do with fear and everything to do with the feelings Brayden coaxed her to feel.

One hand moved from her back, along her ribs, his thumb grazing the side and underneath her breast.

Christian gasped and jerked back.

His eyes stared deep into hers, and the expression in the dark blue was one she'd never seen before.

"I'm sorry. I didn't mean . . . God, Christian, I'm sorry," he said on a ragged whisper, pulling back from her.

He straightened and licked his lips.

The truth suddenly slammed into her. Brayden Kinncaid was as nervous and scared as she was. Christian wasn't stupid, she knew and felt what was between them. It was the same intense feelings she'd carried for the man for the last several years, feelings that had only intensified since they'd finally made love months ago. But now . . . now, the other stood between them, dark and ugly. He was afraid he was reminding her of it, she could see that now.

Clearing her throat, she reached up and touched his cheek. The muscle in his jaw bunched under her hand. He looked at her out of the corner of his eye and she had to turn his head to her. "Brayden, look at me."

Muttering under his breath, he complied, both brows arched.

"Stop it," she said.

"What?"

How could she explain this to this man? The Kinncaids were a different breed of men in her opinion. They often seemed they should be in another time, when men protected and gave all for what was theirs. When nothing and no one stood in the way of what was considered important.

Swallowing, she tried, "Stop it—this. You didn't scare me. You just took me by surprise, that's all."

Wondering if this night would now be laced with tension, she dropped her hand and looked across the water. It was a foggy night.

Finally, she said, "I'll let you know if something you do bothers me." She looked back at him. "Okay?"

With one long, blunt-tipped finger, he scratched the corner of his mouth. "That's just it. I don't want anything to bother you."

"Well, that makes two of us. But I don't want to spoil this between us because we're both worried I might react a certain way." She took a deep breath and confessed, "You keep him away."

"What?"

She realized her dress was slipping and pulled it up. She felt ridiculous, but she needed him to understand. Licking her lips, she tried again. "You keep him away."

He didn't say anything, didn't move. Finally, she chanced a look up at him.

Brayden's head was cocked to the side, studying her in that intense way of his.

Hurrying, trying to make him understand, she rushed through the rest of it. "When I'm with you, talking, laughing, or . . ." She smiled at him. "Or kissing. It's you. Just you. You drive everything else away."

His grin grew. "I guess that's nice to know."

"You guess?"

He pulled her gently back into his arms. The warmth from his sigh tickled the hair at her temple.

"Yeah," he said, "I guess."

"Hmmm." She reached up with one hand and kissed him, ran her hand down the front of his tuxedo. Words she was scared to say hovered on the end of her tongue. She took a deep breath. "I want you to keep him away."

He straightened under her hand. "What are you saying?"

Chapter 14

Christian took another deep breath. Was she ready? Only one way to find out. She hadn't lied to Brayden. When she was with him, things were just them. "Do you know," she said, "I've never seen your room."

She stopped, pulled her hand back, and walked toward his door. Was this foolish? It didn't feel like it, but she was scared. And she didn't want to be scared.

She wanted her life back.

Turning, she looked at him. Brayden stood staring at her, his tux jacket caught behind his wrists, his hands shoved in his pockets and the most confused expression she'd ever seen on his face.

Still he didn't move.

Christian sighed and walked back to him. Maybe she should just let the dress fall. But then another thought slammed into her. What if Brayden didn't want . . . What if when he looked at her . . .

Stop it.

She stood in front of him, looked into his eyes, and wrapped her arms around his neck. A breath away, she murmured, "After the hotel, I would lay awake at night cursing you because I remembered how wonderful it was between us, how precious, how special. I want happy memories again, Brayden. I want to go to sleep tonight and know you're the last man to touch me." Then, she kissed him. Poured all the love, heartache, and hope she could into that one kiss.

He tried to pull back. "This isn't . . . Might not be . . . I don't know . . . You've had a lot of champagne tonight."

"I'm not drunk if that's what you're worried about. You are so stuck on this drunk thing, Brayden. You need to work on that," she told him, grabbing his head and kissing him again.

Their tongues danced and melded, sighs mingled breaths, and their bodies fit, moved, and asked for more.

Brayden jerked back. "Christian, don't."

He held her at arms' length and she could see the uncertainty in his eyes.

She cupped his face, not caring what he saw in her eyes. "I want you, Brayden. I have for a long time. When I moved out, before I moved out, I would wake up thinking you were beside me, feeling your hands on me." She dropped her gaze to his lips. "Remembering what you tasted like, what it felt like to be with you. It was wonderful and beautiful."

One quiet moment stretched, then he whispered, "It's supposed to be."

She ran her thumb over his bottom lip, which was larger and fuller than the top, though not plump by any means. Finally, she looked back into his eyes.

"Now I'm afraid to sleep. I'm tired of him, Brayden. I'm tired of being scared. I want to remember what it's meant to be like." She kissed him again, and whispered in his ear. "Help me forget the nightmare. Make me remember the love."

He pulled her back, his hands hard and strong on either side of her face. "I don't know if this is such a good idea. What if . . ."

"Oh . . ." He didn't want to. Why hadn't she thought of him? "I'm sorry, I didn't mean. If you don't want . . ."

God, this was like before.

"Not want what? What were you going to say?" he coaxed.

"I just didn't think about how this would affect you. If you'd want . . . That is . . ." She couldn't get the words out.

"Christian. Look at me."

Her gaze rose and locked on his and she couldn't define what she saw in his eyes. "You are always beautiful to me and you mean so much, I'm scared of hurting you."

"I'm not scared of you, Brayden. Please? Make him go away. I wake up feeling dirty and I want to wake up remembering sunshine, the warmth of your hands on me, the heat of loving kisses." She felt her lip tremble. "I want my life back. With you."

His eyes burned in their intensity. "You don't ask much, do you?"

She held her breath, afraid he'd tell her no, not sure if she really wanted him to agree.

Slowly, he lowered his face to hers, still clasped between his hands. Against her lips, he swore, "I'll make you remember. It'll only be you. Only be me. I swear it."

Brayden pulled her close to him and lost his fingers in her hair as he deepened the kiss.

Some sane part of him warned him this was a disastrous path, but the echo of her words pleaded through him.

Make me forget. Make me remember . . .

He never wanted a woman so badly in his life, and was so terrified he'd muck it up. Her lips were soft under his. He wanted to dive, to taste, to claim and wash away.

But he wouldn't. Slowly, he had to go slowly.

The kiss went on and on, a slow wave rolling to a shore, only to join and become another. Since they had all the time in the world, he didn't hurry, didn't rush. He skimmed his lips over hers, teased hers with his tongue, ran his along the roof of her mouth and felt her smile and shiver.

Her skin was so soft under his fingers. He trailed a path from her jaw, down over the pulse in her neck, to the prominent collarbone.

She shivered against him.

Christian couldn't think. The kiss robbed her of thought, tossed her into a sea of nothing but feelings. Brayden coaxed a fire deep within her to burn, embers buried under the ash of fear. But now, now they were glowing bright.

Her stomach tilted when Brayden swooped her up in his arms, the silks of her dress rustling. The kiss never broke and she scraped her nails along the back of his neck, felt him shiver slightly. She broke the kiss as he carefully set her down by the bed.

Her stomach tightened. A bed. She swallowed.

"We don't have to do this," Brayden said, his hands on her shoulders, gently kneading.

He pulled back and looked down at her, brushing her hair from her forehead.

The darkened curls looked right on her. This was his Christian. His.

He studied her, saw the skin jump over the blue vein in her neck. On a smile, he traced the telling sign of her excitement. But what if it wasn't? What if she was really scared and forcing this.

"What are you frowning about?" she asked, smiling, rubbing her forefinger between his brows.

He held her chin between his fingers. "I want this to be right."

For a long moment, her smoky eyes looked into his. "I know."

"I don't want to rush you. You shouldn't force this. When you're ready —"

Her cool fingers against his lips stopped him.

"I'm not forcing this, Brayden. Are we rushing it?" She thought about it for a moment. "Maybe. Maybe not."

"We should wait," he told her.

Her eyes widened. "On?"

Brayden shook his head. "I don't know."

Her hands cupped his face. "Brayden, I want this. I want you. You make me feel safe and special and beautiful."

"Promise me if anywhere, at any time, you change your mind, you'll tell me."

For a long minute she didn't say a word, her thoughts shuttered from him by the sweep of her lashes. "I promise. I know you'd never hurt me."

He didn't know about that. He would never *intentionally* hurt her, it was the *unintentional* that worried him.

"You're thinking again," she said on a grin, lying back and pulling him with her.

And he was.

When she reached up and kissed him, wrapped her arms around his neck, he did nothing to stop her.

He let her take the lead. Brayden would only do what she asked.

One kiss turned into another and yet another.

Her hands pushed at his jacket, and he quickly obliged her in taking it off and tossing it to the side. Next to go was his tie. The shirt gave them both hell until a giggle danced out of her at his curse. That one sound relaxed him as nothing else could in this situation. She wanted this. She really, really wanted this. Them. Love.

This night would be one they would both remember with smiles, he vowed.

Christian felt him ease as he kissed her, his mouth gentle and coaxing on hers. She wasn't sure why. Part of her was scared, but the rest of her wanted this, wanted it so badly she could cry. Her hands raced over his wide sculpted shoulders, the muscles in them corded and tight.

Brayden was her strength and rock. Her physical fortress, the shoulder to cry on. He left his pants where they were and pulled her to him, on a deep kiss, sweeping her mouth, filling her with his breath.

He was hers.

She felt his fingers at her back, slowly drawing the ribbon through all the loops as he tried to completely unlace it. At one point, he growled, clearly frustrated. Grinning, she broke away and turned, sitting on the bed, with her back to him. Her heart fluttered.

She wasn't certain she could do this here. In the bed.

He must have sensed something because he sighed and stood. "Perhaps we should . . ."

"No," she said. "I just. I should have already starting sleeping in the bed."

For a long minute, he looked at her, then he grinned and held up a finger. "Wait right here, I'll be back."

Christian waited, the air cooling her. She stood and paced. What was her deal? It was just a bed. A stupid bed, but there it was. She wanted and needed, but mostly just wanted to make love to Brayden. Just not in a bed. Not yet.

In minutes, he strode back into his room. In his hands were all the blankets, quilts, and the large fur rug from her room she'd used as a pallet for weeks before she started sleeping on the couch.

In silence, she watched as he layered them on the floor in front of the fire. He threw the silk duvet from her bed onto the top and then turned, stoking the fire into a blaze. She loved the way his muscles bunched and rippled in the low light.

"Is this better?" he asked.

She only smiled and walked to him, sitting down in front of him. He'd understood. Slowly, she nodded and looked back at him over her shoulder.

Brayden sat up on his knees behind her, gently kneading her shoulders. He leaned over and kissed her cheek.

"You still want to do this?" His breath was hot against her ear and she shivered.

Turning slightly, she leaned up and kissed him. "Yes," she whispered against his mouth.

His fingers played along her neck as he kissed her, those slow gentle kisses that made her stomach flip and the passion in her awaken.

Finally, he pulled back, still kissing her ear as his hands pushed the dress apart, and slowly, so damn slowly she could have screamed, he unlaced the dress all the way down to the small of her back, just above her bottom. Warm knuckles brushed her backbone from her nape to the dent in her lower back. Goose bumps tingled along her skin, and a tremble pooled at the base of her spine.

When the material sagged, she caught it against her. For a moment, she looked at the flames of the fire, and then let the dress fall, pooling at her waist.

Brayden's fingers were warm as they caressed her nape. His hair tickled her ear when he leaned forward and kissed the curve of her neck, his thumbs kneading the muscles of her shoulders.

He mumbled something in Italian. *Bella*? She wasn't sure. Didn't want to ask.

His mouth continued, around to her backbone.

She lay back on the blanket, the silk cool against her bare skin.

Her eyes locked with Brayden's and the breath caught in her throat. So intense. The blue so strong, she was sure it would burn her.

His hands cherished and loved even as he pushed the rest of her clothing aside and off. Her stockings and garters he removed so torturously slow, she started to reach down and help him, but he only swatted her hands away, giving her that charming wicked grin of his before the man used his mouth and fingers to completely undress her. His teeth grazed over her thighs as he unhooked the garters, then his mouth followed her stockings all the way down to her toes. His tongue rolled along her ankle and she gasped.

Even with the fireplace, the room was chilled. She shivered, her nipples tightening.

"Cold?" he asked, reaching down and grabbing another soft cover, tossing it over her.

She only nodded.

"Not for long." His lips were on hers, kissing gently, not demanding, slow and languid.

The longer their tongues danced, lips met and breaths were shared, the hotter she became.

His mouth trailed from hers, kissing down her neck, to her chest. The feelings he brought to life within her were sweet and warm, wrapping her in bliss.

He muttered something against her breasts, but she had no idea what it was, his voice too low. She just felt the deep vibration against her. His breath teased her chilled skin just before he bent his head. The heat from his mouth, from his tongue, from his fingers as he caressed, tasted, and kissed her breasts built a fire within her. Deep within her heart. One finger grazed the undersides of her breasts as his tongue danced wickedly across her nipples before he pulled them into his mouth.

Christian couldn't hold the moan in and speared her fingers into his dark hair, holding him to her.

When he leaned up, he pressed into her, letting his chest connect with hers, and she gasped as his crisp hair crinkled against her. Brayden's ebony hair flickered in the lamplight as he bent his head to her again. Against her lips he whispered, *"Mia bella, Christian. Mia bella."*

God, she loved it when he spoke Italian.

His tongue teased, tasted, dove, made her want for more.

Long warm fingers blazed a hot trail over her breasts, feather light, just the barest of touches, and still she responded, moaning into his mouth. This felt so . . . right. As though she were coming home after a long journey.

She wrapped her hands around the back of her neck, pulling him even closer as his hand continued to meander down her ribs, her hip, her thigh, back up to circle around her navel.

He was being so calm, so gentle, so careful.

When his touch traveled its path again, she arched into him and closed her eyes, relishing in what he made her feel. Warm hands, warm touches, loving touches. She smiled.

His fingers circled her breasts again, slow and teasing.

"God, you're beautiful," he told her, pulling back. His eyes shifted in their blue, the heat storming in them. "Tonight is about you."

So sweet.

She cupped his face and leaned up for a kiss. "No, tonight is about us."

About us.

He heard the words, knew what she meant, but didn't argue. No, tonight was about her.

Already he was so hard, he hurt. For months he'd remembered what it was like to be inside her, to be completely surrounded and engulfed by Christian. But what was a little longer? Nothing to him and everything to her.

Slowly. He wanted to go slowly. Not just for her, but for himself, too.

Tonight was about cherishing, worshipping, loving.

Her hands on his arms smoothed over his muscles and back down, a slight caress that went straight to his gut.

The light in her eyes turned them into deep turbulent smoke. Shifting and roiling.

He traced her brows, her nose, the rise and fall of her luscious lips.

"*Ti amo, mia bella.*" And she was, beautiful and his and he loved her. Loved her so much he wanted this to be perfect.

Her tongue darted out and licked her lips. "What did you say?" she asked.

He only smiled, and bent his head. "I'll show you."

The kiss was from somewhere deep within him. He wasn't good with words, better with actions. Never could he tell her everything he felt for her. Instead, he kissed her, pouring all into that one kiss and hoping she understood.

Her arms tightened around his back, pulling him tightly to her.

Skin as soft as the silks of her dress slid beneath his hand, beckoning, urging him onward. The moans in the back of her throat drove him to the brink.

Slowly.

He kissed his way down her neck, tasting that scent that was hers, that always reminded him of Christian. Something heady and fragrant, complex as the woman in his arms. He loved that dent, just there in her collarbone. The skin pulled between his teeth as he gently suckled.

Her fingers ran through his hair.

Brayden tasted his way back to her breasts. And what absolutely beautiful breasts they were, round, full, high. She always hid them behind too-large shirts and prim clothing. They filled his hands.

"Have I told you what gorgeous breasts you have?" he asked as he cupped them, and blew across the distended peaks.

She only shook her head, her eyes locked with his. While she watched him, he lowered his head, kept his eyes on hers while he cherished the bountiful gift she'd been blessed with.

Watching her watching him was a fuel to his raging libido. Slowly he licked around the centers, watched her eyes narrow, felt the leap in her pulse, around, then he laved the nipple and her eyes slid closed. Brayden pulled her breast into his mouth, suckling, pulling moans from her as she arched against him.

"Please . . . please . . .," she gasped.

Brayden propped on his elbow and looked down at her, at his dark hand against the smooth creamy paleness of her breast.

"Brayden Gallagher Kinncaid, don't you dare stop now," she whispered. Her eyes glazed with passion.

He only grinned and lowered his head again. "Well, if you insist."

In no time, those sexy little noises she made in the back of her throat filled the room again. He smiled as he continued to kiss every last delectable inch of her.

If nothing else, he would give her pleasure tonight, no matter how it ended.

Slowly he traced a line down her leg with his finger, followed it with his tongue. That little spot behind her knee he remembered from before. He kissed it, licked it, had her squirming as he ran his finger over it. He quickly took the rest of his clothing off and settled between her legs, running his hands up the insides to her knees, then back down to her ankles.

She was breathing hard. He hoped to hell she didn't have an asthma attack.

Christian felt like she couldn't breathe and it had nothing to do with a panic or asthma attack.

It was Brayden, his touch, his mouth. Him. Settled there. His hands lit a path up the insides of her thighs. Oh, God. Please.

She felt him shift, come up more and then he touched her. Just the lightest of touches, a feather-light caress.

Her body arched and she couldn't hold the gasp or the moan of his name in. "Braydennnnn . . ."

His breath was hot as he whispered against her thigh, his hair tickling.

Long supple fingers parted her, slicked over her, up and down, around and around. Her world tilted as he wove the magic within her.

Then he muttered something against her and she almost came when he simply kissed her, loving her with his mouth. His tongue laved, licked, promised and drove her to the brink. He toyed with her, alternating between those wicked fingers and that wicked sharp tongue of his. And he was going so incredibly slow.

"*Mia bella,*" he whispered against her, inside her as he stroked her deep with his fingers, his tongue making her forget who she was. The climax beat its arrival inside her, like angry waves wanting to crash against the shore, but he knew just what to do, to hold the tide back, to make it linger, to prolong the need.

Christian fisted her hands in the duvet, even as he lifted her hips in his hands. Still he slowly cherished, worked her till she was sobbing. Whispered against her, into her, words she couldn't understand, until she was begging, so lost in Brayden and what he was doing to her, all she could see was the golden wave he kept just out of her reach.

And she wanted it. Wanted it until . . .

He slid another finger in, just as he suckled her tiny bundle of nerves. The wave roared through her. "Brayden! Oh, God! *Brayden!*"

The wave rolled over her, sucked her back and crashed over her again. She saw stars, bright bursts of lights.

She felt herself pulsing against him, and still he loved her with his tongue, his lips, his mouth. He soothed her with the same kisses as he had aroused her with.

Finally, he kissed his way up her stomach, circling her navel with his tongue, briefly kissing both breasts as his fingers trailed from under them up the sides to her neck.

His fingers dove into her hair, his palms on her cheeks.

"Ah, Christian. *Ti amo, mia bella. Ti amo.*"

She had no idea what he was saying, but in his deep baritone voice, she couldn't care less. It was like thunder promising the softest of summer rains. Gentle, yet cleansing.

His eyes. The emotions burning in them brought tears to her own.

He must have seen them. "Do you want me to stop?" he asked, kissing her eyes, the bridge of her nose.

"No," she whispered and rocked her hips against him.

His shaft was hard and hot against her thigh.

Brayden propped on his elbows and pulled back, his gaze intense. "Are you certain?"

He would stop. If she asked him to, if she wanted him to. She didn't, and she wouldn't.

Smiling up at him, she reached between them and wrapped her fingers around him, satisfaction spearing through her at his sharp intake of breath.

"I've never been more certain of anything in my life. Make love to me again."

Carefully, she guided him to her. Their eyes never strayed from each other.

"I love you," she whispered, letting go of him.

"This is our night, *mia bella*. Ours and no one else's." He cupped her face again, even as she felt him poised at the edge of her. "Say my name," he told her.

"Brayden."

He slid slowly into her, filling her completely with love and hope and promise.

"My Brayden."

He smiled down at her as he slowly began to move. His eyes that intense blue as he lowered his head, whispering to her. *"Desidero fare per sempre l'amore vio."*

She didn't know what he said, but she understood it.

Her eyes closed on a sigh as she began to move with him.

Brayden watched her, the expressions on her face as they rocked together with ease. An age-old dance that only varied in posture or tempo. Theirs was a slow adagio.

God, he loved this woman. Loved the smell of her, the feel of her skin against his, her touch on him, her lips on his, her tight, wet heat surrounding him.

He watched the wonder on her face, the joy as he built her back up to join him.

"Come with me," he coaxed, leaning down to kiss her brow, the tip of her nose, to trace her open mouth with his tongue.

He controlled their rhythm, wanting to prolong their lovemaking.

She was his. His to cherish, to love, to protect.

To protect.

She was his.

Without realizing when or how, the tempo increased.

Christian's moans and pleas filled his mouth, filled his soul.

God, she felt so good, so right. Finally, he felt like he was where he was meant to be.

He would not go without her.

"Come with me," he said again, moisture wetting his face. It was hot, and Christian was hotter still, her fire feeding his, urging his. The need blazed through him.

Her eyes were pools of mercury, emotions shimmering them to silver.

He leaned over and trailed her ear with his tongue, whispering to her, *"Sieta l'amore del mio cuore . . . la mia vita . . . la mia anima."* And she was, the love of his heart, his life, his soul.

He felt her vise around him, tighten, even as she arched and screamed in his ear.

Her scent and yell blinded him to all but being in her. The climax arced through him, so powerful he threw his head back and gave her his heart and soul.

* * * *

Brayden was heavy. But Christian didn't care. She couldn't breathe, but oxygen really didn't seem all that important.

He grunted near her ear and she smiled.

In no time, those eyes pierced down at her as he propped up on his elbow, pulling out of her. Ebony tresses stood up all over his head and she giggled.

He only cocked a brow, and wiped his finger across her cheek. Only then did she realize she'd cried.

"Are you okay?" he asked, concern and worry shadowing his eyes.

The giggle turned into an outright laugh. "Can you honestly ask me that?" she wanted to know.

His knuckle brushed wetness from the other cheek.

"Joy, Brayden. Tears of hope, and joy, and . . . and . . ."

"And?" he asked, tensed.

"Love." She pulled his head down to hers. "Love. Amore. I love it when you use those sexy Italian words."

She felt him relax, his grin hinting at the devilish streak in him. "Really? So now I have to worry about all these Venetian men, do I?"

She rolled her eyes. "Oh, yeah."

He leaned down and kissed her. "Guess I'll just have to keep you busy here with no one but me."

The thought made her heart race. "Wow. You know that many Italian words?"

His eyes narrowed on hers. "Care to find out?" His brows wiggled.

"No, I'm hungry."

He nuzzled the side of her neck, his teeth gently scraping to her shoulder. "So am I."

Christian shoved against him. "I mean for food."

His grin was just as wicked as the twinkle in his eyes. "Dessert should always be eaten first, didn't you know?"

"And it has been, in case you didn't notice."

He settled against her. "Great. Time for the main course."

She only had time to shake her head before he was kissing her senseless again.

It was as if they couldn't get enough of each other. Each wanted more touch, more caressing, more kisses, simply more.

And each gave it.

"What did you say to me before, in Italian?" she whispered hot in his ear.

Brayden paused, arched a brow and grinned. "I'm not really sure."

She shoved against his shoulder. "Excuse me?" Then she laughed. "Here I was thinking it was sexy as hell, and you could have been telling me the canals outside were purple."

Brayden sighed. He wasn't good with words, but he remembered. And why could he whisper it to her in a language she couldn't understand, but hesitated to say it to her?

He cupped his hands on either side of her face. "I said you were beautiful, my beautiful lady. That I love you." He kissed her, telling her, "That I want to make love to you forever . . ." She joined in the kiss, twining her arms around him. "That you are my heart." He kissed down her throat. "My life." Another kiss. God, he loved the taste of her. "My soul." He kissed the pulse in her neck and possessively slid his hand down her. *"Il mio amore."*

His love.

Brayden rolled to his back, bringing her astride him.

This time she controlled it all, the tempo, the race to the shore, the prolonging.

She enjoyed the prolonging.

It was him who was begging while his eyes burned with a deep blue fire.

His hands traced patterns over her, driving her to distraction. Finally, he reached between them and found her, and she was lost.

Completely and utterly lost.

She was his and no one else's. He knew now, he'd never make the mistake of letting her go again.

"Il mio amore," she repeated, her accent pulling a smile from him.

"My love," he answered her unasked question, and proved the words with his actions.

* * * *

A week before Christmas, and still nothing on Josephine.

"What do you mean?" he asked, as he looked up from paperwork on his desk. Damn movers. He had yet to find his Waterford ashtray. He'd have to buy another, but he didn't want another one. He wanted *his*.

The man across from him stood, looking at something behind Richard's head, high above it too. One would think after all the years Ivan Ristovolich had been in his employment, the man could at least look him in the damn eyes.

"Sir, I've searched all their holdings, every listing I could break into, no one is listed under any Kinncaid or Bills or even Montreaux. I checked Louisiana, but no one fitting neither her nor Mr. Kinncaid's description have contacted anyone there," Ivan said, the edge of desperation clear in his voice.

Ivan was an unnoticeable man for the most part, which was a plus for the tasks Richard had him doing. His Slavic features were as heavy and well defined as his accent.

Some people were easily manipulated with fear. It often amazed Richard how incredibly stupid one could be when they were afraid of something. If only they stood back to think, analyze, they might take initiative. Personally, he never allowed them that time.

Which was why he had to find her—no, *needed* to find her. He couldn't allow her to feel safe.

Now the stakes were higher, much, much higher than before. If she decided to tell someone the truth now . . .

Something tingled along his nerves at the thought, but he shrugged it off, rolling his neck.

No, she wouldn't. Josephine was too scared, too worried about her precious Kinncaids. There was no doubt in his mind who they would believe should she decide to give bravery a try. The Kinncaids guarded her like one of their own.

The silence in his study stretched, only broken by Ivan's cough.

Richard sighed. "She'll be back. It's getting close to Christmas, and they wouldn't miss their family holiday. The Kinncaids are all about family, if anything." The leather of his chair sighed as he leaned back and crossed his ankles on the edge of his desk. "Watch their house. Let me know as soon as you find anything out."

"What do you want me to do?"

That was the question, wasn't it? He was constantly reminded what a detriment keeping Josephine alive was, but he couldn't seem to help it. Josephine was Josephine, there was no other like her. He leveled a look on Ivan, noting the way the man immediately lowered his eyes. Power was a heady thing.

Smiling, he sat up. "Why nothing, nothing at all. Just let me know when our prodigal returns, will you?"

With a wave, he dismissed Ivan and turned to look out the windows. Darkness had already fallen, coating the yard and woods in shadows. A flurry of snow late that afternoon had blanketed the grounds in white.

Yes, he had no doubt she'd be home for Christmas.

And when she was . . .

Chapter 15

Dulles International Airport was a nightmare anytime of the year, but three nights before Christmas it was hell. Christian was glad they had come home when they had, and not waited until Christmas Eve.

Brayden had offered to stay in Venice or even Paris another night. But they decided against it and flew home.

Christmas lights glittered from a Christmas tree some employee had decorated. People milled and pushed about. The drone of voices cloaked the roar of the planes taking off and landing. Carols played from speakers, the music interrupted as announcements were made.

It was great to be home.

Someone jostled her from behind and she stumbled. Brayden caught her arm.

"You okay?"

She nodded.

"Sorry," the man said, hurrying by with a bag slung over his shoulder.

"Rude ass," Brayden muttered, scanning the crowd.

Christian glanced around. Brayden was six-four. If there was someone to see, he'd find them.

"There he is," Brayden's deep voice said, his hand tightening on her elbow. "Come on."

The crowd shifted as they walked into the baggage claim area, and she saw Quinlan standing there talking on his phone. She smiled at the familiar sight.

"Isn't that a surprise," Brayden said, grinning.

"Well, as the man is fond of saying, 'When there's work . . .'"

"There's work," Brayden said with her, shaking his head.

Quinlan saw them, waved, and disconnected with whomever he had been talking with. He hurried to them, his long black woolen coat swirling around his legs.

His smile was a single-dimpled one, inherited, Christian knew, from his mother. The youngest Kinncaid stopped right in front of them, hugged his brother and stood staring at her, his head cocked to the side and a question in his eyes.

Christian smiled, anxiety skittering through her, and shook her head. "What? I don't get a hug, too? Did I get demoted?"

Quinlan grabbed her in a tight hug. "God, it's good to have you back, sis."

Tears pricked the backs of her eyes. Of all the boys, he was the one she felt closest to in a brotherly way. Obviously Brayden was a different case altogether. Swallowing past the lump in her throat, she pulled back. "That's more like it."

"Let me see your hand," he said, setting her back and grabbing her left hand. His deep russet brow cocked as he narrowed a look at his brother.

Christian jerked her hand back. "Do you mind?"

He stared a moment more at Brayden, who she saw only smirked back. Men!

"Can we get the bags and go?" she asked.

Brayden hauled her up to his side. "Anything you want, *mia bella.*"

Heat rushed from the tips of her toes to the roots of her hair, prickling her skin. She could only smile, all thoughts completely taking flight.

Quinlan shook his head, still grinning, and said pointedly to Brayden, "Dad's gonna have your ass. He told Mom if she," he said, pointing to her, "came home without a ring on her finger, she better by God not have a baby on the way." Quinlan's chuckle was rusty. "Muttering something about his offspring not keeping their zippers up."

"What did your mom say?" Christian asked as they made their way to the metal slide carouselling luggage for its owners.

"Well, I don't think I was supposed to hear that part," he said quickly and looked at the bags. "So which ones are yours?"

"Quinlan," both she and Brayden said.

A flush started from his neck and stained the edge of his ears. "She—uh—Mom said they only took after their father."

"What?" they asked together. Brayden grinned and she chuckled.

Quinlan laughed again, looking at her. "Glad to hear you laugh again. What did you two do? Take a course on synchronous-rhythmical speaking?"

"I was thinking more along the lines of 'jinx' and a pinky shake," she told him, reaching around both males and grabbing one of her suitcases.

Before long, all their bags were loaded in the back of Quinlan's Lexus.

Christian slid into the backseat, both men in the front. Which was fine with her, gave her time to think, settle her nerves before they got home.

"So, what did you bring me?" Quinlan asked, his gaze directed on her in the rearview mirror.

"What makes you think I got you anything?" she asked him.

"'Cause I'm your favorite brother, and you know I love Italian things, and it's Christmas."

Indeed. She and Brayden had done practically all of their shopping in Venice. Everyone was getting something from either there or Murano. There had simply been too many beautiful glassworks to pass up the fabled island artisans. She'd gotten Brayden a leather jacket. Knowing her luck it wouldn't fit, but she'd worry about that later.

"Did you get the tickets?" Brayden asked from the passenger seat, interrupting their play.

"Of course," Quinlan answered, with that haughty air they all had. Almost as if he were insulted that there might be something he *couldn't* do.

Christian leaned back and watched the lights pass by in the night. Christmas was bright and sparkling in the winter air. By the time they were halfway out of the city, heading toward Seneca, flurries danced in the air.

A white Christmas. That would be nice.

Brayden watched the light snowflakes flutter in the beam of their headlights, noting all the Christmas lights rainbowed with other decorations to shout greetings for the merry season. Celtic Christmas music fluted from the car's speakers.

Tomorrow he planned to take Christian and Tori to see *The Nutcracker*. They went every year, and this year would be no different. Well, that wasn't exactly true. This year, there would be that feeling of family with them. Last year, he'd actually thought about that, but had shrugged it off.

179

But this year. This year everything was different.

They'd bought gifts together. The thought had him grinning. He'd never bought a gift for someone, let alone all his family members, with another woman. It was kind of nice, watching her sign all their names to one card. Even if they were signed: *Brayden, Tori and Christian.* Since he'd made the issue of them buying gifts together, he figured he'd pressed enough not to bring up how her name was supposed to follow his. That would come later, if not as soon as he wished.

He glanced at Quinlan, the dashboard lights glinting eerily on his brother's features as he remembered what his brother had said about a ring.

Brayden's grin grew. A ring? Damn straight. He'd bought it the day he bought her the pendant. But he was smart enough to see when the time was right for things, and as yet, Christian wasn't ready to hear his proposal.

He hadn't gone looking for a ring. He'd been in that shop to buy her the pendant, or something. While the clerk had wrapped the sapphire necklace, he'd browsed. And seen it. Sitting on a bed of black velvet, the ring winked at him.

A single marquise diamond, simple yet not, if he could find the right band to go with it. He had no doubt he eventually would. Three carats seemed perfect; after all, Christian wasn't a flashy or showy type of woman, but that didn't mean he had to get her a plain little diamond either. He didn't want anyone missing what the ring meant when she put it on her finger. With one this size, it should be fairly obvious, though personally, he liked the larger stone. But she wouldn't.

The closer they got to home, the more he looked to the backseat.

Christian sat with her head against the headrest, her gaze out to the cold world. As if she felt his eyes on her, she turned and their gazes locked. Would he ever get used to those pale gray eyes? Probably not. Hell, he hoped not.

A small smile teased her lips and he wished he'd sat in the backseat with her.

"You okay?" he asked, reaching over the console into the backseat, holding his hand out to her.

She grabbed it and laced her fingers inside his. "I'm fine." A frown pulled between her brows before it straightened away. "I'm fine," she repeated. "Just thinking about Christmas and seeing Tori. God, I've missed her."

"Me, too." Talking on the phone every day had in no way made up for not getting to see his daughter for several weeks. The only thing that had comforted his worry was knowing she was in good hands. But it was the first time he'd been away from his little girl since that nightmare with Gavin and Taylor when Tori and Ryan had been kidnapped.

Quinlan turned onto the driveway of their family home.

Home.

Thank God. He couldn't wait to see his daughter. Just as the car pulled to a stop, the front door flew open and the light of his life bounded down the walk.

He heard Christian's sigh as she squeezed his hand, hurrying with her seat belt as quickly as he was. Brayden was out of the car just in time to catch Tori as she launched herself at him.

"I've missed you. It's about time you came home!" she said into his neck, burrowing against him.

Brayden breathed deep, the smell of her sweet and fruity, not masking the child's scent of innocence. He felt a catch in his throat and cleared the words past it as he squeezed his daughter tighter. "Not nearly as much as I've missed you, pumpkin."

She pulled back and he saw her roll her dark blue Kinncaid eyes. "Really, Daddy, I hardly doubt that."

He raised a brow and turned as Christian came up beside them. Tori squirmed to be set down. She wrapped her arms around Christian, whom he saw bend down and inhale deeply just as he had.

Christian's eyes were closed, but he still saw the silvery trail glide over her cheek. "Oh, sweetie, I'm so glad to see you."

Tori pulled back and said, "Well, of course you are! I'm precious."

God help him. She was only eight.

"Why are you crying?" Tori asked, wiping her small hand over Christian's cheek.

"It's a happy, stupid tear," Christian said on a chuckle.

"How can a tear be happy, or even stupid?"

He wondered the same thing. Quinlan strode past them up the walkway and into the crowded door.

"I'll explain when you're older," Christian answered, straightening and looking to him with a small smile.

He smiled back and took Tori's and her hand. "Come on, you two. Everyone's waiting."

"They've been waiting since like yesterday," his daughter informed them. Just as they reached the door, she stopped, halting them all half inside, half outside the threshold. "So, did you get me the Christmas present I wanted?"

She grabbed Christian's right hand, then shook her small dark head and reached for the left one. Dropping that one, she turned a frown on him. "Daddy. Daddy, I ask for one thing? And you couldn't get it for me?"

Some things were not that simple.

"See, Kaitie lass," his father said in his normal booming bark, just to his right as Brayden ushered them all in and shut the door. "I told you. Not an ounce of propriety among any of our sons . . ."

"Oh, Jock, stuff it." His mother smiled and walked to them.

God, it was good to be home.

* * * *

The ballerina twirled and flitted across the stage with a speed and ease that even the most uneducated had to appreciate. The notes of Tchaikovsky's *Sugar Plum Fairy* chimed out in short, sharp bursts. Her stiff tutu bounced to her movements, her sequins flashing silver under the blue stage lights, as her partner ran his hands along her rib cage as she bent back.

Richard found the dancers' movements beautiful and erotic.

Then again, it was probably because *she* was here. He'd seen her the minute she walked in on the arm on that Kinncaid. And a child with them.

He quietly sniffed as he watched them from the corner of his eye. They were in the next section of balcony seats, so it wasn't hard for him to see her, to watch the way she leaned over to whisper something to the girl, or the way her head tilted when *he* said something in her ear.

When the man's arm stretched across his daughter's seat back and his hand caressed Josephine's shoulder, a red haze clouded

Richard's vision.

It was all he could do to watch the performance, let alone not stand up and demand that she come to him.

His fist thumped on the armrest. Estella covered it with her cold hand, jerking his attention back to where they were.

Shifting, she leaned over and whispered, "What is with you tonight?"

He caught the annoyance in her voice.

Looking around, he took note of the other people in attendance, obviously politicians. Senators, Congressmen, government officials. Military uniforms, their braids and buttons catching the light, ordered respect. This was hardly the place to have people wondering. He had a reputation to keep, to build here, to uphold.

Smiling, he patted her hand, and answered, "Sorry, darling, I was just thinking." He kissed her cheek and promised, "I will stop and enjoy our evening."

His wife nodded, straightening in her seat, concentrating on the story unfolding through movements and music.

Kinncaid traced Josephine's ear, and Richard saw them share a smile.

An intimate smile.

Richard bit down, tried to look at the performance, but he couldn't take his gaze away from the couple.

Couple!

And they were clearly that.

No. No. No. This would not work. This would *never* work. He was not about to let her get away, to all but *give* her away now that he had her back.

Silly girl, she knew better, damn it. How dare she let that man touch her! The rage netted his vision, choked his breath.

Time for another tactic. One was already in play, sympathy already given, she just didn't know it yet.

Richard straightened his bow tie and shifted in his seat, wanting to leave.

How could he get her attention?

His plan was, unknown to his wife, already in motion. But in time she would learn. He absently wondered how she would react when she saw her daughter. Knowing Estella, she'd probably ignore

Josephine, but then again, it would depend on the setting. If a performance was needed, he had no doubt his mate could deliver it, she always had before.

He and his wife were a perfect pair, coldly ambitious. He would admit that. But Josephine . . .

She was the fire in his life.

The reason . . . a game . . . *the* enjoyment.

His angel smiled again, a real smile.

Why had she never smiled at him like that? Hadn't he shown her love? Shown her what it was like to be a woman, to be cherished? He'd shown her beauty and she'd hated him.

That man, that man could do no more than graze her shoulder with a finger and she smiled at him.

Anger sat heavy and thick in his mouth, rushed through his veins.

The man would have to pay.

Josephine was his.

With that comforting thought in mind, he focused back on the stage, as his mind calculated, plotted and planned.

He smiled and enjoyed the performance.

* * * *

Christian shivered as Brayden's finger traced her ear. Trying to concentrate on the performance was beyond her. She saw the dancers, the Arabians jumping and leaping to impossible heights, but she could not concentrate.

Pulling her head to the side, she attempted to glare at him, but he had that deceptively bored look on his face. The corners of his eyes told of the smile lurking just at the edge of his mouth. She shook her head and turned back to the stage.

Tori sat on the edge of her seat between them, enthralled as she was every year. Christian ran her hand over the girl's black velvet dress. She and Tori matched, both had on long-sleeved, ankle-length black dresses. She wore her cloak and the pendant Brayden had bought for her in Italy.

The night was wonderful. It was like they were a family. Secretly, she'd dreamed this every year they'd come to see *The Nutcracker*, but this year, it was real. Now, she and Brayden were aware of each other as they'd never been before. Before had been a fantasy for her and not even a thought for him. This year, there were stolen glances, soft touches, promising caresses.

Tori wiggled back in her seat, and Brayden dropped his hand, gently massaging her shoulder.

Intermission came and the little girl had to go to the ladies' room.

The line was long but finally she and Tori were done and heading out one end of the restrooms. There were two entrances. Christian glanced down the way, to the other entrance, and stopped.

Estella Burbanks.

Estella Burbanks.

Her *mother.*

The woman disappeared inside the ladies' room, the flash of her maroon gown and brown hair gone.

No, she had to be mistaken.

What would the woman be doing here? A stupid question. It was cultural, it was a place to see and be seen, a place to make an appearance.

Her heart pounded, and her hand trembled. If Estella was here, then so was *he.*

Oh, God.

A vise tightened on her chest. Before the attack could stake its claim, she pulled her inhaler out of her evening bag and took a puff.

"What's wrong?" Tori asked her.

Christian could only shake her head. Darting quick looks around, she searched for him. He had to be here. No, he *was* here.

She knew it.

The hair on the back of her neck prickled.

"Come on, let's go find Daddy. You don't look so good." Tori pulled her hand, trying to get her to follow.

Her feet were rooted to the spot. A group of men several yards away burst into laughter. The sharp noises grated on her nerves and drew her attention. One man shifted and she could see several of them. She could see *him.* Richard was staring at her. The look on his face was utterly furious, even if he did smile at the man next to him. His gaze was one she knew too well, green eyes all but glittering, the skin pulled tight over his sharp cheekbones.

185

"Christian! Come on," Tori said, impatience clear in her voice.

I love you, everything about you, mia bella.

Brayden's voice guided from her heart, through her soul. Christian raised her chin, looked at Richard, through him, past him.

As they walked by the group of men, nausea greased her stomach, but she held her head high and laughed at something Tori said, though for the life of her, she didn't know what it was.

Seconds after they sat down, the lights dimmed.

Brayden wasn't there. Where was he?

The lights flickered again. And still no sign of him.

First will be Brayden and his little girl . . .

"I wish I could dance like these girls do," Tori said wistfully. "But I'll just stick to the piano."

Christian ran her gaze over the room. Where was Brayden? She scanned the crowd again and saw Richard and Estella sitting down in the next section.

They were so close! She fisted her hands in her lap.

"I missed you two. Where did you go?" Brayden asked, jerking her around.

She couldn't hold her sigh in, but tried to hide her relief.

"Well, I thought we might get a drink, but Christian had to use her inhaler, and I thought maybe we should sit down. I didn't want to miss any of it," Tori chattered.

The lights dimmed a last time, plunging the room into darkness save for the stage lights.

She still heard Brayden's, "Hmmm . . ."

Staring straight ahead, she didn't dare turn her attention to her right for fear Brayden would see her, afraid he'd follow her gaze through the darkness and see who she was looking at.

Brayden's hand rubbed the back of her neck, and though she didn't look once at him, she could feel his cool assessing gaze on her, wondering, studying, watching.

From the other direction, she could feel Richard's hot, angry glare.

She had no idea how much longer the performance lasted. An hour? Over? She didn't remember anything about it, other than Brayden talking to Tori on the way out of the concert hall. His arm, tight around her shoulders, steered them down the steps as he held his daughter's hand.

As they hurried down the steps, out into the cold bitter wind, she heard that voice that haunted her nightmares, that stalked her over the years.

She tried to ignore it, but she must have done something, because Brayden stopped and looked at her, then scanned the crowd.

His look was weighing, tight, and coiled, as though he knew.

But how could he know?

Their limo waited at the curb, the driver standing by the door. Tonight they were staying at the hotel. Christian pulled away from Brayden and hurried to the car. Tori slid in after her. Through the dark glass, she saw Brayden standing on the steps, still looking around, his gaze predatory. She could see the determined set of his jaw from here.

"What's wrong with Daddy? He looks mad," Tori said from her seat along the windows.

"I'm sure it's nothing," she answered.

Richard guided Estella down the steps. It was choreographed perfectly. A slight jostle, and Estella stumbled right against Brayden.

Christian's breath caught as Brayden mumbled something and turned his back on the pair, still searching. They stepped away, but Richard turned back and glared at Brayden.

Finally, Brayden ran a hand through his hair, hurried down the steps without a word to either Richard or Estella as he brushed past them. The driver opened the door for him and he slid in. When the doors closed and the car pulled away from the curb, she sighed and leaned back against the seat, snuggled up next to Brayden.

Too close. Too damn close. God, she felt sick.

Tori's chattering voice saved her from an inquisition but she knew it wouldn't last. Forcing a smile, she listened and tried to concentrate on what the girl was saying.

"My favorite part is the Russian dance," Tori said.

Brayden listened with half an ear to his exuberant daughter.

The ride to their hotel was quiet, save for the slush of tires over the wet asphalt.

Brayden watched Christian while she got Tori ready for bed. She was wound tight as a violin string. Something had happened and he wanted to know what. He was rather impressed with himself for not demanding right away what had happened, but demands didn't really work with Christian. Well, not most of the time anyway.

Whatever it was happened during intermission. She'd been fine when she'd left the auditorium, but pale and jumpy, too composed when she'd returned. And she'd used her inhaler.

He fixed them a drink and set them on the coffee table, before striding to his daughter's room.

Good-night kisses and hugs all around. He flicked the light off and led Christian out of the room and to the couch.

Without a word, he sat, and waited.

Her fingers drummed on her thigh.

"Thank you for tonight. I had a great—"

He stopped her words when he put his finger against her lips, turning her to face him. "Tell me."

The shadows of fear slithered in the smoky depths of her eyes.

She opened her mouth, shut it and shrugged. "It was nothing. Nothing."

"Let me be the judge of that." Gently, he caressed her cheek, her jaw, all the while watching her eyes.

"I just—I just thought I saw someone I knew." She shrugged again.

He nodded once. "Did you?"

Her eyes darted down. "I—I don't know. I lost them in the crowd."

He thought about her words, wondering what part of it was a lie, what part was the truth. "Hmmm."

She wouldn't meet his gaze.

He tried a different approach. He leaned forward and kissed her.

"Tell me," he pressed, whispering against her lips.

She grabbed his head between her hands, spearing her fingers along his scalp.

He tried to stay detached, he wanted answers.

The kiss was ravenous, her tongue dueling with his, parries and forays.

Brayden leaned over, laid her back on the couch, tried to remember where they were and that his bedroom was across the way.

Instead, he kept kissing her, letting her have the lead for the time being. Soon they were both panting.

He stood and pulled her to her feet.

Without a word, he led her to his bedroom. They couldn't continue on the couch, Tori might wake up. He shut the door and flipped the lock.

At the bedside he stopped and looked at her. She looked to him then the bed.

Again, she grabbed him close to her, pulled him back with her toward the bed and whispered, "Make love to me, Brayden."

Make me forget . . . make me remember . . . might as well have been shouted.

There was a desperation in her, one he wanted to question. But her hands and tongue left little room in his mind for thought. Most of his blood had already rushed to lower regions anyway.

"Let me get some blankets," he told her, trying to unwind her arms.

She shook her head, tightening her hold on him. "Banish him. I want the bed. I want you. I just want us."

But the darkness shifting in her eyes, her unspoken cry for help, pulled at him as nothing else did. If this is what she wanted, he would give it to her — for now. Because now he knew what she'd lied about. She knew the person she'd seen. There was no doubt in his mind the bastard had been the same place they had, in the same room they had.

Rage warred with the passion rushing through his veins. He'd banish the son of a bitch from their lives if it was the last thing he did.

But for now, Christian needed love, not anger. With his mouth and hands, with his words, he gave her what she needed.

She jerked him down onto the bed, sat astride him. "I want you."

Apparently the buttons were too much to mess with, and she ripped his shirt apart. Brayden reached up and cupped her face, his other hand bunching the material on her waist, the velvet crushing in his fist.

"It's okay," he told her, his voice tight. "I love you."

She paused, her hands on his chest. He felt their tremble. Looking into her eyes, he quickly undressed her, as she undressed him.

Brayden sat, propped against the headboard on a mound of pillows.

She left on her heels and stockings. A fire burned in her eyes as she climbed back on the bed.

Brayden's gut tightened.

She crawled to him, her features set.

"Christian," he said, reaching for her.

She shook her head, her hands running up both his legs. With a cocky gleam, she leaned down and flicked her tongue over the edge of his erection.

All thought and breath stopped.

He could only watch as she circled him with her tongue again, then closed those kissable lips over his shaft.

Brayden closed his eyes, his chest tightening as her mouth loved him and her hands fondled him. When he could take no more, he grabbed her and pulled her up.

Her eyes locked with his, hot silver, and she straddled him— those black heels making her legs seem even longer, the hose whispering against his thighs and hips as she settled on him.

Brayden tried to keep things gentle, but she wasn't letting him. She wanted more, had to have more.

He leaned back, fisted his hands in her hair. "I want to go slowly, easily."

"I want it now, not long and drawn out. Now, Brayden."

What the woman wanted . . .

He kissed her, ravaged her mouth, scraped his teeth down her neck as she tossed her head back.

He ran his hand down the long line of her body, jerked her forward and kissed her breasts until she moaned, spearing his fingers down between them, working her until she shattered so quickly he couldn't stop. With deft, determined strokes, he built her back up again, biting down when she reached between them and slid down on him.

Their lovemaking was fast and furious, as if through intensity they could drive the darkness away. Or shove it away. She rode him hard until he could see nothing but the hot gray of her eyes.

There was no gentle wave to crest. No spring rain. It was like jumping off a damn bluff. And the free fall was wickedly wonderful.

They both broke, panting and sweating.

Her grin made him wonder if perhaps she could outlast him, not that he even had the breath to ask.

She fell forward onto him and he wrapped his arms around her, felt the thundering pound of her heart against his.

When he could move, he reached down and pulled her shoes off, rolled those stockings off and covered them both.

Christian fell asleep minutes later. Brayden held her to him and stared at the ceiling. *Banish him,* she'd begged. Well, she was relaxed and asleep now, so either he did his job or she did it for him. He wasn't certain, and quite frankly didn't really care for the way things just . . . just . . . tore out of his control.

He wanted to know *exactly* what happened tonight. Thought she saw someone . . . Yeah, he'd bet she did.

Wealthy? Probably, as tonight was one of the more expensive performances. And the man enjoyed the arts. As to whether he was young or old, Brayden had no clue. If she'd been running and running, chances were she'd run as far and fast as she could. Oregon. That was his guess.

Slipping quietly from the bed, he went to the living room, booted up his laptop, and sent an email off to Rob Roy.

Chapter 16

The opera poured out of her, straining, straining to hold that last note.

She didn't want to disappoint him. Never disappoint him. It was worse when he was disappointed.

The stage lights glared, bright and hot. Christian could see nothing other than the empty silent stage.

But she could hear voices.

"Josephine . . . Josephine . . ."

She whirled around, the beautiful ice-blue gown swishing around her legs.

"My Angel . . . Come to me. Come, sing. You are mine, you can't sing for anyone else. Mine."

Where was he? She heard Richard, but his voice moved around her, above her as if he never stayed still. It lingered and stretched so that one whisper ran into the next. The scent of those sweet cigars he smoked swirled with the tangy smell of brandy, a heady fragrance that churned her stomach.

Chills skittered up her back.

"Christian?"

Brayden.

She sighed and turned again, but their voices mixed, rose together.

"Help me, Brayden. Please, help me!" she cried.

"You won't let me," he said.

Richard's smooth, throaty laugh danced around her. "Oh what a tangled web we weave . . . She's mine. Mine. Mine."

"Help me, please."

"You have to let go first," Brayden's voice told her just as he stepped up beside her.

Richard appeared on the other side, holding ropes and a gag; a camera hung from his neck, and that look glinted in his eyes. "Mine," he whispered.

Warm tears trailed down her face.

Brayden held a hand out to her. "Take my hand, Christian. Open up and talk to me, and I can help you."

She was looking from one to the other, one to the other.

Brayden's eyes pulled her to him, drew her attention from all else.

"Let it go," he coaxed.

"Mine," Richard's voice whispered behind her.

She didn't turn around, her attention solely focused on Brayden.

"Christian, don't let him win. Take a stand and fight!" Brayden told her.

For a moment, she stood undecided, then reached for Brayden's hand, their fingers inches apart.

"Funerals are pesky things to plan, aren't they, Josephine?" Richard murmured.

Funerals. Oh, God.

She jerked, clasped her hand to her chest.

"Christian?" Brayden asked.

She took a step back.

"I can't. I'm sorry, I love you too much. I can't!" She backed away again, another step then another.

All she saw was the disappointment and hurt in Brayden's eyes.

"I'm sorry," she whispered.

His hand was still outstretched. "Christian, don't!"

One more step behind. An arm snaked around her, and Richard whispered in her ear. "See, you always come back to me. You will always be mine."

A rope pulled tight around her neck, tighter and tighter.

"Nooooooooo!" she screamed, and realized her mistake too late.

Hands held her.

"No, no, no." She fought them off, tried to pull away.

"Christian! Christian! Wake up, damn it!"

Brayden's voice finally filtered through the haze of terror, jerking her back to reality—back to their dimly lit room.

"Brayden?"

"Yeah, baby, it's me."

She threw her arms around him and held on for dear life.

God, it was so real. So real. She still felt the rope around her neck, cutting off her air.

His arms tightened around her, pulling her closer to him. The hair from his chest tickled her chin.

"It's okay. You're okay, you're safe." His voice was warm against her temple. He lay back down and pulled her with him.

She was tucked up against him, her ear directly over his heart. Hers felt as if it would burst from her chest.

"I'm sorry," she said. "I'm sorry."

"For what?"

"I reached for you. I should have just grabbed hold of you and never let go. Too late," she muttered against him, wiping her wet cheek against the muscles of his chest. "I'm sorry."

He propped up on his elbow, and she turned into him. His finger was gentle yet firm beneath her jaw as he turned her to face him.

"Christian, it was a dream. A bad dream," he said, brushing a kiss on her forehead.

She could only shake her head. She remembered it, and though she wasn't one to put stock in dreams, or omens, or whatever, there was no denying the meaning of the nightmare.

A choice loomed before her, no smaller now than it had been moments ago in her dream, no less nerve-racking now than it had been at any time for the last few months or even years, for that matter.

She could see Brayden above her, his black hair, the lighter contrast of his face. It was dark save for the faint predawn light slanting through the shutters, giving the room a dark blue glow.

His stubble scraped against her palm as she cupped his cheek. "When did you know?" she asked.

She felt him pull back a bit.

"Know what?"

"That I wasn't just Tori's nanny, or the Kinncaids' surrogate sister."

"Heard that term, did you?"

He settled back down beside her, but she rolled to her side. Brayden spooned her, his heat surrounding her. She waited, then waited some more.

Finally, he said, "It was one summer afternoon. That summer before everything blew apart in Colorado with Aiden and Jesslyn. Actually, it was only a couple of days before that. Mom and Dad had already flown out there." He draped his arm around her, and pulled her even tighter against him, her head nestled in the crook of his shoulder. "Anyway, Tori was playing in the pool with Abby, that little redheaded girl that used to live down the lane. The sun was glaring off the papers I was looking over, and I looked up and there you were." His voice softened at the end. "You were holding a tray of lemonade and cookies, and you set it by the side of the pool for the girls. You had on a siren-red bikini and some sort of wrap-skirt thing." A chuckle whispered against her ear, blowing against her hair. "And suddenly there you were looking like a woman straight off the pages of some men's magazine."

She pulled her bottom lip between her teeth, and smiled. "I was always there."

"Not like that," he said, his voice deep and gruff.

Feeling daring, she asked, "What would you have done if the girls hadn't been there?"

Again a murmured laugh. "I have no idea. It's a good thing they were. I might have hit on you." Brayden's lips were soft on her cheek, his stubble scraping her face. "Then again, I probably wouldn't have. I was too shocked at my own reaction. Thank God I had those papers."

Christian smiled. "I first saw you, really you, when Tori was four and had pneumonia. Remember?"

He grunted.

"Anyway, I was so worried and scared, and you'd already left for London. That night, her door opened and there you were. Changed your plans and flew back. You sat beside her bed and told me to go get some rest." She would never forget that.

Brayden hummed. She knew he wondered what she was getting to.

Biting the bullet, she went on. "I was so scared of you, of all of you when I first moved there," she whispered.

He tensed behind her, but didn't move.

Her heart pounded in her chest, he had to feel it. It felt like a bird, slamming against glass, demanding to be free. Tears stung the backs of her eyes.

"You weren't scared of Mom," he whispered.

She could only shake her head. On a sigh, she said, "No. Not really. Your mom is too nice." Time for it all to come out. To let it go. "But all the rest of you . . . You were such big men to me." She sort of shrugged. "You are big men."

Big men.

Brayden closed his eyes, his gut tightening at what he suspected. He didn't know what had happened that Christian was suddenly opening up to him, and he was afraid to even move for fear of her

195

shutting down again.

"Do you know, to this day, I still don't know how I got to your house?" she asked, her voice so soft he had to strain to hear her. "I don't remember. And then, when I woke up, there was your mom and dad and I was too scared to say anything."

"I remember," he whispered. He also remembered how he thought his parents were crazy for taking in a runaway when he'd just brought his baby home and had sold his apartment and moved back to the huge family home with them.

They'd known nothing about her. She was just this silent waif of a girl with large terrified eyes. It had been the eyes that had swayed him, that and once when he was down in the gym and thought Tori was asleep. Christian had ventured down to tell him that his baby was crying and she was afraid to pick her up.

From then on things changed, at least with them. After a time, the fear left her eyes, and after more time, she'd finally lost the haunted look and became part of the family.

"I'd learned the hard way what men could do."

Her words slapped him back.

"Though as a child I didn't know. I had a wonderful father. Sometimes Jock reminds me of Papa, and you boys remind me of my older brother."

Brayden wanted to ask her what happened to them, but he didn't. She was so still, so tightly wound, it seemed she might shatter at the least provocation.

"Josh, my brother, and I are about twelve years apart. He's from Papa's first marriage."

Brayden reached around and laced his fingers through hers, wincing at the grip she had on his hand.

"I should have told him, but I was too scared to, too afraid of what could happen, and too ashamed," she whispered.

Silence fell, settling thick and heavy with each passing moment.

Finally, he asked, "Of what?"

A warm drop fell on his bicep that cradled her head, trickling a wet path down his arm. He tried to ignore it.

"I grew up like Tori, in a big house, my grandparents close by. Anything I wanted, I got, private school, all the proper lessons. Then Papa died and everything changed." She stiffened even more in his arms, though he wasn't sure how.

"She remarried," Christian said, bitterness lacing her words.

"Who?"

"M-my mother."

The room was slowly awakening to the light slanting in across the floor, still he didn't move.

"I wanted to stay with my grandparents, but she wouldn't let me. We moved away."

The wetness on his arm felt like a small river, a constant stream, burning a path straight to his gut, his heart, his anger. What the hell had happened?

"Do you like my body?" she asked.

Where the hell did that come from?

Brayden squeezed her hand and kissed her temple. He started to give some blithe remark, hoping to ease her, but decided against it. Instead, he said, "You're beautiful."

She nodded. "He thought so too."

The picture was congealing, but still he asked, hoping his anger was well hidden, "Who?"

Her hold on his hand strengthened until his fingers tingled. She shook her head once, then again. Her breathing was ragged.

Brayden wanted to stop this, to tell her it was okay, but that wouldn't help her. She needed to get this out.

"My—my st—stepfather," she said, in a strangled voice, as though forcing words out.

Her hand trembled in his, then moved up, until she was shaking against him.

Brayden held her tighter.

"I don't know when it started, a touch here, a look there, a hug that I knew lasted too long. He was so careful, so sly, no one even noticed," she said. "Anytime I said anything, how I didn't like him, how he made me uncomfortable, everyone just told me change was inevitable. They all thought I was still upset over Papa dying and her remarrying. No one listened."

How the hell could they not? "Your brother didn't listen? Your mother?" he asked.

She shook her head. "My mother? I won't even go there. All mothers are not like yours. But Josh? Not at first. He might have listened later, but I never told him later. Later was too late." A sob caught and held.

"Shhh. It's okay. He can't hurt you now. No one will," he told her, hugging her tight.

She shook her head. "It's not okay, it's always there. I never told anyone what he did . . ." She trailed off. "Well, I did, but those I did either . . . Never mind, that's not what . . . It doesn't . . . He raped me."

Her words fell between them, dark and ugly in the air. He'd known, some part of him had known what she would say. But the words still ignited the rage within him, slapped and challenged him to do something.

"I just couldn't—couldn't take it anymore, Brayden. I couldn't. It got to the point I either had to leave that house or just die, and I didn't care if I died." A shudder ran through her, through him at her words. "A friend and her mom helped me get away. I don't really remember too much of it because I hurt so bad. He'd beat me the night before. But I do remember her dad, this one cop, he knew what was going on, tried to help before, but couldn't. I remember riding a bus with him, or maybe a train."

Her hand held fast to his, her other arm wrapped around his that held her. Tears from her eyes wet his arm, tearing out his heart as surely as her words were, and there wasn't a damn thing he could do about it but be silent and listen.

He wanted to roar.

"There was this hospital that I woke up in, they performed a rape kit and set my dislocated shoulder. Wrapped my ribs."

Brayden ground his teeth, wanting to hit something.

"I was too afraid to stay there, so I left and kept running and kept running." She sighed, sniffled and rubbed the side of her face on his arm. "One night in Atlanta, I got fired because I tripped and dumped a plate on a customer. These girls told me I could go with them."

Her voice had softened, but she continued and he listened. "I vaguely remember a party. I don't know what I took or why I even took it. First and last time I ever took anything that a doctor hadn't given me. But then, at that point, I was thinking of slitting my wrists, and the pills, I guess, were easier. Took the edge off, took the pain away."

Christ. Brayden couldn't breathe.

"I woke up in another hospital and they were asking me all these questions, wanting to move me to a psych ward. They were trying to find out who I was and I remember being terrified they'd find out. So when the nurse left, I got out of bed. A woman, her name was Elaine, was in the bed next to mine. I'd never stolen anything before then. But I stole sixty dollars out of her wallet. I wrote her address down from her driver's license, because I knew I'd pay her back. I even jotted an I-owe-you note. I was so careful and quiet. I remember she had these bright green eyes. She looked at me and said, 'Honey, take the hundred behind the Visa. I'm not gonna need it, and I figure if it was bad enough to try and kill yourself over, and run out of here, then you could probably use it.'"

Her tears were hot.

"I don't think I believed in good luck until then. Thought all my religious upbringing was just a fluke. I don't remember getting out of the hospital, let alone on a bus. How I got to Seneca or your parents' house, I still don't know. I've tried to remember, but I can't. Two days from when I ran out of the Atlanta hospital until I woke up on your parents' property."

Brayden was numb. Disbelief, incredulousness muted the anger, but it was still boiling. God in Heaven.

He cleared his throat. "Someone was watching over you."

She half sobbed, half laughed. "Your mom always said that. God guided a daughter to them. I never knew if I believed her or not."

Brayden did. He doubted, very seriously, it was as simple as that. Without a doubt, he knew there was more, much more Christian was leaving out.

"I lied," she said.

"About?" He took a deep breath.

"My age."

Brayden frowned. "How old are you? Aren't you twenty-eight?"

Her head shook on his arm. "No, I lied because I was afraid I would get sent back to that house. So I said I was nineteen."

"How old were you?"

"I was seventeen and several months away from being legal. So I lied." She shrugged, or would have if he hadn't held her so tightly. Instead, his hold only allowed her to shift. "Most girls are worried about boyfriends and hairstyles when they're fifteen. I was worried about not making him mad, wishing I could fade into the shadows so he'd leave me alone. The day I left—it was the day after my sixteenth birthday, and he didn't give me a car. Nope, his was a very special gift . . ." Bitterness speared her voice and it cracked on the end.

Sixteen! Not a word came to mind, not a single one. Well, several did, but he wasn't about to say them to her.

Her tears fell faster and harder. Brayden turned her so that he could hold her, rubbing his hands up and down her back while her silent crying tore him apart. Suddenly, she shoved against him.

"I'm going to be sick." She bolted for the bathroom.

Brayden stood, heard her retching. There could be nothing in her stomach, they hadn't even eaten.

Cursing, he hurried to the bathroom, wet a cloth and handed it to her, but she didn't take it, just laid her cheek on her arm. Bending down, he picked her up and carried her back to their bed. Gently, he wiped her face, then went back and returned with a glass of water.

Her eyes were wary when they met his.

Sixteen! God Almighty! And over a year—where? On the streets?

Her hand shook as she tried to get a drink, and he finally took it from her.

He never said a word, couldn't think of any, and what if they were the wrong ones.

Gripping the glass in his hand, he asked her, "Couldn't you tell someone? Your brother? Your mother? An uncle?" Surely there had been someone.

Why the hell hadn't anyone listened to her? If his daughter felt uncomfortable around someone, he'd damn well listen and want to know *why*. If she mentioned it to his brothers or her grandfather, they'd take heed as well. And whoever the bastard was would be headless, handless, and dickless by the end of the day.

She looked away from him and shook her head. "Sometimes things aren't that simple, Brayden. Not every family is like yours."

He sighed. They never were.

Then her words slid into place, fitting into holes he hadn't even realized were in the whole picture.

. . . *a luscious body you still have* . . .

. . . *always there, just like before* . . .

. . . still have . . .

. . . just like before . . .

Son of a bitch!

His fist rested on his knee. As if watching someone else, he uncurled his fingers and reached out, touching Christian's cheek.

"I want a name."

Her eyes flashed, panic racing through them.

He wanted a name?

Of course the man wanted a name. Had she honestly expected otherwise?

She tried to look away, but his fingers held her chin, caressing her jaw.

"You've come this far," he coaxed. "Won't you finish this? We can put it behind us." His voice was soft, his touch gentle, but his eyes . . . His eyes raged and stormed.

Behind us? God, what a joke. Yet, he made it sound that easy, that final, that definite.

And he didn't even know all of it. Her body shook and trembled; the harder she tried to control it, the harder she shook. Curling tightly into a ball, she wrapped her arms around her knees and put her head on them. She felt him shift and move to her.

His body was warm and hard against hers.

"I love you," he said.

The words always squeezed her heart, no matter how many times she heard him say them. Still she wondered how . . . why . . . her?

He laid back, settled them under the covers, stroking her back, her arm.

Finally, the trembles eased, her muscles loosened.

"Not long ago, you asked me why," he said. "I told you I didn't know, but I do."

His heart beat hard and fast.

"I love your strength, your will, your courage." His voice was gruff and low.

Christian leaned up and looked at him.

"I'm not courageous. Half the time I think I'm a cow —"

His palm against her mouth cut her word off, and she watched as his eyes narrowed, the blue burning bright.

"Don't. Do not even think it, let alone say it." The arm around her back tightened. "You are the bravest woman I know. Look at you. At what happened, and look at the life you've made for yourself. How can you not see your own strength?"

He saw that? Christian shrugged.

"Well, if you don't know, then don't argue with me."

Looking into his eyes, it was hard to miss all the implications of that demanding question.

"You aren't going to tell me his name, are you?" he asked, a muscle bunching in his jaw.

She stretched forward and kissed him, undemanding and gentle. "No."

But she wanted to. God, she wanted to.

His face pulled taut and she saw the flush of rage in his cheeks and deep in his eyes, though his voice was deceptively calm. "Why not?"

Why not indeed. If she told him it was Richard Burbanks, congressman newly elected, Brayden would be arrested and sitting in jail for Christmas.

"Because I know you," she said and tried to move away.

He was obviously having none of that, as his arms tightened around her. "What does that mean? If you know me, you know I'm not about to let this go."

No, he wouldn't and she did know that. "I know," she agreed.

"Again, why not tell me the bastard's name then? Save us both time and energy."

This time, she tried to smile. "One, your family would never forgive me if you spent the holidays in jail. Tori has missed you enough." She traced a figure eight on his chest, and hoped her screaming out in the night hadn't awakened the little girl sleeping in the other room of the hotel apartment.

"So?"

As simple as that, so?

Compromise. "Brayden," she said, taking his face in her hands. "I love you, but I'm not telling you his name, not right now. I love you too much for that. This is big for me. What I've told you . . ." And she still couldn't believe she'd told him. "I've honestly never gotten it all out before. I will eventually tell you everything, but not now."

The niggling thought that Richard would retaliate teased her fear.

"I told someone once," she admitted to him, looking down at his chest, away from those all-knowing eyes. "Well, more than one person. Those I asked for help, they're all dead, Brayden. *All* of them." She'd thought she was done crying, but felt the ache in her chest, in her heart and soul as she tried to keep her emotions in check. "I couldn't bear to lose you because of me. I'd simply die."

And Tori . . . She knew what that bastard would do to such a lovely little girl and she would not share that fear with Brayden either. She knew he didn't understand, few would, but she had to have everything ready . . .

Her eyes rose to his, where anger and frustration warred in their depths, but she could, no would, do nothing to alleviate his emotions either.

She whispered, "I can't believe I told you all this."

His stare was unnerving. She could feel the rage pulsing through his tight, coiled body. The stare held and stretched, daring the silence to continue.

"What?" she finally asked.

"Are you ever going to tell me everything?" he asked, reaching up and tucking a hair behind her ear.

Would she? Yes. She nodded.

One black brow winged up at that. "Really? I don't suppose it's going to be later today or even tomorrow?"

There was enough sarcasm in his words that she grinned. That hard, caustic voice usually got him what he wanted, when he wanted it. She'd seen it happen too many times to believe otherwise.

"You don't scare me," she told him, tapping his chest.

His eyes narrowed, but she caught the tilt of one corner of his mouth. "I don't?"

"No." Christian flopped back down on her pillow and looked at the carved plaster ceiling.

Brayden's grunt calmed her raw nerves as he pulled her back against him. "I'm glad, I'd be really pissed if it were otherwise."

Christian rolled her eyes. "And you're not now?"

"Did I say I wasn't?" There was a fine edge to his voice.

"No."

"All right then." He kissed her temple. "I'll wait you out, if nothing else you're teaching me patience."

Christian couldn't help but snort.

"Yeah," he said, "that's how I thought you'd feel. Well, good, then I won't lie. I'll find out the son of a bitch's name with or without you. But I will find it out." He squeezed her tight. "Now get some sleep."

Sleep? Her heart pounded in her chest. What exactly had she told him? Christian tried to replay it word for word in her mind, but couldn't be sure of anything. Damn it.

Brayden would do exactly as he said, there was no doubt in her mind. She would just have to end it first.

Please let her end it first. There was no way she could live without the man beside her. Simply no way.

Chapter 17

Christmas was always a big event at the Kinncaid home. The air smelled of cinnamon, baked pies and cakes, and entirely too many other things to put a single finger on. A heady, distinctly holiday perfume that lulled and contented the family as surely as the companionship or the sight of the twelve-foot decorated tree in the living room.

The day began early. Christian hadn't been able to sleep last night. Most likely because Brayden had stayed most of the night in his room and she in hers. Tori was known to run into both their rooms to wake them up. She might want them to be married and a real family, but until they were, both she and Brayden agreed they didn't want her stumbling onto them in the same bed. The hotel the other night had just sort of happened.

Since Brayden hadn't been there to hold on to, her mind wandered and planned and worried all night. Christmas. Nine years ago a house in Oregon had exploded because the people inside had dared to help her. She'd shoved that thought away and remembered happier times from her childhood, but that too reminded her of the fact her father was dead. And behind it all was Richard.

Richard.

Richard.

Damn the man. He was *not* going to ruin her holiday.

Christian looked over to where Brayden sat on the floor by the fireplace laughing with Aiden. The jacket she'd bought for him fit perfectly.

Brayden gave her entirely too many gifts, her favorite the charm bracelet with a champagne flute charm. New beginnings.

Jesslyn, Aiden's wife, sat beside her, a baby on her shoulder. The couple had been blessed with twins, both dark-headed and blue-eyed like their father. If the attention the boys already garnered was any indication, they would be too handsome for a mother to sleep well at night. Jock Kinncaid held the other one on his massive shoulder.

"I see you two have finally come to some sort of understanding," Jesslyn whispered while she gently rocked baby Ian.

At least Christian thought this one was Ian; it might be Alec. She had trouble telling them apart.

"Here," Jesslyn said, passing the baby to her. "You hold Ian for a bit. You might as well get used to it."

Christian took the baby. "What's that supposed to mean?"

Little Ian gave her a gummy grin.

"Oh, please. I bet you two are married before . . ." Jesslyn thrummed her fingers on her thigh. "Valentine's Day. Yeah, that's what? Two months away?"

"More like six weeks," she answered.

Jesslyn's one-sided grin and cocked brow said it before her words. "So you two *are* actually planning on getting married? I notice there was no denial in all that."

A smile pulled at the edge of Christian's mouth as she bounced the baby on her knee. For a moment she thought about what Jesslyn said. Finally, she shrugged. Who knew? First, she had to put all the rest of this behind her.

"All this darkness in your life will pass, you know," Jesslyn said softly.

Christian didn't look away from the baby, only nodded. One day it would all be over. Hopefully very, very soon.

"Besides, Tori told Ryan she wants a baby sister. She's tired of being the only girl."

A fist squeezed her heart. A baby girl. That would be . . . wonderful. Turning, she smiled at her friend, and realized with a sudden jerk that Jesslyn was the first female friend she'd had since Susan. Reaching out, she covered Jesslyn's hand with her own. "Thank you."

"For?"

"For being my friend. I haven't had many, so thanks."

Jesslyn smiled, her dark eyes narrowing. "Well, that makes two of us. I'm not the friendliest person around."

"You can say that again," Aiden said, coming up behind his wife.

Jesslyn rolled her eyes. "Was I talking to you?"

Christian smiled as Brayden sat at her feet, tickling little Ian's chin until the baby gave a deep belly laugh.

Her eyes met Brayden's and something shot between them, heavy and strong, a tug of longing. Brayden's eyes crinkled at their edges as he gave her a small grin. Voices shouted and laughed as more people came into the room.

"I don't want a baby brother," Tori said as she sat in front of the mammoth tree.

Brayden's bark of laughter echoed with everyone else's.

"First they have to get married, Tori Bori," Ryan, her cousin, informed her.

"I know, I know. I keep after them." Her small shoulders lifted on a shrug. "But what do I know?"

Kaitlyn Kinncaid clapped her hands. "How about we open presents?"

The kids shouted their agreements and the gifts were quickly passed around to their recipients. Christmas music played softly on hidden speakers.

Laughter rang in the air, mixing with the rip of paper, the toss of a joke, the shout of a thank-you. Christian absorbed it all, as thankful for this family this year as she was the first Christmas she'd ever shared with them. With the Kinncaids, peace reigned.

"Incoming . . ." Gavin threw a small package in their direction, which Brayden caught easily.

Well, theirs was a different kind of peace.

* * * *

Richard glanced at his wife reading on the couch. The diamond bracelet he'd given her winked in the sunlight. Fire crackled in the hearth, and the Christmas symphonies she liked to listen to softly played on the stereo.

The heavily decorated Christmas tree was almost gaudy, but he didn't say anything. Gold blinked and shimmered on the boughs of the branches. Looked as if Midas himself had reached out and touched the damn thing.

Shrugging, he turned and gazed across the lawns. The French doors were closed, but the sunlight shot off the snow and poured into the room.

His tracks leading into the trees were clearly visible, but then, they always were. It was, after all, a habit for him to walk or jog in the mornings or evenings. Everyone was used to seeing him take that direction and he wanted them to be.

He smiled.

And what he'd seen this morning, hours before dawn . . . The Kinncaids had an impressive home. Larger, by far, than this one, and at least a century older.

Richard, however, was only interested in the layout, which his newest golfing buddy was only too happy to show him.

Jock Kinncaid was a big man, if a bit lacking in intelligence. He'd become complacent in his old age. Mr. Kinncaid was, after all, only a few years older than Richard himself, but one couldn't tell it. Jock wasn't as healthy as he should be. Richard thought it imperative to keep in shape. Perfection must always be maintained.

The truly sad thing, Jock used to be a killer in business. Someone Richard could have admired once. Now the Kinncaid sons seemed to have that go-for-the-jugular instincts. The old man gave others control of what had once been his.

Richard would never be that stupid. God, the damage that could be wrought. He shook his head, his gaze drawn back to the tracks in the snow. Tracks that led through the woods and straight to the Kinncaid home.

There was—as far as he'd been able to tell—no alarm system. Foolish that, probably the old man's idea of too much hassle.

Around four this morning, Richard had stood in the shadow of the large home and waited, counted the windows down to the room he'd known was hers. His host had given him the grand tour a few weeks ago. Since then, he'd even eaten over at the Kinncaid home several times.

And because of that "friendship," he knew exactly which room was Josephine's. The thought of her not in her room, but in Brayden Kinncaid's, had him raging. That was when he'd noticed the lights come on in the indoor pool. The blue haze bounced and shifted through the glass of the solarium.

He stood in the shadows, shifting so he could see through all the interior trees and plants circling the indoor pool. Finally he'd found a place so that he had a clear view. It was in the corner where the solarium met the house. Bushes grew heavily against the glass, hiding him from anyone outside as well as from her inside.

She'd cut through the water with the grace and ease he'd remembered of her. Sleek and wet, her body had called to him. The siren's perfection sang out to his blood. The thought of going in, waiting and watching while she swam, of turning the lights off, of getting in the pool with her had taunted him.

But that would be stupid, stupid indeed.

He'd watched as lap after lap she'd swam. His groin tightened when she'd climbed out of the pool, water sluicing down her centerfold body.

A body that someone else had touched.

A body she *let* someone else touch.

". . . but I don't know. What do you think?" Estella's voice pulled him back to the present.

"What do you want to do?" he asked ambiguously, turning back at her.

"Well, they seem like nice people."

He had no idea whom she was talking about.

Richard wondered if the Kinncaids had gotten his package yet. Special presents he'd left the last time he'd gone to visit with Jock.

Jovial Jock.

"But they're not really in our circle. Though I like Kaitlyn, she seemed nice enough at the country club party. She did invite us to their New Year's party." Her sigh grated on his nerves. "I suppose it would be rude of us not to go, wouldn't it?"

Sometimes his wife could be rather trying. Clearing his throat, he only said, "I rather like the Kinncaids. We're going to their party."

With that, he stood and strode from the room, his heels clicking on the hardwood floors.

He wished he could have been at the Kinncaid home when they opened their gifts.

Richard smiled, chuckling to himself as he walked to his study.

* * * *

Brayden hugged his mother.

"The vase is just beautiful, darling. Thank you both so much," she said.

"You're welcome, Mom."

Seemed everyone like their glass gifts from Murano.

Brayden leaned against the sofa Christian sat on. He draped his

209

arm over her knee, incredibly conscious of where his elbow rested high up on the inside of her thigh.

Christian shifted.

He leaned his head back and grinned at her; she narrowed her gaze at him.

"Miss me?" he asked.

She snorted and reached for another package.

"Christian, I see you didn't get a certain Christmas gift you *should* have," his father pointed out, then turned a glare on him. "You don't know where a jewelry store is?"

Several chuckled. Brayden did not.

"You know," Jock continued, "I think this is your fault, Kaitie lass."

Kaitlyn Kinncaid arched one perfect brow. "Care to share that brilliance with us, dear?"

"Well, it's your curse."

She sniffed lightly. "I recall the epithets were actually hurled at you."

What?

None of them asked, as they were used to their parents' vague jabs, but their faces were all a collective look of question.

Jock Kinncaid waved a hand as he explained. "Well, whichever, she was *your* grandmother. The old bitty." He shook his head. "You see, your mother lived in America with her parents until she was fifteen."

They knew all this. Before her sixteenth year, their grandparents had been killed in an auto accident. Then their mother had moved back to Ireland, where she lived with her paternal grandmother, whom they all referred to as Grammy.

"Dad, we know this," Aiden said.

"No, you don't. You and Jesslyn battled a serial killer, Gavin and Taylor that . . ." He looked at the kids. "Witch of a woman. And now Brayden and Christian—this monster. It's the curse."

Jock Kinncaid was a practical man, believing in what he could see for the most part, but old family legends were the exception for him. However, this was one Brayden had never heard of before, and from the looks of his brothers, neither had they.

"A curse?" Brayden asked.

"Well, your mother's other grandmother was a bitter woman. She never liked the man her daughter married, and liked even less that he moved her baby girl off to America. She was upset after the accident when your mom decided to live with Grammy instead of with her. And she liked me even less than her late son-in-law." He shrugged his massive shoulders. "So, a few days before your mother and I married, she said we'd be cursed. Our road would be hard and our children would fight to find peace and happiness with their own marriages."

Brayden had never heard this before. His mother walked over and sat by her husband.

"She was just unhappy. Surely you've never put stock in her words," his mother said.

Jock only humphed.

"A curse?" Quinlan asked.

"Well, that explains it," Aiden said, chuckling.

"Hell, better than thinking it was something *we* did," Gavin agreed.

"And how come we're just now hearing about this?" Brayden asked.

Both his parents shrugged.

"Well, at least I'm saved," Quinlan remarked. "Either I won't marry at all, and save myself the trouble, or I'll just find a mail-order bride."

"I don't think those are still around," Brayden told his brother.

Quinlan shrugged. "Well, good, I'm off the hook."

Christian said, "You, brother dear, are going to be brought to your knees by some slip of a woman who's going to turn your world upside down."

"God forbid," Quinlan muttered, opening another gift.

Brayden patted Christian's thigh, trailing his finger from one side of her knee to the other before leaning up to see what Tori wanted to show him.

"Look. Isn't it cool, Daddy?"

The grow-sugar-crystals kit was every parents' dream. Educational, yes, and bound to reward the kids with plenty of sugar.

"It is that."

"Ryan gave it to me."

"Did he now?"

"Yes, and I got sheet music and a pennywhistle from Grams and Pops and this makeup kit from Aunt Taylor and Uncle Gavin."

"Makeup?" he asked, turning to glare at his brother. Makeup? Over his dead body.

Gavin in turn glared at his wife and said to Brayden, "I didn't get Tori any makeup."

Taylor shrugged off her husband's glare. "Every girl needs makeup, even if it's only to play."

Jesslyn laughed, while all the men grumbled about daughters and makeup.

Makeup?

Tori had migrated over to her grandmother, showing her the trove of lip gloss and shadows and . . . God only knows what else.

He turned to see what Christian thought of it all, but she wasn't paying attention.

Pale and silent, she stared at an angel she held in her hand.

"Oh! How . . . interesting." Jesslyn said, reaching over to run a finger down the little figurine. "Who gave you this?"

One of the wings fell off. As it toppled in Christian's palm, the other wing leaned to the side.

Christian did nothing but stare at it.

Brayden crouched in front of her.

"Christian?"

Her chest rose on a deep breath, and she dropped it down in the box it came in.

He noticed the cracks in it then, and the fact it was missing its eyes. Miniature black holes marred the face where eyes should have been.

An angel.

His angel.

"Son of a bitch!"

"Brayden Gallagher Kinncaid!" his mother said; only then did he realize he'd cursed out loud.

He tried to take the box from Christian, but she gripped the edges and wouldn't let it go.

"What is going on over there? There are plenty of presents. You have years to argue over things. I hardly think a gift needs to be one of them," his father said, a mixture of befuddlement and amusement.

Brayden didn't care. He saw her haunted eyes, the anger and determination burning in them.

But no fear.

No fear.

That alone had him letting go.

"Bray?" someone asked.

She shook her head, leaned close and said, "Please, please don't spoil it for them. It's not important."

He kissed her forehead and sat down beside her, crowding both her and Jesslyn in between him and Aiden. "The hell it's not," he told her. But she was right. Not now. Looking to his mother, he only said, "Sorry, Mom. I forgot something."

A single russet brow rose in a look he knew all too well. "Your manners?"

"Can I see it now?" he asked Christian, his arm going around her shoulders.

"Why?"

He looked straight at her. "Don't push me."

A sigh huffed out. "Here then." The small box jostled as she shoved it at him.

Carefully, he picked through the pieces, not really touching them as much as moving them around with a shake of his wrist.

Jesslyn struck up a conversation about what they were going to do after all these presents were opened. The kids each had several ideas. He tuned it all out. Christian opened another gift.

"Let me see it," Aiden said over the women, both of whom shook their heads.

Brayden passed the morbidly offensive and broken figurine over.

What did it mean? The man had always referred to Christian as his angel. At least that was what all the cards had written on them. He'd even seen a photo of the painting the man had sent her. So what? The man wanted to break her wings? And what was with the damn eyes? Or, for the simple fact that the whole thing was shattered.

Did he now see her as fractured, broken?

Fallen angel?

And if the man saw her as fallen?

Brayden pulled her tighter against him, a cold settling down his spine while the sunlight warmed across the room.

"Open another one and forget about it for right now. We'll talk about it later," she said absently.

Damn right they'd discuss it all later. He looked around to see if any of his brothers had noticed what was going on, other than Aiden. Quinlan's brow quirked in question. Brayden only shook his head.

Gavin was talking to both Ryan and Taylor, keeping Tori busy by asking them all questions. The quick glance said he knew something was up, but he was deflecting the attention.

The next present Christian opened was from Quinlan and it was a music box. Brayden quickly looked over her cards, noting whom the gifts were from.

Sighing, he leaned back and grabbed one of his own. Out of habit, he tucked the card in the gift and reached for another one, mumbling a thank-you to his twin.

How had the bastard gotten the gift in here in the first damn place? Maybe it was delivered. The Kinncaids had friends far and wide, the front door saw many a delivery man around the holidays. He watched as Aiden placed the lid back on the box with the angel before handing it back to him. Brayden put it on the side table by the lamp.

Christian seemed fine, if somewhat angry. Upset, yes. But more annoyed. She wasn't reaching for her inhaler, crying, or trembling.

Her smoky eyes looked up to him. "What?" she asked.

Leaning close, he gently kissed her. "I'm so damn proud of you."

"I thought you were mad at me." Her brows furrowed.

"A little."

Her smile was brilliant and sucker-punched him right in the gut.

Brayden picked up another gift. There was no card. It was about a foot long and a foot wide. Shaking it told him nothing. It wasn't really heavy either. Huh.

Carefully, he slid his finger under the gold and red diamonded paper. The big red bow slid to the floor.

Inside was a box.

Unease slithered around him.

Someone laughed.

"Daddy! Look, Grams and Pops got Ryan a pennywhistle too!"

His daughter's exuberant voice turned his head.

Hoping no one noticed his unease, he said, "Now we can hear whatever duet you two come up with next."

"Grams, can we look through your Irish music? We've already opened our gifts," Ryan asked.

"Yes, I suppose if you just can't wait another moment."

The two youngsters ran out of the room in a whirl of chatter and laughter.

Brayden lifted one flap, then another. Inside was packing and tissue paper.

"Look, Brayden." Christian nudged him. Inside her music box was a locket and inside was a miniature family picture of all the Kinncaids, and the other was a family picture of him, her, and Tori. "See, Quinlan even had it engraved. 'Sis.'"

Her eyes lighted and twinkled. She looked down. "What do you have?"

"I have no idea." He shoved the packaging out of the way and lifted the tissue paper. A frame?

He tossed the bubbled covering aside and looked in.

The roar that filled his head stopped his heart.

Mother of God!

His gaze narrowed to the gold-framed picture in the box. In harsh black-and-white detail, Christian lay naked, blindfolded, gagged, and spread-eagled on a bed. Across the glass: *Mine.*

He couldn't touch it. No way in hell. The urge to rip it, to shatter it, to destroy it clawed through him.

"Don't," Christian whispered in his ear, her breath jerky. "Don't. He—he—he wants to up—upset you."

Upset? Blinking, the world fell back into focus. He turned to her. She was as white as the snow outside, and he noticed her breathing was ragged. "Upset? No. No, I'm not fucking upset. I'm *way* beyond that."

With a muttered curse he stood, but the box slipped from his hand and tumbled to the floor. Careful that no one saw what was inside, he picked it up and realized there was more.

Another brown packet. He cursed.

Brayden Kinncaid was neatly printed on the front.

Looking around, he noticed everyone was watching him, but at least the kids were out of here.

"I dearly hope you have a good reason for talking that way," his mother said.

Brayden ignored her. There on his haunches, he put the photo back in the box and shut the lid, keeping the envelope under his arm.

"What's got you so riled?" his father asked.

Brayden looked up and no words came to mind. Not a single damn one.

"What's that under your arm?" His father's shrewd blue eyes narrowed on the brown envelope, now drawing the attention of all.

"Give it to me," Christian said from behind him.

Standing, he ignored her, walked to the window, and ripped the packet open.

Eight-by-tens slid easily into his awaiting palm. Deftly, he flipped through them. More of the same. Christian tied and helpless, some just of her face, pulled tight in fear. One of no more than her blindfold and bridge of her nose. All of them made him sick. On each and every one was the word *Mine*. Knowing what had happened to her, hearing her tell it, seeing her bruised and fearful face had been bad enough. But this—this slapped him in the face with her terror and the reality of what she'd gone through.

Bastard!

He bit down until pain shot up his jaw, and still rage roared through him.

Without a word, he shoved the photos back into the envelope. His hands were shaking.

He turned and stared at Christian. By God, she was going to tell him the man's name.

Brayden's eyes launched flaming arrows at her. She'd bent down and picked up the box and looked inside while he flipped through the photos by the window.

Immediately her chest seized, her heart slammed, but then she closed her eyes and breathed deep.

It was only a photograph. She wanted the power and this game was all about power.

He couldn't hurt her anymore. He couldn't hurt her anymore. Neither could his gifts or bad memories.

She wouldn't let him. Period.

If she wanted the power, she had to act like it. Otherwise she would always be his victim. Always be his.

But it was hard.

She opened her eyes and met Brayden's angry glare.

He didn't say a single word, but he didn't have to. He might as well have just roared, *"Who?"*

Chapter 18

A knife could have cut the silence of the living room.

"Are those more photos of Christian?" Jock asked.

Brayden didn't say a word, nor did a single flicker cross his eyes.

"This is just what he wants," she told him, trying to ease the tightness in her chest. That framed photo was bad enough, brought it all back. But it was in the past. Behind her.

Still Brayden didn't move, barely blinked. She'd never seen him this angry. She knew he wasn't mad at her, but Brayden's anger had been known to spill on those around him. And maybe he was a bit pissed at her.

"As you told me, you're letting him win."

That got him moving. He hurled the photos away and strode to her, ripping the box from her hands.

"Letting him win?" he yelled. "Good God, woman! I'm not the one still protecting him!"

That's what he thought?

"Brayden, calm down," Quinlan said.

"I agree," Jock said. "There's no cause to act this way or yell at her."

Brayden whirled on his father. "She knows the son of a bitch, Dad. She knows the bastard, but God forbid she tell me his name."

All eyes turned to her. Christian raised her head and looked straight at Brayden, who was so angry, so enraged for her and at her.

"Why do you want to know?" she asked.

Both eyebrows rose on that one. "Excuse me?"

"I asked," she said, standing her ground, "why you want to know."

"You need to even ask?" His voice was hard and low.

She shook her head. "That's why."

"You know the man who did this?" Jock asked.

"Why didn't you say something?" Kaitlyn butted in.

Christian closed her eyes and counted to ten. Finally, drawing a deep breath, she looked straight at Brayden.

"Yes, I know this man. Yes, I know his name and no, I won't tell you. Any of you." She glanced around the room, noting the shocked faces.

"I. Want. His. Name," Brayden said, spacing each word.

For a long moment, she stared at him. Finally, she said, "And you'll get it."

"Now."

"No."

"Now!"

"I said no!" She walked to him, jabbing him in the chest with her finger. "You're pissed? Fine. You're angry? Fine! Do you like these pictures, Brayden? Do you like what you see here?"

She didn't expect an answer and she didn't get one.

His eyes burned dark and blue, a witch's raging caldron. Still, she didn't back down. This was too damned important.

"You want a name because of what you see, what he did, what I told you. But your anger is nothing, *nothing* compared to mine." She should probably stop before she said something she might regret, but she couldn't stop the flow of words. "You think I'm protecting him? Well, you're wrong. You *were* right. I protected him for too long, lost in my own fear, from threats and dark memories. But no more! No more!"

Christian stalked past him to the French doors. The glistening snow offered no advice. "My fury could swallow yours. I've hated this man for far too long to let you or anyone else take this away from me." She turned and stared back at him.

"You're not taking him on," Brayden said. "This." He held up the box with the frame. "Was sent to me. Me. Not you. He's angry at me."

That he was, and Christian wasn't about to let Richard turn on Brayden or any of the rest of them.

"I'm not hiding behind you," he bit out. "And if you believe anyone else in this house is, you don't know us nearly as well as you think."

Silence stretched and stretched some more. Kaitlyn was the one that broke it. "Why didn't you ever say something? We would have helped you."

They would have. Or they would have started to. No. Hell. Even as well as Christian knew the Kinncaids, she also knew how persuasive Richard could be. Doubt whispered mockingly at her. She only shook her head.

"No?" Kaitlyn asked. "No, what? You didn't want our help? I'm trying to understand."

Christian sighed and looked at the older couple she thought of as her own parents. "It'll all be over soon, it doesn't matter."

Both their faces hardened. "Do not insult us like this," Kaitlyn said. "You are just as much one of our children as any of the boys. And if one of them is in trouble or hurt . . ." She trailed off as her voice cracked.

Christian didn't know what to do to make it better. She couldn't tell them, not yet. It was too close to being completed, if she could just get the damn documents in the mail. But she was hurting them and she didn't like that or the fact they saw it as an insult.

"If any of our kids are in trouble," Jock picked up, "we damn well know about it and what the hell to do about it. We no more let them stand between us and trouble than we will let you."

"You don't understand," she tried.

"Because you won't explain," Brayden said.

"No, I won't."

"Why? We don't need protecting!"

She couldn't hold in the harsh chuckle. "No, you think you're invincible. He thinks so too, but he doesn't like to be crossed. The only advantage I have right now is that he still thinks I'm too terrified to do anything. But if he didn't . . ." She only shook her head. "If I told you, you'd go off half-cocked. He'd be out before you knew what happened suing this family for slander, if he was in the mood. Or maybe he'd be sympathetic and play the oh-those-poor-deceived-people card and show you the evidence of how very unbalanced I am." At Brayden's raised brow she continued. "What? You don't think I'm delusional, Brayden? Don't think I'm a liar? Well, that can be disproved right off, can't it?" She counted off on her fingers. "There's my age, my name, my omission of the truth. He'd produce file after file, document after document over how unstable I was as a teen, of the lie I've clearly led up until now, clearly deceiving you good people. His own pocketed psychiatrist would vow before a court he'd seen me twice a week for hour-and-a-half sessions and would vouch for how unstable I am."

She ground to a halt. No, she was not going there.

"And did you?" he asked.

"What? See the illustrious doctor? No. I never saw him."

"Then what did you do during that time? Where were you?"

Even as he asked the question she saw something flicker in his eyes. She should have known he wouldn't let it go. Damn it!

"Where was I? What was I doing? Use your imagination, Brayden." She bent down and picked up the packet of photos. "And if that fails, flip through these, they'll give you a good enough idea." She tossed the envelope on the couch. "Why did I never say anything? Why? I have to have every shred of proof I can. He's not getting away this time, because if he did . . ."

God, the repercussions . . .

"Do you honest to God think I never asked for help?" She shook her head. "People were bought off. Or worse. He *killed* those that helped me. You don't understand him, the lengths he'll go to. He'd do the same again because this time he has so much more to lose. Maybe you'd turn on the coffeepot one morning, only to have the shop burst into flames. Or perhaps Jesslyn would flip a light switch in the nursery and the house would go up." At his look of disbelief, she said, "He's done it before. I tell, someone dies. Or in one case, an entire family, who not only dared to believe me, who wouldn't take his money, but helped me escape. All of them, parents, grandparents, children, Christmas morning. Ka-boom. And before you think you're better equipped, that man was a cop, a decorated veteran cop. Or maybe your parents would get in the jet to fly somewhere, only to have it explode. He told me he was rather partial to fires, very cleansing, he said.

"Then there's Jock, who likes to play golf. What's a new friend? One that might have a heart problem too and wants to know what meds Jock takes, compare notes, gripe about age, that sort of thing. Maybe he'd slip your dad something that would prove fatal, switch out his nitro with a sugar pill. Or Quinlan could get shot in a mugging gone bad. Though he tries not to repeat the same crime, so maybe he'd just have Quinlan run off the road. Oh, no, wait, he did that too. Hell, maybe this time he'll just have someone take your mom out with a rifle shot while she's out walking. Are you getting the picture now? Am I protecting you? You're damn right I am."

She looked around at all the questioning, confused and angry faces. "You're my family." Tears clogged her throat and she looked back at Brayden. "My family. He made it impossible for me to have anything to do with the relatives I have left. I survived what he did once. Not the beatings or the rape, but to those I cared about, those I loved. I couldn't do it again."

A muscle jumped in his jaw. He wasn't listening. Christian threw up her hands.

"How can you not understand I have to have this? That I *need* to see him stripped of his life, of how everyone sees him after everything I've told you?"

Brayden's eyes stormed, and she could see he was grinding his teeth. He shook his head, raised his hands and dropped them. "I can't let you do this alone."

Christian shrugged. "Well, it's not really your choice, Brayden."

He took a deep breath, probably trying to calm down, but his bunched fists told her it didn't help.

"That makes you mad. I'm sorry for that. But I can't let you take this away. I've waited too long, come too damn far. He's going down. And I'm going to be the one that jerked his perfect little rug out from under him. You don't like that, I understand. But he started this twisted game long ago in his sick mind. I'm going to be the one that finishes it. He created this storm of rage in me, and by God, that bastard is going to reap what he sowed."

With that, she turned and walked out of the room, Brayden's mumbled curse mixing with someone else's the only sound she heard over the pounding of her own heart.

* * * *

Later that week, Christian sat outside the police station.

The Kinncaids were barely speaking to her, and she couldn't really blame them. She'd gone to see her doctor earlier that day for a follow-up. Everything thankfully was fine, other than she needed to work on her stress.

Stress? Yeah, she was rather familiar with that emotion.

She flipped the visor down and checked her appearance. Satisfied, she got out and hurried inside.

For some reason the police station made her nervous, but she figured it probably had that effect on everyone. People shouted and laughed. Some cursed. Printers whirred and phones rang, papers shuffled, and people jostled.

Chaos, plain and simple in her opinion.

"Lieutenant Morris, please?" she asked the desk sergeant, who told her where to find Gabe. Checking her watch again, she took the stairs as fast as traffic would allow.

Once in his area, she spotted him. Gabe sat at a desk with his feet propped on the corner. His partner, Emma Laurence, said something to him that pulled at the corners of his mouth.

He looked up and saw her.

If she wasn't head over heels in love with one Brayden Kinncaid, she could easily fall for this guy.

Gabe waved her over. Taking a deep breath, she figured it was now or never.

"I'm glad you made it back here to the good ol' U.S. of A." His gaze ran over her. "How are you doing?"

She sat in the chair he motioned to, set beside his desk. "I'm better, much better. Thanks. Hello, Ms. Laurence. I'm sorry, but I forget your rank."

"It's lieutenant, but call me Emma."

Christian shook the woman's hand and turned back to Gabe.

Dark eyes assessed her, and she could read nothing in them. "You're not moving back to the condo, are you?"

The condo . . .

She could only shake her head.

He gave a nod. "Didn't figure you would want to, let alone that those bodyguards you have would let you."

"Bodyguards?"

"Is there another name for those Kinncaid males?" One brow cocked.

She smiled and laughed. "Bodyguards, they'll get a kick out of that."

He only grunted.

Clearing her throat, she tried to think of what to say.

"So, what brings you to us without one of them hovering?"

With a shrug, she answered, "Probably because they don't know I'm here."

She hated that supercilious lift of his brow. "Still keeping secrets, Miss Bills?"

"I have to, Lieutenant."

He shook his head. "So?"

Christian took a deep breath. "Have you gotten the DNA results back from the attack yet?"

"As a matter of fact, we did."

Her heart slammed in her chest, and without realizing it, she latched on to his arm. "You did?"

Gabe looked from her to her hand on his arm, then back at her.

Christian snatched her hand back and put it in her lap.

"Yes, we did. Strange thing, once in the database, it matched up to the offender in two other unsolved rape cases, one filed in California on an Oregon case, and the other in Arizona. Both minor Jane Does, no names given. Which is not all that uncommon . . ."

His words faded.

They matched. They matched! Even he hadn't been able to change that with bribes or terror tactics. Christian was still waiting on notarized documents from the lab in Arizona and San Francisco. But apparently the doctor, or the lab, whichever, filed one case, and a forgotten cop, the other. Thank you, God.

They matched.

". . . With the time difference, we're checking dates with prison incarcerations and releases. Cross-referencing and waiting."

Christian nodded.

"Do you know anything about this?" he asked.

"How long does the cross-referencing take?" she asked instead. "You will find him, right?"

"Do you think I'm going to drop this?" he asked, clearly insulted.

What was it with her and stubborn men?

"No, that's not what I meant. I just mean, I'll feel . . . I don't . . . Once I know he's behind bars, maybe I can sleep safely," she told him. Which was, essentially, the truth.

A moment passed, then another. Gabe shoved some papers aside and leaned up onto his elbows. "You're safe now. Though I don't like the fact you're out alone."

"Well, I'm sure no one else would like it either," she said. "I needed to come see you without going through an inquisition."

And she would undoubtedly pay hell for it. Brayden was at the shop, where she had supposedly been for hours, at least as far as Kaitlyn was concerned. He, however, thought she was out at Seneca and would ride in with Kaitlyn and Tori later. Another small white lie, as they didn't intend to come to town. Today was golf day for Kaitlyn and Jock; how she'd forgotten that fact, and Brayden hadn't picked up on it, was beyond her. 'Course, she hadn't *exactly* lied to Kaitlyn, she'd just needed to meet Gabe before going to the shop. Which, technically, was the truth. First off, she hadn't wanted anyone with her at the doctor's office. And she was glad now she'd stuck with that idea. Second, she didn't want anyone with her when she came here. But, Brayden would likely not have understood.

"Anyway," she continued, "I needed some time."

"For?"

She looked at him. "Stuff."

"Are you always this helpful?" he asked with a grin.

"Hmmm."

She needed to think. She hadn't come in today to spill all to Gabe. When she told him everything, it would be hard enough. She knew the evidence Richard would produce against her and she didn't want to seem flighty, confused, or scattered.

"Can you find a man?" she asked.

"The man who attacked you?"

She shook her head. "No, but this man knows all his moves, all his plans, or most of them." Deciding to chance it, she said, "I need you to find an Ivan Ristovolich."

In long easy strokes, she wrote his name out. Then she took a photo out of her purse that she'd ripped out of a newsmagazine. The original copy was a photo of Richard waving to fooled constituents and Ivan was standing beside him. She'd cut Richard off and copied the picture of Ivan.

"Here's a photo of him."

He took the paper and the photo and passed them to his partner. "This isn't your attacker?"

Christian shook her head. "No, but if you can crack him, you'll have your guy."

"Why the middle man? Why not just tell me the bastard's name?"

She stood and thought about how to phrase it. Finally she

shrugged. "You won't get that man," she said, pointing to the file on his desk with her name printed neatly on it, "unless you get Ivan. Trust me, I know. The bastard's gotten away with it"—she looked pointedly at the report about the Jane Does—"twice before, and without Ivan, he probably could weasel his way out again."

"What the hell does that mean?" Gabe asked, standing, anger tightening his rugged features.

She shook her head, leaned over and kissed his cheek. "I never thanked you, did I?"

That caught him off guard. "That doesn't matter," he said with a wave.

"Yes, it does. So, thank you." She pointed to the paper. "I promise, soon. I'll answer all your questions soon. I just have to find the courage somewhere."

"Is it going to be anytime soon?"

She couldn't help but grin. "You and Brayden are so much alike sometimes."

"Why the wait?"

"Because I need some time to think." She smiled at him.

"I could arrest you for obstruction of justice." His glare could melt steel.

"But you don't want to have to explain that to my bodyguards, do you?" She turned and walked out of the police station. Though Brayden was currently so mad at her that he might just help Gabe snap the cuffs on.

Another silver lining.

She could have kids, and Richard's DNA matched. With a rueful smile, Christian climbed in her car and drove to the shop, realizing that this was a good day.

* * * *

Richard checked his watch.

"And then we'll meet again later in the month," a man across from him said.

The two other men were congressmen—one a senator and the other a representative.

Why hadn't he heard anything yet?

The plan he'd set in motion was sure to have Josephine doing *exactly* what he wanted. She'd be too scared not to.

She'd forgotten her place and it was time she was reminded of it.

Josephine answered to him and him alone. Not Mr. Brayden Kinncaid, but that was soon to no longer be a problem between them.

Wondering again why Ivan hadn't called, he sat up and offered the men a drink.

"No, thank you, Congressman Burbanks. We really need to be going. You mentioned you had a golf game you needed to get to, and we're keeping you. Thank you for inviting us out."

They all shook hands and he led them to the door.

Again, he checked the time.

What the hell was taking so long?

His obstacle should have been eliminated by now.

* * * *

Brayden ushered the clients to the table nestled in the corner window of the shop.

"We were really hoping we could find a nice Edwardian armoire, but so far, nothing is what we're looking for."

The Arlingtons were some of his pickiest clients. Some had the picture of a "perfect" piece in their minds, and if whatever was found did not match up, they didn't want it. Which was fine with him. It just didn't make his job easy. But he was almost certain he'd finally found one they would like. Of course, that had been a nice Regency, and now they wanted Edwardian. Oh, well, he'd show them the photo and information on the furniture he'd found. Who knows, maybe they'd buy both. In his business two was always better than one.

He asked if they wanted any refreshments and wondered again where in the hell Christian was. She wasn't answering her phone. He'd only gotten her voice mail.

Idiot woman. Going out alone. Was she insane? No, just stupid apparently.

He was going to have to permanently attach her to his wrist. If he'd known she'd run off first thing out of the box, he would have brought her along this morning. Which had him asking again where she went and why she had to lie about it; not that he told his mom when she called that Christian wasn't here. No, he just played along that she was here and had run out to grab something.

The bell over the door tinkled.

Christian stood there in her black peacoat, a smile on her face and trouble shifting in her eyes.

He wanted to shake her. Smiling to his clients, he excused himself and jerked his head to the back.

Without a look behind him, he knew she followed as her boot heels echoed on the floor.

In the kitchenette, he whirled. "Where in the hell have you been?"

Her brows furrowed then cleared as she smiled at him. "I'm sorry for lying to you and your mother, but I had some things to do."

"Such as?" he asked, pouring coffee so quickly it sloshed onto his hand. Damn it.

A heavy sigh filled the air. "Soon, Brayden. I promise I'll tell you everything. Soon."

Slamming the carafe down, he asked, "When?"

Her head cocked to the side. "Tomorrow night?"

"Tomorrow night's the New Year's Eve party." What was she up to?

"I know what day it is, Bray."

He took a deep breath and counted to ten. It did not help. Nothing helped anymore when it came to Christian.

"Why I want to marry you is completely beyond me at the moment." As if in battle, he all but tossed the cups on the tray, jostled the sugar and creamer on there, and threw a couple of spoons down to complete the arrangement.

Well, hell. Grabbing a towel, he straightened the mess and tried to make it presentable.

When he looked at her, she was as still as the bronze siren standing just outside the doorway.

"What?" he asked.

"What did you say?" she asked him, in a small voice.

He ran back over the words, and smiled. Then frowned. "Are you married?"

Her brows rose in shock. "No."

"Is your name Christian? Or do I have to get used to calling you something else?" This was *not* how he'd planned to go about this.

"No, it's Christian."

Her face was a mixture of hope, befuddlement, and confusion. The expression pulled a smile from him. Quickly, he leaned over and gave her a peck. She never moved. Good, it was about time he caught her off guard. Lord knew that's where he spent most of his time.

"Don't lie to me again, or go running off by yourself." With that he picked up the tray and walked out the door.

Several minutes later, she walked to the register. He was jotting down what the Arlingtons were looking for in their Edwardian search. He wanted the file on the Regency he had for them.

"Christian," he said.

"Yes?"

"Could you get me the file on the Arlingtons' last request?"

She left and came back. "It's not in the filing cabinet. Did you take it home?"

Brayden thought. "Yeah, I did. It's in my backseat." He remembered taking it out when he'd been looking for something in his briefcase.

"Keys?"

Quickly, he dug them out of his slacks pocket and tossed them to her.

Christian smiled at the Arlingtons. "You're going to absolutely love this piece. It's in mint condition, owned by and passed down through an aristocratic family in Lancashire. They all died out and the last remaining in the line auctioned off the estate."

"Oh, really?" Mrs. Arlington said. "Did you just get the one piece from the estate?"

Christian looked to him.

"No," he said, "we purchased several. They just arrived in the last couple of weeks."

"I'll be right back," Christian said and walked to the back door, or more aptly, side door.

The shop was on a corner and had two doors. One led into the kitchen, the one he always used as he parked on the side. The other door was, obviously, the front.

"This is the Regency armoire we asked you about before?" Mr.

Arlington asked, drawing his attention back.

"Yes. And Christian's right, it's a wonderful piece. If you don't take it, I'm thinking of keeping it myself."

The clang of keys dropping to the floor had him turning. Brayden leaned back and looked down the aisle to see Christian bend down and pick up the keys as she opened the side door.

"Grab anything else I might have left," he hollered.

She nodded and smiled as she pointed the keypad.

He saw her thumb press it.

An explosion rocked the shop. Windows shattered, missiling glass. Christian flew back into the cabinets as someone screamed.

Chapter 19

"Is your family cursed or something?" Lieutenant Gabe Morris asked him.

Brayden only glared at the man. Could his day get any better? What was the cop doing here? Morris worked special crimes. Did this fall under that heading? Then again, it was a bombing in D.C. Every law enforcement person from any branch milled about.

They stood at the back of an ambulance, where Christian was being treated for shock. She refused to go to the hospital. Since the EMTs convinced him that she was fine, for the most part, he didn't press the issue.

Smoke singed the December wind, and heat from his blackened Hummer still melted the air. Fire trucks blocked the street, red lights flashing. Someone had finally turned off the damn sirens.

"You two okay?" Morris asked.

No, they were not.

"We're fine," Christian mumbled.

Brayden's breath caught as it hit him yet again how close, how very damn close he'd come to losing her. Again. If she'd been a few feet closer, God forbid right at the vehicle, when she'd pressed the button . . .

He squeezed her hand. His own were riddled with cuts, one long slash down the side of his face from a piece of glass. The Arlingtons had been okay. But since they were an older couple, and Mr. Arlington had heart trouble, Brayden had been glad to see them in another ambulance heading to the hospital. Other than some windows blowing out in the shop across the street, nothing else was damaged and no one was hurt. Thank God.

Blowing out a breath, he tried to calm the rage pouring through him.

Maybe you'd turn on the coffeepot one morning, only to have the shop burst into flames. Christian's words from Christmas echoed in his mind.

"All right, you'll probably be sore for the next couple of days. Don't be surprised if you have some bruising. If something else comes up, go see your doctor," the EMT stated.

Christian nodded and Brayden helped her up, pulling the brown blanket together at her collar.

He looked around. Morris's partner—what was her name, Laurence? Yeah, she was shoving journalists out of the way. Reporters stood off to the side behind a barricaded area.

He cursed. His parents, he needed to get hold of them so they wouldn't see or hear about this on the news. With Dad's high blood pressure, he'd simply rather not take that chance.

"Brayden!"

He turned to see Aiden and Quinlan shove their way through a group of policemen.

"Could you tell them to let my brothers through?" he asked Morris.

"Doesn't look like I have much of a choice," Morris said as the two barreled their way toward the ambulance. "It's okay," the lieutenant told the following uniforms. "They're family."

"God, are you two okay?" Aiden asked.

His oldest brother looked pale, in his opinion, and Quinlan, always perfectly attired, was rumpled, his red hair standing up. Probably from—Quinlan ran a hand through his hair—that right there.

Aiden grabbed him in a tight hug. "We were at the hotel when we saw this on the news."

"It's already out?" he asked, pulling back.

"Yes."

"Damn it. What about Mom and Dad?"

Aiden shook his head. "I already called Jesslyn and gave her a heads-up." His phone rang and he quickly answered it. "Yeah. Jessie. Could you go by and tell Mom and Dad everyone is fine. Stress that last bit so they know neither Brayden nor Christian was hurt."

Brayden turned to see how Christian was holding up, but she was staring at the mangled, burned remains of his vehicle, the end of her blanket gently swaying in the cold December wind.

"I don't know," Aiden said, impatiently. "What time is it? Okay, check the country club. Dad mentioned something about a golf game. I don't know if Mom went to the club or not. Tori will be at the house with Becky, but Mom might still be there. Could you go over?" Aiden caught his eye and nodded.

Good, at least they might not hear about this on the news. Jesslyn would tell them.

"Love you, too," Aiden told his wife. He slapped his phone shut. "Now, what the hell happened?" his brother demanded.

Brayden looked to Christian. She still stared blankly at what was left of his Hummer.

"Christian?" Aiden asked, his voice hard.

Brayden grabbed his brother's arm. "I'll handle this."

Aiden's angry blue gaze pierced him. "Will you? Can you?"

"What the hell is that supposed to mean?"

"It just means . . ."

"Stop it!" Christian's furious whisper cut through the air.

"So, Lieutenant Morris," Quinlan said into the yawning silence. "What exactly are you doing here?"

They all turned to the cop, all but Christian.

Morris rubbed the corner of his mouth with his finger. "Well, I was on my way to talk to Christian when the call came in on the radio. I'm not a big believer in coincidences."

"Join the club," Aiden barked.

Quinlan raised his brows and walked off.

Morris looked to Christian, and Brayden couldn't help the spurt of possessiveness that shot through him. Taking a deep breath, he stepped closer to her just as Morris did.

"So? You came to talk to Christian, about what?" He stood between the two of them, noting she never so much as shifted.

Morris smirked. "That's between Christian and me. But right now, it's not at the top of my list. If you'll excuse me, I'm going to talk to Chief Mayben and whoever is in charge of this case. Don't any of you go anywhere." With that, the smug man walked off.

Prick.

He turned and pulled Christian against him. She was stiff, reminding him of how she'd locked into herself weeks ago. Her hair smelled like smoke, but he didn't care. God, he'd been beyond himself by the time he'd reached her. She'd been on the floor, dazed for several moments, stunned from the blast, covered in glass and wood from the door. In those seconds she hadn't answered and he'd tried to find a pulse . . . He hoped to the Almighty he'd never, *never* have to go through anything like that ever again.

Finally, he pulled back and cupped her face. For a moment, her eyes lost that blank stare. The flash of emotion in them was too fleeting to pin down, but he'd seen it. Gently, he shook her.

"Don't. Don't do this again. I'm here. I'm right here, damn it."

Her eyes shifted, filled. "But what if it had been you?" she asked on a broken whisper.

She swallowed once, then again.

"What happened?" Aiden asked him yet again.

Anger at her, at what could have been, at some faceless coward all built together and he lashed out toward his brother. "What the hell does it look like?"

"It looks like you have an enemy," Aiden replied, crossing his arms, his look as chilled as the day.

"Ya think?"

"I'm sorry," Christian whispered. "I'm sorry."

Tears ran down her cheeks. Brayden pulled her against him. "It's okay."

"No, no, it'll never be okay. Even if I put him away, he'll get out one day. It'll never, ever be okay." Her words were hot against his chest. "If I went away, he'd leave you alone and—"

"Don't even fucking think about it," Brayden snarled.

"Sorry to interrupt," Morris said, returning.

Brayden didn't want to like the guy, he really, really didn't. But the cop had helped not only when Tori and Ryan were missing, but had saved Christian before and was trying to help now.

Christian pulled out of his arms and turned to Morris, wiping her eyes.

"I need to talk to you," Morris said to her, the lines of his mouth tight. "Can I drive you home?"

Brayden didn't let her go completely. "I'll take her to the hotel." Gently he started toward his brothers, but said, "You can meet us there."

A fireman walked up. "Mr. Kinncaid?"

"Yes," he and his brothers all answered.

The man had *Chief* on his fire coat and hat.

"I'm Chief Mayben. I need to speak with you, forms to fill out, reports and whatnot. There are several questions that need answering, and after me, the lieutenant here wants to talk to you."

The man held out his hand.

Brayden let go of Christian to shake it. Damn. He didn't want her here, and the hotel was convenient. Checking his watch, he saw it had been almost an hour since the explosion.

An hour? It felt like an eternity, and apparently it would be longer until he got out of here.

"Why don't you and Aiden stay and work this all out, and I'll take Christian to the hotel?" Quinlan asked.

Brayden thought that was a great idea.

"No," Christian said. The tears were gone, replaced by determination. "Gabriel? Will you give me a ride?" she asked, turning to the lieutenant.

Gabriel? Brayden ground his teeth at the purely male smile the cocky cop flashed her.

"Sure. I need to discuss a lead with you anyway."

Aiden's phone rang, but Brayden was listening to Christian and Morris.

"Shit," Aiden said, drawing his attention. "Yeah, thanks, Jessie girl. No, stay there, I'll be home later. You too, bye."

He hung up and said, "Mom and Dad are on their way here. Apparently they saw it on the news."

Damn.

"Jessie said they were headed to the hotel," Aiden continued

"I'll get over there and meet them," Quinlan said. "I'll call Gavin too."

Brayden nodded.

"You riding with me?" Quinlan asked Christian.

She only shook her head. Turning on his heel, Quinlan left.

"I'll see you later? Or do you need me here?" Christian asked.

On a resigned sigh, he asked, "Where will you be?"

"With me," Morris said. "Relax. I just need to ask her some questions while I drive her to the Highland."

Brayden took a deep breath and nodded.

She licked her lips, and he noticed they trembled before she firmed them.

"Mr. Kinncaid?" the fire chief asked.

Brayden held up his finger for the man to wait just a minute.

Leaning up on her tiptoes, she kissed him. "I love you. Please,

please be careful."

"Don't worry, I'll take care of him," Aiden remarked.

Brayden looked over her head to Morris.

"She'll be fine. I give you my word," the cop said.

He kissed her once more before he watched her walk away with Morris. She was going to tell the lieutenant something. She *wanted* to talk to the man.

* * * *

"You're serious about going over everything later?" Gabe asked her yet again. "You're not going to back out on me, are you?"

She shook her head. "No. I just want Brayden there, and I'd like to shower. I also want to go up and make certain that Kaitlyn and Jock are all right."

Gabe had taken her for a cup of coffee, updating her as much as he could on the case, questioning her on the bombing. She'd answered what she could.

She told him some of the things she'd mentioned to Brayden, enough to let him know she was serious about getting it all over with, but not enough that he could do anything yet.

"Thanks for the coffee and the ride," Christian told him as she climbed out of the car.

"I can walk you in," Gabe told her.

She shook her head. "No, that's okay. I know you want to get down to the shop and I know Brayden's still down there." She stepped up to the front doors.

Gabe checked his watch. "Yeah." Thumping the top of the car, he told her, "Look. Stay around the Kinncaids. Don't go off by yourself. We've assigned a couple of plainclothes to watch things. Just be careful. I'll call you soon. Who knows, with any luck we might pick up Ivan tonight."

She had told him that Ivan was the one that knew about bombs.

"If you find him, tell him Josephine asked for his help."

"Josephine?"

She only smiled. "I'll talk to you later. Can Brayden and I just meet you at the station? I don't want to do this here. I don't want it here."

He lifted the corner of his mouth in a rueful grin. "Yeah, that's fine. Give me a call on my cell and I'll meet you there."

"Thanks."

"Don't mention it. It'll be over soon."

She hoped so, but her life couldn't be that easy.

He climbed back in the car and she watched as his taillights blinked when he pulled out onto the street.

"Ms. Bills," the doorman said, opening the door for her.

"Thank you."

The private elevator behind the mirrors was warm and silent as she rode up to the family's penthouse suites.

Jock and Kaitlyn were already here. She knew that from talking to Brayden. Quinlan had been here to meet them; as far as anyone else was concerned, she had no idea.

The elevator doors slid open.

A hot shower beckoned, but she could see the doors at the end of the long hallway stood open. Jock and Kaitlyn's suite. With a sigh, and wondering what she was going to say to them, she decided the shower could wait.

She was just inside the entryway, when a voice halted her steps.

"Jock," the man said calmly, "I'm certain they're fine. Patience, my friend. It won't do to excite yourself with your blood pressure."

Oh, God, no.

Her heart slammed against her ribs and the bands around her chest tightened.

Richard! Damn the man.

What was he doing here? Pictures, memories and terror rushed through her.

It was okay. It was okay. What could he do right here in front of everyone? Nothing.

Fear mixed with anger, and rage conquered.

On a deep trembling breath, she strode into the room, and didn't so much as look at him.

"Christian!" Kaitlyn was off the couch and hurrying toward her.

"Hi, Mom," she whispered in her ear. "I'm sorry."

Kaitlyn squeezed her tight then leaned back and brushed hair off her forehead. The touch was feather-light.

"Nothing to be sorry for. My God, you could have been killed.

Are you all right?" she asked.

They were the same height. Christian hugged this woman, who was more a mother to her than the woman who gave birth to her, and said into her ear, "I will be soon. Very, very soon."

Her eyes met Richard's, and she didn't look away from the pale green depths.

He looked . . . relieved. Yes, relieved and angry. There was no masking the anger burning bright in his jaded depths.

"Where the hell have you been?" Quinlan asked from behind the bar.

Christian shrugged. "Answering questions."

"I hate that crap," Jock grumbled. "Questions, always questions. Why can't they leave the good guys in peace?" He stood and walked to her, wrapping her in a tight bear hug.

Her ribs folded together, but it hardly mattered, Jock was happy to see her.

"I'm okay," she told him, patting his back.

He set her away from him and stared at her. "They've been badgering you again, haven't they?"

Not now. She didn't want Richard to know she'd been with the cops planning to spill all.

"I'm fine."

"You don't look fine, Chrissy."

She smiled at the name he sometimes called her. Chrissy. It was a truly horrible nickname. But it was better than Jesslyn's, whom he referred to as Missy. Or even Kaitie lass. Jock had a thing with ending nicknames in *ie* or *y*. But it was who he was and it was as comfortable as her favorite pair of jeans.

"Quinlan," Jock barked, "fix your sister a drink."

The man then guided her to the couch, where Richard stood.

Taking a deep breath, she held his stare, noting the smirk at the corner of his mouth.

"Jock," he said, tsking. "You didn't tell me you had such a lovely . . ." He trailed of as his gaze ran over her. "Daughter?"

Jock stood a bit straighter. "Well, it's a long story, but yes, Chrissy is ours. She's a Kinncaid."

Richard's eyes ran over her again, and she could no more stop herself from crossing her arms than she could from inwardly cringing.

She couldn't help wonder what he thought of learning his grand plan almost killed her. Was he happy? Relieved or angered? Or had that been the plan?

Jock continued. "Christian, this is a friend who moved into the old Cooley place, just up the road. He was the one who heard about it at the club. Kaitie and I were sitting in the lounge. Anyway, he drove us here."

"Yes, we can't thank you enough, Dickie," Kaitlyn said, coming to stand with them.

Richard's smile grew as he stretched his hand toward her.

Christian looked at it, but didn't take it, and decided to snatch the ball from his court. Meeting his gaze again, she asked, "Congressman Burbanks, isn't it?"

"You know Dickie?" Jock asked, turning to her.

Dickie? Christian arched a brow, and looked as slowly over Richard as he previously had her. Dickie? He must *hate* that. With a chuckle, she only said, "Oh, yes." She cleared her throat. "Um . . . *Dickie* and I have met before."

Richard cocked his head to the side. "Have we?"

The smug son of a bitch. God, she wanted to tear into him, claw his eyes out. He could have killed Brayden, hurt Tori, and she knew none of that mattered a damn to this man. No, he was more worried about the perfect crease being arrow-sharp down the front of his golfing chinos. Arrogant ass.

It would be so easy . . . so easy to just let something slip.

Silence stretched. She could feel everyone's eyes on her.

As much as she wanted revenge against him, now was *not* the time. DNA they had. But she wanted it all. Every last shred of evidence. Maybe even a confession.

There was a thought.

"Yes, our previous meeting was a charity, I think." Smiling only slightly, she hoped no one could see how flustered she was. "A charity event a while back." Inspiration struck. "For sexually abused children and laws of limitations."

Something flashed in his eyes. A muscle bunched in his jaw, and he only nodded.

"That sounds about right," Kaitlyn said, guiding her to the bar, where Quinlan had her drink—something in a mug. Probably tea. Christian hopped up on the stool, turning back to face Jock and his new friend. No way in hell was she turning her back on Richard.

Kaitlyn continued to chatter. "Christian here is always doing something to help kids."

"Really?" Richard asked.

"Oh, yes, too many things to go into." Kaitlyn turned back to her and asked, "Hon, is it sweet enough? Quinlan, how much honey did you put in it?"

Christian shared a sibling smile with Quinlan.

"A teaspoon and a half, just like you taught us all, Mom."

Kaitlyn Kinncaid nodded just as the phone rang and Quinlan grabbed it.

How long was Richard planning to stay here? Had Brayden met the man yet? The Cooley place? My God, he wasn't even a mile from them! So Brayden could have met him.

After maybe three seconds, she discarded that idea. Brayden was hardly stupid. If Brayden had met a man named *Dickie* he would have immediately known it was a diminutive for Richard. And that would have been enough for her Kinncaid to set some plan in motion.

Dickie.

Richard Burbanks, hated, *hated* and despised nicknames.

Bless Jock's simplifying heart. It was enough to make her smile.

Quinlan hung up and said, "That was Aiden. He and Bray should be here soon. They're on their way."

A sigh escaped her.

Richard shifted. "I should probably be going. Looks like everyone is fine and headed this way." He held his hand out to Jock, who took it with a hearty shake.

"No need to run off," Jock said.

"Well, now that your family is all here, and I can see you're fine, I think—"

"What do you mean, he's fine?" Christian asked.

Quinlan stood stiff beside her, having come around the bar to sit on the other stool.

"Oh, it's nothing." Jock waved his hand.

Richard gave a harsh chuckle that grated on Christian's nerves like nails down a chalkboard. "Nothing, Jock? You could have had a heart attack."

"What?" both she and Quinlan asked.

"He's fine," Kaitlyn assured them. "We just had a bit of a scare in the car on the way here. We were in Richard's car, since he insisted on driving us; he didn't think either one of us should be driving. Anyway, Jock started to have chest pains and couldn't find his nitro pills."

"I don't know what happened to them. I had them in my damn pocket, Kaitie."

Kaitlyn only shot her husband a hard stare, her green eyes like shards of emeralds. "Anyway, luckily I had some in my purse and gave him one." Looking from her to Quinlan, Kaitlyn said, "He's fine. He's fine. Nothing to worry about."

But it could have been something to worry about. Oh, God, it could have been. Missing pills. Jock never, *never* went anywhere without his pills. He always carried them in his pocket. It was like his wallet.

Christian looked to Richard and felt nauseous.

He only smiled, a sharp-bladed grin, walking toward her. Christian tried, but she must have stiffened because suddenly Quinlan stood just a bit in front of her.

Richard cocked a brow and said, "It was good to see you again" — he paused — "Christian."

She couldn't talk to him, or even nod. My God, both Brayden and Jock?

It was all she could do not to roar off the stool and rip his head off. Anger pulsed through her, thick as the blood in her veins.

"Dickie, thank you again for everything today," Kaitlyn said, blessedly drawing his attention.

Christian stared into her mug of tea, the smell of chamomile wafting with the steam. She listened as the Kinncaids walked Richard Burbanks, the monster in her life, to the door and felt self-loathing at the fact she'd brought the wolf to the sheeps' pen.

When the door clicked shut, she closed her eyes and leaned back against the chair, chills racing through her. She tried to stop the tremors, but her hands shook.

Jock and Brayden.

Oh, God, forgive her.

"Hey, you okay?" Quinlan asked, his voice jerking her back to where she was.

She started to nod, but knew he'd see through it, so she only took a sip of tea.

"Did you really know him?"

Where had that question come from?

"Why do you ask?"

Quinlan's gaze was studying, weighing. Finally, he said, "Because the closer he'd get to you, the stiffer you became. And you didn't shake his hand."

The look in his eyes said he saw more than that.

Hell. Grabbing the first thought that came to mind, she said, "I just . . . I don't know. I'm fine around all you guys. But others . . ." She trailed off and let him think what he wanted. Shaking her head, she added, "I just didn't feel comfortable around him."

Quinlan humphed and climbed on the other stool. His hand thumped on the bar. "Well, I don't like him at all. He's too . . ." The corner of his mouth quirked. "I don't know. Too something."

"Who are you two talking about?" Jock asked, sitting on the couch, pulling Kaitlyn down with him.

"Your buddy," Quinlan answered.

"You don't like him?" Jock asked.

Quinlan shook his head. "No, I don't. Slick. He's too slick. You can see it in his eyes."

Jock frowned. "I'll admit he's a bit stiff, but I hardly think he's slick or whatever it is you're implying. Though he's a politician, so he probably is slick."

"I'm not implying anything, Dad. Something about him just seemed off."

Christian stared at her tea. No message floated on the surface telling her what to do or say.

"If you think he's bad, you should meet his wife," Kaitlyn added.

Could this get any better?

"Kaitie lass."

"Well, I'm sorry, Jock, but I see what Quinlan means, and Ms. Burbanks is a cold woman. You can't argue that."

Jock's heavy sigh could have felled a tree. "No, I can't. And she wonders why her daughter ran away. Can't say I blame the girl at all."

Christian's cup shattered on the floor.

Oh, God. What did they know? Surely she hadn't heard right. Daughter? Estella talked about her daughter, about *her*.

She couldn't stop shaking.

"Christian?"

Jerking back from Quinlan's touch, she slid off the stool and stooped to pick up the broken pottery.

"Oh, honey, ignore us," Kaitlyn said, right beside her. "Here we are talking. You need a hot shower and a bed. After everything else and now this afternoon."

Kaitlyn took the pieces Christian had picked up.

"Go on. Go take a shower or bath. I'll order you some room service. Or all of us some, I guess, since no one's had dinner."

The thought of a shower was heavenly. But what if Richard didn't leave? What if he knew which suite was hers? He would. Or he could be waiting in the hallway near the elevators. Hell, he would, wait to pounce. What if he was in there now? Waiting on her.

"Christian, honey," Kaitlyn said, setting the broken cup on the counter. "You're shaking like a leaf."

And she was. She couldn't quit.

Kaitlyn's hands were warm.

"Your fingers are like ice. Come on, I'll run you a bath." Kaitlyn started to pull her toward the door, but she stayed rooted to the spot.

"Christian?" Kaitlyn asked.

What had Estella told them? What if when it all came out, they didn't believe her? They were already friends with the people who had hurt her most in the world.

The path that seemed so very clear earlier now was shadowed, uneven, and overgrown.

Brayden. She wanted Brayden.

Chapter 20

At that moment, the door opened, and as if from merely needing him, he was there.

"I don't care," he was saying over his shoulder to his older brother, Aiden.

His eyes met hers and for some stupid reason, hers filled with tears. Without stopping to say a word to anyone, he strode to her. Kaitlyn, thankfully, let go of her hands, right before Brayden crushed her to his chest.

Neither of them said a word. His arms held her so tight, she couldn't breathe, but she didn't care. He could have died. What if she had been late and he'd run out to get the papers. She knew his habits. He waited till he was at the hood to unlock his vehicle.

A shudder danced through her.

Brayden pulled back. "How come you haven't had a shower yet? You still smell like smoke." A frown crinkled his brow.

Christian just shrugged, but Jock put in, "Probably because she just got here not half an hour ago."

Brayden shook his head and she let him steer her toward the door.

"I'm ordering room service," Kaitlyn said. Which translated to: *You will eat.*

"Thanks, Mom," Brayden replied as he ushered her out the door and into the hallway. "Come on, we both need a shower."

"You're finished?" she asked him.

Brayden opened the door to their apartment suite. "No, I simply told everyone there I was leaving. Gabe showed up about the time I was leaving and mentioned something about us all going down to the station later. That you wanted to meet?"

Christian stopped in the living room, looking toward her room. She really didn't want to go in there alone. Though she had a perfectly fine bathroom and her fear was more than likely completely unfounded, but still . . .

"So, we'll shower, I'll make certain you're all right, we'll eat, since Mom's ordering, and then go to the station. Though I don't know why he can't come here." He pulled her to his rooms on the other side of the living room.

"I'm fine, Brayden." And she didn't want to eat.

He only shoved her toward the bathroom. "And then I'll make sure you get to sleep tonight, and I need to make a few calls."

"Brayden . . ."

He flicked on the light, stepped around her and turned on the shower. With quick, deft fingers he shed their clothing, then pushed her toward the stall.

She closed her eyes and sighed as the hot water sprayed her, enveloping them both in steam.

Damn, he'd turned the water up too hot. Brayden started to turn it cooler, but her words stopped him.

"No, leave it. It feels great." Still she didn't open her eyes.

Water trickled over her face, dripped off her chin, ran down the long column of her neck, slid down her fantastic body.

Brayden's control snapped. When he'd seen her fly through the air, couldn't get her to respond . . . those seconds had been absolute hell.

He kissed her hard.

What if he'd lost her today?

He wasn't stupid, he'd been the target, but the bastard could have killed her or Tori.

God. Pulling back, he leaned her against the wall.

"I could have lost you today," he said.

She shook her head. "I could have lost you."

Their mouths were hot and fast, demanding and giving in turn. His teeth skimmed over her as quickly as hers did him. Mouths met and fought for control. Water slicked over them, heated the air around them as the blood, the need to appease roared through him.

He slid his hands down her body, pulled her nipples between his fingers. Grabbing the soap, he lathered them both up, until they slid and moved against each other in a glide.

Her nails bit into his shoulders as he lifted her, bracing her against the tiled wall. He kissed her breast.

"I can't take much more of this," he muttered against her.

The fear and anger clawed and taunted the lust in him.

He spread her with his fingers, flicked his thumb back and forth until her eyes clouded and she moaned.

"Please, Bray." She wrapped her legs and arms around him.

Brayden surged into her, their mutters and pleas mixing in the steam. She vined around him, vised all of him, until he couldn't breathe, couldn't see, could only feel the tight pulsing of her inner muscles. He groaned and emptied himself into her, bracing one hand on the wall and praying they wouldn't fall to the floor.

Under the heated spray of water, they washed away the horrors of the day.

* * * *

That had been too damn close.

Richard pulled his car up in front of the garage door.

How in the hell . . .

He leaned his head on the steering wheel. She could have died today. His Josephine could have been killed because she'd been with *that* man.

And Ivan.

Where the hell was the bastard? Stupidity was not a reason. Richard accepted no excuses, only results. He'd yet to get hold of the Lithuanian, but he would find him. The idiot was probably hiding. Smart, now that he thought of it. With his present frame of mind, Richard would probably kill the incompetent fool if he saw Ivan.

And Ivan would damn well do the job again—right this time—without a penny more.

Richard had paid him enough the last time, and for what?

A mistake. A costly, almost deadly mistake.

It would not happen again. Perhaps it was time to find a new tiger. A new man he could use. Someone with a bit more stomach for things that needed doing.

Richard wasn't a fool, he knew Ivan did not like the jobs he did. It was that fearing stupidity again. If the man had only stepped back enough to question, he could have easily seen the lies.

Idiot.

Carefully, Richard let go of the steering wheel, his fingers cramped from holding it so tightly.

Everything had gone wrong today. First the son, then the father.

Jock should be dead. He'd planned it all so damn perfectly. He should have anticipated the fact Kaitlyn would have extra nitroglycerin pills. The woman was a retired doctor, after all.

Sighing, he got out of the car. The cold air held a tint of wood smoke. Lights blinked from inside the windows. He called and let Estella know what was going on and where he was going.

She was worried about whether or not the party was still on tomorrow night. Shallow woman. If she only knew . . .

Not that she didn't care about the Kinncaids. However, if the party were canceled, there were more career-promoting events to attend. Ones for which she needed to inform the hostesses they would be attending.

His career.

Richard ran a hand through his hair. Perhaps it would have been better if Josephine had died today. The thought pierced his heart.

When she'd walked into the room tonight, he'd wanted to take her away with him and take care of her. Clean her up, fix her. She looked sad and tired. Not at all like Josephine was supposed to look.

But even exhausted, she hated him. He could see the fire of it in her eyes, burning the smoky color to pure mercury. There had been no fear. No fear until the end when she'd learned about Jock.

She knew. She knew. Josephine wasn't stupid. She knew him and the lengths he'd go to for her.

His love, his light, his reason . . . dead?

No, no, regardless of the threat to his career, he couldn't kill her.

He couldn't, at least not yet. She was simply too precious to him.

Mr. Brayden Kinncaid, or any of the Kinncaids, however, was another matter entirely. Checking his watch, he took out his phone and dialed the number he'd gotten from a contact. It was time to find a man who would do what he wanted, when he wanted, and one who would do whatever job right.

* * * *

A man, brown-haired, brown-eyed, with a neatly trimmed goatee, shifted through some of the rubble at the shop.

He'd asked questions of the firemen, the chief, the police and the medics. Everyone was all right, for the most part, if not a little shaken.

His insurance company needed all the pertinent facts for the report, he'd told them, flashing his ID, which sat beside the picture of a woman and a smiling child.

Yes, Robert Royson, representative of Oakly, Danze, and Rife Insurance, carefully jotted down things on his clipboard. For all those present, he was as he should be. An insurance man, checking out a claim. A calm, quiet man, who was shaken at what he was seeing and wishing he were at home with the woman and child that several had glimpsed beside the perfect credentials.

But then, that was what they were supposed to see.

Brayden's Hummer was still too hot to get close to, but he knew enough already that he didn't need a firsthand look.

Oh, he'd like one, to see the handiwork, the switch used, the placement of wires, what type of materials were used. Each of those things told him a bit more and a bit more. Altogether, they were as telling as a person's handwriting. If he saw the layout, the arrangement, he might know the man.

Those things would, at the very least, lead him to the bastard who dared to plant a damn bomb on this car.

With his head bent to the clipboard, he carefully scanned the crowd. No one seemed out of place.

His contacts told him little more than he already knew and suspected.

Miss Christian Bills was not all she appeared to be, but then he already knew that, too.

It was by absolute chance he was here at all. He'd planned to come next week. But plans change, and he ended up having an appointment earlier today.

The news blurb on the radio, as he'd made his way to his hotel, was enough to draw his attention. The address had him pulling his car off at the nearest exit and thumping away information into his laptop.

Brayden Kinncaid and Christian Bills were lucky to be alive.

His pager vibrated.

He glanced down at the numbers. Well, they would just have to wait. He'd get back to them.

"Find everything you need?" a plainclothes cop asked.

He knew this one, remembered him from a few months back

when Ryan and Tori had been kidnapped.

In a truly wonderful Southern drawl, if he said so himself, he replied, "Why, yes, yes, thank you." He scanned the mess around him. "It is amazing what some people will do, isn't it?" He held out his hand. "I'm sorry, I didn't get your name."

"Lieutenant Morris, of the DCPD."

Shrewd dark eyes assessed him and saw only what they were meant to see; at least, he hoped so.

"Robert Royson."

They shook hands.

"Lieutenant!" a uniform shouted, drawing Morris's attention.

"If you're done here . . ." Morris let the sentence hang.

"Oh, I think I have enough for the report. If my superiors have a problem with it, I'm sure they'll let me know." He clipped his pen to the clipboard. "Do you have a number I can call you at? In case of questions or something?"

Morris pulled out a card and gave it to him, before turning to see what the beat cop wanted.

With another scan of the crowd, Ian Kinncaid walked across the street and disappeared into the crowd. He had a meeting to get to.

* * * *

Gabe Morris turned from the sergeant working the case. The night wind cut through his coat. He wanted to be at home, warm and relaxing.

Instead, he'd spent the last ten minutes convincing Sergeant Mifflin that he wasn't going to try and take over the case. Gabe knew, *knew* the stalking and sexual assault case were linked to this one. No doubt in his mind. But Mr. I-Wanna-Impress-My-Captain did not believe any such thing.

However, the guy finally agreed to share whatever his findings were. Since the sergeant was acting all territorial, Gabe didn't feel the need to share the information that he knew what the probable bomber looked like.

Gabe turned to see what that insurance man was doing. Claimer — what the hell were those guys called? Probably had some neat little title, but as far as he was concerned, insurance man covered it.

The man was nowhere to be found. He couldn't be done already.

Gabe scanned the crowd again looking for the brown hair and goatee.

A familiar face stood out.

Looking quickly away, he felt his heart slam in his chest.

Criminals could be so damn stupid.

"Emma!"

His partner hurried over to him. "What?"

"Suspect, three o'clock. Blue coat, toboggan cap."

"Got him," she said, nodding to him and walking away.

He saw her unclip her gun as she made her way around the crowd and toward the back of it.

Gabe headed straight for the guy.

Ivan Ristovolich was perhaps five feet eleven inches of muscle, graying hair, wide-set cheekbones, and a bladed nose. The man turned to look to his right, his profile harsh.

Hurrying forward, while the man's attention was diverted, Gabe stopped right beside him, his hand on his gun, and said, "Mr. Ristovolich?"

Ivan turned, his eyes rounding, then he darted through the crowd, shoving people out of the way.

"Stop, police!" Gabe shouted.

Ivan ran, finally clearing the crowd.

Gabe saw the top of Emma's head. Then Ivan fell to the sidewalk.

When he got there, Ivan was cussing in another language. Well, maybe not, but the man sounded like he was cussing.

"Need some help?" Gabe asked his partner.

Her look said the question was insulting. One brow cocked. "I brought him down." Then she leaned over and said, "Mr. Ristovolich, we just wanted to talk to you." Emma straddled the guy, cuffing him.

For a little lady, Gabe knew she could handle herself.

"What do you want?" Ivan asked, his accent heavy.

"We just wanna talk to you." Gabe reached down and hauled the guy to his feet.

"I don't have to talk to you."

Gabe sighed as he led the guy to their car. "No, you don't. But then it would be easier on you, and Josephine seems to think that you might actually help her." At the car door, he stopped and looked Mr. Ristovolich in the eye. Gabe shrugged. "I think she's wrong."

For one long moment they stared at each other. Like the guy would say a word. Mumbling to himself, he put his hand to the top of Ivan's head as the guy got in the car.

Slamming the door, he wondered if Ivan would cooperate. Like life would be that easy.

* * * *

Brayden could no more stop asking her if she was all right than he could quit breathing.

"Brayden, I'm fine. Just a bit sore is all." They were on the way into the police station.

She stopped, stood on her toes, and kissed him. "I'm fine."

He kissed her back, ran his hands down her arms, her chenille sweater soft as down under his fingers. Aside from the knot on the back of her head and little cuts on her face, she looked fine, just as she said.

Sighing deeply, he laced his fingers through hers and followed her up the stairs of the noisy cop shop.

A cop leading a handcuffed man down the steps staggered toward him as his prisoner shifted and tried to run.

Brayden jerked Christian back out of the way.

"Schupit, pigs. Don't know shit," the dirty, probably homeless, drunk said.

Leaning up, he whispered in her ear, "Why did you want to do this here?"

"Because I don't want this filth in our home any more than it already is." She straightened and walked up the rest of the stairs. At the top she waited.

She licked her lips. "When we do this . . ."

"Yes?"

"I need you here, but please don't . . . Don't . . ."

"What?" he asked her, cupping her face.

"I'm afraid you're going to be mad at me."

He laughed. "Hell, woman, I'm pissed at you half the time. If you're worried that anything you say will change how I feel about you, that *will* piss me off." He studied her eyes. "That wasn't what you were thinking, was it?"

"I don't know. I don't know. Just today with the explosion, and then . . ." She stopped.

"And then?"

"You'll find out soon enough."

Brayden sighed. "What, Christian, tell me now."

"Your dad. He had a bad time of it on the way here and couldn't find his pills. I think . . . I think . . ."

"Dad's fine. I know about that. I talked to Mom while you were getting ready." He threw his arm around her, seeing Gabe coming down the hallway. "Let's get this over with so I can take you home, okay?"

She took a deep breath and let it out on a huff. "Okay."

* * * *

Christian sat in the chair and held the cup of water between her hands. Brayden's arm around her shoulders anchored her.

"I don't know where to start. It all began so long ago." She looked down at the scarred wooden tabletop. At least she wasn't in some interrogation room. Gabe had known this was not going to be easy so he found them someone's meeting room or something. At least it was private.

Taking a deep breath, she said, "It began in New Orleans, when a thirteen-year-old daughter sang her father a birthday song . . ."

She went on from there, telling him how a man in the audience heard her and simply wanted. There was her father's death shortly thereafter—killed in a mugging supposedly gone bad.

She told him everything she told Brayden, and then some.

"He swore he'd never let me go, and I was too scared after no one believed me the first time to try and say anything again." The room smelled of cigarette smoke. "That's not exactly true. One cop and his partner believed me, but . . ." She shook her head. "I'm getting ahead of myself.

"First off, I did try and report what was going on, but it didn't matter, he just bought them off. One day, a friend of mine, and I didn't have many, noticed a bruise on my wrist." Danny

Williamson . . .

"For some stupid reason that I still can't fathom, I didn't deny it when Danny asked me right off if it was my stepfather who gave me the bruise." If she had . . . That didn't matter.

Christian ran a hand through her hair.

"Anyway, Danny apparently lost control of his motorcycle about a mile from the house."

"He's dead?" Gabe asked.

She could only nod. "Seventeen." A wasted life, all because he'd wanted to do the right thing. "At first I tried to believe it was an accident." Richard's voice slithered through her memory.

"Such a sad thing, accidents. They silence people forever, don't they, Josephine? You should have kept our little secret. Though I must give the boy credit for courage if nothing else." He'd laughed.

"Who's Josephine?" Brayden asked, speaking for the first time.

"What?"

"You said Josephine. Who did he mean?"

She'd spoken aloud. Licking her lips, she stared at the tabletop. "Me." She took a deep breath, then turned to look at Brayden. "My name is Josephine Christian Clara Montreaux. My father was Phillip Montreaux of New Orleans, Louisiana. We own banks. Or my brother does, now."

That was the first time she'd said those words in years. Montreaux. Brayden's eyes narrowed, but the hand on her shoulder gently caressed.

"So this man killed your friend?" Emma asked.

"He said he did, but he's never dirtied his hands with anything other than the times he beat me. Always had Ivan do his dirty work."

"How do you know this?" Gabe asked, the corners of his mouth tight.

"Because he told me, and he wrote it all down." She shrugged.

"Wrote it all down?"

She thought about what to say. "Yes, he wrote it all down. Did he kill Danny Williamson? Probably. All because Danny knew the truth and wouldn't listen to my stepfather's lies. All because he tried to help me."

Poor Danny.

She jumped ahead. "He raped me in July when I was fifteen.

Though he was so drunk . . . That's the San Francisco case."

"But it was filed . . ." Gave checked his notes.

"Buddy Michaels filed it, though he may have used another name. He was a cop, maybe he still is. His partner was Frank Smith, my friend, Susan's, father."

"Was?" Emma and Gabe asked.

She nodded. "When I turned sixteen, he raped me again. On the night of my birthday. That had been the plan all along. Make me a woman on my sixteenth birthday. He'd just 'lost control' before. But once done it can't be undone and it's easier to 'lose control' again after that. But after the party he was so angry because I had talked to my brother. Joshua had wanted me to spend the night at the hotel with him and God, I wanted to go," she finished on a broken whisper.

Taking a fortifying breath, she squeezed Brayden's hand, which at some point he'd laced with hers. "They didn't let me go. Joshua didn't want to cause problems, so he didn't push it. But I'd made a big enough deal that . . . That night when he . . . It wasn't . . . He was angry," she finished. Tears welled in her eyes, stupid as that was. They didn't do any good now. Brayden's arm tightened around her and she took strength from him. "The next day I could barely move. Someone, Maria, our maid, I think, called my friend, or it could have been Ivan. Susan and her mom came and got me out of that house and into their car. I do remember Ivan carrying me. Then Frank, Susan's father, rode a bus or train with me. I can't remember for sure. I woke up in the hospital with a letter from him not to tell anyone where I was, not to call home. He left me some money. It was November."

She remembered the relief at escape, and a flood, a tidal wave of gratitude for the Smiths' help, and fear. Always the fear that Richard would find her. Licking her lips she said, "I was in San Antonio, Texas, I think, when I learned they'd all died Christmas morning."

"They?"

"The entire family."

She went through it all. How Frank helped her, how the house must have had a gas leak. The fact that Frank was a cop bothered the hell out of Gabe, which he told her.

Nausea greased her stomach. "I never thought it was an accident.

They'd helped me, you see. And somehow he must have known. If you find Ivan and crack him, he'll roll on my stepfather. Then you can get a search warrant maybe?"

"Couldn't you get one now?" Brayden asked, the edge in his voice sharp.

"Probably."

Christian shook her head. "No, he'd stop you. He'd find a way to. He was the district attorney and the state's attorney general." She leaned up on her elbows. "My stepfather had something on Ivan. I overheard Ivan once talking to the maid that he wrote everything down. Something about not spending blood money. I think Mr. Ristovolich didn't really like what he did. I've often believed he was just waiting for the right time to escape. If you don't get Ivan, it'll only be my word against my stepfather's, and he'll find a way to stop the search warrant. He'll have to."

"Why?"

"Well, if you searched wherever he lives here, you probably wouldn't find anything, though you might. But if you searched his home back in Oregon, you'd find all sorts of . . ." Christian trailed off.

"Of?"

She took a deep breath. "Things. Things. He liked to brag. He's rather egotistical. There's a room . . ." God, her hands were shaking. "Or there was, and probably still is . . . There's a room up—up in the attic. The right sconce on the back wall turns, and a door that looks like a wall opens. And behind it is—is a—a room."

Christian swallowed.

"What's in it?" Gabe asked softly.

Shoving back, she stood and walked to the window. The day was dying. Shadows stretched across the streets and buildings. Christian gripped her elbows. "There's a bed, or there was. Pictures all over the walls . . ."

"Of?"

The sharp image cut through her haze, of things she tried to forget.

He couldn't hurt her now. She was strong. She was strong.

Clearing her throat, she continued. "He'd drug me and I'd wake up in that stupid room. I hate that room. The rape was the worst in many ways. Yet, he'd led up to it for so long . . . It was almost a relief he'd finally gotten it out of the way so he couldn't taunt me with it anymore." She took another deep breath. "After a while you try to— try to go away, try to forget what he's doing, the things he's trying to teach you." Tears fell, and the words felt like they were ripped from some dark hole, deep, deep inside her. "That's when he put pictures up. So that even staring at the wall, you couldn't go away. You couldn't get away. There was simply no place to go."

No place to go.

No, that was before. This was now. She pulled free of the talons that threatened to pull her back down into the despairing fear.

With a sniff, she realized she was crying. "They were photos of me. Mostly like the ones you got from the house on Christmas. I think that's how he made the border, or frame or whatever on that painting. There's also other paintings in that room."

Silence greeted her, but she didn't turn around.

"There's also a desk in there. He liked diversity, after all. But that's neither here nor there. In the desk is a journal. A journal of everything. How he paid people off, how keeping me was his main goal even if he had to kill to do it, his plots and plans and schemes."

"Is that where he raped you?" Laurence asked softly.

Christian sighed and nodded. "The first time, yes. The times after. That was 'our' room. It's what he always called it. There's lots of things a man can do without actually . . . without . . ." She swallowed. "It was where he tried to teach me . . . to teach me . . ." She couldn't get the words out. She heard a chair scrape across the floor and then Brayden's arms were around her.

His heart hammered against her ear. She couldn't break now, she couldn't. Biting down past the swirling emotions, she pulled back and gave him a watery smile.

Finally, she turned to face the two policemen sitting at the table. Emma's brows were pulled in a frown. Gabe had no expression whatsoever on his face.

"What?" she asked. "You don't believe me?"

His eyes sharpened. "Why do you ask that?"

"Because no one else ever did, and if they did, he just paid them off or scared them so bad they moved."

"Like Buddy"—he checked his notes—"Michaels?"

She nodded.

"Well, I don't scare easy and I can't be bought off, so that's covered."

A muscle bunched in his jaw. She figured she should probably tell him what else he'd find.

"In the desk—there's also a file on me."

There went that sardonic brow of his. "And what is in this file?"

"A doctor's file. Telling how unstable I was. Still in denial over Papa dying, drugs, sex. Any and everything to paint me as the rebellious teenage slut in case he ever needed it. Dr. Stevens." She answered the question she saw in his eyes. "And no, I've never met the man. Though the file will document that I met with him twice a week."

She sat back down in her chair and took a drink of water. It didn't calm the nauseous storm rioting in her stomach.

"Where were you during this time? It wouldn't do to say you had appointments if people saw you," Emma said.

The cup turned smoothly between her palms. "Good point. No, I had appointments, just not with a Dr. Stevens in his office."

"Then where were you?" Gabe asked.

She looked up and into Brayden's raging eyes. "I was detained in a hidden room by one, now, U.S. congressman, Richard Burbanks, learning all the tricks of the trade."

Chapter 21

They took another shower once they were at the hotel. Brayden had to stop on the way home because Christian got sick.

Rage roared through him.

A congressman? A damn congressman. And the man lived only a mile — one fucking mile — from his family home.

Once he'd known that, he'd called Aiden, who had driven back to Seneca earlier, and gave his brother a shortened version. He wanted Tori safe. The urge to go up there and get her himself rushed through him, but Aiden talked him out of it. Told him that he'd call a security agency and hire a bodyguard, and he was going right then to get Tori.

Thank God for family.

He knew his daughter was safe. Christian was safe, if emotionally drained. Tonight had been so damn hard for her and there hadn't been a thing he could do about it. The idea of having a speed bag here appealed to him, but it did no good right now. He'd already punched another hole in the wall. He closed his eyes and leaned his head back, wondering what was taking her so long in the bathroom, though it was probably a good thing since she didn't see him lose his temper.

Brayden left the bedroom and went into the living room. He paced by the bar, his robe flapping around him, and finally poured himself a drink.

God, the things he'd heard tonight.

The pain and despair that had poured up out of Christian had made his heart break and his hatred burn.

If he found the son of a bitch . . .

Morris was not a stupid cop. The lieutenant told him point-blank that he did not want to have to arrest him for such a lowlife scum.

That was debatable. But then the smart-ass informed him that he was being tailed — for his protection. Yeah right.

He wanted to find the bastard.

He wanted to rip his heart out.

He wanted to . . .

The glass shattered in his hand.

Damn it.

He looked around, grabbed a dish towel and swept the mess into the trash can.

"Did you cut yourself?"

Her soft voice startled him.

Swallowing, he didn't turn to look at her. "No."

"Are you okay?" she asked him.

Was he okay?

He turned to her, incredulous that she'd even ask him that. "Me?"

She was dressed in a pale blue silk robe. Her dark wet hair stood up all over her head and she looked so perfect, so innocent his breath froze.

"You're angry," she said.

Did the woman think he wouldn't be? Her remark didn't even need a response.

"I don't blame you for being angry with me," she whispered from across the room.

He threw the towel down. "What the hell kind of thing is that to say?"

She shrugged.

Brayden cursed himself and strode around the bar, walking to her. "Christian, I'm frustrated and disappointed that you didn't tell me this all before." He saw the dejection in her eyes. "But," he said, cupping her face and tracing her jawline, "I understand why you didn't, baby."

"You do?"

"Yeah, I think I do." He wasn't for sure if he did or didn't. "I mean I do, but I don't. With his position, he had a lot of clout, a lot of power and a lot of people and favors he could call in to make your life hell." He raked a hand through his hair. "I suppose, in a way, I do get it."

She nibbled on her lip. A grin peeked out of the corner of her mouth. "Is there any champagne over there?"

He smiled. "Why?"

Her finger ran over the vee of his robe. "Well, because I would like some."

"I think there might be."

She hugged him tight. "Thank you. Thank you for going with me, for being there, for understanding, even if you don't completely."

Her words humbled him and he kissed the top of her wet hair.

"You don't have to thank me."

She pulled back. "Yes, I do."

God, he loved her eyes.

"Yes, I do," she continued. "If not for you, I wouldn't have been able to get through tonight, through the last few months. I love you."

Brayden ran his hand over her face. "I love you too."

"Champagne?" she prompted.

"I'll get it."

When he turned back around she was gone.

Sighing, he got two flutes and walked to the bedroom.

The cork popped and the bottle fogged out a stream. He filled the glasses and sat on the bed beside her.

"To us and new beginnings," she whispered, clinking her glass with his.

He stared deep into her eyes and noted the fear, if not all the shadows, were gone.

Her lips were soft beneath his.

"To us and new beginnings."

* * * *

Christian lay awake watching the play of nightlights across the ceiling. Brayden's deep, even breathing told her he was asleep.

He was warm against her and she snuggled deeper.

She smiled into the darkness. For the first time in years she felt free. Well, not exactly free, but she was getting there. It was like black chains had been worn away and now all that was left were memories and the threat that something could happen. But the story, the whole horrible story was out.

The stone on her heart and soul was gone. It was a relief and it was . . . empty.

Now, now maybe life could really, truly go on.

Brayden turned and pulled her tighter against him, kissing her neck. "I missed you."

"You just had me."

He laughed, rich and deep. "Yes, I know, and I'd love to again."

"Now?"

"Always, but there's something I want to give you."

"What? You've given me enough."

He sighed and squeezed her tighter. "I love you. I was going to do this earlier, but we got distracted, thought I'd do this after dinner. Which, come to think of it, we never ate."

Brayden's mouth covered hers. She tasted wine and mints.

He turned her gently around and propped on his elbow above her.

"Close your eyes," he whispered.

What was he up to? She studied his eyes for a minute, only seeing a smirk hiding. Finally, she complied.

Something cold and hard grazed down her nose, over her lips, across her chin. She giggled when it slid down her neck.

"You're such a bad boy, Brayden Kinncaid. Sex toys? I thought I was enough for you."

"Oh, you are. And this isn't a sex toy." His laughter rumbled through her and she shifted against him.

Whatever he held he ran over her shoulder and down her arm. The cold metal sent shivers down her spine as it grazed the sensitive flesh of her inner arm.

Down and around her wrist.

What was it?

Over her pinkie, down the valley of her finger.

Up her ring finger.

He stopped.

"Open your eyes."

A ring.

Her eyes shot open.

There, held above her left ring finger, was an engagement ring. A huge, beautiful marquise diamond solitaire.

"Oh, my God. Brayden?"

His smile was devastating in its charm. "There is so damn much going on right now, I don't know what the hell tomorrow is going to be like. I just want to know you'll be there. That you'll still be mine."

Tears filled her eyes and it felt like a hundred butterflies flitted in her stomach.

"Will you be mine? Christian? Will you marry me?" He

swallowed and a muscle jumped in his jaw, even as those intense blue eyes of his stared down at her.

She couldn't look away. "You really want me? With all that you know?"

He only cocked a brow. "I'm waiting."

She swallowed. "I know you love me, but some part of me, some part . . . I don't . . . Are you sure?"

His eyes narrowed. "You're right, I love you. I will always love you, no matter what you say, what I learn." He traced her face with his eyes. "You are as you have always been to me. Beautiful. So beautiful and so strong it scares me. I just want you to be mine."

She bit her bottom lip, then smiled. "Yes. Yes. Yes. Yes." Christian pulled him down for a kiss even as she felt him smile against her lips, felt the slide of the ring down her finger.

"I love you," she said, breaking the kiss.

"And I love you, *mia bella*," he whispered softly.

Their kiss was long and passionate. His hand slid up from her hand, to cup her face.

"You're talking Italian again."

"Of course, got things to show you."

She laughed as he kissed her senseless. His hands cherished and shoved the bedding away so that nothing kept her from him.

Christian brought her hands up to cover herself, but he took them in both of his. "I want to see you. All of you."

He kissed every inch down her body.

Brayden loved making love to this woman; it was a need he could never satisfy, a bottomless pit of need that fed off her.

He propped up on his elbows and watched her, sat back kneeling between her spread thighs.

She lay open and inviting for him. He grinned, ran a finger up the inside of her leg, paused as he reached the tender skin between her thigh and body, skimmed it with his fingers and drew circles up to her breasts. He loved her breasts. He ran his hands over them, smiled when she arched into his palms, sighed as his fingers played over the nipples. He wanted her every which way he could dream up. But that was for later. Now, he knew what she was comfortable with. And since she'd agreed to be his wife . . .

They had years to play in bed . . .

That didn't mean he couldn't have her begging now.

"You're exquisite." Her soft skin, warm as he slid his hands down her belly, fluttering over her hip bones. He raked his nails lightly over her thighs.

She gasped and opened her eyes. Brayden scooted a bit closer to her, spread his knees wider, in turn opening her more for him.

Slowly, he ran his hands back up the insides of her thighs.

"Bray?" she asked.

"What?" He watched his hands skim up the soft supple skin.

She scooted, her bottom against his knees.

His gaze rose to hers.

His eyes were so hotly blue, the center of flames. Christian took a deep breath and smiled. "What are you waiting on?" She wanted him to touch her.

A grin lifted one corner of his mouth. "I want to go slowly."

"I just want . . ." She trailed off as his eyes darkened.

"What? Tell me what you want." His voice was deep and dark as the shadows.

"Whatever you want," she whispered.

His brows rose, and the grin grew. She felt his hands go higher up her thighs, felt his cool thumbs spread her for him. She watched him watch her and knew she was getting warm.

Christian closed her eyes.

"I just want you. To please you. To make you smile."

His thumbs ran over her back and forth, back and forth. She shuddered out a breath. Then he spread her further open and played, his fingers dancing wickedly, wherever he pleased, stroking as he pleased, as deeply as he pleased.

The feelings in her coiled, tighter and tighter. She locked her gaze on his, saw the hardened set of his jaw.

"Bray . . ." She wanted him in her.

His hands grasped her hips and he pulled her up his thighs and entered her in one sure thrust. He rocked them, the feelings he brought to life within her so powerful she could only hold his forearms and arch, accepting.

"I love you," he whispered, his hand running from her face, over her chest, down to her center.

He thrust again, and she shattered, stars bursting behind her lids.

Brayden groaned, leaned over even as he stroked her still. Mumbling against her lips, he said, "That smile. I love that smile I can give you."

Her grin grew then faded on a moan as he took her back up . . .

* * * *

Lieutenant Morris sat astride a chair in the interrogation room.

"Come on, Ivan, talk to us," Gabe coaxed.

Mr. Ristovolich had been in jail for hours, while his prints were run and they tried to ascertain whether he was even a U.S. citizen, which he was not. No visa, no passport, not even a green card.

Gabe shook his head. At least the man should have a fake one, wouldn't he? For God's sake, his boss was a U.S. congressman.

Or maybe Ristovolich did, indeed, have fraudulent papers. Ivan had been in this country long enough to know that he couldn't go anywhere without some sort of identification.

So why had he?

Unless he wanted to get caught?

Gabe frowned down at his watch.

Four a.m.? God, could it be?

"Why did you want to kill Mr. Kinncaid?" Gabe asked.

Something flickered in the darkened depths of Ristovolich's eyes.

"Or maybe you didn't?"

Eyes shifted from his.

Gabe ran his hand through his hair. Why couldn't the guy talk? Ivan knew English. They'd been in here for over an hour.

A knock at the door preceded the person walking through it.

"Who the hell are you?" Gabe asked, standing.

The man extended his hand, and for a moment Gabe experienced déjà vu. Running through his memory, Gabe tried to place the face, but nothing came to mind.

Something about the man . . .

"I'm Duncan Gregor, from Immigration and Naturalization Services." He propped a briefcase on the table. "I'm here to represent Mr. Ristovolich." The locks on his briefcase clicked in the small confines of the room. "We wouldn't want anyone crying 'foul' for any reason later, would we?" Gregor asked, sitting down in a chair beside Ristovolich.

Duncan Gregor had burnished red hair, rosy cheeks, as if he didn't get out in the sun much, bright green eyes, and was a bit overweight. Yet something about the man was familiar.

Shaking off the thought, Gabe cleared his throat. "No, that's true."

Gregor shot off a stream of some guttural language.

Ivan, after a moment, shook his head and answered in the same tongue. The conversation between the two men flew and every bit of it was beyond Gabe. Though he thought he heard a *niet*, and thought that was "no." Maybe not. Gregor shook his head and said, "English."

Ristovolich ran his tongue around his teeth. Finally, he tilted his head toward Gabe and said, "I want deal."

His accent was so heavy, the man sounded like he was swallowing the *l* on the end of his last word.

"A deal?" Gabe asked.

Ivan nodded. "A trade. I get deal, you get dirt."

"How much dirt?" Gregor asked, then looked at Gabe. "I read through the file. A U.S. congressman. I must say you have balls."

Gabe found his first smile in a long while. "That's what they tell me." Standing, he strode to the door, then around the room.

"What dirt?" he asked, leaning on the table.

Ivan shrugged. "Depends."

"On?"

A furrow appeared between Ivan's bushy brows. "You said . . . you said . . ."

"I said?" Gabe asked.

"You said, she thought I help?"

Christian.

"Does it matter?" Gabe inquired.

Ivan nodded.

Gabe sighed. "Yes, that's what she said. We got your name and visual I.D. from her. She seems to think you want to escape."

Deep lines appeared on either side of the man's mouth. "I want deal. I want immunity, if I can. If not and I must go to prison, it is no less than I deserve. I want asylum here in United States and I want my family brought over from Lithuania. I have wife, two daughters and son. I want us all to be able to live here."

Gabe thought for a moment. "You won't do this out of the goodness of your own heart?"

Ivan sighed. "I do have family. If he got away, he would hurt them. They are all I have in this world."

Gabe looked to Gregor.

What the hell kind of last name was Gregor, anyway? Four a.m. God, he needed sleep.

Gregor shot off another burst of indiscernible words. Ivan shook his head, his hands gesturing while he said something back.

Gabe leaned against the wall and waited. After several moments he cleared his throat.

Gregor looked up, frowning. "Sorry, he speaks Russian easier than English."

"What did he say?" Gabe asked.

The man smiled. "Client-attorney privilege, Lieutenant."

Prick.

"But," Gregor continued, smoothing a hand down his perfectly buttoned suit, "I would advise you to push for a deal. I think we both know he's full of all sorts of information."

Gabe knew that.

"I can get it through INS, but you need to push it with the powers that be, here."

True.

It would be another couple of hours before the captain was in, but he could call him. This was a big case, or would be once it was blown wide open. God, the headlines danced in his head like poisoned sugarplums.

Striding through the door, he said over his shoulder, "I'll see what I can do."

* * * *

Duncan Gregor, to those present, waited through the interview, and was not all that shocked at what he heard.

He'd known coming in that either Ivan Ristovolich hadn't known a hell of a lot about bombs or he knew enough that he'd rigged the Hummer purposefully the way he had. Come to think of it, Ian had never heard of anyone wiring the device to the door locks. And his suspicion was proven.

"I did not want to kill the Kinncaid man. He's a good man with a little girl. I have gotten old. I never liked the blood money Mr. Burbanks gave me. I put it all away, could not use it. So I wired car to explode with locks. Everyone has little pad today to unlock door way before." Ivan leaned up on his elbows.

Well, that right there might save Mr. Ristovolich's life, though he didn't know it.

Ian typed things into a laptop. He wasn't about to actually write something. That was far too telling. Writing scribbles on the clipboard at the crash site with his left hand was one thing. In here, it was too confined and he knew they were being watched. Call him paranoid.

So, it was the laptop that he plugged everything into.

"Why didn't you ever just leave?" Lieutenant Morris asked.

Ian looked over his screen as Ivan muttered a Russian curse.

"Fear is strange thing, Lieutenant," Ivan said.

Morris's look said he honestly couldn't understand that.

Lieutenant Morris was a black-and-white kind of guy, an either/or man. For him there were no shades of gray.

For Ian—there was nothing but. The lieutenant might be a decorated special crimes detective, but he still didn't understand the basis of human emotions that led to actions.

Fear fed power, an entrée Ian had seen too many times to discount with a shake of his head.

No, Ian understood power, and probably entirely too well. He shrugged as he typed in more information. Power was in a gray realm, with a hierarchy all its own.

"What was the threat the congressman held over you?"

Ivan sighed. "He promised he would help me become a citizen if I helped him."

"But he never did, did he?" Morris asked.

Ivan shook his head. "And he promised to bring my Tatiana over with the children. I have never met my son."

If Ian had a heart left, he might feel sorry for the guy, but he had no such qualms.

"Take us through it all again," Morris said, sitting down.

Hell, once was good enough for Ian, and they'd already been through it twice, but not for the good boys in blue. Ian knew when a man told all and when he'd lied about something. Mr. Ristovolich had not lied about anything. Ian really didn't need any more information. He had all he needed.

"Problem, Gregor?" Morris asked him.

Ian checked his watch. "No, but I have another meeting in an hour."

After the first run-through, Morris had put in for his warrant to search the Burbank home in Portland. A judge only listened to about half the evidence before signing it.

God bless older judges with three young granddaughters.

Morris was not a stupid man, he knew who to call to get the ball rolling. And since it was a United States congressman who allegedly committed crimes in three states, Morris even got permission for the best crime scene team in Oregon, out of Portland. They worked for both the locals and the feds and all of them were new, the task force having been created only a couple of years ago by none other than former state's attorney general Richard Burbanks.

Irony was a wonderful thing.

Morris, the not-so-stupid man, was studying him again. Ian only raised a brow. "Problem, Morris?" he asked.

"Have we met?"

Inwardly, Ian laughed, but he only smiled to the lieutenant. "No, I don't believe so, why?"

"Something about you is familiar."

"Well, if you figure out what it is, let me know."

Someone knocked on the door. "Sir?"

"Yes?" Morris answered the uniform.

"You have a call in the conference room from Portland, sir. A Detective Stalinski says it's urgent."

Morris left the room and Ian wondered how he could find out the contents of that phone call.

Chapter 22

Christian and Brayden laughed as they got on the elevator the next morning.

They thought they'd give his parents the good news, but Kaitlyn and Jock had already left.

"Wait up," Quinlan hollered.

"Getting a late start this morning, aren't you? It's almost six thirty, Quin," Brayden said.

"I've been up and solving problems for over an hour, brother dear." His gaze ran over them and Christian couldn't help but grin.

"No need to say why you two are just now getting up and about," Quinlan mumbled.

She laughed. "Aw, come on. Don't you want to know?"

He actually blushed.

Both she and Brayden laughed.

"We had some celebrating to do," Brayden said, leaning down to kiss her.

And what a celebration it had been.

"Really? And what is there to celebrate? Did I miss the news flash that this guy had been caught?"

Christian straightened and watched as the humor fled from Brayden's face.

"Well, actually, we did talk to the cops last night and Christian finally gave them a name."

She looked down and swallowed.

"And his name would be?" Quinlan said.

Brayden's hand on hers tightened. She cleared her throat. "Richard Burbanks."

"The congressman?"

Brayden started against her. "You know him?"

"Hell! I shook the bastard's hand." Quinlan's eyes burned at her. "Why in the hell didn't you say something yesterday. He sat right there. Right there in the . . ."

"In the what?" Brayden asked, looking from her to Quinlan.

"I forgot to mention something yesterday."

"Did you, now, babe?" he asked quietly.

269

She threw up her hands. "Yes, I did. Scared the hell out of me when I walked in and saw him. Heard his damn voice. But you know what? I got mad, Brayden. I was so furious, I didn't care. And I felt good, because I knew what I was going to do, knew what evidence there was against him, and he had no clue. No clue."

Quinlan was muttering as they reached the bottom.

Again she threw up her hands. "I'm sorry. But I'd do it again. There."

"Hey." Quinlan reached out and grabbed her hand. "What is this?"

He smiled his one-dimpled grin.

"And here I thought you were so smart," Brayden said.

"Most people call it an engagement ring, dear," she said.

Quinlan rolled his eyes. "'Bout damn time. Congratulations." Then he shook his head, muttering about bastards and sons of bitches.

He strode off through the lobby.

"Well, that went well, don't you think?" she asked.

"Come on, and try to remember if you forgot to inform me of anything else."

* * * *

A warrant? There was a damn warrant out for his arrest? *His?* He was a Representative to the United States Congress! His career and reputation were spotless. How in the ever-living hell had this happened?

He wouldn't even know about it, if not for someone in the Portland police department. The sergeant had called him, but then he always had. Greed was a wonderful motivator.

The girl had guts. She'd always had guts.

Richard looked at his watch, trying to decide what to do. He could stay and fight it, but by God, they'd been to his house. His damn house.

He knew what they'd found.

He should have listened to Estella all along and destroyed what was in that room and just killed Josephine. But damn if he had been able to let go. Estella was right, he was weak. Josephine made him weak.

This storm . . . The fallout . . . God. D.C. was a place of survival; the first to turn on the unwary, the unlucky, the revealed were colleagues and former friends.

The headlines . . .

Thinking quickly and estimating the time he had left, Richard grabbed his wallet, checking the amount of cash he had on hand. Not enough. He reached for his cell phone, but that would never do, neither would his car keys. They'd find him too damn easily then. Entirely too easily.

He hurried down the stairs. Looking back up toward his wife's room. No need to wake her. She'd slept through the phone, and if he did tell her, he'd only have to hear how she'd told him so. How she would never be able to hold her head up. How no one would like her now . . .

In his study, the early morning light slanted through the windows. No snow today, thank goodness.

He swiveled the Renoir out of his way to reveal the safe behind.

It must be going on seven. He had to get out of here.

Quick and deft, he spun the lock. Inside, he took out several thousand dollars.

No one knew of his place off the North Carolina coast, a cottage on a lonely island. He'd bought it earlier in the summer under another name, right after he'd learned of Josephine's location, long before he won the election. It was going to be his and Josephine's special place. Now, she'd get to see it. He could take her out on his boat. Just the two of them.

He shoved the money into his coat pocket and shut the safe.

From the back of his chair, he grabbed his coat.

The French doors opened and shut silently. The frozen ground crunched under his shoes. He turned and looked back, noting his tracks were visible. Hell.

Cursing the season, he ran around in circles. To the edge of the woods, around and around, scuffing his feet along the ground to make a muck of things.

Finally, satisfied at the chaos he'd made of the frosted and dead grass, he took off through the woods, careful to brush away tracks.

It took him longer to get through the woods than he would have liked.

At the edge of them, he looked toward the large gray stone house sitting on the rise.

How was he going to get in?

Same as before, he supposed.

But the police would suspect he'd been here.

A plan.

Damn if he didn't have a plan, and he'd always had a plan. But he never thought she'd actually betray him.

Josephine wasn't even here. She was in town with the family at the hotel. Taking a deep breath, he watched as his exhale fogged in the early morning light.

He would bet the party was still on. No one had mentioned otherwise, and even if it wasn't, they had to come home at some point.

The trick was in finding a place to hide until things settled down. And in a house that size, there were many hiding places.

Sliding away from the cover of the forest, he hurried to the side door.

No wait.

Test the waters.

Taking a deep breath, he quickly changed his plans.

He walked up to the front door and rang the bell.

* * * *

Dressed in gray clothing, so as to blend into the early morning light, Ian Kinncaid slid quietly up the stairs. His hunch was that Mr. Burbanks had already fled. Someone had tipped the bastard off. The safe had been opened, its contents rifled through, and not very thoroughly.

Was the congressman agitated?

He smiled as he eased around the corner and down a hallway. Voices and clatters drifted up from what Ian assumed was the kitchen. The house was getting ready to serve its master his food.

Too bad one of them hadn't laced it with a little arsenic. He shrugged. Though cyanide would work too. Either or, they both got the job done.

Whatever got the job done.

Ian was determined to get this damn job finished.

Time was running out. He could feel it. He needed to finish this, not only for his family, but there were people waiting on him. People who did not like to be kept waiting.

Focusing on the task at hand. He listened at one door, the silence beyond beckoning. Carefully, he cracked the door. The soft scent of a flowery perfume drifted on the air. Mrs. Burbanks.

He gently eased the door shut.

At the next one, he listened and opened it. The heavy smell of aftershave, mixed with the dark leathers, told him whose room this was.

A quick check and scan confirmed what he already knew. Mr. Burbanks had left.

No wallet, though a cell phone rested on the dresser, along with car keys. Smart man, those two were easily traceable. Credit cards were scattered along the mahogany top. Ian picked them up and flipped through them.

Ditch the car, the phone, the credit cards. All traceables. That left cash.

Did our esteemed congressman have a passport? Not under Burbanks, the man wasn't stupid.

Ian was rather impressed. Most people who ran just panicked and ran, no clear thinking.

This was not so with his current prey.

At least the hunting would be more interesting.

He heard car doors shut.

Sliding to the window, he stood at the edge of it and looked out.

The sharp Lieutenant Morris.

Time to go.

Besides, he found out what he came for. Now it was time to hunt.

* * * *

"He's not here," Gabe said. He could feel it. They'd waited too damn long. He'd known that.

"He might be, but I think you're probably right," Emma agreed.

Yeah, well, lot of good agreeing with him did. Gabe wanted this bastard, wanted him badly.

"If he's not here, he won't get far."

Several cruisers pulled up, the uniforms getting out.

"Surround the house," Gabe said, motioning to half of them. "I don't want anyone coming in or going out."

He removed the legal documents that were sure to make this elected government official's life a living hell. Gabe smiled. "The rest of you come with me."

At the door, he knocked.

And waited.

He knocked again.

A short woman answered the door.

"Yes?"

"Are you Ms. Burbanks?"

"No, she's still asleep, I believe. Can I help you?"

"Mr. Burbanks?"

She shrugged.

"You might want to wake them. We have a warrant to search the house and premises, and to arrest Mr. Burbanks."

As they filed into the house, he handed the papers off to the woman, whoever she was, and started barking orders as he took the stairs two at a time.

At the top, he drew his gun, Emma right behind him.

One door swung open, and both he and his partner whirled.

The woman, dressed in a robe, screamed and kept screaming.

"Ma'am? Ma'am? We're the police."

While Emma tried to explain the situation and calm the high-strung woman, he went to the next door, easing it open with his foot.

The room was empty. He quickly checked the bathroom. A quick scan of the room showed him the discarded credit cards, cell phone and keys. But no wallet.

"Where's your husband?"

"What is this all about?" Mrs. Burbanks asked. She was a pretty woman, with brown shoulder-length hair, fairy-like features, and blue eyes.

Marry the mother to get the daughter. It was just sick.

Looking at her, Gabe wondered just how much this woman had known about what was going on. Did she know that her husband had abused and raped her only child, that he was still tormenting Christian? And if she had, had she cared? Though the beauty was there for all to see, there was a stillness, an icy control that told him this woman had been a match for her mate.

It was the eyes. Her eyes were empty. No, there was rage in them, but he didn't think it was at him. She wasn't yelling, or cursing, or throwing a fit. She simply stood there with one hand grasping the edge of her robe together.

"Do you mind if I get dressed? I will be down shortly." With that, the woman turned and walked toward her door.

"Lieutenant Laurence will be waiting right outside the door for you."

She stopped and turned to him. "My husband will have both your jobs. Do you have any idea who he is?"

Gabe rolled his head on his neck. "Not a very nice man?"

"Richard Burbanks is a United States congressman! I'm calling our lawyer."

Gabe nodded at her chink in that icy veneer. "You do that, ma'am."

He hurried downstairs to see how the search was going. He wondered if there was a secret room here. A quick look at his watch told him he probably should call the Kinncaids. Or at least Christian.

The hotel said the Kinncaids were not in residence.

Flipping his phone shut, he realized they must be on their way home, or were already there.

It was a mile down the road. Time to update and get back here. Burbanks wasn't here, the boys outside hadn't seen him. No one inside had seen him.

Ms. Potts, the woman who answered the door, did remember an early morning phone call from a sergeant with the Portland police, but for the life of her, she couldn't remember the man's name.

Didn't matter, Gabe would find and nail the dirty cop to the wall. Portland or not, he didn't care where the man was, he'd tipped off a criminal.

At the bottom of the stairs, he hollered up to Emma.

They met halfway on the staircase. "Is she ready yet?"

Emma shook her head. "No, I don't think she's going to come out, actually. I heard her talking on the phone, yelling on the phone, and our sweet politician's wife knows some interesting curse words."

"Can you handle things here?" he asked.

Her look told him she wasn't even going to bother answering that one.

"Sorry," he said. "I'm going to run over to the Kinncaids' place and give them a heads-up. Especially since we're missing a suspect."

"Did you put out an APB?"

He gave her the same look she'd given him.

"It doesn't feel good to be treated like you're stupid, does it?"

Gabe rolled his eyes. "It's not a stupid thing."

"Yes, it is."

"I don't have time for this." He hurried down the stairs. "I'll be back in a bit."

Her chuckle answered him. As he was walking out the door, he heard her yell, "Carter! For God's sake, this is a search, not a damn tea party."

Yeah, Emma could handle it. He had some news to break to another woman, and he wasn't looking forward to it.

* * * *

Christian hugged Tori to her and said, "I missed you, too."

"How come everyone else gets to know everything that's always going on, and no one ever tells me anything?"

She wasn't sure how to answer that one.

"Because you don't need to know everything, squirt," Brayden told his daughter as they sat down to eat.

It was almost nine and they'd gotten home about half an hour ago; a round of congratulations went around as soon as it was known they were engaged.

Quinlan had stayed at the hotel, and would be here for the party tonight. Aiden and Jesslyn were at their home, several miles down the road, where Brayden had stopped and picked up his daughter. Gavin, Taylor, and Ryan would arrive to the party a few minutes late. Gavin had some appearance to make at another party before coming here.

So it was rather a quiet breakfast with only Jock, Kaitlyn, Tori, Brayden and herself.

"It's not fair," Tori whined.

"That's enough, Victoria, drop it," Brayden said, flipping his napkin out before putting it in his lap.

People were already all over the house. The caterers had arrived a few minutes before the family, the florists were carrying in arrangements. The whole thing was the normal chaos of having a lavish party.

But the family was ensconced in the breakfast room, with only the occasional interruption.

"Will any of you be needing anything else, then?" Becky, the longtime housekeeper, asked, her voice lilting with Ireland.

A round of nos and thank-yous answered her. At the French doors, she stopped.

"Almost forgot. This old age is for the birds. Mr. K., your new friend stopped by bright and early this morning. Said he needed to leave you a message in your study. He was heading out of town." She nodded and patted down her graying hair.

Christian carefully set down her glass.

"I swear, Becky, I don't know why I let you stay with us all these years. Could you be a bit more specific? What friend? What the blazes was he doing here?" Jock leaned back in his chair.

Becky waved absently. "That pompous senator, or whoever."

"Dickie?" Jock barked.

"Are they talking about who I think they are?" Brayden asked her.

Becky tsked.

Christian's mind flew. What had he been doing here? Laying another trap? He'd said he didn't want to kill her. But what if he lied? What if he delivered some gift that would explode like yesterday?

Voices faded and swirled around her.

"Christian?" Brayden shook her arm. "Honey, calm down. It'll be okay."

"Well, I don't care who he is," Kaitlyn was saying. "I don't like him and I don't like that he was in our home with us not here."

"Now, Kaitie," Jock tried.

Something shifted deep within Brayden's eyes even as the skin tightened over his features. Without looking away from her, he said to his father, "I agree with Mom. You have no idea who the bastard is."

"What the hell is wrong with him? You know him? He and his wife bought the Cooley place about a month ago, while you two were away. Nice man, comes from Oregon, Washington? I forget."

Christian licked her lips.

"Son of a bitch," Brayden muttered. "Oregon, Dad. The bastard's from Oregon." His fingers tightened on her arm, then loosened. The doorbell chimed.

"I'll just be seeing who that is," Becky said as she hurried out of the room.

"Victoria, go play in the music room," Brayden said.

Christian opened her eyes and looked at him.

"But, Daddy, I haven't even eaten yet."

"I don't care. Go."

She shook her head. "No, Tori, wait until Becky gets back and then stay with her. Go eat in the kitchen. Don't ever be by yourself. Do you understand me?"

The little girl nodded, looking from one of them to the other.

"What the hell's going on?" Jock asked.

"Later, Dad," Brayden said. "Tori, do what your mother says."

Tori huffed as she slid out of her seat. "I will, even if she isn't my mother *yet*. Not that it's *my* fault. You're the one that's just now getting around to asking her to be a real part of our family."

Smart girl that she was, she quickly left the room, stopping at the door and grinning back at them. The little twit.

Becky stepped up and said, "There's a policeman here to see you. That same cute copper that was here before."

"Miss Becky," Tori said, pulling on the older woman's sleeve. "I'm supposed to go with you and not be out of your sight. I have to eat in the kitchen 'cause Daddy's mad at, as he said, *my mother*. Though I don't know why, it's more of that adult stuff they won't let me listen to. Though I told him she's not my mother yet. 'Course, that's not my fault, now is it?" Tori chattered as Becky led her away.

Gabe stood in the doorway, his coat rumpled as if he'd slept in it, and she knew just by the hard look on his face.

"We need to talk," he said to her.

She started to rise, but Brayden held her hand, squeezing tighter and tighter until she turned to look at him.

The look in his cobalt eyes showed her the mix of emotions swirling in him.

Turning back to Gabe, she said, "You might as well just sit down and spit it out."

As Gabe did take a seat, Brayden said, "Did you arrest the congressman yet?"

"What the hell is going on?" Jock asked.

Brayden turned to her, and waited. He didn't say a word, but then, he didn't have to.

Christian cleared her throat. The orange juice she drank earlier burned a hole in her stomach. Taking a deep breath, she looked to Kaitlyn and gave a brief rundown of the story she'd told the cops last night. Jock and Kaitlyn both had questions once they got past the initial shock.

The hand holding hers was gentle now, Brayden's fingers softly rubbing the back of her hand. He was trying so hard to get past his own anger to be there for her.

"It's over. It's over," he whispered to her.

Christian nodded and looked at him, saying softly, "It will be."

Morris leaned back in the chair he'd sat in. He too answered questions

Brayden looked at the woman beside him and was so damn proud of her. He knew that his parents thought of Christian as their daughter, but right then, it hit him like a slap to the face.

"I'm so sorry he hurt you," his mother said, wiping at her own tears. "Why did he come after you again?"

He put his arm around Christian as she answered, "He swore I was his, and I always would be." She shrugged. "He saw a picture of me a few months ago during the Ryan-Tori-Fisher incident."

"And he found you again. Oh, my poor girl." His mother, who had walked around the table, cupped Christian's face in her hands. "Why, why didn't you tell us? We would have helped you."

Christian nodded, and swallowed. "I know. But I know what he did to people who helped me."

Jock's muttered curse filled the air. "To think I let the bastard into my house, my home, that I thought he was a friend."

"I'm sorry," Christian said.

His father waved a finger at her with his eyes narrowed. "You,

Chrissy, have nothing to apologize for, though from now on, try and remember that families help each other out. I should string the coward up by his balls."

"Get in line," Brayden said.

His mother leaned over and kissed the top of Christian's head. "Jock's right. It doesn't matter now, the whys or how-comes. Now the important thing is stopping him. What about your mother, will she help us?"

Christian's mother was still an enigma to him.

"Actually, if I can get a judge to go for it, we're trying to get a warrant for her arrest too, but it'll be your word against hers," Morris said.

"What?" Jock asked.

Christian sighed. "I told you, my family is not like yours. Did my mom know what was going on? At first, I thought no, and how could I tell her? What was I supposed to say, 'Hi, Mom. Did you know your husband comes to my room every night?' When I finally did get the guts to tell her" — she shook her head — "I thought she didn't believe me, the things she said. He laid the groundwork well, so that if I ever did tell her, she wouldn't believe me. But that morning I left, I found out differently. She knew, she just didn't care."

"Are you certain you didn't misunderstand? I can't imagine a mother not caring," his own mother said.

"You're more my mother than she ever was. I spent more time with Papa or my grandparents growing up than I ever did around her. The only reason I moved with them after the wedding was because of Richard. Yes, I'm certain she knew. That last morning, she came to my room, dressed for the country club. She was looking for a pair of earrings that she accused me of stealing."

Her voice softened and trailed off. Brayden knew, but he knew his parents didn't.

"How does that make her know what was going on?" his father asked.

Christian looked right at Jock and said, "I was still bloody and beaten from the night before, tied to my bed. I think it was kind of hard to miss."

Her breath caught and held. Brayden pulled her close to him, kissed her temple.

His mother just stood there, tears rolling down her face, her hand to her mouth. "How could she? How . . . What kind of . . ."

"Kaitlyn," his father said, holding his hand out. His mother took it and sat in Jock's lap as he kissed her temple.

No one said a single word. Finally, Christian looked to Gabe, and Brayden held her trembling hand. He hated this. Hated that she was having to go through it again.

Brayden shook his head and studied Christian, not at all satisfied at what he saw. Every time he thought about everything, the rage in Brayden beat harder and faster. A bodhran drumming out the call of war. Brayden wanted quite simply to kill the man. And he would. If it were the last thing he ever did.

Chapter 23

"What are you doing here?" Brayden asked Morris without preamble.

Morris cleared his throat. "We have a warrant out for the congressman's arrest."

Answered but not quite.

"Again, what are you doing *here*?" Brayden asked.

Morris pursed his lips and leaned up on his elbows, staring at Christian. "I don't know why I doubted you on the police there in Portland."

"Someone tipped him off," she guessed.

Morris nodded. "Looks like. He's not at the house. We've got an APB out on him."

"Son of a *bitch*!" Brayden glared at the cop.

"He was here earlier," Jock said. Then, ringing a silver bell furiously, he bellowed, "Becky!"

She came puffing around the corner glaring at him. "One day, I will get you, Mr. K. I know where you sleep, I do."

He waved her away. "What did the congressman want this morning?"

Becky frowned. "Well, he knocked on the door almost at seven. I thought it was someone for the party here early, but it was him. There was no car, but then you know as well as I, Mr. K., that he usually walks over. In any case, he said he needed to leave you a message and a gift in your study. Had somewhere he was needing to go and wouldn't be back for a good bit, he said. I asked him where he was off to, just making conversation as I led him down the hallway, but he was vague. Said he was just needing a trip."

"Did he mention where?" Morris asked her.

She shook her head. "At the study door, he took a little box out of his coat pocket and said he'd leave it on Mr. K.'s desk. I told him if a thing was missing, I'd be knowing who to call and I knew where he lived." She waved her hand. "The phone was ringing by then and I was on it in the entryway when he came back out, kinda waved to me and left." Becky shrugged. "That's all there was to the whole thing. I know I shouldn't let him into the study, but he just put the gift down and picked up a pad to leave you a note, so I didn't see anything wrong with it. Why're ye asking?"

"You're certain that was it?" Morris asked her.

"I may look old, but I know what I know, thank you very much," the housekeeper huffed.

"Yes, ma'am. And for the record, I don't think you're old."

Her plump cheeks dimpled on her smile. "You're a charmer, ye are."

Brayden shook his head. Enough of this.

"Where is he?" Christian asked, worrying her bottom lip.

Jock pushed his chair back. "I'll go see what he left."

"No, Dad," Brayden said.

Morris stood in the doorway, having moved there to block Jock's path. "With all due respect, sir, this being your house and all, I'd feel better if we had someone take a look at what he left you first. This is a vindictive man, who tried to kill your son because Brayden here has what Mr. Burbanks considers his."

His father frowned, then nodded. "All right."

Morris pulled out his phone, ordering a bomb specialist here to the Kinncaid home as there was a possible situation.

Brayden knew whether his father had agreed or not, Morris would still do what he was doing now.

"This is never going to end, is it?" Christian softly asked.

Brayden pulled her to him, and kissed the top of her head. "Yes, it will. He can't run forever. It'll end one way or another."

Of that, he was certain.

* * * *

Richard was surrounded by the smell of Josephine, she filled his senses. He could hear the muted sound of people downstairs from his place in her closet.

When the housekeeper had let him into the study, he'd unlocked the terrace door and put Jock's gift on the desk. Then he'd left the way he came, waving to the woman as he'd walked out the front door.

Then he'd hurried around to the side of the house and slipped back into the study door that led out onto the terrace. Once inside, he'd locked the door again, waited till it was clear and bided his time for a chance.

It came with the decorators and florists. What was another arrangement going up the stairs?

Once upstairs, he was in her bedroom, surrounded by her things, her scent, by *her*.

He might not have had a plan before, but he did now. He just had to figure out how to get her out of the house. If he couldn't, then he'd end it here. After all, she had betrayed him.

And no one betrayed him.

Patience, patience. He'd strike and none would be the wiser.

A smile lightened the heaviness of his heart. His career was gone, that was a given.

But Josephine was still his.

She would always be his. He'd kill her before he let her go.

* * * *

Marque DuBouis looked around the entryway and clapped his hands.

"Florence! Florence!" he all but shrieked. This was his best disguise ever. Even his mother didn't recognize him dressed in his neo-Regency outfit, complete with ruffled shirt and a long brocade dress coat.

"Yes? Mark?"

He sighed and propped his hand on his hip, flipping the long mane of dark hair back over his shoulder. In a high-pitched voice he said, tinted with a French accent, "It's Marque. Like the diamond. Honestly, Florence. Marque."

"Sorry, *Markie*."

"*Merde*, Americans!" He shook his head and said with a flick of his wrist, "Where are the fire and ice roses? These are simply beyond help." He gestured to the blooms at his hand. "Bring me more! We're trying to impress, for the love of God. Not scare clients away!"

The college girl hurried off, muttering under her breath.

Marque watched as Lieutenant Morris paced the entryway. What was going on?

"Did anyone go in the study?" Morris asked him.

Marque glanced around and behind him, then turned back to the cop. "Moi? Are you speaking to me?"

The All-American cop narrowed his eyes and rolled his head.

Could the florist be getting on his nerves?

"Is there anyone else here?" Morris asked.

Marque pretended to ponder the question. "I don't believe so, no. The study? Why? What's wrong with the study? Does it need decorating too? I'm sure we can spare an arrangement or two to go in there, though I'll have to survey the room first to decide what goes best. I cannot be expected to work miracles!"

Morris shook his head. "I don't want flowers! Just stay away from it."

Marque thrummed his fingers along his cheek. "Are you gay by any chance?" He almost laughed aloud at the shocked look that flashed over Morris's features. Marque tried to sashay over to the cop, rather impressed with himself at his hip roll. It wasn't exactly as easy as one might expect, but he thought he did a good job. Running his gaze up and down the cop he said, "Normally, I go for the more artistic type, but you are just sooooo . . . Mmmm. I don't know. Something in a rough sort of way."

"I'm not interested, but thanks. And no, I'm straight," Morris said stiffly.

Marque sniffed and turned away. "All you hunky heroes are. Is anyone interested in me? I hate the holidays, just hate them! My partner left me for a construction worker. A construction worker." Fluttering his hands, he asked, "*Where* is the beauty in that?" He shook his head, even managed a tear on a shuddering breath.

Morris looked frantically around. "Just stay away from the study and the back of the house."

With that, the man quickly escaped out the door.

The study, was it?

Marque, chuckling to himself, left, hurrying down the hallway. If all else fails, play stupid.

Inside his father's study, he scanned the area, saw the note and the box on the desk. With a quick look over his shoulder he listened for the sound of footsteps.

No one.

At the desk, he read the note:

Jock, found your pillbox in my golf cart and figured you'd like it back. Sorry for any pain their loss might have caused you. ~ A friend.

Pills? His nitro pills. The son of a bitch. Morris was probably terrified it was another bomb.

He knew that was unlikely. No. Ivan was in jail, and he would bet their dear congressman had no idea how to build a little bomb. After all, Burbanks hired out.

Marque hurried to the door, looked both ways and started down the empty hallway. Nearly there, he almost collided with Brayden coming out of the living room.

"Oh!" Marque shrieked.

Brayden shook his head, dismissing him.

Ian chuckled.

Brayden stopped and turned slowly, his eyes widening. "No," he whispered.

Ian only smiled.

"I said I need you close, but good God!" Brayden whispered.

"You remember what I asked you in Venice?"

Brayden's eyes narrowed and he said, "I want this bastard."

"You sure?"

The look in Brayden's eyes was one Ian knew well. He'd seen it enough in the mirror.

He nodded, then walked on, clapping his hands and asking for his flowers.

He could hear his brother's muttered musings.

Florence came hurrying back into the house with two containers full of fire and ice roses, his mother's favorite.

He looked at his watch. There were things he needed to get. Things he had to have ready and in place by nightfall. But for now, he was in the house, making certain nothing happened.

Life was interesting.

* * * *

Brayden walked Morris to the door, though he didn't move to open it just yet. His parents stood at the bottom of the stairs, his mother talking to the people she hired, his disguised brother included—Heaven help them all. Christian stood off to the side.

"Keep her in your sight," Morris said to him.

"I will."

"At least it wasn't a bomb," the cop said.

That was true, thank the Lord. A note meant to show, to make a person realize the danger that had been so unknowingly close. Brayden hated this, hated this all. He couldn't wait to end it. If they could just find the bastard.

"There will be a couple of patrolmen here. I'm heading back over to the Burbanks' estate. I'll be back later with an update. I want to go over tonight with you. As many people as will be here, it'll be the perfect time to make a move." Morris shrugged. "It's when I'd make one anyway."

Brayden agreed.

"Gabe?" Christian asked.

"Yeah?" The cop turned and stepped toward her.

"Thank you for everything. For all you've done."

Morris smiled at her, closed the distance and hugged her. "Aw, shucks, ma'am. I'm just doing my job."

Her laughter danced out, warming Brayden.

"You're hopeless, you know that, don't you?" she asked Morris, pulling back.

"Yeah, so the girls all tell me. It's hard to be a man in uniform."

Christian rolled her eyes.

"Seriously," Morris added. "Be careful. Don't go off by yourself, stay around the family, and—"

"I know, I know," she interrupted him, shoving him toward the door. "Go catch him so I don't have to be a prisoner, please."

"The ungratefulness of it all," Morris mumbled.

Christian walked over to him and Brayden pulled her against him.

"I'll take care of her."

"If I didn't think so . . . Well, never mind."

The door burst open and a brunette woman came tearing into the house.

"Where is she? Where is that little, conniving bitch?" she screamed.

Christian coiled tightly in his arms.

Morris had his hand on his gun. "Ma'am, you shouldn't be here."

The woman turned blazing eyes to Morris, then past him to zero in on Christian.

"You!" she spat, striding toward them. "I should have known you'd be with some rich man. You've really outdone yourself this time, Josephine."

Christian took a deep breath and stepped forward. "Hello, Mother."

Morris had ahold of the woman's arm, but she shrugged him off, continuing on to them. Brayden tried to push Christian behind him, but she stood beside him.

"Lieutenant, if you don't want a harassment suit, I'd suggest you take your hand off me. Now!" She might dress in Chanel and wear a fur, but the woman was a snake.

Brayden could see it in her eyes.

His mother stepped forward. "Get out of my home. Immediately."

The two women looked each other over, his father coming to stand beside his mother.

Mrs. Burbanks stood not two feet from him and Christian, and she slowly turned to them. "I told him what would happen. But would he listen to me?" she screamed, slapping her chest. "Did he *ever* listen to me? No! It was always *Josephine*. Josephine, Josephine. It was always, always about you! And his lust for you. You! I hate you." The woman spat on her. "I hate you. I wish I'd killed you before you were ever born. I never wanted you."

Enough!

Brayden took a step forward.

The woman's eyes rounded. "Going to protect her? Someone should have warned you. She's nothing but a tramp, a gold-digging little tramp. She knows enough tricks, Richard could have called her out to his friends and made a nice little side profit."

Brayden had only ever wanted to hit one other woman and that had been last summer. Now? Now, he'd happily deck the bitch in front of him. He wanted it so badly just then, so badly, he actually balled his fists. Realizing the temptation, he shoved his hands into his pockets.

Mrs. Burbanks looked back to Christian. "I knew this would all happen as soon as he found you again. I'd hoped that by letting him keep that damn room it would be enough. But no. You almost ruined him before with the ruckus your brother raised over the possible murder, but he survived. He survived and he won, because of me. Me!" She laughed, a cold, harsh and ugly sound. "When he found you again, he asked what I thought when he realized I knew. Men can be stupid. All the while he thought I never knew what was going on. I knew. I always knew. Do you know what I told him?"

Christian took a step away from him. "The suspense is killing me. Please, do tell."

"You haven't changed a damn bit."

Brayden looked to Christian, who didn't so much as blink, the look in her eyes vague and distant but edged in anger. He reached for her, clasping her hand in his.

"I told him he should have Ivan kill you. You would ruin him, ruin his career and his future. But he didn't listen to me, did he?"

At her words, he shoved Christian behind him whether she wanted to be there or not, all the while keeping hold of her trembling hand.

"Leave," he said, afraid of what he'd do if she said more.

His mother walked up to stand beside him, her hand in his father's.

Christian shoved her way around him and in a low voice he'd never heard her use, she said, "Leave. Get out of this house." She took another step closer to the woman who should have, in his opinion, helped, but didn't. "I used to wonder how in the world I could be cursed with a mother like you—now I just don't care. You're worse than he is. You knew all along what he was doing and you didn't care. Tell me, did you have Daddy killed? How much did it cost you?"

"You were always the bane of my life."

"The feeling is mutual, Estella, believe me. You aren't fit to be a mother. You are nothing to me."

"I will not tell you again," his own mother said. "I'll have you arrested for trespassing and slander."

Mrs. Burbanks whirled on his mother, but his father stepped in front of her. "My wife asked you to leave. You don't want me asking."

Morris grabbed her arm. "Come along, Mrs. Burbanks. Don't

make this any harder than it already is."

Again she jerked her arm free. "She's my damn daughter."

"No, she isn't. Christian's ours, she's a Kinncaid," Kaitlyn said.

Mrs. Burbanks laughed again, and this time hysteria danced in the grating sound. "A Kinncaid? No, she'll always be a Montreaux. Through and through. A damn voodoo Creole is all she is, straight out of Louisiana slums. Look at her eyes. Just like her grandmother. Just like her father. It's all in the eyes. In her eyes."

The woman was laughing and sobbing. Cursing one minute, pleading the next.

"Get her out of here," Brayden said.

This time, Morris's hold on her didn't lessen. "Come on, Mrs. Burbanks. You and I need to have a little chat about negligent child abuse, accomplice to sexual assault of a minor, and conspiracy to commit murder." He turned and passed her off to two uniforms who'd come into the house after hearing all the commotion.

Brayden turned and pulled Christian against him. Felt her trembles and wished he'd actually slapped the bitter woman.

No one said a word, silence cloaked everyone. Brayden looked around and caught his brother's eye—though they were black instead of blue.

Ian barely shook his head.

"Well," his father said. "That was interesting."

He felt Christian chuckle.

"Chrissy, love," Jock said. "Please tell me you don't have any more hiding relatives."

Christian pulled back, wiped a trembling hand under her eyes. "Only normal ones. My grandparents and an older brother."

"This is the same brother that raised the ruckus?"

She nodded.

"Good for him. Are we going to get to meet them?" his father asked.

Again she nodded. "Yeah, when this is all over." Christian's voice cracked at the end. Brayden reached for her, but she shook him off. Looking at his mother she said, brokenly, "Thank you."

His mother smiled softly. "Silly girl, there's nothing to thank me for. We'll get all this straightened out. One day, this will all be behind you." She hugged Christian. "I meant what I told her."

"That's why I'm crying."

His mother brushed the tears away. "I thank God for you every day. Don't ever doubt it."

Christian only nodded.

"Come on," Brayden said, pulling her with him. "You need to rest."

"But . . . The party . . ."

"Forget the damn party."

"Brayden's right," his mother agreed. "You need to lie down. I feel like I need to lie down. What a morning. Go on, hon. Go with Brayden. The party will work itself out." She then turned to his father. "Jock, there's been lots of excitement this morning. You go rest, too."

"Now, Kaitie lass."

"Don't you 'now, Kaitie lass' me."

Brayden pushed Christian up the steps and left his parents to their own debate.

"I don't need to lie down," his father repeated.

Then a high-pitched, French-accented voice said, "Why, Mr. Kinncaid! You look positively ghastly." A gasp.

Brayden had to stop and turn to look.

Ian stood in his deep purple brocade frock coat with a hand clasped to his chest.

"What will your sweet wife do if you have to be rushed off to the hospital? Why, the party will be ruined. All my lovely flowers — pshew — gone to waste. No, it is not a good thing, not a good thing at all." Ian sashayed over to Jock.

Brayden barely kept from laughing.

"Here's what you do to relieve stress . . ."

Shaking his head, Brayden all but shoved Christian up the rest of the stairs. If he watched anymore, he'd bust out laughing and have to explain. Ian would never forgive him for blowing his cover.

* * * *

The rest of the day seemed to fly by. Christian stood in her bedroom trying to decide what to wear. It was about three hours before the party was to start, at eight — which was when dinner would be served.

After the family reunion in the front entryway, Brayden took her to his room, where they spent a couple of hours making love.

She smiled at her reflection in the mirror as she held up a black dress. The tension Estella caused ceased to exist once she'd left Brayden's room. He had a way of working all the stress away, of working all the kinks out.

No, this dress would never work.

She tossed it on the bed and reached for another one, her hand stilling. A chill danced up her spine and she whirled around, half expecting to see someone behind her, but there was no one there.

Nerves. Just her nerves.

There, in front, was the dress Brayden bought her in Italy. Why not just wear the blue one? It was appropriate and it was her favorite. Yeah, she'd wear that one.

She pulled it out and hung it on the bathroom door. Hopefully, some of the wrinkles would work themselves out. Reaching into the shower, she turned on the hot water.

Steam filled the stall. She checked to make certain her robe was on the hook by the shower stall door. The hot steam filled the bathroom. Good, she hated to get out of a hot shower to a cold bathroom.

She quickly undressed and stepped into the shower, adjusting the temperature of the water, but still she liked it very hot.

Her sigh carried tensions with it. Soon, it would all be over soon. Then she and Brayden could get married. And as soon as they had Richard in custody, she was calling her grandparents. Or better yet, she'd go see them.

She slicked the water back from her face and thought she heard something.

"Brayden?"

No answer.

A shiver danced down her spine. They still hadn't found Richard. One reason she was getting dressed so early tonight was so that the police could wire her, just in case he showed up, which they seemed to think he would.

Just a whisper of a sound.

"Brayden?" She leaned out the stall door and looked around—

nothing.

She was being paranoid. There were more cops downstairs than the local Seneca P.D. employed.

"Idiot," she muttered to herself.

Shutting the shower door, she let the hot steam and water clear her head.

Chapter 24

Richard listened to the water rushing in the shower. He could picture the liquid sluicing over her luscious body.

It had been so simple.

Cat and mouse. He did love this game.

The police were all over the county and D.C. area; they'd given a joke of a search to the house.

No one looked in the most obvious of places.

He heard the policewoman open Josephine's door earlier that day, and he'd been so far back in her closet, hidden behind the evening gowns, that no one saw him.

So easy.

Again, help was so close, yet unattainable.

He waited until he knew she was in the shower before moving from his hiding place. He'd locked the bedroom door and slipped quickly and quietly into the bathroom.

And she'd called out Kinncaid's name. If he could, he was going to kill that bastard for daring to touch what was his. For turning Josephine against him.

But his first priority was getting Josephine out of the house, taking her away and reminding her of her place with him.

She was humming a song.

What was it?

Pachelbel's *Canon*.

A wedding song that. Why was she humming a . . .

No.

No.

Josephine was his. He fisted his hands, the blood pounding in his head.

Coming from behind the wall to the right of the shower, he decided to have fun with her first.

Richard leaned over and wrote a message in the mirror.

She would never be anyone else's.

* * * *

Brayden stood downstairs with his brothers, though where Gavin was he didn't have a clue. He, Quinlan and Aiden were talking to the new bodyguard. The security agency, since this was an emergency situation, sent two bodyguards in rotations.

The first one was John. That was it. John. The man had reminded him of his brother, quick assessing glances and controlled energy. And he was the same man that had guarded Jesslyn two summers ago in Colorado.

Whereas John reminded Brayden of Ian, the new replacement, Sean . . . Well, Sean *was* Ian.

At least Brayden suspected he was. Sean was the right height with pale, icy blue eyes, a bald head and a bladed nose. He'd done something to his jawline, or had he?

Brayden had seen the man in so many different guises it was hard to remember exactly what was real and what wasn't.

Lieutenant Morris walked up.

"Hello, gentlemen."

"Morris," Brayden answered. "I'd like you to meet the bodyguard we've hired. He works out of a security agency."

"I called them last night and they sent someone early this morning," Aiden supplied.

"I was worried about Tori being here alone and everything."

Morris nodded and looked around the room. "Good idea. What agency is that with, Mr. . . . ?"

"Sean, just Sean. We're with Banockburn Security. A new agency. Some retired government agent set up the service. Or so rumor goes."

Morris looked him over. "You have a card?"

Sean smiled, a dimple appearing in his cheek. Amazing. Ian didn't have a dimple. Creepy. Downright creepy. He handed over a card and Morris pocketed it.

"Where's Christian? We need to go over a few things, and Emma wants to get her wired," Morris said.

Brayden nodded up the stairs. "She's getting ready."

Morris nodded and moved off through the crowd to the nearest waiter — who was actually a cop.

"This, boys, will be fun." Sean slapped him on the back, then straightened as their parents made their way over to them.

Damn.

* * * *

Christian turned off the water and opened the shower door. She probably needed to hurry.

The wall was smooth as she reached for her robe.

It wasn't there.

She grabbed the towel off the shower door and wrapped it around her hair, picking up her robe. Must have been what she heard. She knotted the belt and tightened the towel on her head, securing and tucking the ends under at her nape.

Her engagement ring caught her eye and she smiled. Brayden. She'd wear the pendant tonight too, and the charm bracelet. He would like that.

Everything was finally falling into place.

If they could only find Richard.

She looked up, intending to wipe the mirror. Her heart froze.

MINE slashed across the fogged glass.

Oh, my God. Oh, my God.

She spun around.

Richard stood behind her, dressed in black.

She opened her mouth to scream, but he struck out, his hand snapping across her throat so that she coughed as pain gripped her. Then he grabbed her, his fingers tightening, cutting off her oxygen.

Christian gasped, stumbled, as the momentum slammed her into the shower door. It flew back, hitting the towel rack, and shattered. Glass tinkled around her, down the back of her robe.

"Josephine. Josephine." Richard sighed.

God, her throat. She couldn't breathe, couldn't swallow.

"You've been a very, very bad girl," he calmly stated.

She clawed at his hand, at his arm. God, she couldn't breathe. Pain burned in her throat as she gasped for breath. He was going to kill her.

She raked her nails down his face and he lifted her higher, up onto her toes.

Spots danced before her eyes. Richard dropped her and she gasped for air, her hand flying to her throat. Gasp. Wheeze. Gasp. Wheeze.

Not now. Not now. Not that an inhaler would do her a bit of

good. Think. She had to think. Glass bit into her knee and palm.

She opened her mouth to scream and nothing came out.

Richard's smile iced her blood. "You made me angry, Josephine. I could have crushed your windpipe. That would be a tragedy, considering the gift you have. I expect your larynx is bruised." He squatted beside her. "The larynx is an interesting thing. Hit hard enough, no sound comes out. And what does is basically unheard." He laughed. "Don't worry though, in a few days your voice will be as good as new. And you can sing for me."

"Go to hell," she rasped out.

His eyes narrowed on her as she tried to stand. She backed up and winced, slicing her foot on a piece of glass.

"You do look wonderful." Those pale green eyes roved over her and he smiled. "Something about you wet always turned me on, all those little droplets of water."

Terror clawed at the back of her mind.

Gasp. Wheeze.

God, she hated this man. She looked at him, deep into his eyes, and hoped he saw how much she loathed him. "You are nothing but a pathetic coward."

A flicker in his eyes warned her just before he lunged. She dove to the side, slamming into the vanity.

She reached for the door, threw the lock as she screamed. But the sound was muted, garbled and lost.

He grabbed her robe, jerked back, and spun her around.

Christian fought. Kicked, clawed, hit. Skin gave way under her nails.

"You bitch."

He hit her, hard enough she stumbled again, tearing out a vanity drawer. Objects scattered and bounced all over the plush rug.

"I had hoped we could do this the easy way."

He was on her, straddling her. Just like before. Just like before. Time stopped. Terror exploded inside her, reverberating down her spine, freezing her of all thought, of all action. Her mind screamed for her to do something. Something inside her shattered.

Never again.

Never again!

She bucked, twisted, and fought, but pinned as she was, there was little she could do.

"I hate you," she bit out, no more than a soft whisper.

He only smiled, thin and straight as a dagger. The fire in his eyes burned with an unholy intent.

"I'll ask a question and all you have to say is yes or no. Or rather," he said, reaching behind him, "just nod or shake your head. I'd hate for you to strain your voice." His switchblade hissed open.

The blade winked in the lights, wicked sharp.

"Now, Josephine. Is that a ring I see on your finger? An engagement ring?" His knee was on her left wrist, his hand holding her right one down.

"Is it?" he asked, his breath hot against her face.

What was he going to do? Did it matter? She couldn't, wouldn't bow to him ever again. Besides, she wanted the satisfaction of him knowing she belonged to someone else. Looking straight into his eyes, she smiled. "You're damn right it is."

He tsked and stabbed the blade into her shoulder.

She screamed, a garbled, high whispered sound. Christ.

The pain blinded her. Oh, God. She bucked and twisted, tears leaking out. He jerked the blade free and blood flowed. She felt the slide of it as it soaked her robe. Bile rose in the back of her throat and the lights dimmed and tilted.

She looked at the wound, the red was growing.

"Let's try this again, shall we?" Richard asked. "You know my rules. I don't share."

He'd released her left hand. God, her arm hurt.

The room spun and all she saw was the red spreading over the blue silk of her robe.

The objects eye level with her drew her attention. Makeup tubes, combs, brushes, odds and ends. A cord. She followed it up. Her curling iron balanced on the edge of her vanity. Had she plugged it in?

"Are you going to marry him?" Richard asked. "Do you think I'll let you?"

The light winked off of silver on her floor. Shears. Antique barber shears. Sharp blades. If she could just . . .

Slowly she inched her hand along the carpet.

"Josephine," Richard practically whined. "Why can't you love me? Why? I want you to say my name, whisper it, like you do his."

She looked at the shears. No, a distraction, first. The curling iron.

* * * *

Ian watched and waited. He needed to get upstairs and check things out.

"Sean, do you like what you do? How long have you been a bodyguard?" Jock asked him.

It was amusing to him that his own parents didn't recognize him. He didn't expect them to and was glad that they didn't.

"Several years, sir," he answered.

"I guess you stay busy then, huh?"

Ian nodded. He watched as Brayden headed up the stairs to get ready. Brayden was going to shower and then bring Christian down to get her wired.

"Honey, leave the man alone, I'm sure he has things to check," Kaitlyn said, coming up and smiling slightly at him.

She tilted her head to the side. "I could swear I know you, but I guess not."

He smiled.

"I thought the same thing," Jock muttered. "In fact you remind me of . . . Well, never mind."

Sometimes he missed home. At least this trip he'd actually managed to come back here, to this house. It had been years since he'd been here. The last time was when his father disowned him. Call it perversion, but he liked the idea that his father was now shaking his hand and welcoming him into the house as a bodyguard.

But that's what he did.

So that is what he would do.

The spatter of a police radio whispered across the room. The server in the back. They needed to work on the volume a bit. 'Course, considering police department budgets, they didn't have the equipment he did.

He turned and walked out of the room. Time to run a search. He could feel it. Things were drawing to a close. First, he'd scan the downstairs, then the upstairs.

* * * *

"Do you love him?"

It would be smarter to say no. *Say no.* But she couldn't. Never again would she bow to him, no matter what.

She licked her lips.

Lie. Lie. Lie.

She nodded. The words scratched her throat. "He's a real man. Why wouldn't I?"

The blade came down again, embedding to the hilt. She felt the skin on the back of her shoulder break. Again he jerked the blade free and she felt the blood flow.

God Almighty! A wave of dizziness washed through her, and she fought not to throw up, sobbing at the pain.

"No, you are not," Richard hissed. "No one will have you but me."

Christian looked up at him as he lowered his mouth to hers. When he was almost there, she reached out, moaning at the pain in her arm, stretching for the cord.

Before he turned, she spit in his face.

There. She jerked. The iron landed with a clatter. She picked up the black end.

"You shouldn't have done that," Richard said, wiping the spittle off.

She slammed the iron up with all her might, holding the heated metal against his forehead.

He cursed and leapt up from her.

Christian rolled and grabbed the shears, her arm hanging at her side, blood dripping off her fingers.

Richard yanked on her hair. "Stupid bitch. I would have given you everything, everything. You're nothing, nothing now."

She turned and shoved the scissors up to his groin, but he met her move and twisted. The blades slid into the flesh by his hip bone.

Still he yelled and struck out at her. Her head hit the wall, glass bit into her palms. The world rang in her ears.

Hurry. She pulled herself up, listening as he moaned, pulling the shears free. Her blood smeared along the wall.

She jerked the door open and stumbled through her room.

"Help! Help!" she screamed. Nothing but a strangled whisper.

God, where was everyone?

At her door, she twisted the knob. Blood slicked her hands, but she unlocked it, throwing the door open. He was coming. She could hear him.

The hallway spun and tilted. Not now. She was not giving up now.

She staggered through the doorway, just as he stumbled through after her.

His hand slammed down on her shoulder and the pain brought her to her knees, sending her into a little side table. It wobbled, tilted, and sent the dainty china figurine crashing to the floor.

An arm locked around her throat and pulled her up; something stung down her arm twice as he stumbled.

The world grayed. Blood dripped from her fingers.

Someone screamed.

* * * *

Brayden heard Tori screaming. He threw his shirt aside and tore out the door.

The sight that met him halted him in his tracks.

The bastard held Christian. Blood covered an entire side of her robe, trailed from her fingers.

Mother of God.

He saw men racing up the staircase.

"Shut her up. Shut her up!" Richard yelled.

Brayden picked Tori up and shushed her. "It's okay, sweetie. It'll be fine." Someone came up behind him and he turned.

Emma Laurence. "Take your daughter out of here."

"Not a chance." He shoved Tori into the woman's arms.

"Congressman, calm down. No one needs to get hurt," Morris tried, his gun held at his side.

Brayden edged closer; chills raced over him at the sight of Christian bleeding. Richard spun from the men in front of him on the staircase, to Brayden standing behind him.

When Richard stopped and looked at him, he could see the intent in the man's eyes. Evil as the devil's heart, and cold as a grave.

"We had a little disagreement."

He heard Christian wheezing.

"Want to know what it was over?" Richard asked.

Brayden looked at Christian's ashen complexion. How much blood had she lost? He noticed blood stained the front of Richard's pants.

"Do you!" Richard yelled.

Brayden licked his lips. "If you want to tell me."

The bastard leaned over and nuzzled Christian's ear. "Do you want to tell him, Josephine, or should I?"

His laugh slithered across the hallway. "Oh, I forgot. She can't talk, not really. She's been a naughty girl. So I took care of that problem."

What the fuck did that mean?

"Christian?" Brayden asked, looking at her. Her eyes were glazed.

All he could hear was her wheezing.

Hang on, baby. Just hang on.

God help him.

"Well, since she can't tell you, I guess I should. Our disagreement was over you." The man smiled. "I told her I didn't share, and here she is wearing your ring." He tsked. "I almost cut her finger off for that, but that would disfigure her, so I can't do that, now can I?"

Brayden shook his head, always sliding toward them. "No, you wouldn't want to do that."

"I told her she couldn't love you. She can only love me. Only me!"

What reasoning was there with a madman?

Brayden moved closer, almost to them, but the guy kept pulling Christian with him along the wall, closer to the staircase.

"I can't let you have her. I can't let her go."

Well, Brayden wasn't about to let the bastard take her.

"She is," Richard continued in that silky voice, "my angel. My beautiful, lovely angel."

The glint of a bloody switchblade hissed right before the son of a bitch pointed it at her neck.

"I don't want to steal such beauty from the world. But dead, we would be together. Forever."

Christ.

"You—you don't want to do that," Brayden tried, keeping his voice calm. Out of the corner of his eye, he saw Ian poised at the entrance of the other hallway just off the stairs. Everything, all the wings intersected at the head of the staircase.

"Why? Because you want her?" Richard taunted.

Brayden saw the pearl of blood at the tip of the blade as it pricked her skin.

Christian wheezed again, jerking Brayden's gaze to her. Her eyes fluttered shut and she slumped in Richard's hold.

Two shots fired, both spinning Richard around. He lost his hold on Christian and Brayden rushed him.

Brayden growled as he flew at the monster.

He hit him, mid-torso, the momentum carrying them both back toward the banister.

"Brayden, move!" Ian shouted.

He saw the blade coming and ducked, reached up and grabbed it. For a bleeding man, Richard was strong, stronger than Brayden had given him credit for.

The blade glinted as it wavered between them. "You're a low-life son of a bitch," Brayden bit out between his teeth. "It's time to reap what you sowed." With a prayer and a curse, he used his strength to turn the blade toward Richard. Closer and closer.

The man's eyes glinted and he smiled. "She will always be mine."

"She was *never* yours." Brayden shoved his weight against the knife, felt it slide in, nick a rib, and pop the heart. Blood flowed over his hand. "Burn in hell."

He heard the wood crack, felt it give and tried to jerk back.

Richard grinned and locked his hand around Brayden's wrist.

The railing gave way and Brayden pitched forward.

"Stupid, hotheaded ass," someone said.

Hands jerked him back, grabbed hold of Richard, but the other man slipped and crashed to the hardwood floor below, blood spreading in a dark pool around him.

Brayden turned and looked at his brother. The disguised icy blue eyes were furious. "Don't ever pull a dumb stunt like that again."

Brayden huffed out a breath. "Thanks."

He turned and rushed to Christian, who lay crumpled on the rug, her bloodstained robe sticking to her body.

Gavin was working on her, bending over her, checking her pulse and his watch. He must have come up the back stairs.

Brayden knelt beside her. She was almost gray. Oh, God, please, no. Not after all this. He couldn't lose her now.

The look on Gavin's face was serious. Gavin said, "She's been stabbed twice, has other smaller cuts, lost a lot of blood and has a bruised larynx. Ambulance is on the way and FlightStar is waiting at the local hospital. We're going to medevac her to Georgetown Memorial."

Brayden sat down and dropped his head. Gently, he leaned over and kissed her cheek.

"I'm sorry, baby. So damn sorry."

Why couldn't it have been him the bastard went after?

People shuffled and moved around them. He heard his parents, thought he heard his daughter, but none of it registered. All he saw was Christian. All he knew was that he failed her again.

Epilogue

Christian opened her eyes. The stringent smell of a hospital stung her nose. Then she realized it was the oxygen hose.

The bleep of a monitor pierced through the haze. What was she doing in a hospital?

She turned and saw Brayden sitting by the window, his arms crossed over his chest, dark stubble on his jaw.

Her arm and shoulder throbbed. Licking her lips, she realized she was thirsty.

"C-can . . ." Only a whisper came out.

Memories slammed back into her. The bathroom. Richard. The knife. The fight. Brayden.

He turned and hurried to her bedside. "You're okay. Calm down. You're safe." His hand on her forehead was feather-light. She leaned into the comfort.

"You've been out for a good while. Scared me to death, though the doctors tell me this is all normal, considering your wounds."

Stabbings.

"Richard?"

Brayden's face hardened. "You'll never have to worry about him again."

What did he mean?

"He's dead. Shot twice."

Well, that was nice to know. A smile caught her off guard. The monster in her life was banished.

"Rest, you should rest." He leaned over and kissed her cheek again. "Don't try to talk. The doctor said it would be several days before any normal sound came out as long as you don't push it. Are you thirsty?"

She nodded. A machine hummed beside her.

Sunlight slanted through the window and across her bed.

Water sloshed in a glass, dripped off the bottom and onto her hand as he moved it over toward her. The straw felt awkward, her mouth as dry as sawdust. But the water was wonderful.

Too quickly he took it away. "The nurse said only sips."

She rolled her eyes, or tried too. Suddenly the throbbing in her arm stopped and she felt light and floaty.

"Go back to sleep."

Christian reached out and grabbed his hand. "Don't leave me," she rasped.

"Never." He sat in the chair beside her, and held her hand.

"I love you," she tried to whisper.

"I love you, too."

Blackness swirled and swept her into a painless oblivion.

* * * *

Ian slid into the car and shut the passenger door. The police had badgered him, but his story was rock solid, even if one of his bullets was in Richard's upper chest, the other from Morris. All the numbers they called were answered by an answering service for Banockburn Security. Of course, Sean McClean worked for them. And they were sad to hear someone died, but at least the little girl, who he was hired to protect, was all right.

The police had no choice but to buy it. He had to come back for some interviews. He told them fine. Even went so far as to write them down in a neat black organizer. No one in that department would ever see Sean McClean again.

"Can we get the hell out of here now?" John asked him, his British accent clipped to a point, as it often got when he was tired.

"What, didn't you enjoy your vacation?" Ian asked, looking over at the only man he'd trust his back to. Well, besides his brothers. But he needed someone in the business to help with this operation, and John was it.

"Oh, definitely." John continued, "Nothing I like more than stings. What, after all, does a beach, a tanned woman, and lots of fruity drinks have to compare with excitement like this. Blood, lies and bullets. My kind of fun. Personally, I'd go for the sand, the drinks and sex. Lots and lots of sex with tanned women, fruity drinks on the beach."

They pulled away from the curb.

"All things considered," John continued, "I think that all went rather well. We even managed to cover our arses."

"Went well?" Ian asked him.

"Everyone lived, didn't they? Too many variables to cover. We try."

"Trying's not good enough."

"Not when it's our own, is it, boyo?"

The early morning D.C. lights whizzed past. Silence stretched between them. They were almost to the airport when John spoke again. "Time to get back, she's already been calling wondering what the hell is taking you so long."

"She'll wait," Ian added. "We had to finish this. I didn't want to have to come back later and clean up."

"You could have just ended this much earlier. You knew who the bastard was weeks ago."

He could have, yes. "I should have, after the way it fubared there at the end. Almost lost Christian."

"You just wanted your brother to have a go at the bloody bugger."

Damn John anyway. "Would you shut up."

"Yeah, it went damn well. And almosts and should'ves don't make a fuck, mate. God, I love job success."

* * * *

When Christian opened her eyes again, she couldn't believe what she was seeing.

"Grandmere?" Damn her voice.

"Ah, you're awake." The old raspy voice held a hint of French Creole. "Don't strain your voice. Your man explained it all to us. Scared us, Joshua showing up with that Quinlan Kinncaid in the wee hours of the morning. Knew right away we'd found you again."

A cool, weathered hand cupped her cheek.

Christian felt the slide of tears.

"Child, don't cry. Don't cry. The darkness has passed. All you have now is the light." The hand was as soft as she remembered, the white hair pulled back in a bun, eyes as gray as her own held the wisdom of age. "How we've missed you. I knew. I always knew we'd find you one day. And then there was Josh and Quinlan. That man flew down and found us, flew us back up here. Didn't want your granddad and I, or even your brother, to hear this all on the news."

"I'm sorry," she whispered.

Her grandmother sighed. "Regrets are only good for regrets. Look forward. Always forward." She shifted. "I have to tell you, I love your man. Very strong, very honorable, very handsome. He reminds me of your grandfather. That one will last you a lifetime."

Christian nodded and pulled her hand out to hold her grandmother's.

Her grandmother smiled. "Now, I should tell you the wedding plans we've come up with . . ."

The door opened.

"I'm sorry, didn't mean to interrupt," Brayden said, pulling her attention around.

"Why, you're not. Come over here and give me a kiss, young man, then give one to Christian."

Brayden smiled, did as she asked, then stood by the bed.

Christian smiled up at him. "Thank you."

"You're welcome." He leaned down and kissed her on the mouth.

"Are they still fighting?" her grandmother asked.

Christian looked to Brayden.

He was glad to see she had color back in her cheeks, but she was still too pale. It would be a long damn time before he didn't have to know where she was and what she was doing. He held her hand, rubbing the back of it, noting how dry it was. He'd bring her some lotion.

"Dad and your granddad," he answered the question he could see on her face. "Mom and Clara—"

"That is Grandmere to you," the elderly woman interrupted.

Brayden smiled. "Mom and Grandmere have been making wedding plans. Your brother and I duked it out, not that I blame Josh."

Her grandmother muttered something about self-blame. Hell yes, he blamed himself. Why wouldn't he? If her brother blamed him for Christian getting hurt, that was fine by him. At least they were speaking to each other now. And Joshua Montreaux knew where Brayden stood with the guy's sister.

"Anyway, Dad and your granddad are fighting over where the wedding will be. You have an opinion?"

She smiled and nodded.

"You do?"

She looked at her grandmother and shared another smile.

Clara's eyes were as gray as her granddaughter's. She said, "All Montreaux women wed at Montreaux Meadows. It blesses the union, or so legend goes. You don't want to rebuke a legend, or blessing, do you?"

Brayden thought for about five seconds. His mother might not believe in the family curse, but he'd washed Christian's bloodstains off his hands. "No, ma'am. I think a Southern spring wedding will be wonderful."

Christian shook her head.

"No?" he asked.

"No," she whispered. "No later than Valentine's Day."

He smiled. Fine with him.

"How about *on* Valentine's Day?"

She nodded and smiled.

Clara stood. "I think I'll leave you two to iron out details." She patted Christian's bed. "Don't worry, I'll be back."

Brayden waited until the door shut, then he sat on the bed beside her.

"A Valentine's wedding. Are you sure?" he asked.

"Well, I'm not drunk, and I miss playing house with you."

He smiled. "Do you?"

She nodded and he leaned over and kissed her lips.

"Well, then, it is house we shall play."

Coming soon!

Read on for more of the Kinncaid family
in an excerpt from *Deadly Games*!

* * * *

Chapter One

Thirteen years later
Czech Republic
October 28, 10:00 p.m.

The Prague club roared with the sounds of vices better left unknown, but too tempting for most. This Czech city was Janas-faced. Two faces of the same coin—its beauty and old world for the discerning tourists, but flipped, the red-light districts rivaled those in Amsterdam or the worst hells on earth. An evil, black and thick, rolled through the Prague underground, plumping its greedy fist from those who sought pleasure in unconventional ways.

So much for a quiet evening at home. Though quiet might not be found for a couple more days. Most residents were out celebrating— this was, after all, Czech Independence Day. The pop of fireworks burst through the air, laughter rang out and motorists zoomed by. Tonight was full of revelry. Fireworks still shot from Prazsky hrad, bursting the castle walls with color, and people still gathered in *Stare Mesto*.

Dimitri Petrolov, also referred to as the Reaper, strode to the front of Nero's Nightclub. Ivan, the bouncer, only nodded to him and let him pass. But then Dimitri really hadn't expected anyone to try and stop him. There was, after all, a good reason for his nickname. He was Viktor Hellinski's enforcer. And everyone who was anyone knew Hellinski was not a man to cross.

The club pulsed. Rammstein beat against the smoked-tinged air from hidden speakers. Strobe lights flashed through the darkness, and dancers, revelers, drug users alike took on a macabre glow. The club was painted black, with the only relief burning murals on the walls that seemed to glow and flicker in the black lights.

"Hey, Dimitri, baby," a sultry voice called.

He looked to his right, where one of the night waitresses weaved between bodies with a platter of empties. Debromil. Or was it her twin, Elsa? They were both blonde and stacked like Viking goddesses. Hopefully, they would simply remain waitresses and not wind up in Hellinski's other jobs. He merely smiled at her. Her silicone breasts, all but bursting from the corset she wore, didn't move as she gyrated to the music, her platter of empty drinks never wavering.

Dimitri wove his way to the staircase at the back of the club. Women, men, college kids moved out of his way. He ignored the drugs, probably ecstasy, being passed between two girls. Another couple kissed openmouthed. His foot on the bottom step, he heard the sounds of an argument between a man and woman, but ignored them. At the top landing he looked below at the strobing, spandex- and leather-clad figures, dark in the shadows of flickering bright lights. The smell of cigarette smoke, the tinge of stronger chemicals mixed and melded with too many perfumes on too many bodies, and glossing it all was the permanent smell of alcohol. It was the fragrance of greed and vice. Well, one he associated anyway. Most here tonight were simply out for a good time. At least this was Nero's and not one of the other clubs.

He closed his eyes for a moment before turning to the hallway, guarded by two men he personally thought of as Pit and Bull. Their jackets did little to cover the holsters or the semiautomatic weapons harnessed there. But who the hell was he to raise a brow at a weapon. His SIG Sauer P226 was in his own shoulder holster beneath his suit jacket.

His skin itched with the knowledge that something was up. He didn't even look at them as he walked down the hallway. The black door at the end was marked *Private*.

Dimitri ignored this and shoved the door open, walking into the dark office. A low light spilled from a lamp on the desk. The tall leather chair was turned away from him, facing the large picture window that overlooked the floor of the club below.

"What took so long?" Viktor asked, not turning.

"I was otherwise . . ." Dimitri paused. ". . . engaged."

Viktor scoffed. "Were you? Hope she gave you a good time, my friend."

Dimitri chose not to answer. Instead, he walked to stand at the edge of the window looking at the melee below. They reminded him of chaotic ants. Too much confusion.

"Nice profit tonight."

"Yes," Dimitri answered, not bothering to look at his boss. The man was reflected in the glass. No one could see them. As a viewer below, it looked like a giant wall of mirrors that only reflected the dancing, blinking scene back to the revelers. He studied the man sitting in the chair, his hands resting on the arms, a glass of vodka in his hand.

They both stared out at the scene below them. Dimitri waited. He never pressed for details, never asked. Questioning, in his opinion, led to others questioning him. Questions often gave more away than silence. And silence, he had learned, afforded him more.

He watched as one man and woman screwed against the wall in the shadows. The bouncers and guards didn't notice, and if they had, nothing would have been done.

People gyrated on the dance floor; to him, they all looked the same. A sea of black ants. Drugs, sex, booze — just a good time, they'd say.

If they only knew.

"I have a job for you," Hellinski said.

Music from below barely pulsed through the floor or walls; there was a soft vibration from the base, but that was it. Dimitri knew these rooms were soundproof.

As was the rest of the building.

People came to play downstairs and some went upstairs and to the adjoining building for a different taste in entertainment that had little to do with dancing on the dance floor. It was only one of the many businesses that Dimitri helped his boss oversee.

These days he was gone more than here, only called in for specific jobs.

Dimitri waited in silence again.

"'Tis annoying habit you have, Dimitri. Silence. I don't like silence. I've killed others for their arrogance, you know."

"Yes, I know." And he had been the one to put the bullet in many of them.

"I'm also aware I'm not the only one who gives you orders."

He kept looking at the dancers and partygoers below. He saw a group of young men slip something—probably roofies—into the drinks of their dates.

"No, sir. You told me when I was brought in that I would answer to Elianya as well as to you."

The older man grunted and Dimitri turned to study him. Viktor did his Slavic ancestors proud. Wide slanted eyes, like those of a lion, watched him from their amber depths. Viktor's nose was slightly crooked, broken God only knows how many times. Scars slashed across the right side of his elongated face. The ash-blond hair was pulled back in a queue. The man was one of the most feared in the Prague underground, and in time, Dimitri knew, he himself would be on Viktor's hit list. It was simply the way the game was played.

Those amber eyes narrowed on him, even as Viktor straightened in his chair and pulled at the maroon silk shirt he wore. "Tell me what you would do if I ordered you to kill someone you might not want to."

Dimitri merely arched a brow. What game was the man setting into motion now?

He walked to the sideboard, reached into the small refrigerator, and pulled out a frozen glass. The vodka poured in smoothly. He set the decanter aside and turned back to his boss, sipping the clear liquid.

"When do I learn the name of this . . . problem?" Someone *he* wouldn't want to kill? His pulse sped. No way the man could know. Dimitri glanced at him as he sat in the chair to the side of the desk, his back against the wall, facing the rest of the room.

Viktor frowned and propped his left ankle on his right knee, his foot bouncing.

"Perhaps," Dimitri ventured, "the person is not one whom *I* might have a problem eliminating?"

Those eyes snapped back to him. Silence settled between them.

"Perhaps."

Dimitri nodded. And waited.

With a curse, muttering of whores, Viktor stood, his hands clasped behind his back as he stared again out the window.

Apparently someone had angered Mr. Hellinski. Not wise, but then who was he to complain. This was what he did.

On a deep breath, the other man shook his head. "Come back tomorrow night. I will give you a name then. I want it done as soon as possible."

It was Dimitri's turn to frown. Why the hesitancy?

"Hellinski." When the man faced him, he said, "You're a hard man, with a business to oversee and protect, and as far as friends go, I consider you one."

Viktor smiled, his scarred face more distorted. "And I you, Dimitri. And I you."

"You don't like people to cross you." Dimitri stared at him. "And you have no mercy for those who betray you."

Viktor inclined his head.

"I'm of the same mind." Dimitri stood, set the glass down.

Viktor's eyes widened in shock. "You think I would betray you?"

Dimitri smiled. "For enough money, yes."

Viktor laughed, but they both knew the words to be true.

"I'll be back tomorrow night."

Viktor nodded. "You're right on what you said of betrayal. I'll give you the name night after tomorrow, as I just recalled I have a prior engagement. I do want the job finished within the next week."

Dimitri strode out of the office, seemingly not paying any more attention to anyone than when he walked in.

He slapped Ivan on the arm as he walked out of the club and put his head down against the cold autumn wind. He waited for a cab, noted that Ivan took out a cell phone and made a call.

* * * *

She set the phone aside and bit on her thumbnail. Now what? Damn it all to hell. She had not worked this hard to see it all go up in flames. Not now.

One stupid mistake.

But she held the cards. She knew, she held the winning hand.

Kill someone whom Dimitri might object to?

She chuckled. For all the hard-won reputation, for all the crimes the man had committed, all the lives he had taken, she knew Mr. Petrolov for what he really was.

A savior of the weak, a champion of the downtrodden.

The Reaper? More like the Saint.

Oh, he killed all right. And Elianya Hellinski had no doubt that when her brother ordered her hit, Dimitri Petrolov—or so he was called—would not hesitate in carrying out that order. And probably enjoy doing it.

Things had not ended well with them. Damn the man, they could have ruled and created their own dynasty if he'd only listened to her.

But no. Elianya was a good fuck, but nothing more. Fine. She'd had others turn her down. Of course, they were all dead. He would be as well. Pity though, the man was the best lover she'd ever had. But a woman had to do what a woman had to do. If the bastard didn't want her, that would be his loss. No man, no matter how much he amused her, would reject her. Period. She simply didn't allow that.

Besides, if he lived, he might be a problem. Might? She sighed. If Dimitri Petrolov was anything—it was a threat. She knew without a doubt Mr. Petrolov would kill her in a split second if he found out what she was really doing. For all his darkness and fear, the man was one of the most honorable she'd ever met. It was very sad. Honor was well and good in certain aspects— business, business where millions could be made, no. She had no use for such as the likes of him. Besides, she'd given the man his chance and he'd turned her down.

Ball-less wonders. Women were, without a doubt, the stronger, more driven sex. Men waited on orders, let too many things tie their damn hands.

No one tied her hands. No one. Not Dimitri, not Viktor, not any man.

Her heels clicked as she paced her office, the hardwood floors gleaming.

Stopping, she looked out the window, over the inky black waters of the Vltava River. She loved the nights. The night was the only time the truth shone in this world.

People hid behind daylight.

She grinned. And in daylight she would make certain it happened.

Walking back to her mahogany desk, she sat down and clicked on the address she'd paid dearly for. If this failed, there was always a backup. One should always be prepared.

Time to hire her own enforcer and make certain at the end of the night she was the one left standing.

* * * *

New York, New York

The Raven clicked her way through wasting time as she waited on her plane, reading headlines via the Internet.

Her heart still slammed against her chest, but she knew enough to go slowly, to stay calm.

The last job went smooth as butter, and all the better for it.

Her eyes skimmed down the page, reading the weather reports. Good thing she was leaving New York and flying back home to Dublin. A storm was blowing in and she had no wish to stay here longer than necessary; already her flight was delayed. It would be early tomorrow morning when she arrived. She sighed.

An icon popped on-screen for Raven. Three messages.

She wanted to open it, but it was hardly safe. Not here. There were high-powered cameras all over airports these days. Though perhaps many would call her paranoid, she preferred the term *cautious*. Caution had saved her life more times than she cared to count and she wouldn't toss it aside now.

Once on the plane, however, she pulled the computer back out and clicked on her mailbox. The return address was probably as bogus as the one she herself created, but it served its purpose.

B-Widow only had one thing to say.

I've a job for you.

Raven closed her eyes and leaned back against the soft, plush, first-class seats. The black Atlantic thousands of feet below did not soothe her.

Nothing soothed her these days.

Nothing.

She took a drink of her ginger ale.

Perhaps it was time to call it quits.

God knew she had enough bloody money that she never had to do another thing in her life again.

And yet . . .

She was good at what she did. Never one to mince words, she knew she was damn good.

But she rarely took jobs back-to-back. Not wise.

And yet . . .

Something called to her.

Since the fiasco two years ago, she demanded names and information, gathering her own before she ever agreed to take on a mark.

A little unorthodox to some, especially to her trainer, Nikko.

But it was what she did and the way she preferred doing things.

After all, she didn't want some innocent man to die just because an ex-wife was pissed at him. She might kill for a living, but she had her own code of ethics, though most would never see them.

What the hell.

She set the glass aside and typed a reply back to B-Widow, wondering who, wondering what, how much, and wondering what excitement this next job would bring her.

About the Author

Jaycee never really grew up—she still enjoys playing with imaginary people on a daily basis. Sometimes those people are nice, sometimes they're not, but in the end the girl gets the guy, so all is well. Jaycee earned her degree in Elementary Education from Eastern New Mexico University. She lives in Texas with her family, who puts up with her when her characters demand more of her time and appreciates her weirdness—or so they claim. There are also the cats and the corgis, who, in truth, rule the family. When she's not chained to her keyboard, she's doubling as a parent, a teacher, a maid, a chef, a chauffeur, a therapist, and promoting her education in human development while finishing her masters in plant elimination.

You can learn more about Jaycee by visiting her website at www.jayceeclark.com or emailing her at jaycee@jayceeclark.com. Her newsletter and blog subscriptions can be found on her website, along with links to follow her on Twitter, Facebook, and various other sites.